Prai...
USA TODAY bestselling author

KASEY MICHAELS

"Michaels can write everything from a lighthearted romp to a far more serious-themed romance. [Kasey] Michaels has outdone herself."
—*Romantic Times BOOKreviews*, Top Pick on
A Gentleman by Any Other Name

"Non-stop action from start to finish! It seems that author Kasey Michaels does nothing half way."
—*Huntress Reviews* on *A Gentleman by Any Other Name*

"Michaels has done it again.... Witty dialogue peppers a plot full of delectable details exposing the foibles and follies of the age."
—*Publishers Weekly*, starred review, on *The Butler Did It*

"Michaels demonstrates her flair for creating likable protagonists who possess chemistry, charm and a penchant for getting into trouble. In addition, her dialogue and descriptions are full of humor."
—*Publishers Weekly* on *This Must Be Love*

"Kasey Michaels aims for the heart and never misses."
—*New York Times* bestselling author Nora Roberts

"A cheerful, lighthearted read."
—*Publishers Weekly* on *Everything's Coming Up Rosie*

KASEY MICHAELS

A Most Unsuitable Groom

HQN™

ISBN-13: 978-0-373-77191-2
ISBN-10: 0-373-77191-6

A MOST UNSUITABLE GROOM

www.HQNBooks.com

Printed in U.S.A.

Dear Reader,

Some people are seemingly born already knowing who they are, and instantly feel secure in their place in the world. Maybe they're the lucky ones. Maybe not. Maybe the not knowing, and the journey, the discoveries along the way, are what make many lives worth living. Spencer Becket has gone searching for himself, or so he thinks. But what he finds–and who he forgets–will change him forever.

Spencer intrigued me from the moment I first "met" him. The dark, brooding one. The angry one. The odd man out. The one who didn't fit, couldn't seem to come to terms with his past or be comfortable with his expected future. How could he know that all his answers would be found in a fiery-haired stranger and an infant who'd clasp a tiny hand tightly around Spencer's finger...and capture his heart?

The Beckets of Romney Marsh are such a unique family, filled with diverse personalities, all striving to live their lives in peace, even as an old enemy jeopardizes everything each has gained, every person each loves.

We've seen Chance Becket in *A Gentleman by Any Other Name*, Morgan Becket in *The Dangerous Debutante* and Eleanor Becket in *Beware of Virtuous Women*. Their stories are ongoing. Now it is Spencer's turn at center stage. This September, October and November we'll see the Beckets again in *A Reckless Beauty*, *The Return of the Prodigal* and the culmination of the saga, *Becket's Last Stand*.

I hope you'll continue to enjoy reading about the Beckets of Romney Marsh, just as I've enjoyed "meeting" them and writing their stories.

Warmest regards,

Kasey Michaels

To Daniel Edward Seidick
Welcome to the world, Danny!

A Most Unsuitable Groom

BECKET HALL, ROMNEY MARSH

August 1813

AINSLEY BECKET sighed, then removed the spectacles he'd lately found necessary for reading and tossed both them and the letter on the desktop. "Well, I'll say this for the boy. They didn't execute him."

"Execute him? Our Spencer? Our so mild, even-tempered Spencer committed a hanging offense? Imagine that. I know I can." Courtland Becket reached for the letter that had taken several months to arrive at Becket Hall, most of them, judging from the condition of the single page, spent being walked to Romney Marsh stuck to the bottom of someone's boot. "What did he do, get caught bedding the General's wife?"

"If it were only that simple," Ainsley said, getting to his feet to walk over to the large table where he kept a collection of maps he consulted almost daily, tracking the English wars with both Bonaparte and the Americans. "He's in some benighted spot called Brownstown, or he was when that letter was written, nearly five months ago. From reports I've read in the

London papers, if he's still there he's in the thick of considerable trouble."

"Sweet Jesus," Courtland swore quietly, scanning the single page, attempting to decipher Spencer's crabbed handwriting and then read the words out loud, as their friend Jacko was also in the room. "'Forgive my tardiness in replying to your letters, but I have been incarcerated for the past six weeks, courtesy of our fine General Proctor. Allow me to explain. Against all reason, Proctor left only our Indian allies to guard several dozen American wounded we'd been forced to leave behind at the River Raisin after what had been an easy victory for us. I was sent back a few days later to retrieve them, only to discover that the Indians had executed every one of them. Hacked the poor bastards to pieces, actually. You, I'm sure, know what this means. There will be no stopping the Americans once they learn what happened. And that's the hell we face now. How do you fight an enemy that's out to seek revenge for a massacre? They'll fight to the last man, sure that to surrender means we'd turn them over to be summarily killed.'"

"The boy's right," Jacko said from his seat on the couch. "When it's kill or be killed, a man can fight past the point of reason. Now tell me what our own brave soldier did that should have gotten him executed."

"I'm getting to it now, I believe." Courtland looked down at the letter once more, turning the page on its end in order to read the crossed lines. "'I returned to our headquarters once I'd seen the bodies, walked straight into Proctor's office and knocked him off his chair. I should have been hanged, I suppose, and it would have been worth it to see Proctor's bloodied nose. But Chief Tecumseh, the head of all the Five Nations, agreed that this mistake could cost us heavily in the long run, and Proctor settled for stripping me of my rank and throwing me into a cell on starvation rations. Now I'm assistant liaison to Tecumseh—Proctor considers that a punishment—and I don't like the way the Chief is being treated. Mostly, I don't like that he's smart enough to see through Proctor, which could end with a lot of English scalps hanging from lodge poles. In truth, I have more respect for these natives, who at least know why they're fighting. And, yes, thinking fondly of my own scalp, I have been careful to be very friendly and helpful to Tecumseh. Rather him than Proctor.'"

"I don't see a career in the Army for that boy, Cap'n," Jacko said, winking at Ainsley, who had returned to sit behind his desk once more.

"Spencer hasn't the temperament to suffer fools gladly, I agree. Truthfully, I'm surprised he only bloodied the man's nose."

"And, for all we know, Spence is still squarely in the thick of the fighting," Courtland said, picking up his wineglass. "This Tecumseh might leave the English, leave Spencer, to their fate. Or, yes, turn on them, kill them. No matter what, I can't believe nothing's happened since Spencer wrote this letter. But what?"

"Exactly," Ainsley said as he stood up and quickly quit the room.

"He'll be walking the floors every night again until we hear from Spencer, searching the newspapers for casualties in the 51st Foot," Courtland said, taking up Ainsley's seat. "Damn my brother for wanting to be a hero."

"A hero? Spencer? No, Court, not a hero. A *man*. Spencer wanted to be his own man, not just son to the Cap'n or brother to you and Chance and Rian. Time the rest of you figured that out. Ah, I feel so old, Court. How I long for the feel of a rolling deck beneath my feet, just one more time. Running with the wind, the Cap'n barking out orders and the promise of sweet booty at the end of a sweeter battle. I envy our young soldier that, at the least. I never planned to die in my bed. Yes, bucko, land or sea, I envy Spencer the battle."

MORAVIANTOWN

October 1813

TO DIE, TO DIE very soon, seemed inevitable. To die for stupidity, for incompetence, was unforgivable. He should have done more than bloody the man's nose.

Spencer Becket stood half-hidden behind a large tree, waiting for the Americans. He didn't look much like a soldier in the King's Army, having divested himself of his bright uniform jacket in favor of an inconspicuous buckskin jacket that had been a gift from Tecumseh himself—not because the man loved him, but so Spencer wouldn't stand out like a sore thumb, making himself an easy target.

To his immediate left stood the skinny-shanked Clovis Meechum, who still liked to consider himself Spencer's batman, even though Spencer had long since lost his rank and was now nothing more than another highly disposable infantryman like Clovis and his constant companion, the Irishman, Anguish Nulty. They still wore their uniform jackets, but the material was so filthy as to be nearly colorless.

Behind the three soldiers, melted into the trees, were Tecumseh and his warriors.

All of them were waiting for the Americans. Waiting to die.

"They'll be coming up on us soon, Lieutenant?" Clovis asked quietly, fiddling with his powder horn. "We'll turn 'em back?"

Spencer went down on his haunches to look straight into Clovis's eyes, not bothering to remind him that he was a lieutenant no longer. Clovis made his own distinctions. "No, my friend, we won't turn them back. But perhaps we'll slow them down, give the civilians a chance to put some more distance between themselves and the main American force. Are you prepared to die today, Clovis?"

"No, sir, I don't think so, at least not today. How about you, Anguish? You ready to cock up your toes for king and country?"

The Irishman scratched beneath his thatch of filthy, overlong hair. "And that I'm not, Clovis. It's still longing to see this Becket Hall I am, what we've heard so much about. Sturdy stone walls, a warm fire at my feet, the Channel to m'back and nothing but nothing to do today and nothing more'n that to do again tomorrow."

Spencer smiled, showing even white teeth in an otherwise deeply tanned and dirty face. He looked a rare hooligan, as Anguish had been so bold as to inform him, his thick black hair grown uncared for and much too long—releasing fat, waving curls, Clovis had added, that would be the envy of any female. "You forgot to mention the mug of ale at your right hand, Anguish."

"That, too, sir," Anguish agreed. "I'll be sorry to miss it, that I will."

"Then let's be sure we don't end our days here, all right?" Spencer stood up and looked across the river to the other bank once more. He was so tired. They'd abandoned Detroit, the soldiers and more than ten thousand men, women and children with all their belongings, all of them heading for the safety of the western part of Upper Canada before the worst of the winter arrived.

But they'd left their retreat too late, and the Americans were catching up to them. Spencer could already taste the bile of defeat at the back of his throat. Tecumseh's idea was a good one—fighting with the swamp to their backs while the English forces pushed the Americans back to the river—but any hope of outflanking the Americans was just that, a hope.

"Here they come, Lieutenant. It's been grand knowin' you."

Even as Clovis spoke, Spencer felt the earth begin to tremble beneath him, signaling the imminent arrival of the American cavalry. Above the rumble of hooves pounding against the earth, the battle cry "Remember the Raisin!" rolled through the air.

And then hell and all its fury came straight at them, and there was no more time to think.

Anguish went down, but Spencer couldn't stop to

examine the man's wound. There wasn't even time to curse Proctor, as he saw the man commandeer a wagon and drive off with his family, leaving the troops to raise the white flag.

With Clovis standing at his back, Spencer tried to load his rifle one last time, only to discover that he was out of powder. Spencer threw the weapon at the American running toward him, bayonet fixed to his own rifle, then ducked as Clovis's knife found the man's throat...but not before the bayonet had sunk deep in Spencer's left shoulder.

"Sir!"

"I'm fine," Spencer shouted, pushing Clovis away from him. "Our troops have surrendered, but there will be no surrender for the Indians. No surrender, no quarter. We have to get clear of here if we hope to save ourselves."

"But the women, sir," Clovis shouted back at him, pointing to the near-constant stream of English women and children, and Indian squaws and their children, all of them running blindly, terrified, racing deeper into the swamp.

"Hell's bells, what a disaster!" Spencer pressed his hand to his shoulder, felt his blood hot and wet against his fingers. The pain hadn't hit him yet, but he knew it would soon, unless he was dead before that could happen. "Where's Tecumseh? Is he dead?"

"No, sir," Clovis said, pointing. "There! Over there!"

Even now, the chief was ordering some of his

warriors to their left, to fill a breach before the Americans could take advantage of it. And then he seemed to pause, take a deep breath and look to where Spencer stood. Slowly, he moved his arm away from his body, revealing a terrible wound in his chest.

"Christ, no!" Spencer shouted above the din, knowing that if Tecumseh fell, the Five Nations would all fall with him; the battle lost, the coalition broken. "We've got to get him out of here! Clovis! With me!"

But Clovis had slipped to his knees in the deepening mud and, when Spencer bent to pull him upright, he felt the sting of a bullet entering his thigh. Falling now, he never felt the fiercely swung rifle butt that connected heavily with the side of his skull....

"SIR? LIEUTENANT BECKET, sir? *Sir?*"

Spencer awoke all at once, his mind telling him to get up, get up, find Tecumseh and carry him away. But when he lifted his head the pain hit, the nausea, and he fell back down on the ground, defeated.

"Get him away...we can't let them see...leave me...must get Tecumseh away..."

"He's gone, sir," Clovis said, pushing Spencer back as he once again tried to rise. "Dead and gone, sir, and has been for more'n week. They're all gone, melting away into the trees like ghosts, even leaving some of their women behind to make their own way to wherever it is they've gone. It's just us now. Us and poor Anguish and some others. Women and children who hid or were lost until the Americans took off again. They left us all for dead, but you're not dying, thank God. You just lay still and I'll fetch you some water. Water's something we have plenty of. Cold and fresh."

Spencer lay with his eyes closed, trying to assimilate all that Clovis had told him. Clovis was alive? Anguish was alive? Tecumseh…the great chief was dead? *Damn, what a waste.* He opened his eyes, wincing at the bright sunlight that filtered down through tall trees, their leaves already turning with the colder weather.

He moved his right hand along the ground, realized that he was lying on a blanket, realized when he tried to move his left arm that it was in a sling. He moved his legs, wincing as he tried to stretch out the right one. His head pounded, but he was alive and supposedly would recover.

But where was he? Still in the swamp? Yes, of course, still in the swamp. Where else would he be? A week? Clovis had a said week, hadn't he?

"Here you go, sir," Clovis said, holding out a silver flask as he raised Spencer's head. "Don't go smiling now, because it's water I'm giving you. We used up the last of the good stuff on Anguish before we cut his arm off. Cried like a baby, he did, but that was the drink. He wouldn't have made a sound, elsewise. Now hush, sir. It's herself, come to look at you."

"So he's finally awake. Very good, Clovis."

Spencer looked up toward the sun once more to see the outline of a woman standing over him, her long, wild hair the color of fire in the sunlight. A woman? But wasn't that the scarlet coat of a soldier she was wearing? Nothing was making sense to him. Was she real? He didn't think she was real. "An angel?"

"Not so you'd know it, sir," Clovis whispered close to Spencer's ear. "One of the women, sir. She's been nursing your fever all the week long. Her and her Indian woman. They're stuck here with us and she's, well, sir, she's the sort what takes charge, if you take my meaning. Other women are camped here with us, children, too, who hid out until the Americans left. We've been living off the dead, which is where I found the flask and blankets, but not much food. We've only three rifles betwixt us, and not much ammunition anyway. It's a mess we're in, Lieutenant, an unholy mess."

Blinking, Spencer tried to make out the woman's features, but now there seemed to be two of her, neither one of her standing still long enough for him to get a good look, damn her. "English?"

"You're not a prisoner, if that's the answer you're hoping for," the woman said, her accent pure, educated. "We'll give him another day, Clovis, and then we have to be on the move north. Onatah says we'll have snow within a fortnight, and we can't just stay here and freeze as well as starve, not for one failed lieutenant. As it is, it will take us at least that fortnight to get to civilization. We'll make a litter, and we'll simply have to take turns dragging him."

Then she was gone, and Spencer squeezed his eyes closed as the sun hit him full in the face. "You're right, Clovis. Not an angel," he said weakly, and then passed out once more.

CHAPTER ONE

Becket Hall
June 1814

"CAN YOU SMELL IT, Spencer? There's a considerable storm churning somewhere out there. I imagine Courtland will have noticed, and won't bring the *Respite* back from Hastings until it passes. That's unfortunate. I was hoping to hear any war news he and Jack may have picked up while visiting my banker." Ainsley Becket turned away from the open window overlooking the increasingly angry Channel to look at his son. "How's the shoulder? Does it still pain you when a storm's on its way?"

Spencer shook his head and returned to his glass of canary. Well, Ainsley had slipped that question in neatly, hadn't he? "No, sir. If it did, I wouldn't tell you. Because then you'd tell Odette and she'd be after me again with her damn feathers and potions. I'm fine, Papa. Truly."

"And bored," Ainsley said, seating himself behind his desk. "You won't be leaving us again, will you, now that you're recovered? Or should I refrain from mentioning that Jacko has compared you to a lion incessantly pacing in its cage? All that seems missing is the growl, but I doubt that will be the case for long."

Spencer avoided Ainsley's intense eyes, pretended to ignore the inquisitive tilt of the man's head. He knew he was being weighed, judged. Even goaded. Quite the devious fellow, Ainsley Becket, for how smoothly he poked at a person. That was the trick with his papa—don't trust the smile, don't pay attention to the mild tone. Watch the eyes.

"No, I'm not leaving, Papa. I've had enough of Canada for one thing and now that Bonaparte has abdicated there's nowhere else to go, no one else left to fight. I'll just sit here and rust like everyone else, I suppose."

"And the headaches?"

"Sweet Christ!" Spencer leaped to his feet and began to pace. So much for trying to keep himself in check. He remembered Jacko's comparison and quickly stopped pacing, ordered his temper back under control. "I told you, I'm fine. Fully recovered, I promise."

Ainsley kept pushing. "So you remember now? How you got to Montreal, how you were loaded on a boat and then onto the ship that brought you back to us? You remember more than being in the battle and then being at sea? You remember more than either Clovis or Anguish has told you?"

Spencer stabbed his fingers into his hair and

squeezed at the top of his skull with his fingertips until he felt pain. "No, damn it, I haven't. Odette says the good *loas* kindly took away my memory of those weeks, so that I don't recall the pain. *Loa* protecting me or not, I got a whacking great bang on the head, that's all. And I'm damned tired of being treated like an invalid."

"And you're bored," Ainsley repeated, palming a brass paperweight as he continued to look at Spencer, the man who had once been a defiant orphaned boy of hot Spanish blood, wandering the streets of Port-au-Prince, barefoot and close to starving, yet ready to spit in the eye of anyone who looked at him crookedly. Ainsley had been forced to stuff him in a sack to keep the boy from biting him as he took him to the island and handed him over to Odette and Isabella's tender mercies, the seventh of the orphans Ainsley had felt it necessary to take on to ease his increasingly uneasy conscience over the life he'd chosen. He'd named the boy Spencer, in memory of the sailor they'd lost overboard on their most recent run.

Within months of his joining them, they'd fled the island, Spencer still mostly wild, a wildness that had never really left him. What a long way they'd come. How little he still knew about his adopted son. The timing had been wrong. He'd brought Spencer into his world only months before he had wished himself out of it, and Spencer had been left mostly to his own devices for the past sixteen years.

"Spencer? You can say it. I do understand."

"Then, yes, damn it, I'm bored! How do you bear it, living here, day after day after day, year after year after year? At least when the Black Ghost rode out, there was something to break the monotony. I'd almost welcome the Red Men Gang back to threaten us, just for the excuse to ride out, bang a few heads together."

"There will be no more smuggling from these shores, Spencer, and therefore no need for the Black Ghost to ride out to protect our people. With Napoléon contained, the government is able to use its ships to set up a blockade all along the coast. Smuggling has become much too dangerous an enterprise. And I won't commit the *Respite* again. It's too risky for us."

Spencer knew they were getting into dangerous territory now, and spoke carefully. "Not everyone in this part of the Marsh is willing to give up the life."

"I'm aware of that. But we took more than a few chances these past few years, and I don't believe in pushing our luck, so those who persist in making runs will have to do so without the protection of the Black Ghost."

Spencer kept his gaze steady on his father. "A few of the younger men are restless, confined here the way they are. They want their turn outrunning the Waterguard. They want their own adventure."

Ainsley steepled his long-fingered hands beneath his chin as he looked at his son. "You had yourself an adventure, Spencer. Killed your share of men, watched friends die. Do you really long for another such *adventure?*"

"You coming, Spence?"

Spencer turned his head to see that his brother Rian had poked his head inside the room. "Oh, right. I forgot the time," he said gratefully, getting to his feet, careful to look Ainsley full in the eyes as he added, "If you'll excuse me? A few of us are meeting at The Last Voyage. Would you care to join us?"

Ainsley smiled, shook his head in the negative, just as Spencer had known he would—or he wouldn't have invited him. Not this evening. "No, thank you, I think not. And watch for the storm. You wouldn't want to get stranded in the village for the night."

"Because to walk home along the beach in the rain might serve to melt me."

"Probably not, but neither of us really needs to have Odette ringing a peal over our heads about her poor injured bird, now do we?"

Spencer grinned. "It's gratifying to know I'm not the only one afraid of Odette's mighty wrath. I promise you again, I'm fine, completely healed," Spencer said, sighing. "Good night, Papa. I'll see you tomorrow. And the day after that, and the day after that…"

Spencer motioned for Rian to precede him into the hallway, and then the two brothers sought out woolen cloaks and made for the front door, hoping to avoid Jacko and anyone else who might ask where they were going.

"You saved me there, you know. Papa was being his usual self, asking questions for which I have no answers."

"You can thank me later. They're probably all waiting for us now," Rian told him, donning his cloak with a flourish that seemed to come naturally to the almost poetically handsome young Irishman, with his riot of black curls and clear green eyes, the almost feminine, soft curve of his cheek. Less than two years Spencer's junior, he seemed so very much younger…possibly only because he was so damned inconveniently pretty. He needed a few scars; that's what Rian needed, if he was ever going to convince anyone he was a man, even at the ripe old age of twenty-five.

"Good. If we can all agree tonight, the Black Ghost will soon be riding again," Spencer said, stepping onto the wide stone landing, pausing only to look out over the endless flat land that was Romney Marsh. On a clear day a man could see for miles, see distant church spires taller than any tree, as the few trees that grew here could only rise so high before being bent over by the ever constant wind from the Channel.

This place was so different from the North American continent with all its tall trees, rolling hills, rushing cold, clean waters and bluer-than-blue skies. Romney Marsh was stark, not green.

Spencer had lied to Ainsley. He did miss America. It was an old land and yet also new; young and raw and vibrant. When Tecumseh had spoken of his land, he had made Spencer see it through his eyes. An all-glorious land of bounty and promise. And freedom. Maybe he would go back some day. Not to fight, but to explore, to find his place. Because much as he'd tried, as much as he'd attempted to conquer his discontent, his place wasn't here at Becket Hall. That Ainsley knew this concerned Spencer, but he knew his father would not stop him when it came time to leave.

Rian hefted the lantern they'd need to guide them along the path to Becket Village. "Spence? They're all waiting on us. You looking or moving?"

He shook himself back to attention just as the skies opened up and the dark night turned extremely wet in an instant. "Right. Sorry. Rian? Do you think Papa knows what we're up to?"

His brother involuntarily backed up a pace, nearly tripping down the steps. "Knows we're planning some freetrading across the Channel? Please God, no. Why would you ask that?"

Spencer pulled the hood of his cloak up over his already drenched head as they headed down the stone steps. "No reason. We were having a conversation just before you came to get me, that's all. I'm imagining things."

"But Papa does have this way about him," Rian said and then sighed. "He never goes anywhere, never does anything, and yet he seems to know everything. Spence? Damn this rain. Look out there, see if you see what I think I see. Is that a coach heading this way? By God, it is. Spence?"

Instantly on the alert, for visitors were rare at Becket Hall and never arrived uninvited, Spencer motioned for Rian to go alert their father as he watched the coach lurch to a halt and a groom hop down to open the door and let down the steps.

He squinted through the dark and the slashing rain, watching as a female form emerged from the doorway, holding tight to the groom's hand as she stepped to the ground, a small moan quickly cut off as she thanked the servant.

Now what? You don't turn away a woman, not late at night, not in the middle of a growing storm that could last for days. But who the hell was she, and why was she here? Was she alone?

That unspoken question was answered when the groom shut the door without anyone else having stuck his or her head out the doorway.

The groom looked good only for hanging on to and probably would have let the woman stand there until she drowned in the downpour, so Spencer advanced until he was in her line of sight, such as it was on this starless, moonless night. "Good evening, madam. Lost your way on the Marsh? This is Becket Hall."

Her head lowered, the woman replied crisply, "What a happy coincidence. I fully intended to *be* at Becket Hall, albeit much earlier in the evening. Do you make it a point to keep visitors out in the rain, sir?"

"A thousand apologies, madam," he said, gesturing

with his left arm that she should walk ahead of him, climb to where Rian now stood in the open doorway, light spilling out onto the wide stone porch.

He followed her up the steps, the newly supplied light not quite bright enough for him to be able to inspect and perhaps admire the woman's ankles as she lifted her gown and cloak in order to navigate those steps. Pity. He hadn't been with a woman in a long time. Long enough to have forgotten both the time and the woman.

He shook his head, trying to clear it. He had to start thinking like a Becket, and a Becket would be calculating how dangerous this unexpected visitor could prove to be, not hoping for a glimpse of shapely ankle.

"Ma'am," Rian said, bowing slightly to the hooded figure that brushed past him as he looked to Spencer, his expressive eyebrows raised. "Yes, of course, ma'am, please do come in," he ended, the woman having already disappeared into the house. "Spence? Who in hell—?"

"Did you alert Papa?"

"I did. He'd just gone up to his bedchamber. He's throwing on a jacket and will be down directly. Spence?"

"Good, he can handle our unexpected guest. I have no bloody idea who she is," he told his brother as he shrugged out of his sopping cloak, looking toward the woman who had her back to him as she surveyed the large entry hall.

As she lifted her head the hood of her cloak fell

back and Spencer looked hard for a moment, then squeezed his eyes shut as a memory flashed into his mind. Sunlight. A halo of golden red fire. And a voice. *We can't just stay here and freeze as well as starve, not for one failed lieutenant.*

He shook his suddenly aching head and opened his eyes again to see that the woman had turned around and was looking at him now. *God.* Hair the color of golden fire was only the beginning. Her green eyes were those of an imp of the devil, tilted up at the edges and penetrating as a pitchfork to the gullet. Her full lips were slightly parted over straight white teeth; her skin was the color of fresh cream. With her masses of wavy, disheveled hair, she looked like a woman who would bed well. A passionate woman. One who might even bite…

And then she shrugged out of her cloak, allowing it to drop to the floor, which exposed an out-of-fashion plain gray gown and the fact that she was—good God, the woman was *pregnant.*

"As you can see, Lieutenant, I don't arrive alone," she said just as Ainsley Becket descended the last step to the marble floor. "Congratulations, sir," she added, her green gaze fastened on Spencer. "It's possible the coach ride from Dover so soon after my sea journey may have been ill-advised. I do believe, Lieutenant, that you're about…to…to become a father."

Spencer opened his mouth to hotly deny her ridiculous accusation. But his words were cut off when the woman swayed like a sapling in a breeze, then gracefully collapsed into Ainsley's waiting arms.

"Rian, you help me get her into the drawing room. Summon Odette, Spencer," Ainsley ordered tightly. "Spencer. *Now.*"

CHAPTER TWO

SHE WAS LYING on a couch now, in a large, splendidly appointed room. How lovely, after so much time at sea and then in that terribly sprung coach, to be somewhere that didn't move. "Thank you…thank you, sir. I'm fine now, really. Perhaps I'd…I'd simply overreacted. The jarring of the coach, you understand. I must apologize. I'm not by nature a blatantly dramatic person and hadn't planned quite so intense an entrance." She then quickly placed her hands on her swollen belly in surprise as another pain gripped her. *"Oh."*

"Sweet Jesus," Spencer said, fairly skidding into the drawing room after flagging down Anguish in the hallway and sending him to fetch Odette. "She's really giving birth?"

She rolled her eyes toward the ceiling. "Oh, dear. I had hoped for at least some small modicum of intelligence from the man. For the child's sake, you understand," she said, looking at Ainsley. "I…I should introduce myself, shouldn't I? My name is Mariah Rutledge. I, um, I met Spencer in America."

"A pleasure to meet you, Miss Rutledge. I am Ainsley Becket."

"Would someone be so kind as to go out to dismiss the coach and bring in my maid, Mr. Becket? Her name is Onatah. And she won't scalp any of you, I promise, which is something I had to swear to those idiots whose coach I hired. If you're nice to me she won't, that is."

Rian grinned at Spencer. "Onatah? Is that an Indian name, Spence? Did she bring a red Indian with her from America? Yes, of course she did. Oh, this is beyond splendid. Except for you, I imagine. Sorry," he added quickly, losing his smile as Spencer all but growled at him. "You stay here. Let me go get her. Yes? Well, I'm off, in any event."

Spencer advanced on the couch, to get a better look at the woman. No, he didn't recognize her. Just the hair. Just that voice, a little low, faintly husky, the disdain in it flicking hard at his memory. "Miss...Rutledge, you said?"

She looked up at him, then returned her gaze to the older man, attempting to sort out the people in the room with her. His father? No, she saw no resemblance. "He truly doesn't remember me, does he?" she asked, pushing herself up slightly against the pillows now that the pain had eased.

"I don't think so, no," Ainsley told her kindly. "He has no memory of anything between his last battle and being at sea, on his way back to us. Where, may I ask, did you two meet?"

"Actually, sir," Mariah said, embarrassed but truthful, "we were never formally introduced."

"I tried to bring her but she—Miss Rutledge? *Here?* Our Sainted Lady of the Swamp? Oh, now and isn't this a fine kettle we've got boilin' now."

Spencer wheeled about to see Anguish standing just inside the door, his ruddy Irish complexion gone white. "You recognize her, Anguish? And where's Odette?"

"I was just about to say, sir. She was all dressed, Lieutenant, and waitin' on me, but still at her heathen altar, prayin' and such, and won't budge until she's done. That's what I came to tell you. It's knowin' I was comin' for her that chills my marrow," Anguish said, his bug-eyed stare still riveted on Mariah Rutledge, who had wrapped her arms around her belly once more. "Is she…is she…oh, Lord God, she *is!* Crikey, and her woman's here, too? Ah, the sight of that takes me back to where I don't want to go no more, lessen it's to visit my poor arm, because at least my arm I miss seein'."

Anguish stepped back sprightly as the latest addition to this insane farce entered the room behind Rian, who was grinning like the village idiot, as if he'd just brought home a Christmas surprise. The woman was small, thin, bent—wizened, Spencer supposed—with wrinkled skin the color of mahogany and black bean eyes that would give small children and many grown men nightmares. She wore a dark gingham dress over moccasins, her thick grey hair twisted into a single braid falling halfway down her back, a patterned wool blanket clutched tight around her shoulders by one heavily veined hand.

"Iroquois," Spencer said quietly, recognizing the design on the blanket. "Bloody Iroquois."

Onatah paused a moment in her advance, just long enough to say something gruff and pithy to him, before she moved on toward the couch.

"What did she say?" Rian asked excitedly. "Did you understand her? Do you know the language? God, Spence, this is magnificent. I never dreamed I'd ever see a real red Indian. Tell me, what did she say?"

Spencer's jaw was set tight at an angle as he shook his head. "I hate to disabuse you, brother mine, but I'm not that familiar with the dialect. I spoke mostly to Tecumseh, who knew our language better than half the men living on this island. However, and only for your amusement, I do think I've just been called the fornicating son of a three-legged cur."

"Oh, well, that's understandable. I suppose. Ah, and here comes more trouble. I really should go wake Jacko and the girls. I shouldn't be having all the fun."

Odette shuffled into the room in her aged carpet slippers and one of Courtland's old greatcoats over a rusty black gown, her wiry silver hair also hanging down her back in a single braid, her skin ebony to Onatah's mahogany and only half as wrinkled. She stopped, took in the scene—her attention centered on the Indian for several tense seconds—and then walked over to Spencer.

"I was wrong," she said sadly. "The good *loa* didn't steal your memory. The bad *loa* took it, so that you would not know you're to have a son. I only saw that in my bowl tonight, as she drew closer, too late to warn you. I ask your forgiveness for my failing."

And then, surprising Spencer even more, Odette lifted her hand and slapped him hard across the cheek, her unexpected strength knocking him back on his heels.

"And what was that for?" he asked, holding a hand to his stinging flesh.

"For thinking the boy isn't yours," she told him. "Now, come, help get this girl upstairs. Your son wishes to be born tonight."

Mariah was speaking quietly to Onatah, who had placed a hand on her mistress's stomach, waiting for the next contraction. "They'll stop now that I'm not in that coach, won't they, Onatah? It's too soon."

"Babies come when they come," Onatah pronounced with all the gravity of Moses tripping back down the mountain with stone tablets in his hands.

A gnarled black hand joined Onatah's on Mariah's belly, and Mariah blinked up into the kindest eyes she'd ever seen. "Foolish child, to hide the pains from your nurse. You've had them all day, since you first rose this morning. There is time yet, but not much. We will allow no harm to come to you or to Spencer's son.

Now come. Rise up, walk with us. And better you do it now, between the pains."

"Onatah?" Mariah asked, feeling suddenly very young again, and quite frightened.

"Old women know best," Onatah said and, between the two of them, Mariah was on her feet once more, being led toward the hallway.

She had taken only a few steps when she could feel the pain begin in the small of her back once more, long, strong fingers advancing around her hips to grip tightly against her lower belly. She'd had the pains since that morning, but not like this, not so intense, so frequent or lasting so long. "Ohhh," she said, her knees buckling slightly. The hallway looked miles away, the tall, winding staircase a mountain she could not possibly climb.

"The devil with this!" Spencer exploded, storming across the room to take hold of Mariah's arm and pull her toward him, then scoop her up in his arms. He turned toward the hallway. "Where? What room?"

"Yours, of course," Ainsley said smoothly, motioning with a sweep of his arm that Spencer should carry Mariah up the stairs.

"No," Spencer said flatly. "Morgan's chamber."

Mariah moaned again, her eyes shut tight. "If I had a pistol, I'd shoot you," she told Spencer quietly. "Just put me *somewhere*—and then *go away*."

"Go away, is it? Should have said that sooner," Anguish whispered to no one in particular, unfortunately not that quietly. "Would have saved us all a boatload of bother."

Spencer's last sight of Rian as he carried Mariah toward the stairs was of his brother sliding down the wall, clutching his stomach as he laughed uproariously at the Irishman's assessment of his brother's predicament.

Mariah kept her eyes closed as Spencer carried her up the stairs, holding her breath against the pain of the contraction and the added pain she felt each time he jostled her as he climbed the stairs, not opening them again until she felt herself being laid on cool sheets.

When his arms left her, when he stood back from the bed, she felt curiously abandoned.

"When?" he asked her, his dark eyes boring into her. "Where?"

"What does it matter?" she asked in return. "Believe me, it was considerably less than unforgettable. Go away."

"Do as she says," Odette told him as the Indian woman stepped between them to begin stripping Mariah out of her clothing. "Go downstairs and fall into a bottle. It's what men do. Women know what to do here."

"But—" Spencer knew when he was beaten. "All right. But she and I have to talk. I have to understand how this happened."

Odette's white teeth flashed bright against her dark face. "Boy, I think you already know how. Now go."

Spencer stomped out into the hallway to see Jacko

standing there in baggy brown trousers, his nightshirt hanging over his large, tight belly and dropping all the way to his bare knees. The man's eyes were fairly dancing. "Rian came to tell me your news. Congratulations, *papa*."

Spencer spoke without thinking, because a wise man never gave Jacko an opening he could slip his tongue through. "I don't even remember her."

"You bedded what Rian tells me is a fine-looking woman and you don't remember? Ah, bucko, there's all kinds of hell, aren't there? But I think you've managed to conjure up a new one."

"As long as I can amuse you, then it's all right," Spencer said, heading for the stairs only to be stopped by his sister Eleanor, who had come out into the hallway in her dressing gown. Had Rian run from chamber to chamber, ringing a bell and banging on every door, eager to tell everyone?

"Spencer," Eleanor asked, "is there anything I can do to help?"

He thought about this for a moment as he looked at his sister. So small, so fragile and beautiful. Yet Eleanor and her Jack had almost single-handedly dismantled the Red Men Gang last year. If there was anyone whom he could count on to move mountains, it would be Eleanor. Calm, steadfast Elly.

"Odette's in with her, Elly, and her own Indian nurse. But," he said, a thought just then striking him, "you could answer a question for me, one Odette would box my ears for asking. How long, um…" He hesitated, waving one hand in front of him. "You know. How long from…beginning to end?"

Elly blinked, then smiled. "You're asking me the length of a pregnancy, Spencer?"

He nodded, looking back at the door to Morgan's bedchamber, to see Jacko stepping forward to hold open the door for two of the Becket Hall women, Edyth and Birdie, to enter with pots of steaming water and an armful of towels. This was happening. This was really happening.

"I would say approximately nine months, Spencer," Elly told him. "So that would be…last September?"

Spencer shook his head. "No, that can't be right. We didn't meet the Americans at the swamp until the beginning of October. So that's…that's…" He began counting on his fingers, then looked at his sister before looking at the closed door, his stomach suddenly uneasy. "It's too soon, isn't it? If it's mine."

"*If* it's yours? Spencer?"

He held up his hands to ward off the harder tone of Eleanor's voice. "It's mine. Odette says so. The woman says so. I'm the fornicating son of a three-legged cur. I just don't remember. Why don't I remember?"

"You had that knock on the head," Jacko reminded him. "Your shoulder, your leg, the knock on the head, that fever that hung on for months according to Clovis. Damn, boy, I'd say the woman had her wicked way with you when you couldn't fight her off. You lucky devil."

"Jacko."

One word, just one, from Eleanor and Jacko lost his smile and much of his swagger. "I was just saying…"

"Yes, and now that you have, you will forget you've said it, please," Eleanor told him as if she were a governess scolding her young charge. "Now, you boys go downstairs to Papa, who had the good sense not to come up here, and I will go in with the ladies and offer my assistance if it is needed as I introduce myself to your young woman."

"She's not my—" Spencer gave it up as a bad job. "You'll let us know what's happening?"

"I will," Eleanor said, her smile soft. "What's her name, Spencer? I should most probably know that."

"Rutledge. Mariah Rutledge. And she's English. But that's all I know. Damn it all to hell, Elly, that's all I know."

And that hair, that voice…

Spencer pressed his fingers against his temples, hoping for more memories to assert themselves. But there was nothing. He did not know this woman, remember this woman. "Go downstairs, everyone, before we wake Fanny and Callie. I'm…I'm going to go talk to Clovis."

He walked briskly toward the servant stairs and climbed to the top floor of the large house to where Anguish and Clovis had been installed upon their arrival at Becket Hall.

Ainsley had given them the run of the house if

they'd wanted it, in thanks for bringing Spencer back to Becket Hall, but neither man had felt comfortable with that sort of free and easy arrangement. After all, as Clovis pointed out, they were only doing their duty. Hiding them from an army they didn't wish to return to was thanks enough for both of them.

Still, Becket Hall wasn't like most English homes, made up of a strict hierarchy of master, master's family, upper servants, lower servants. No, that wasn't for Ainsley Becket.

He had run a taut ship but a fair one, and he ran a fair house. The servants were the crew, each lending a hand to whatever chore was necessary at the moment, and each still very much the individual...individuals who refused to see Ainsley as anyone less than their beloved Cap'n.

There was no butler or major domo at Becket Hall. Whoever heard the knocker and was close opened the door. When beds needed changing they were changed; when rugs needed beating they were beaten.

The only area of the house Ainsley considered to be off-limits to himself and most of the household was the kitchens where the cook, Bumble, reigned supreme by means of a sharp tongue and a sharper knife that had been waved threateningly a time or three over the years, and anyone who thought the man's wooden leg had slowed him soon learned their mistake.

When Clovis and Anguish were moved in nobody

blinked an eye. The Cap'n said they could stay, so stay they would and welcome aboard. Clovis had insisted upon acting as Spencer's right hand and, since Anguish no longer had a right hand, he had offered his left to Bumble and now spent most of his day sitting on a high stool in the main kitchen, telling tall tales to make the females giggle behind their hands and sampling all of the day's dishes. It was an arrangement that worked well all around.

Spencer knocked at Clovis's door, because personal privacy was also very much a part of living at Becket Hall, and entered only when he heard a grunt from the other side of the thick wood.

He walked in to see Clovis sitting on the side of his bed, still completely dressed, an empty bottle in his hand.

"Sir!" Clovis said, quickly getting to his feet. "I'm wanted?"

"In several countries, no doubt," Spencer returned with a wan smile, indicating with a wave of his hand that his friend should sit once more, and then joining him. "You're still worrying about our decision to guard the freetraders?"

"That I am, Lieutenant, sir," Clovis told him, then sighed. "You and Anguish see adventure, and I see only trouble. I think I'm old, and I don't know which worries me more."

"No, not old, just prudent. But I'm here on another matter. Clovis, do you recall a woman named Mariah Rutledge?"

Clovis shot to his feet once more. "You're rememberin', sir? Well, sir, that's above all things grand."

"No, I'm not remembering anything, more's the pity. She's here, Clovis, at Becket Hall. Miss Rutledge. And she's giving birth to my child in my sister's bedchamber. Odette says it's a boy, so I imagine it is."

The older man sat down once more with a thump that shook the bed. "I shouldn't drink so deep. I thought you said—sir?"

"I know, Clovis. It's a lot to swallow. I don't remember Miss Rutledge. I damn sure don't remember bedding the woman."

Clovis wrinkled his brow, deep in thought. "Well, sir, we were all together for more'n three weeks. First in the swamp, then movin' north. Forty-two of us, forty-one after little Willy died. Sad that, him being only three years old. You remember that, sir?"

Spencer shook his head. "No. Nothing. How did he die?"

"Caught a stray bullet during the worst of it, sir. We laid him atop you when we drug you along in the litter the Indian women made up. Until he died, that is. You suffered something terrible, sir, when we had to take his little body from you. I didn't want to tell you. There are things best not remembered. Mr. Ainsley said as much himself when we told him. Either you'd remember or you wouldn't."

Spencer buried his head in his hands. War. What a stupid, senseless way of settling disputes. Governments shouldn't rise or fall on how many people their soldiers could kill. "I don't remember, Clovis. I don't remember any of it. Tell me…at least tell me about Miss Rutledge."

"Miss Rutledge, sir? Now there's a woman. General Rutledge, Anguish called her. Standin' up, takin' charge, barkin' out orders, everyone steppin'-to just as if they knew it was right, that she was goin' to save us all, lead us out of there. And I'll say this for her. She did it, sir. A fine, rare woman. She was the first to begin strippin' the dead for what we could use, sayin' prayers over each one, thankin' them for what she took. It was her what sang to our Anguish the whole of the time we was cuttin' off his arm. Holdin' his head in her lap, singin' loud enough to shoo the birds from the trees. Don't hear the saw workin' down on the bone so much that way, you see, or hear Anguish cursin' and screamin'."

He shook his head. "I ain't never seen the like, not from a woman. Walkin' around in that scarlet jacket she took for her own, givin' us all what-for, tellin' us what to do. Our Lady of the Swamp, Anguish called her, too, when she couldn't hear him. I think he half expected her to be growing wings at any minute— when he wasn't thinking she should be sprouting horns. A hard taskmaster, Miss Rutledge. But she saved you, sir. Her and her Indian woman. She saved us all."

Spencer wished he could remember, hated that he'd

been a burden rather than a help. "So Miss Rutledge was in charge of me, Clovis? Not you?"

Clovis went red to his hairline. "I did…the personal things, sir. Bathing you and such like. Don't fret about that. But nights, sir? There were only a few of us men and we had to stand guard on the camp, you understand. So Miss Rutledge would watch you then. Give you water for the fever, lend her body to heat you when the chills took you, shook you. The night…the night after Willy died, you were shakin' bad, sir. Really bad. I was sure you were dyin' on us then."

"So she laid with me, sharing the heat from her body," Spencer said, imagining the scene. The dark woods, the chill October night air, their two bodies close together in the middle of nowhere, hope fading, young Willy dead, their collective future looking bleak. Sometimes you just needed to hold on to someone, believe you were alive…

"I see." He got to his feet. "Thank you, Clovis. You won't speak of this to anyone."

"No, sir, Lieutenant," Clovis said, standing to attention. "Not a word to anyone. She's a good woman, sir. Daughter of the quartermaster at Fort Malden, him cut down in the first volley. A world of hurt she had that day, but she never gave herself a moment to mourn, never gave us a moment to think on our dire straits. A true soldier's daughter. Just movin', keep movin', and she got us safe out of there."

"And then?" Spencer asked. "How did we become separated?"

Clovis lowered his head. "Well, sir, it's like this, sir. Anguish didn't want no more of the Army, and I could agree with him, seein' as how General Proctor made a holy mess out of everythin' he touched. We saw a boat, stole you out of the cabin they put you in that first night, and off we went, fast as we could."

He looked up at Spencer pleadingly. "They were safe, sir, everyone was safe. But we wanted to be gone before everythin' froze and we was stuck there all the winter long, and we couldn't think to leave without you. But she found you, so that's all right, isn't it, sir? A baby you said, sir? Doesn't that beat the Dutch for somethin'?"

"That it does, Clovis, thank you," Spencer said as he walked out of the room, ducking his head under the low lintel, for the room was tucked into the eaves of the large house. His head stayed down as he walked the length of the hallway to the servant stairs, then slowly descended to the next floor. He paused for a moment, looking down that wider hallway toward his sister Morgan's room.

The woman had saved his life. She'd saved many lives.

And he'd rewarded her by impregnating her, leaving her and then forgetting her.

She was here now, straining to bear his son, and he still didn't remember her, couldn't remember her.

"Bloody hell," he swore, and turned his back, headed all the way down the servant stairs to the kitchens. He walked past a startled young cook's helper he didn't recognize and slammed out of the house and straight into the raging storm, the wind-blown rain plastering his thick black hair to his head and his shirt against his skin in mere moments.

He half walked, half staggered to the slippery sand and shingle beach. He didn't stop until he was standing knee deep in the angry Channel, where he punched his tightly fisted hands high above his head, lifted his face to the wind and rain and screamed out his frustration at the lightning-streaked sky.

CHAPTER THREE

MARIAH SENSED someone looking at her and slowly opened her eyes. She'd slept, only a little bit, but couldn't seem to tamp down the strange exhilaration she felt, as if she'd just accomplished something wonderful. And she had, hadn't she?

"You," she said, seeing Spencer, and closed her eyes again. He looked so solemn; please God he wouldn't feel some compelling need to ask her again if he was truly the father of her son. And if he was, then it was just too bad for him. Odette said there was no doubt and he'd simply have to come to grips with the situation, wouldn't he? "Come to see the fruit of my labor, have you?" she asked him, unable to restrain a smile at her genius. Goodness, she felt good. Sore, tired, but good, very good. And fiercely protective of her son…their son.

"Madam," Spencer said, looking a bit awkward. "He's a fine boy. Small, but Odette promises me he's strong and healthy. And you? How do you feel this morning?"

Mariah opened her eyes once more, even summoned another smile. He looked rather like a boy who'd been caught with his hand in the candy dish and was now weighing the consequences as to the reward and the possible punishment. He also looked exhausted, as if he hadn't slept all night. "Much like a horse that's been ridden hard over rough country and put away wet, I imagine. How do you think I feel?"

"Abandoned," Spencer said. "Clovis told me what happened."

Her smile turned rueful. "Oh, I highly doubt that. He wasn't there at the time."

The corners of his mouth twitched slightly. "You might be down at the moment, Miss Rutledge, but you're most assuredly not out, are you? Are you always this blunt?"

"I've just given birth to your child, Lieutenant. And I've no time for niceties. If you're at fault, so am I. It was a...a frightening time. You really don't remember? Eleanor swears you don't. I wish I didn't." She regretted those last words as soon as she said them, for Spencer seemed to stiffen his spine as if she had just physically threatened him. "He...the baby has such a thick thatch of black hair just like yours. Did you see?"

"I did. A humbling sight. And I'm sorry that I questioned you last night. He's mine, there's no doubt."

Mariah plucked at the bedcovers, avoiding his dark, intense gaze. He looked so different and yet so much the man she remembered. A handsome man, there was no denying that. Fiery. Exotic. All that was missing was the vulnerability. Healed, sound once more, he was rather formidable. But she could be formidable, too!

"He's also mine, sir. I cannot, however, provide for him, not now with my father dead, our few possessions gone and with no other family to take me in. After paying for the passage, the coach, I have precious little left but what I can stand up in, once I can stand again, and Onatah to care for. I can't…" Her voice broke slightly and she took a deep, steadying breath in order to say what she had to say. "I can't even nurse him. Onatah has decreed that I'm too weak from our journey, that I need all my strength and that he needs more than I will be able to give him. Your Odette agreed and has kindly arranged a wet nurse. I hate both of them for that, but they both said I was being womanish, which I hate even more."

Spencer felt even more uncomfortable. What could he say in answer to a statement like that? All he could do was reassure her, he supposed. "We'll marry, of course. As soon as you're recovered. You have no worries about your future, madam, I promise you that."

Those green eyes flashed in quick anger, anger being preferable to tears. "Aren't you generous," she said, her voice all but dripping venom. "It's not my future that brought me here."

"Perhaps not, madam, but that's what is going to happen. No son of mine will be a bastard, never knowing his father. Or did you simply think I would hand you money and send you and the child on your way?"

"I didn't know what you'd do," she admitted quietly. "Yes, marriage had occurred to me. It seemed a logical answer." She looked up at him again. "Until now."

"How did you find me?" Spencer asked, to avoid an answer to her last words, not that he had one.

Mariah shifted on the sheets. "There was a letter in your jacket. Bloodstained, but I could make out some of it. Someone named Callie signed it, adding the words Becket Hall, Romney Marsh to her signature. No one knew you when we landed at Dover but the closer we drove, the more people were able to direct the coach on the proper roads. It's difficult to believe this is England. The landscape is so singular. I lived with my father in the Lake District, until we left for North America eight years ago."

"Clovis tells me your father was the quartermaster at Fort Malden. Yet we never met."

Mariah caught her bottom lip between her teeth for a moment, the mention of her father, who would never see her child, obviously piercing her heart. "Papa kept me fairly well isolated from the men once we were moved into the fort as our losses mounted. And the Indians, of course, no matter what Onatah told him to the contrary. He was certain they'd be after my hair if they had a chance."

Spencer looked at the mass of golden-red curls spread out on the pillow; living fire. His fingers itched to reach out to stroke that hair, to learn whether it was as soft and warm to the touch as it appeared. "I remember your hair. I don't know why, but I do. Your hair, your voice." He shook his head. "But that's all. I'm sorry. Clovis told me you were very brave and that he doubts anyone would have survived without you. Me, most especially. So I thank you."

"You're welcome," Mariah said, wishing he'd leave the room. She was going to cry. She wasn't exactly sure why, but she was definitely going to cry. She wanted, needed, to cry.

"He also told me about the child who died. We…we have a small tradition, us Beckets. When I was brought to…when Ainsley adopted me, I was given the name of a sailor who had died. With that in mind, I thought we might name the child William. William Becket."

Mariah squeezed her eyes shut. Would he please just go away? "William Henry Becket. After my father, as well."

Spencer laughed shortly. "William Henry? As in William Henry Harrison, the American general who beat us so soundly?"

Now Mariah was caught between tears and laughter. Thankfully, laughter won. "General Proctor's name is Henry," she pointed out, grinning at him. "Perhaps we need to reconsider this whole thing?"

"No," Spencer told her. "William Henry Becket. And he'll grow to be his own man, as we all must. Now, madam, I think you should rest."

"I was just about to suggest the same thing," Mariah

said, sighing. "But I would like to see William again, please. Just for a minute?"

Spencer looked to the door to the dressing room, then to Mariah. "He was sleeping when I looked in on him a few minutes ago. And alone. Um…I'll go find somebody."

"Why? Just bring him to me, Mr. Becket."

"Spencer, Mariah. I think you'll agree that we're a bit beyond formalities."

Just when she thought she could begin to relax, he was looking at her that way again. So intense. She had to look away and hated him for making her so nervous. "Yes, of course. Spencer. Just pick him up and bring him to me. You can do that, can't you?"

He'd rather juggle siege cannonballs. With their fuses lit. "Yes, certainly." He looked toward the door once more. "Is there…is there anything I should know about him?"

"I don't think he'll break, if that's what you mean," Mariah said shortly, then took pity on him. She threw back the coverlet. "Oh, let me do it."

Spencer held out his hands to stop her. "I said I'd do it, damn it."

"Thank God," Mariah said quietly, falling back against the pillows. She really was exhausted and more than a little sore. "Support his head, please."

"What?" Spencer asked, already halfway to the dressing room. But he kept going, knowing that if he stopped he'd probably turn into a complete coward and simply run away, like Proctor. So he opened the door slowly and looked into the dim room at the cradle someone had brought down from the nursery.

Their ship's carpenter had made the cradle for Callie, so many years ago. Pike, dead now, one of the first casualties in their personal war with the Red Men Gang. But the cradle was still here, the magnificent carving done with such talent, such love, the oils of Pike's hands as he stroked and smoothed the wood permeating it, giving it color and life. In this cradle, Pike lived on. They all lived on, every last lost man of the Black Ghost and Silver Ghost crews, if only in the memories of those who had sailed with them.

Just as young Willy would live on in William Henry Becket.

For the first time Spencer truly understood why he and the others had been taken to the island, taken in, been fashioned into a family by Ainsley Becket. By Geoffrey Baskin, who had died sixteen years ago, come to this most deserted area of Romney Marsh coastline, and become Ainsley Becket. If he could be half the father Ainsley was, he'd be a happy man.

Spencer looked down on his sleeping son, a cotton-wrapped warm brick snuggled against his back. There was a small brown cloth bag tucked into one corner of the cradle, tied with colorful ribbons and with a single feather protruding from the top. Odette and her charms and amulets. The child would soon probably have his own *gad*—an alligator tooth dipped in powerful potions to ward off bad *loas,* bad spirits. Spencer believed he might have some small trouble explaining that to Mariah. Ah well, as long as Odette was happy.

William's incredibly small hands were in tight fists, hanging on to this new life with fierce tenacity, already looking as if he knew there would be times he'd have to fight.

But not alone; never alone.

Something drew up hard and tight in Spencer's chest, just like William's fists, and he marveled at the feeling, at the fierce protectiveness he felt all but overwhelm him.

My son. My God, my son.

"Spencer? Just put one hand beneath his bottom and the other behind his head," Mariah called to him from the other room.

Spencer blinked, realized his eyes were wet. He'd been alone for so long. Alone, amid the crowd of Beckets. Always looking for his own way, some reason for being here, for being alive at all. Always angry, always fighting and not knowing why.

And now, William.

And now, in an instant, everything made sense.

He bent over the cradle, carefully scooping up the closely wrapped infant, pressing him against his heart. The knot in his chest tightened even more, then slowly dissolved, filling him with a warmth of feeling that threatened to completely unman him.

Slowly, as if he were carrying the most precious of treasures, he returned to the bedchamber and crossed to the high tester bed. "He's so small. It's like holding air."

Mariah reached up her arms. "Amazing, isn't it? For the past few months I would have sworn to anyone who asked that I was carrying a sack full of rocks wherever I went. Please? Give him to me?"

Spencer handed the child to her and immediately felt the loss of that slight weight. "He stays here," he said firmly. "You stay if you wish, marry me, or go if you like. But the boy stays here."

Mariah ignored him, gazing in wonder at her child who, until she'd actually seen him, held him, had been considered little more than yet another problem to be solved in a world filled with problems. "He has my eyes. See? Tipped up at the edges a bit? That won't make him look too girlish, will it?"

"*Madame*, I'll have your answer," Spencer said, feeling fierce and wishing himself civilized. But then, he'd never been all that civilized.

She tightened her hold on the infant as she glared up at Spencer. "I liked you better when you were nearly senseless. You didn't talk so much. Yes, I'll marry you. For William, for what appears to be your very kind and concerned family, I'll marry you. But attempt to touch me again, Spencer Becket, and I'll gut you like a deer. Do we understand each other?"

Spencer watched her eyes, those tip-tilted green eyes that had looked so lovingly at William and now stared icily at him. The fire of her hair, the sudden ice of her eyes.

He remembered Jacko's joking comment and unashamedly used it. "I could say the same to you, Mariah, as I was hardly in any position to fight off your advances, was I? Another man might say you took unfair advantage of me."

"But another man didn't say that, did he? You did. Another man might not have been fevered and distraught and reaching out to someone, to anyone. And another woman might not have been so frightened, so alone...so foolish as to yearn for someone to hold on to, for someone to tell her that, yes, she was still alive, she could still feel...and that being held, being kissed, being touched, was so natural, so human a need..."

"Sweet Jesus," Spencer said, rubbing roughly at his aching head. She'd just said exactly what he'd thought last night, put those thoughts into words that sliced at him, humbled him. "I don't remember, Mariah. I *can't* remember. I'm...I'm so, so sorry. Was it so terrible?"

"You? Were you so terrible? Is that what you mean?"

Spencer attempted a smile. "Consider it manly pride, madam. If the thought of me touching you ever again upsets you so, I must imagine that the experience wasn't exactly a maiden's dream."

Mariah didn't know what to say, where to look. "I'm sorry. I didn't mean...that is, I didn't know what to expect."

"But, whatever you did expect, it wasn't what you received?"

"No, I suppose not." She kissed William's head. "When you were gone, I was glad. I knew I couldn't face you, not after what we'd... And then, when I realized what had happened...that I was... Can we please discuss this some other time?"

"When you realized you were carrying my child," Spencer finished for her. He was pushing her, he knew that. But there was so much he couldn't remember. How in hell could a man forget bedding this woman? "You must have hated me then."

"I can't hate you now. Look at him. Something good, coming out of something so terrible. So many lives lost, and now there's him."

Spencer sat on the side of the bed, laid his hand on the small, tightly swaddled infant. "Let's begin again," he suggested quietly, then smiled. "No, let's *begin*. There's no *again* about it, is there? For William?"

Mariah pressed a hand to her mouth to stifle a sob. "I'm so tired. I feel as if I've been fighting forever, fighting the entire world. I don't want to fight with you now, too." She managed a watery smile. "Besides, Eleanor tells me you're all bluster and heat and hot passions, but really a very nice man. Of course, she's your sister so she probably doesn't really know you all that well."

"You're right," Spencer said, grinning in relief. "I'm actually a blackguard who sold his soul to the devil years ago. We just don't tell Elly because she likes to think the best of everyone."

Mariah returned his smile. "You look nothing like her or the man I met downstairs last night. You said you were adopted. And Eleanor?"

Spencer made a small face. This was going to be difficult. There were things he could tell her and much more he could never tell her. Giving birth to his son did not make Mariah Rutledge a Becket.

The baby stirred in her arms and he pressed a finger against William's opening hand, only to have the child grasp that finger tightly.

"Our son has Spanish blood," he began slowly, feeling his way. "At least that's what we believe. I'm told that I spat some fairly choice Spanish at Ainsley the day he found me, took me home with him. Unfortunately, I've forgotten most of it."

"I don't understand."

"I wouldn't expect you to," Spencer told her, smiling even as he sorted facts in his mind, deciding what to reveal, what to conceal. "Ainsley isn't my father or father to any of us except Cassandra—Callie—whose letter you found. The rest of us? Flotsam and jetsam he picked up along the way when he was living in the islands. Haiti. Have you heard of it?"

Mariah nodded. "I think I could point it out on a map, yes. To the south and east of the American Florida, yes? It must be warm there."

And then it got hot…too hot to remain there.

"Papa…Ainsley owned sailing ships. Trading ships," he said, keeping to the story that had been told for so long that he sometimes even believed it.

"And you all lived on the island. Haiti."

"No, not on Haiti itself. We, um, we had our own island. There are several to choose from in the area."

Why, the man sounded positively embarrassed. Or leery of telling her about his youth. Which was it? "Oh, my. That does sound important. And wonderfully warm weather for all of the year. No snow, no ice freezing over the rivers every winter so that you are virtually isolated from the world. How could you bear to leave?"

"The girls were beginning to grow up, so he decided it was time to return to England. And here we are."

"And who are *we?*"

Spencer felt on firmer ground here. "I told you that Callie is Ainsley's own child. Her mother died shortly after she was born. Callie's—good God, she's about sixteen now. You'll meet her soon enough, I'm sure—it's difficult to keep Callie away from anything she wants. And then there's Morgan. This is her bedchamber, hers and her husband's, when they visit here from Ethan's estate. Morgan's the Countess of Aylesford now and the mother of twins I've yet to see, now that the earl is making himself useful at the War Office and a nuisance in Parliament—but that's another story."

"One I hope to hear," Mariah said, committing the

names to memory. "And the young man from last night? Rian, was it?"

He nodded. "You'll have to excuse him. He isn't usually so silly. Ainsley gathered up Rian and Fanny from the rubble of a church that had taken cannon fire." He smiled wanly. "Another long story, I'm afraid."

"Fanny and Rian," Mariah repeated. "Are they brother and sister?"

"No, not by blood." The baby stirred slightly, made a small sound, and Spencer's heart lurched in his chest. "Is he all right?"

"I think so. He may be getting hungry, poor little scrap. You should probably call someone. And that's all? You, Rian, Callie, Morgan and Eleanor, who has already told me that she lives here with her husband, Jack…"

"And Fanny," he added helpfully. "Then there's Chance, the oldest of us all. He has his own estate north of London and is married, with two children of his own. And Courtland. God, let's not forget Court. He still lives here and probably always will. You'll recognize him by the perpetual scowl on his bearded face. The world sits heavily on Court's shoulders, you understand."

Mariah lifted William's hand to her mouth, kissed it. "Why?"

"Why?" Spencer repeated, inwardly wincing. Damn his tongue for running too hard. Explaining his family without exposing his family was difficult in the best of times. "No reason. Court just likes to see himself as being in charge of all of us. Elly, too, come to think of it. But they're not. Ainsley is the head of the family, very much so."

"Such a large family. I had only my father," Mariah said. "It must be wonderful, having so many brothers and sisters."

Spencer smiled. "Many would think so, I suppose."

"But you don't?"

"That's not—of course I do. But I'm a younger son and sometimes I feel as if I'm standing at the end of a long queue, awaiting my turn to—never mind."

"No," Mariah said, truly interested. "Waiting your turn for what, Spencer?"

My turn to live. The words were in his mind, but he didn't say them, ashamed of his desire, his *need,* to be his own man, unburdened by the shadow of Ainsley's past and the dangers that past still held for them all. Because he'd always believed there was a life away from Romney Marsh and, now that he'd seen it, he felt more confined than ever. Because to say the words out loud would brand him as an ungrateful bastard.

Mariah felt the sudden tension in the room and raced to fill the silence. "So Ainsley was once in the shipping trade, you said. What do you all do here? Farm? Herd sheep? What do people do in Romney Marsh?"

Free trade. Ride hell for leather across the Marsh after midnight as the mist rises all round, outrunning the militia as the casks of brandy and tea are moved inland. Race ahead of the wind on the Respite *upon occasion, just for the thrill of it, playing cat and mouse with a French frigate patrolling the Channel. Cool their heels two weeks out of every four and stare at the choppy sea, aching to see what lies beyond the water.*

Spencer bit back a smile. "We keep ourselves busy," he said, standing up once more. "I'll go find Odette."

"They've already bound my breasts," Mariah heard herself say, and then lowered her head, her cheeks hot. "They won't even let me try. But if it's best for William, I suppose I understand."

"I'm…I'm sorry," Spencer said, sure that Mariah was upset. "You haven't had an easy time of things. I'm sure your woman is only thinking of your own health, as should you. I don't remember most of my voyage home. Was yours an easy crossing?"

She shook her head, wishing away these silly tears that kept threatening. "We had storms most of the way. For six long weeks I spent the majority of my time with my head over a bucket, I'm afraid." She lifted a hand, let it drop onto the coverlet once more. "I know they're right." Her face crumpled slightly. "But I'm his mother."

Spencer felt as useless as a wart on the end of Prinney's nose and sighed in real relief when the door to the hallway opened and Odette came sailing in, a young woman following behind her.

"Here now," Odette said, taking in the scene. "Is

this what you're good for, Spencer Becket? Making the girl cry? Take yourself off and be glad I don't turn you into a toad and step on you."

"But I—oh, never mind. Who's this?"

"I'm Sheila, sir," the small brunette said. "Jacob's wife."

"Jacob Whiting? Morgan's Jacob?" Spencer asked, remembering how Jacob had followed Morgan like a puppy for years, the poor besotted fool.

"Not no more he ain't, sir," Sheila said, raising her chin. "I'm weaning my own little Jacob now, and Odette asked for me to nurse the new little one, and that's what I'm doing. Sir."

It seemed he was being put in his place every time he opened his mouth, so Spencer merely nodded and quit the room, promising to return later to see his son again, adding to himself: *when there weren't so many damned women around.*

Mariah sniffled, still feeling sorry for herself, and watched him go, because asking him to stay would make her appear weak and she had the feeling that, no matter how rosy a picture Spencer had painted of Becket Hall and its inhabitants, she would need to be very strong in order to survive here in this strange place. What was odd was that she was beginning to think that Spencer thought the same thing about himself.

CHAPTER FOUR

FOUR DAYS PASSED with Mariah sleeping almost constantly, regaining strength dissipated by the long journey and the hours of labor. And she was content, except when she was complaining. She could see William. He could be laid on her bed. She could stroke his head, kiss his fingers. But she couldn't hold him because, Onatah explained, to hold him would be to draw more milk into her breasts.

She saw Spencer twice during that time, as he seemed to be avoiding her chamber, even as he used the separate door from the hallway to the dressing room to see his son. *He* could hold William and, irrational as she knew her feelings to be, she hated him for that.

On the fifth day, Mariah decided she'd had enough. Remain in bed for ten long days? What nonsense! She had given birth. Surely a natural process for a woman. And she felt fine. Well, as fine as anyone could possibly feel, being deprived of most fluids in order to keep the milk away, her breasts strapped tight to her—not to mention the layers of folded cloth between her legs as she continued to bleed, also something she had been told was perfectly natural.

Onatah and Odette had already come and gone, fussing over her, subjecting her to the indignity of washing her, just as if she couldn't do such basic things for herself—it was an amazement to her that they let her clean her own teeth! William was back in his cradle, sleeping the sleep of the well fed; Sheila Whiting had gone back to her own baby.

Mariah was alone. Blessedly alone.

She pushed back the covers and swung herself into a sitting position, ignoring the fact that lying prone for five days could tend to make a person slightly dizzy when that person first attempted to stand up. She took a few deep, steadying breaths, then looked down at the floor, which seemed quite far away.

There was a knock at the door moments before it opened. "Damn it!"

"Mariah? Mariah, what are you doing?"

"Shh, Callie," Mariah called quietly. "Come in here and close the door. Lock it, if necessary. I'm getting up. I'm getting up, I'm getting dressed and I'm going downstairs to see something besides these four very pretty but confining walls before I go stark, staring out of my mind. And it wouldn't be quietly, I promise you."

Callie closed the door and padded across the room to stand at the bottom of the bed. Such a petite, pretty child, all golden-brown curls and huge velvet-brown eyes over a small, pert nose and bee-stung mouth. An angel of a child. Except that, as Mariah had learned to her delight over the past days, Cassandra Becket had the heart of a warrior. And all the deviltry of a born mischief-maker.

"Odette won't like this, you not obeying her orders. Everyone obeys Odette, you know, and is afraid to take a step wrong around her," Callie pointed out and then grinned. "Should I get your clothing for you?"

"Would you?" Mariah asked, sliding off the mattress until her bare feet connected with the carpet. "Everything has been washed and pressed, thank God, not that there's much I didn't strain at the seams these past months." She looked down at her belly beneath the voluminous white night rail. "Oh, would you look at me? Do you think there's another babe still to come out? I still look as round as a dinner plate."

Callie giggled. "Oh, you should have seen Morgan after the twins were born. Ethan called her his pumpkin, which earned him a shoe tossed at his head. Do you ride? Morgan was back on her horse before anyone could say differently and she swears it helped. I've always been a little plump, although it's finally going away—Odette said it was baby fat. But I know how you feel. Not that I'd want to be all bones like Elly, but no one wants to have someone else shaking their head and tsk-tsking, just because you've reached for a second muffin."

While Callie was chattering she was also opening

drawers and cupboard doors, pulling out undergarments, hose, a yellow and white sprigged muslin gown that had been one of Mariah's father's favorites—and one of the few personal possessions she had insisted on dragging through the woods after the battle—and a pair of black kid slippers that, alas, had seen better days.

"Would you like anything else?" Callie asked. "I can turn my head, but it would probably be easier if I just helped you, don't you think? I helped Morgan the day she sneaked out of bed. I think she lasted one more day than you, though."

"Thank you." Mariah believed she may have left her modesty somewhere, because she couldn't seem to muster much at the moment, and began stripping out of her night rail, allowing it to drop to her feet, so that she stood there in her cloth-wrapped bosom, pantaloons that held the cloths between her legs in place, and not much else. "There are a multitude of indignities associated with giving birth, Callie," she told her seriously, "beginning with the moment a woman you once thought to be perfectly rational kneels on the bed between your spread legs and shouts excitedly, 'I can see the head! Push! Push!'"

Callie giggled again. "Morgan says she wouldn't have cared if the whole world had been standing there watching while her bottom was bare, just as long as someone for God's sake got that baby out of her. Of course, she had two babies in there. Morgan does nothing in half measures."

"She won't mind that I've been using her chamber?" Mariah asked as she began unwrapping the cloth binding her breasts and then sighed in blessed relief once it was gone, feeling as if she was now taking her first full breath in days. She cupped her bare breasts in her hands, rather marveling at a new heaviness, gained during the pregnancy, that hadn't seemed to have abandoned her. "Oh, that feels so much better. Would you please hand me my shift?"

"Mariah, I thought I'd see how you—*oh, bloody hell.*"

Mariah looked toward the door to the dressing room, to see Spencer standing there, looking at her as if…well, she really didn't want to consider what he might be thinking.

She grabbed at the shift Callie was holding and pressed it against her breasts. "Some people knock and then ask permission before entering a woman's bedchamber, sir," she said, hoping the tremor she heard in her voice wasn't apparent to him. She wouldn't even think of the way her nipples seemed to have tightened the moment she realized he had seen her bare breasts. She had never suckled William, but that night, that wild and insane night, Spencer Becket had fastened his fever-hot mouth to her as she'd given herself over to the moment—and the man.

Spencer was looking at the floor as if there might be something of great interest lying there. "Some people, madam, were supposed to remain in bed, resting. What in blazes do you think you're doing?"

"Oh, for pity's sake, Spence," Callie said, rolling her eyes at Mariah. "She's getting dressed. What did you think she was doing? Go away."

As quickly as it had come, Spencer's embarrassment left him. "No," he said, raising his eyes to look at Mariah. "You leave, Callie. *Now.*"

"But, Spence, she's not even dressed. I can't, oh, for pity's sake, don't *glower* at me like that." She looked apologetically at Mariah. "Ten minutes. I'll be back in ten minutes," she promised. Then she stomped past Spencer, glaring at him, and left the room.

Mariah turned her back to the man. "Are you always such a bully?" she asked, fumbling with the shift, trying to cover herself better even as she knew her back was bare to her waist.

"Probably, yes," he said, reaching around her to take hold of the shift. He should have left the field, retreated, but not yet. Definitely not yet. "Here, let me help you."

"No," she protested, knowing that the bundled shift was all that covered her breasts. But he wasn't listening to her or at least he wasn't obeying her.

She couldn't struggle or else his hand might slip. The shift might slip.

"Mariah, you just gave birth," Spencer told her, his breath warm against her bare shoulder. "I'm not a monster."

She closed her eyes, nodded. And let go of the shift.

"Ah, that's better. Raise your arms, Mariah."

She'd rather die. She felt so vulnerable. "Just…just

drop it over my head, please. I can manage from there. And turn your back!"

Spencer smiled, then realized he was probably fortunate Mariah couldn't see that smile. "Would turning my back come before or after I lower the shift over your head? After all, my aim might be off, and I'd end up dressing the bedpost."

"Oh, for pity's sake! You're perfectly useless, aren't you? I'll do it myself." Keeping her right arm pressed across her bare breasts, she turned on him, grabbed the shift from his hands and then turned her back to him once more, struggling with her free hand to find the head-hole of the damned, uncooperative shift.

He didn't know why he did what he did, even as he knew he was being, as so many told him, so often, *impossible*. Because what he did was perch himself on the side of the mattress, right next to Mariah, fold his arms and say with a grin, "Have at it, my dear. I'll just watch."

"I could cheerfully hate you," Mariah told him honestly, then gave up all modesty in order to turn the shift about with both hands, locate the head-hole and finally drop the damnable thing over her head, shoving her arms into the armholes. And tug. Tug again. "It doesn't fit. Did you open the buttons?"

Spencer looked at her, her head poking up from the bodice that seemed stuck halfway over her lush, full breasts. Even her arms were stuck. "I believe I've seen scarecrows in the field that look much as you do now, madam. But you're correct. I do think I neglected to open all of the buttons. Would you like me to do that now?"

"No," Mariah groused, knowing she must look exactly like a scarecrow, damn him. She was hot, she was frustrated, her hair was tumbling into her eyes, and if he didn't help her she'd be stuck in this ignoble position until Callie came back into the room. "What I'd *like* is for you to go straight to hell, Spencer Becket."

"I'll take that as a yes, in any event," Spencer said, pushing away from the bed and stepping behind her to open the last half dozen buttons on the shift, then giving the material a yank, settling the straps on her shoulders. "There, you're decent now."

"Not in my mind, I'm not," Mariah told him honestly. "In my mind, I'm committing murder upon your person, in several unlovely and definitely painful ways. But as long as you're here, now you may button me again. Please."

"Ah. Please. How can I possibly refuse?"

Mariah stood still, fuming as he began buttoning the shift, from bottom to top. His fingers kept brushing against the skin of her back and for some reason that incidental contact—please let it be incidental—served to tighten her nipples, so that she felt her breasts to be actually straining against the material.

Which was nothing compared to the way her insides reacted when, finished with the buttons, he put his hands on her shoulders, then bent to lightly brush his lips against her nape. "Thank you, again, Mariah, for William."

She whirled around to push him away, completely forgetting that she was still standing within the puddle of her night rail, and ended by crashing against his chest, her hands on his shoulders to support herself.

"My God," Spencer said, his senses swimming as he looked at her; that swirl of living fire that was her hair, those bewitching green eyes. "How in bloody hell could I have forgotten you?"

"I...I don't know. As you said, I took advantage of you," Mariah said, closing her eyes as his hands slipped down to cup her waist. "Don't...don't do that."

"We're to be married," he reminded her, his concentration centering on her full, slightly parted lips.

"And?" Mariah asked, arching one brow at him. "You sound as if you're purchasing a horse. Pay the price, and I'm yours to...to do anything with?"

Spencer removed his hands, held them up at his sides in mock surrender. "Clearly we don't know each other very well yet, do we? Will you feel better if I tell you that I don't believe marriage makes you my possession?"

Mariah stepped out of the tangle of night rail and walked to where her robe hung over the back of a chair. "Yet you said I could leave, but William would stay. I think we should see this marriage for what it is, don't you? It will be for William. As for anything else?" She slipped her arms into the robe and turned to face him, the material of the robe held tight over her breasts. "I should wish to be recovered from William's birth before we even discuss the idea of marriage again."

At the moment, Spencer believed he would agree to anything. His palms still burned from where they had made contact with Mariah's soft skin, so pale beneath his tanned hands, and the mere thought of her creamy breasts, how she had seemed to be holding, weighing them in her cupped palms—as if offering them to him, or at least that's how he'd always remember that sight—would probably haunt his nights. "You want time, Mariah. I understand that. How long?"

She shrugged, wondering how much time she could reasonably ask for without daring his refusal. "A month? Two?"

He nodded. "A compromise, then. Six weeks, Mariah. But we will be married."

"For the child," she reiterated.

"For whatever reasons may occur to us. The gutting me like a deer, Mariah, will remain negotiable," he replied, and then turned his head as Callie knocked lightly on the door and then reentered the room. "Callie, help Mariah finish dressing, please."

"You say that as if that wasn't what I was doing when you first stumbled in here and sent me out of the room," his sister reminded him. "Or have you forgotten that?"

Spencer rolled his eyes. "No wonder Court calls

you his unholy terror," he said before bowing to Mariah. "Don't overtax yourself, madam. Good day."

"I'll be very careful, sir," Mariah shot back at him. "Just as you will be careful to knock next time you come to visit, and then wait for my permission to enter my chamber."

The door had slammed on Spencer's back before the last words left Mariah's mouth.

She looked at the closed door for a few moments and then at Callie. She raised her eyebrows.

Callie raised her own eyebrows.

The corners of their mouths twitched as their eyes danced.

And then the two of them laughed out loud.

"Did you see his face when he first came barging in here?" Callie said, wiping at her eyes as their laughter subsided. "I thought he was going to swallow his own tongue."

"Well," Mariah said, removing the robe, "I was standing there, holding on to myself, just as brazen as you please. Oh, Lord, Callie, *what* am I laughing at? He *dressed* me! I'm so embarrassed. *Mortified.* Quickly, help me on with my gown before I'm tempted to crawl back under the covers, never to show myself again. As it is, I'll never be able to look at the man again."

"I don't know. He certainly was looking at *you*," Callie said, helping Mariah into her gown. "Turn around and let me button this, if I can see the buttons through my tears. Mariah, I'm so glad you're here. With Morgan gone, we're so stodgy and boring these days. But I think that's about to change."

Mariah slipped into her shoes and walked across the large room to the dressing table where Onatah had laid out her brushes. She sat down in front of the three-piece mirror and fairly goggled at herself. Look at her hair! She looked like a wild woman. Why hadn't Spencer run screaming from the room, convinced he'd been compromised into wedding a witch?

She picked up a brush and began attacking the mass of hair that fell well past her shoulders, waving so wildly that it was almost as if only half of her face could peek through to the world. Which might not be too terrible, if she didn't want to look at Spencer. "It's all so thick and heavy and a terrible nuisance. I should have Onatah just cut it all off," she said as Callie picked up another brush and began working on the left side of Mariah's head.

"Cut this beautiful hair? Are you mad? I've never seen hair this color. It's so alive. It's like…like a candle flame. I heard Spencer the other night when he thought I wasn't listening. He was telling Rian that he remembered your hair. 'Like fire in the sunlight,' he said. It's not like Spence to be poetical."

"It's not?" Mariah asked, daring to open the drawers in the dressing table, then borrowing a dark green ribbon she discovered in one of them. She was so curious to learn more about the man who was to become her husband. "What is it like Spencer to be?"

"Angry," Callie said, taking the ribbon and tying back Mariah's hair in a thick tail at her nape. "He's always angry. Papa says he's got the passions of a hot-blooded man and chafes at the confines of Becket Hall, of how we live. There! Doesn't that look pretty? Are you ready to go downstairs now, before Spencer finds Odette and tattles and you're slapped back into bed?"

"Certainly," Mariah said, rising to her feet and brushing down the front of her gown. "I'd like to go outside, if that's possible. Breathe some sea air. The world should smell good after three days of storms."

"Only if the Channel didn't spit up something terrible from the bottom," Callie told her, grinning. "We'll use the front stairs. Odette never uses them, even though Papa told her she could. But he gave that up as a bad job years ago. Odette does what Odette does. She's a *mamba,* you know. A real voodoo priestess. She's taught me a lot, but says that I'm not a chosen one, so she won't teach me more. Maybe she'll teach you. She likes your hair, you see. Says it's a sign from the good *loa.* Magical living flame. I wish I had magical living flame hair. Mine is just brown. So depressingly ordinary, and there's so very much of it. If only it wouldn't curl so, like a baby's hair. I detest ringlets...."

Mariah let Callie chatter on as they walked and she examined her surroundings, as she'd been otherwise occupied the first time she'd entered the very large, impressive foyer of this huge house. Squire Franklin's manor house had been the grandest dwelling she'd seen at home, and she'd lived in her share of small, cramped quarters, following her father to North America.

But Squire Franklin's prideful possession paled in comparison to Becket Hall. Most anything would, she imagined. In fact, at least half of the Squire's domicile would probably have fit comfortably in the foyer of Becket Hall.

They passed Edyth in the hallway, and Mariah asked if she would please sit with William for an hour. The woman's smile was all the answer she'd needed to assure herself that the infant would be in good hands.

Odette had been kind enough to explain how Becket Hall was run, and the whole arrangement seemed very democratic. Almost American in the way everyone was free to do what he or she did best, and with responsibility placed on each person's shoulders by that person him- or herself. Odette had also told her of the years of slavery in Haiti before the slaves had risen in their own version of the French Revolution and Ainsley Becket's abhorrence for anything that even vaguely resembled forcing anyone to do anything.

Mariah would have thought that everyone would just lie about, doing nothing, yet Becket Hall was pristine, beautifully organized. And the maids, if they had to be given a title, sang as they worked.

Callie descended the wide, curving staircase slowly,

looking back at Mariah every few steps, as if she might faint and topple on her, but then they were crossing the wide foyer and Callie's slim shoulders seemed to relax.

"Papa is in his study most days at this time, reading all of the London newspapers that he has shipped to him, and everyone else is out and about somewhere—and Spence is probably hiding his head somewhere in shame. Do you want to see the drawing room first?"

"You seem to be enjoying your brother's discomfort," Mariah pointed out, smiling.

"Oh, yes, definitely. It's lovely to not be the one Odette will be giving the hairy eyeball for this once. That's what Rian calls the way Odette *looks* at us—the hairy eyeball. I have *no* idea what that means. Well, here's the drawing room. You probably didn't notice much of anything the night you arrived here."

The furniture in the main drawing room was massive, much of it, Mariah believed, Spanish—she'd once seen a book of drawings on such things. The ceilings soared, the windows rose from the floor to nearly touch those high ceilings and the fabrics that covered those windows and the multitude of furniture in the drawing room were of sumptuous silks and vibrant brocades. She strained to take in the fine artwork hanging on pale, stuccoed walls and to count all the many vases of exotic flowers and acres of fine Turkish carpets spread out over gleaming wooden floors the color of dried cherries.

"All these flowers," she said, cupping one perfect pink bloom in her palm.

Callie nodded. "We have a conservatory and Papa is always adding new flowers and plants he has shipped here. But it's Jacko who cares for them. I'll show it to you later, if Jacko says it's all right. He's very possessive of his babies. Not that he calls the flowers his babies, but that's what Rian says."

"Then I'll wait for his permission," Mariah said, continuing her examination of the large room.

None of the four immense crystal chandeliers, each hanging from a different coffered area of the ornate ceiling, had been lit, as all the draperies had been thrown back so that only sheer ivory silk panels with fleur-de-lis woven into them covered the windows that poured with sunlight.

One enormous glass-fronted cabinet placed between two of the windows displayed a collection of jade that was probably worth a king's ransom. The far wall—it was very far away in this large room—actually had a highly ornamental black metal grille hanging on it, the entire piece nearly the size of a barn door. And yet it didn't overpower the other furnishings. Little could.

"It's humble," Mariah said cheekily, "but I imagine that, to you, it's simply *home*."

Callie frowned at her, not understanding, and Mariah wanted to slap herself for speaking so plainly. This was a fine home and she should be on her best behavior…and she would be, if she knew what that was. But she was a quartermaster's motherless daughter, brought up in some rather rough-and-tumble locations, and she was probably both more unsophisticated and more blunt than most young English ladies.

The paintings on the walls were magnificent: landscapes, seascapes. And, when she walked toward a fireplace that could probably comfortably roast an ox on a spit, it was to see something else she had missed that first night—the nearly life-size portrait of one of the most beautiful women she'd ever seen. Her hair was a mass of dark curls, her smile lit up the room and her striped, full-skirted gown was bright, colorful. *Exotic.*

"Mama," Callie said as Mariah walked closer for a better look. "Her name was Isabella. I don't remember her and I don't look like her. Everyone says I do, but I'm not half so…so vibrant. I'm the pale English version, I suppose. Papa bought most everything in this room and many of the others while he lived in the islands and had it all shipped here on his boats, for years and years, to be stored until we found Becket Hall. Oh, and I meant ships. Jacko winces if I don't say ships."

"Jacko again." Mariah returned her attention to Callie, who could prove to be a fountain of information—if she could only find the correct way to ask her questions, that is. "I don't recall that name in the list of Becket siblings. But he is a Becket?"

"Jacko? Oh, no, he's not a Becket. Jacko is Papa's

business partner. Most everyone came here with Papa when he decided it was time to return to England. Why, they even broke up the ships and used the lumber to build the village. We're very self-sustaining, Papa calls it."

"And quite isolated," Mariah said, now heading for the hallway again. "This room seems to be at the front of the house. I want to see the water. I don't know why, as I saw much too much water for six long weeks. I think I'm simply attempting to get my bearings and I'm all turned about at the moment. Which way would I go?"

"This way," Callie said, leading the way down another wide hallway, Mariah following slowly, taking time to peak into several other large rooms, all of them furnished in equal grandeur. The Beckets were obviously not worried where the pennies for their next meal might come from. She stopped at one doorway, leaning a hand against the jamb. "A piano! Oh, and a harp! Do you have musical evenings, Callie?"

Callie backtracked to look into the room done all in golds and reds, just as if she'd never seen it before this moment. "The music room. The piano is mine. Papa gave it to me one Christmas, as soon as he learned of the invention. What sort of present comes with an obligation for daily practice? Elly plays much better than I could ever aspire to do. And Spencer sings. But never ask Court to sing. He will, most willingly, but he's not very good. Now come on. We can't be safe for much longer before someone will see us and—oh, good morning, Jacko."

Mariah turned around to see a huge man standing in front of her. Not that he was overly tall, but he was, as her father would have said, a door-full of man. Broad, with a hard, rounded stomach that she felt certain she could bounce coins off, if she dared. He was dressed simply in white shirt and tan breeches, his muscular calves straining at white hose. His dark hair had begun to thin atop a huge head and he had a smile that seemed to be full of amusement and a joy for life.

Until, that is, she looked more closely. Because that's what he was doing—looking more closely at her, his head forward on his neck, his heavy, slightly hunched shoulders hinting at an aggression his smile would put the lie to only for anyone who wished to believe in fairy tales.

This was the man who had grown all those beautiful flowers? The idea seemed incomprehensible, as he looked more like the ogre who would invade a town, frighten all the children and stomp on all the pretty posies.

Mariah fought the urge to step back a pace and instead lifted her chin even as she dropped into a slight curtsey. "Mr. Jacko, I am Mariah Rutledge. I'm pleased to make your acquaintance."

Jacko reached up his right hand to scratch beneath his left ear, a curious gesture, but one that now had his head tilted to the right, so that he seemed to be looking at her now out of the corners of his bean-black eyes. "Just Jacko. There's no *mister* about it. So, you're the one who gave us that fine boy upstairs. I haven't laughed so long or hard in a long time."

Mariah lifted her chin even higher. "You find my son amusing, Jacko?"

Now he tipped his head from side to side, as if weighing how he would answer. A fascinating man, but perhaps fascinating in the way a North American rattlesnake could be fascinating. "No, Mariah, girl. I find the fix Spencer's in amusing. You've just tied him fast to Becket Hall, didn't you now? Tied him hard and fast, when we couldn't find a way to make him stay. The Cap'n's over the moon, though he'd never say so. He likes to know where his chicks are."

Mariah knew her cheeks had gone pale. "Spencer...Spencer didn't plan to stay here? Where was he going to go?"

Jacko shrugged those massive shoulders. "Which way is the wind blowing today, Miss Rutledge?" He lifted a hand to his forehead in a blatantly mocking salute. "But he won't be sailing off now. What with the fine great anchor you tied fast to his ankle."

"Jacko," Callie said quietly. "That was a mean thing to say. Go away."

And, to Mariah's amazement, that's just what the man did, turning his back on the pair of them and heading toward the front of the house. Her body inwardly sagged in relief.

"Did he mean that, Callie? Was Spencer planning to leave?"

Callie shrugged. "Spencer has always talked about the places he'd like to see. China. America. I think he'd cheerfully sail off to the moon, if it took him away from Becket Hall. That's why he went off to the Army. He wanted to fight Napoléon, see the Continent. But he was sent to Canada instead." She smiled. "But that's how he met you, Mariah, and now you're going to be married. Elly says Spencer has to grow up now, stop chafing at living here. I don't know why he chafes. I think it's lovely here. But Spence was ten years old, I think, when we came to Romney Marsh. He remembers the islands and I don't. I only know Romney Marsh."

"But Spencer knows other places exist," Mariah said as they began walking once more. "Whole other worlds he hasn't seen. And now, because of William and me, he won't see them."

"Nonsense. He hasn't even been to London. You can take William and go to London, surely. That's another world, or at least that's what Morgan and Elly say. Come on, we'll go outside, let you smell the fresh air."

Mariah nodded her agreement, knowing she'd just heard an opinion straight out of the innocence of youth. It would serve no purpose to argue that she, Mariah, had put an end to all of Spencer's dreams, whatever those might be. A wife and child meant responsibility and, if she knew nothing else about Spencer Becket, she knew he was a man who took his responsibilities very seriously.

She'd had time, around their nightly campfires, to listen to Clovis tell her about Spencer Becket, the man who had bloodied General Proctor's nose. She'd heard the same story from her father, who'd believed the man had deserved a medal, not two months in the small gaol and being stripped of his rank.

Was it any wonder that the night she'd crawled beneath the blanket to share her body's warmth with Lieutenant Becket, and he'd reached for her, felt her softness, began to fumble with the buttons of her gown, that she'd welcomed that touch, sought...sought *something* in that touch? Not only allowed what the feverish man was doing, but aided and abetted him?

Even the pain that had come when he'd entered her had been welcome, proving to her that, yes, she was still alive and she could still *feel.*

And now she had tied an anchor to the man's ankle; he felt duty-bound to marry her, care for their son. She'd quite possibly saved his life; he'd quite possibly saved hers without knowing it and his reward was to be a lifetime in this house, on this land—where he didn't want to be.

"Mariah, what do you think?"

Mariah blinked, surprised to see that she was now standing on an immense stone terrace overlooking a stretch of sand and shingle beach, the Channel lapping quietly at the shoreline, the blue sky seemingly limitless.

"It's…it's beautiful," Mariah said honestly and walked over to the railing, placing her palms on the cool stone. How did Spencer see this view? Did he recognize it for its own beauty or stand here to look longingly toward the water and all that lay beyond it? "Oh, and two ships. Aren't they sleek-looking?"

Callie also looked to her left to where the sloops rode at anchor offshore, about one hundred yards apart, their sails rolled up and firmly lashed to the masts. "The first is Papa's *Respite,* and the other is Chance's *Spectre.*"

"Spectre? You mean, as in *ghost?*"

Callie's smile suddenly seemed awfully bright. "Yes, that's it. Chance, um, Chance says that with a wife and two children now and his estate to oversee, he has only the *ghost* of a chance to go sailing on her more than twice a year. He says that and then Julia gives *him* the hairy eyeball and he laughs."

"The hairy eyeball and an anchor firmly tied to his ankle. Well, they're beautiful ships." She leaned forward slightly, still looking to her left, to see a few peaked roofs peeking up behind a rise in the land. "And there's the village, I suppose. I'd like to walk over there someday, but not just yet."

She then looked to her right where there was— nothing. Only some tall grasses waving in what must be a constant breeze from the water. Even the shingle slowly faded away, leaving only a wide stretch of sand.

"You aren't allowed to walk there," Callie said, suddenly serious, as if she knew where Mariah was looking. "The sands can shift and swallow you whole, the way the whale swallowed Jonah. But the sands never spit you out again. Long ago, someone told me, some local freetraders taking their wool across the Channel used the sands to beach their boats where the Waterguard wouldn't dare follow, and then offloaded the contraband they brought back with them. There are so many legends. But the smugglers knew the sands and we don't. They're not safe. Nobody goes there. And nobody smuggles from these shores anymore, of course. Not for years and years."

"Really?" Mariah asked, still looking at the sands, fascinated by them for some reason she didn't understand. Perhaps it was the stark beauty of waving grass and sand and water…and the danger hidden beneath that beauty. Or perhaps it was the rushed way in which Callie had told her small story and then added even more warnings.

"Oh, yes. There's no smuggling here. There's no need."

"But it must have been so very exciting, don't you think, Callie?"

Callie sniffed. Quite an adult sniff, at that. "That's just romantical. Smuggling is…smuggling was what they did to survive, nothing more. Nobody smuggles for the adventure of the thing. That would be silly."

"Yes, of course it would be," Mariah said, stepping back from the railing, ready to return to the house, as she was beginning to feel as if her legs were fashioned out of sponges. But then she caught a movement in the distance, and moments later Spencer Becket appeared out of the tall grasses. He was striding surefootedly across the sands toward Becket Hall, a staff taller than himself in his right hand. The young man she recognized as Rian Becket from that first night walked along behind him.

Rian Becket had a small wooden cask hefted up and onto his shoulder and he was whistling. The sound carried to her on the stiff breeze.

She felt Callie's hand on her arm. "We should go inside now."

Mariah blinked, closed her mouth, which had fallen open at the sight of the two men. "Yes, yes we should. I'm afraid I've done too much too soon." She allowed herself to be led back across the wide terrace to the French doors they had used earlier, turning only at the last moment to take one last look to the beach.

He carries the staff in case the sands try to take him. To either hold out to a rescuer, or brace it lengthwise against the sands and employ it to crawl to safety. But he carries it carelessly, because he already knows the way.

What had she asked him? How did he amuse himself here on Romney Marsh? And what had he answered?

Oh yes, she remembered now. *"We keep ourselves busy...."*

CHAPTER FIVE

"SHE SAW ME, saw what I was doing."

"Is that so? And precisely what did she see you doing, Spencer?" Ainsley asked coolly as he continued to slowly move the magnifying glass across the map on the table.

Spencer fisted his hands at his sides, trying to hold on to some semblance of calm, remaining at least marginally civilized. "I saw her hair. That damn hair, burning in the sunlight. She was on the terrace when I came through the sands, and Callie with her."

He closed his eyes. Yes, he'd seen her hair. He'd seen considerably more of her earlier. No wonder his eyeballs burned in his head. Just as his soul should be burning in hell for lusting after a woman who'd just given birth. To his *son*. And he couldn't even remember impregnating her. What a damnable mess. He could barely wait to be shed of this place for a space, concentrate on something other than his own confused feelings. And if that made him a coward, then so be it.

Ainsley put down the magnifying glass and looked

at his son who, as he'd expected, didn't so much as blink, even as he was sure Spencer would like to be pacing, seething, perhaps even shouting—anything but standing still in front of Jacko and his father. Standing tall, never cringing. Personal bravery had never been an issue with Spencer. Good sense, however, had. Still, he had gone away a lad, and come home a man. "How nice that Mariah feels strong enough to be up and about so soon. You'll arrange for the wedding now, of course."

"No, not yet," Spencer said, thinking back on the promise he'd made to Mariah. "She'd, um, she expressed a wish to be fully recovered from the birth before we hold the ceremony."

"I see. And you've agreed?"

"I've agreed. Hell, it was the least I could do."

Ainsley nodded. "Very well. Was there anything else?"

Spencer dropped unceremoniously onto the leather couch, taking a moment to glare at Jacko, who sat at the other end. He loathed subterfuge, and Ainsley was so very good at it. "Don't pretend you both don't know what I've been planning, Papa. You made it clear the other night that you knew and warned me against it."

Ainsley looked levelly at him and then smiled slightly. "Clearly my powers of intimidation have gone sadly missing then, because you still plan to leave for Calais tonight to arrange for the first smuggling shipment."

"You know even that? Clovis told you," Spencer

said, smacking his fist against his thigh. Mariah's arrival had delayed his first trip across the Channel, but he would go tonight or know the reason why. "He's turned into an old woman, afraid we'll all be caught and hanged. But I never thought he'd betray me."

"And I doubt he ever would," Ainsley said, lifting the wine decanter, wordlessly offering the other men a drink, which only Jacko accepted with a nod of his head. "Please allow me to flatter myself that I still hold the loyalty of my own people, who are kind enough to keep me informed when they consider I should know what goes on beneath my own roof. And beneath the roof of The Last Voyage. Now, as you already know I will not discuss my sources any further, tell me about your soon-to-be bride. Exactly what did she see?"

Spencer would not involve Rian. "I was told that there were still a few casks hidden away beneath a hollowed-out log just beyond the sands, left behind from one of the last runs. I went looking for them and found only one, its contents ruined, of course, but felt it better that the cask be disposed of before anyone else stumbled over it. Mariah saw me carrying it across the sands."

"Takes you back, doesn't it, Cap'n? Like Chance's Julia all over again, and him needing to find a way to keep her silent," Jacko said, chuckling. "Except Spencer's already bedded this one, Cap'n, so we'll have to think of something else."

Spencer leaped to his feet and turned to physically confront Jacko; why, he didn't precisely know.

"I think we're done with reminiscences, Jacko, thank you," Ainsley said, seating himself behind his desk. "Spencer, sit down if you will? We've more to discuss than your Miss Rutledge, who is here in any case and not going anywhere else anytime soon. Let her busy herself making brides-clothes or whatever she might feel it necessary to do before your wedding. I'm confident Eleanor will keep her occupied."

Spencer sat again, but only reluctantly. "You're going to order me not to go to Calais. Not to ride out as the Black Ghost. Not…not to involve Rian or anyone else in my mad attempt to amuse myself with a dangerous enterprise before I blow out my brains from sheer boredom."

Ainsley smiled, surprising Spencer by suddenly looking much younger than his more than fifty years. Perhaps it was the slight gleam in the man's eyes? "Not really, no."

"No? Wait a moment. You *want* me to go to Calais. Why?"

Ainsley picked up the heavy brass paperweight and began to turn it in one hand. "It has come to my attention that there are more than a few Frenchmen—and others—who are not happy to see Bonaparte exiled on his minuscule new empire of Elba. If you don't know the island's location, there are maps on that table, not that this is important for the moment, except to know that if Bonaparte were to leave that island he could make landfall in Cannes in rather short order, where he could rally his former soldiers to march on Paris. Perhaps before his lax jailers can notify anyone that he has even escaped."

Spencer sat up straight, his arguments as to why he wanted to help the smugglers forgotten. "He actually could do this? I thought he was chained to Elba."

Ainsley sat forward on his chair. "We've heard that he advised the Bourbons to change nothing but the palace sheets, sure the people of France will call him back to Paris within six months. That leaves five months, at my count, before all hell could break loose on the continent."

Spencer nodded. "And us? Where would Bonaparte's escape put us?"

"France, far from thriving, is falling into dire straits with their Emperor gone. There are those here in England who would like nothing more than to see the mad king and his proliferate, spendthrift Regent son sent to the Tower and beheaded, and a new order come to power. For some, a freed Bonaparte begins to look like a viable option to many Frenchmen. And many Englishmen."

"For some, you say? Some Englishmen? Those who see Bonaparte's power as their power, correct? And their profit," Spencer said, his mind now fully engaged. "That's all very interesting. But Bonaparte, if he did escape, would have his hands fully occupied solidifying his hold on France, without planning another invasion here, on England's southern coast. No, I don't see it. The two don't really connect, not unless it's from a great distance. This has nothing to do with us, our safety."

"Tell him, Cap'n," Jacko said, levering his bulk up and out of the couch so that he could go refill his glass.

Spencer looked from Jacko to Ainsley, felt the tension in the room. "Tell me what? What is it I'm not seeing?"

Ainsley carefully put down the paperweight. "Not what, Spencer. Whom. Edmund Beales."

Ainsley paused to let the name sink into Spencer's consciousness. A name from the past and one that, until last year, they'd believed buried in that past. The man who had sixteen years previously destroyed their world, who had caused them to flee to Romney Marsh. The man who had led the Red Men Gang. The man who had yet again disappeared to God knows where and for the devil only knew what purpose.

"But…but Beales was operating from these shores," Spencer said, trying to sort everything in his head.

Ainsley looked at him levelly. "There are two sides to the Channel, Spencer. An ambitious man like Beales would work both of them. It doesn't matter to him who wins, just as long as he doesn't lose. He could give Talleyrand lessons on playing both sides of a fence."

Talleyrand. Spencer knew that name: Bonaparte's greatest friend, unless he was Bonaparte's greatest critic and enemy, and gathering new fortunes to himself every time he turned his coat, from France to

England to America to even the Russians—Talleyrand cultivated them all at one time or another for his own profit. What had the Emperor called the man? Oh yes—filth in silk stockings. To which Talleyrand had said—only after Bonaparte had quit the room, of course, for Talleyrand was a prudent man—that it was a pity the man had been so badly brought up.

It was the sort of intrigue, game playing, that Spencer abhorred. On this he agreed with Bonaparte. If you dislike someone, tell him so, and then knock him down. Don't play with words.

His head was beginning to ache. "And you think Beales was working with Bonaparte?"

"Beales gravitates to the winners," Ainsley said quietly. "We've learned, thanks to Chance's friends in the War Office, that Beales's Red Men Gang transported precious little wool across the Channel. He favored gold. Gold that would eventually make its way to Bonaparte to pay his army, to supply him with weapons. Beales doesn't give up easily, not when he sees a profit for himself. The allies already have begun fighting amongst themselves, with all of them jockeying for the most power and influence, which means that chaos and unhappiness reign in France. And Elba—Elba and the Emperor—are not that far away."

Spencer mentally sifted and sorted all that had been said, and then tried to apply it to himself and to his plans for the Black Ghost Gang. "And where are we in all of this? Beckets are loyal to Beckets. We watch the world, but we're not really a part of it. Even as I fought the Americans, I knew that. Our only real enemy is the possibility of exposure, being connected to what happened so many years ago. That and Edmund Beales himself."

Ainsley stood up and walked to the window to look out over the Channel. "I'm convinced there are already plots afoot to rescue Bonaparte from his plush prison. I could be very, very wrong, but I can imagine Edmund Beales and his ambition being a part of one of those plots in some way, either from this side of the Channel or over there, across that too-narrow strip of water."

He turned to look at Spencer. "Information will pass back and forth between the shores of the Channel. Covertly."

"Using smugglers, the way it was done during the war," Spencer said, nodding his head. "But why us? There are small gangs all up and down the coastline. Nobody needs us."

"True. But they might *want* us, if you were, while in the waterfront bars of Calais, to make it known that your sympathies reside firmly with Bonaparte. And, of course, that statement will be proved rather handily when you offer gold coin to help with the cause."

"And you expect me to sail to Calais and dangle gold I'd willingly give to aid in Bonaparte's escape. A gamble, a possibility—you can't be certain anything you're thinking could ever really happen. Papa, I've got that woman and child upstairs. She's probably already suspicious, seeing what she saw this morning. I'd planned to go to Calais only the one time to set up suppliers and purchasers at that end. But if I am to disappear for days at a time…?"

"I've given you a portion of my affairs to manage," Ainsley put in smoothly. "I've commissioned another ship, this time a frigate."

"And that would be a lie?" Spencer asked, fairly sure it was not.

"That I need you to oversee the building of the ship, which is very nearly complete? Yes, that would be a lie. The frigate, however, would be a reality. There is only one gun deck, but more than three hundred souls can easily be accommodated aboard ship."

"Three hundred? That's more than we have in the village, counting the women and children—and the goats." Spencer looked at Jacko, who was busily inspecting one ragged fingernail, probably gotten while digging in the dirt with his beloved flowers. "Have I had blinders on since I've come home? What's going on here? Are we planning another retreat? Hell, we don't even know if Beales was the person Jack caught sight of in London."

"Spencer, to wait until we're certain could be courting disaster. Better to be prepared for all contingencies. For anyone who inquires, and some have," Ainsley said calmly, "I am now engaged in the ship building business. That I am only building one ship is my concern and nobody else's. And yes, we do sit here with our front exposed and nothing at our backs but the Channel. If it becomes necessary to leave— only if, Spencer—it is always prudent to have a convenient back door."

"And you'd do that? You'd leave all of this, turn your back on it? Just like that? After sixteen years?"

"Certainly not without regrets," Ainsley told him. "But we will be safe, all of us, yes, to the last goat. The events that took place on the island will never be repeated." He smiled without emotion. "Edmund Beales isn't just one man. He has his followers, some of whom were at his side sixteen years ago. He'll have gathered more, for evil always finds it easy to attract evil. I want him dead, Spencer, it's that simple. I want them all dead. But I will not endanger our women and children. Not again."

"So you go smoke him out for us, bucko," Jacko said, clapping a beefy hand on Spencer's shoulder. "Go to Calais, dangle your gold and see if you can find Beales for us. If anything will get the Cap'n back on a ship where he belongs, it will be to learn that Beales is chomping down frogs in Paris."

"We find Beales by taking gold to France, hopefully to have it end in Bonaparte's pocket? How high do they hang you for that, I wonder?" Spencer said, feeling the excitement of the thing beginning to course through his veins. "What do I tell Rian?"

Ainsley smiled one of his rare smiles. "Goodbye should be sufficient. We're no longer at war, remember, so you'll be taking the *Respite* quite openly. A week for you in the bars of Calais should be sufficient. After what you've just told me, I believe you should avoid being in Miss Rutledge's presence. I'll speak to her, explain your absence. And remember that boy upstairs and your responsibility to him. I expect you home here in one piece. To be too careful is to invite disaster, but the hotheaded, reckless behavior of your youth is no longer an option you or your son can afford. Do you understand?"

"Yes, sir," Spencer said, finishing off his wine. Then he hesitated, looking to Ainsley. "Why me? I'm flattered, definitely. Chance has more experience at this sort of thing, but he's got his wife, his children. And his face is known in London. I understand that. But why not Courtland? He's the oldest here."

"You both, thanks to Chance and Jacko and their tutelage, are equally proficient handling the *Respite*. In many ways, save age, you and Courtland are equals. The men will follow you. Court, however, is a steward and a good one," Ainsley said, having considered both men for the project. "He's dependable, intelligent and courageous. Solid. You, on the other hand, while also being intelligent," he continued, smiling yet again, "have the heart and soul of a rogue. For this project, that will require not only the skills of a good fighter, but also a touch of larceny and a glib, lying tongue, I prefer the rogue. You even look the part. Where Court could make anyone believe he is a fine country squire or masterfully play the part of a government official, you, son, possess all the flash and fire of an adventurer."

"What Cap'n's saying is that Courtland's a stick," Jacko said, then laughed. "A boring stick, bless his heart. Sure, he was the Black Ghost there for a while, but his heart was never in it. Just his belief that he's responsible for the Marsh and every chick in it. *You* rode out for the thrill of the thing, bucko."

Spencer grinned, then nearly fell over as Jacko clapped him heartily on the back. "I'll be ready to sail the moment the sun sets, sir."

He headed off to find Clovis and Anguish, the two men he wanted by his side in Calais. He believed he should talk to Mariah before he left but, when he remembered their fairly intense interlude in her bedchamber and how she'd looked at him when she saw him on the beach…well, a week's absence before they met again seemed a reasonable alternative.

"Which would make me a coward," he told himself as he paused outside the door to Morgan's bedchamber on his way to his own chamber to pack a bag for his journey.

So he knocked on the door, and a moment later, Mariah opened it, looked at him and then turned her back and left him standing in the open doorway.

"I'll consider that an invitation to enter," he said, stepping inside and closing the door behind him.

"You can consider it whatever you wish to consider it," Mariah told him, retreating to the bed and picking up William, who had been lying there, wonderfully awake, as she had cooed to him. She was using her son as a shield and that was shameful. But what other shield did she have? "At least this time you knocked."

"And at least this time you're clothed," Spencer replied, walking over to bend and kiss his son's downy head. Then he straightened, not backing up an inch, and looked into Mariah's too-observant eyes. "I'm going away."

Mariah's arms tightened around William's small body. "You're leaving? Why? When will you return?"

Spencer nudged at William's hand with his finger, and the child caught on to the tip, squeezing it tight, just as Spencer's heart seemed to be squeezed tight in his chest. "Ainsley's commissioned a ship, and I'm to go to Dover to check on its progress. I'll be gone for a week, possibly more." Then he looked at her again. "Will you miss me?"

"I haven't been in your company long enough to miss you if you're not here," Mariah told him, wishing that were true. "A week or a little more, you said?"

William let go of his finger and Spencer took that opportunity to put a bit of distance between himself and Mariah. "Probably a little more, to be honest."

"Honest? Oh, you're being honest?" She laid the baby back down on the coverlet. "Now there's a novelty. I saw you, you know. Earlier, walking easily across sands Callie had just warned me were treacherous. Rian was carrying a—"

"Cask of brandy. Yes, Mariah, I know," Spencer said, cutting her off. He hated subterfuge, talking around a subject when both parties knew bloody full well what the other was saying. But the damnable thing was, he couldn't simply confess that he and everyone at Becket Hall had been spending these last years aiding and abetting the local smugglers who engaged in freetrading in order to supplement their meager incomes to feed their hungry children. It sounded too much like a noble excuse to commit a dangerous crime.

Mariah twisted her hands together in front of her, cudgeling her brain for something to say, something that would tell him that she wasn't about to betray him. "William is your son," was all that she said. "You have a responsibility."

"Meaning?" Spencer shot back, testing the waters as it were, trying to find out how much she thought she knew.

"Oh, for pity's sake, Spencer, you're *smugglers*. The lot of you," Mariah said, exasperated. "This house itself was built with money your family gained by shipping wool across the Channel. It's obvious. Why else live here, at the back of beyond, isolated from the world?" She lifted her chin. "I will not have my son a part of this. I won't."

Spencer stabbed his fingers through his hair, frustrated by Mariah's assumptions. Angered that they were at least partly correct. "How noble you are," he said, his smile more of a sneer. "You can't be bothered to ask questions, listen to answers. You simply go forward with your assumptions, damning people who have been nothing but kind to you, nothing but kind to me."

Mariah had been so angry, so frightened to think she was all but a prisoner here, she and her son both. "Then I'm wrong? I've seen a cask of brandy, listened to a few things a young girl has said and then come to an incorrect conclusion? Spence? Answer me. Am I wrong?"

He stepped closer, cupped her chin in his hand, looked levelly into her anxious green eyes. "You're wrong, Mariah," he told her in all sincerity, employing the glib, lying tongue Ainsley had so recently mentioned, as if it was an asset, not a fault. Yet he wasn't lying, not really, not directly. He was merely taking the truth and giving it a twist. "I would never do anything that could harm William. Or you."

Mariah closed her eyes, sighing. She so wanted, needed, to believe him. "Onatah says that a woman who has just given birth is prone to…to melancholy and to thinking fancifully." She opened her eyes again and smiled up into Spencer's face. "Actually, she said only a fool looks for misfortune in the face of good fortune. Oh, Spencer, I'm sorry. I saw you out there, the way you were walking…something about the way you looked, so confident, so at your ease…so…no, don't—"

But he had stopped listening, fascinated by her mouth, by the softness of her skin beneath his hand, so easily remembering how she had looked earlier. Earthy. All woman. Lush and full. He brought down his mouth and captured hers, sliding his arms around her, holding her close as he slanted his mouth first this way, then that, easing her lips open, sliding his tongue inside, kissing her as a man hungry for the taste of a woman. This woman.

Mariah gave up the battle, gave herself over to this kiss, this sweet invasion. She wasn't going to win, she already knew that. Her body already knew that.

He had been a handsome man, even as he lay wounded and feverish, his eyes burning dark in an unnaturally white face. He spoke the King's English like a native, but had the touch of the exotic about him…something foreign and intriguing and, as she had to admit to herself, exciting.

Now, healed, strong once more, she knew he was the most dangerously attractive man she'd ever seen, and she'd seen her share, living so close beside the army all of her life. It wasn't the uniform; it was the man who wore it, and Spencer Becket could be clad in rags and still be the most striking man in any room. He exuded danger and excitement. Then and now.

She raised her arms to slide her fingers up and into the dark tangles of his hair.

Wasn't this how it had all begun? With her stroking his thick black hair back from his fevered brow, feeling the silk of it, then being startled when he'd opened his unfocused eyes and she'd glimpsed the mystery of the man—a mystery she would probably never unravel. When she'd unbuttoned his shirt to see his shoulder wound, she'd also seen the slightly olive hue of his fevered skin that covered smooth, rippling muscles, the dark thatch of hair that arrowed down to his waistband. So elementally male.

He'd lain there, unprotected, vulnerable, helpless, and still he exuded strength she could feel beneath her fingertips. She remembered placing the palm of her hand against his chest to feel his heart beating strongly but much too quickly and her palm had tingled.

At that moment, saving Lieutenant Spencer Becket had become the most important thing in her world, more important than saving herself. Turning into his arms when all her hope felt gone had seemed so logical at the time.

But where was logic now? Where was her sense of self-preservation? Hers, and that for the safety of her own son? Why was this man more important than anything and anyone else in this world? Was it because, deep in her heart, she knew that without him, she and William would never be complete?

"No," she said at last, pulling away from him. "Not again, Spencer Becket. I won't allow this to happen again. I don't even know you, you don't even know me. This is insane, was insane the first time it happened."

"A time I can't remember," Spencer said, collecting himself, for he had very nearly forgotten that this woman had only recently given birth. What was it about her that made him lose all reason, want nothing more than to kiss her, touch her, take her? Again and again and again. "Forgive me. I should be courting you, shouldn't I?"

Mariah gave a short, nervous laugh. "Courting me? Really? With our son as chaperon, I suppose?"

The tense moment was broken, saved by Mariah's teasing remark, and Spencer laughed, that laugh ripe with relief. "I've got to go. You'll…you'll be all right here?"

"They're your family, Spence," Mariah said, lifting up William, who was now asleep. "You'd know the answer to that better than I."

His smile disappeared. "You'll be safe. We protect our own. Believe me when I say we've learned that lesson well."

And then, before he could say anything else, before she could ask him what he meant, he turned and left the room.

CHAPTER SIX

MARIAH WAS STANDING at the far corner of the terrace as the sloop anchored offshore, peering through the glass she'd seen days earlier in Ainsley's study and commandeered later that same evening, hiding it away in her room. After all, if there was one thing a quartermaster's daughter knew how to do, it was how to *appropriate* necessary supplies with a clear conscience. Hadn't her father told her that a quartermaster, especially in time of war, was actually little more than a thief with stripes on his uniform sleeve, gathering supplies for his troops by any means available?

Ainsley probably knew she had taken the spyglass. There didn't seem to be much Ainsley Becket didn't know, and if he didn't, Odette did. Or Eleanor. Or Callie. Or Fanny. Or Rian. Or Courtland.

So many people. She was surrounded by people who saw everything, noticed everything…and commented on very little.

They were all so friendly and welcoming, all of the Beckets. And yet, after a full week of being in their company at meals, in the drawing room after supper,

Mariah knew that they had garnered much more information from her than she had managed to nudge out of any one of them.

She felt she had all the names and even the faces of the many Beckets straight in her head now, thanks to fine drawings Eleanor had made of her siblings and their mates and children. In return, Mariah had sketched Tecumseh's likeness for them all in colored chalks, and Rian had begged for the page, planning to hang it in his bedchamber.

They were all rubbing along well, quite well.

Yet Mariah knew only one thing for certain and that was that she still knew next to nothing. Fort Malden, any of the outposts she had lived in with her father, even those surrounded by stout wooden walls, felt more open and free than Becket Hall. If Spencer felt confined here, she could understand his feelings. But who were the hostiles the Beckets felt it necessary to protect themselves from, to keep at bay?

Eight days had passed since she'd seen Spencer walking across the sands; eight days since he'd lied to her, kissed her and then left her.

The Beckets were freetraders, smugglers. There was no other explanation, no matter what Spencer had tried to make her believe. A family living outside the King's law. Had they lived outside the law in the islands, as well? Privateering—or worse? It seemed quite plausible. Even the furnishings of Becket Hall were the stuff of which pirate booty was made.

A few kisses, a few moments of madness, hadn't held up well when she'd been left alone for eight long days to think.

She and her son were now a part of this nefarious, fascinating family. Which, Mariah had to admit to herself, still far outstripped giving birth at a crossroads and living under a hedgerow, which was what she would have been reduced to if she hadn't been welcomed at Becket Hall. The last of the money her father had carried had gone for their passage to England and the traveling coach, and she had little more to her name now than the clothes she stood up in. Everything else, a broken wagonload of furniture and pots and even a few portraits of her mother, had been left behind at Moraviantown to become part of the spoils of war that went to the victor.

Spencer Becket may have lied to her, but he'd only delayed the inevitable and perhaps even made that inevitable even worse, for she had gathered up a list of questions as long as the man's arm, all waiting for his return.

And now he was back.

The glass pressed firmly to her eye, Mariah held her breath until she saw Spencer's dark head in the longboat rowing toward the shore in front of the village. His head was bare and the greatcoat he'd slung around his shoulders blew about in the cool, early-evening breeze. It had to have been even cooler out on the water, where she had been told earlier by Fanny a storm was most certainly brewing.

Ah, never fear, sir. You have no idea how very warm your homecoming is to be, Mr. Spencer Becket.

Onatah was with William, so Mariah felt free to descend the steps to the beach and walk toward the village to meet Spencer halfway, before he could be swept up and taken into his father's study, away from her. Outflanking the Beckets. After all, in any war, logistics were crucial.

He stood on the beach for a minute, speaking to the men who had landed with him, and then turned, heading for Becket Hall, so that Mariah stopped, waited for him to approach her.

She thought his step was a little slow in the now rapidly fading daylight and his shoulders seemed to slump a bit under the weight of the greatcoat. He walked with his head down, his wavy black hair blowing every which way in the wind. Surely he hadn't exhausted himself simply overseeing the construction of the frigate.

If that's where he'd been, and Mariah didn't believe that as much as she'd wanted to believe that it was true, that his absence had been innocuous…and not outside the King's laws.

Did they really expect her to turn a blind eye, pretend she was an idiot, allow her son to become a part of whatever was going on here?

Did she really think she could leave? Would even be allowed to leave? Certainly not with William. Spencer had made that very clear from the beginning.

"Hello, Spencer. Welcome home."

"Mariah," he said, at last looking up, seeing her standing not ten feet away from him, the hood of her cape fallen back, her amazing hair free and dancing about her face. His heart lurched a bit crazily in his chest. "Is something wrong? William?"

How wonderful, his first thought had been of William. Not that it should have been of her. That would be ridiculous. "He's just fine. He's passed from hand to hand all the day and night long, as if he's the most remarkable infant to have ever been born. At this rate, I doubt his feet will even touch the ground until he's at least three years old."

Spencer's dark eyes seemed to light up with this news, except that those eyes then swept down and up her body, as if he was taking some sort of mental inventory. "So you've come down to the beach to greet me, just like a good wife. How gratifying. Even if we're yet to wed."

Mariah swept her hair out of her face. "A lapse your family seems eager to rectify, although they've agreed that I should have these next weeks to…to prepare," she said as he began walking once more and she turned, falling into step beside him.

Spencer nodded, pushing his windblown hair out of his eyes. "Yes. Elly took me aside and explained to me about brides-clothes and embroidered handker-chiefs—and a woman's body after giving birth."

Mariah felt herself flushing with embarrassment. "She shouldn't have told you about that."

"No, you're right. I should have known. And are you...recovering?"

"I'm not an invalid," she shot back angrily. "Perhaps *I* should be more concerned for *you.* You look exhausted."

"Only because I am. We ran ahead of the storm all the way, but it will be here soon. Tell me more about William, if you please."

"He's an infant. They really don't do much, you know, save eat and sleep. He's ravenous twenty-four hours a day," Mariah told him, smiling in spite of herself, for her love for that infant seemed to grow by the hour. "Piggish, like his father."

"Not quite like his father. I'm more hungry for the taste of your mouth than for any food."

Mariah quickly lowered her head. "I wish you wouldn't say things like that. We...we were getting along so well there, if just for a moment."

"Just for a moment, yes, we were," Spencer said, turning away from her to look back at the *Respite,* the painted name of *Athena* on the bow in order to disguise the ship now covered by a length of draped sail. He'd enjoyed being aboard the sloop, but solid land remained his preferred location. "I imagine that, in a fit of fantasy, I had thought you'd be eager to welcome the sailor home from the sea."

"I have welcomed you," she reminded him. "I most distinctly remember saying *hello, Spencer, welcome home.*" And then, because the questions had been building in her for over a week and she couldn't hold them back any longer, she asked, "Are the casks of brandy still in the hold or did you off-load them somewhere else along the coast?"

Spencer looked at her owlishly, trying to keep his lips from twitching. God, she was a magnificent creature. And braver—or more foolish—than most. "I beg your pardon?"

"You heard me. Or did you think I would believe that ridiculousness you told me about you traveling to Dover? I may have allowed myself to be convinced once—but not twice, not now that I've had time to sort through your clever lies and evasions. You're smugglers, freetraders, all of you Becketts."

He stopped walking and turned to face her. "Freetraders, are we? And you think I'd take the *Respite* out on a smuggling run? You'd best read again whatever marble-backed novel it is that put such foolishness into your head, madam. Smugglers do not advertise their presence by sailing willy-nilly across the Channel in well-marked sloops. Not unless they've a strong desire to be hung in chains at Dover Castle."

Mariah winced slightly, acknowledging the hit. But then she rallied. "You weren't in Dover, though, were you? Where did you go?"

Spencer rolled his eyes at her. "Not even wed and the woman has turned into a fishwife. Clovis told me you like to be the one in charge. Our Lady of the Swamp, I believe Anguish christened you. Am I to kowtow to you, too, now, as did my men, list all my comings and goings, ask your permission before I blow my own nose? I think not, madam."

Mariah opened her mouth to protest, then hesitated. "He…he called me that? Why?"

"Part angel, part taskmaster. Did you really cock a pistol at one Private Angus MacTavish, telling him either he took his turn on the watch or you'd add another hole to his head? I remember Angus MacTavish. He probably survived the battle by hiding his fat backside behind a tree."

"They told you I did that?" Mariah felt her cheeks flushing at the memory, even as part of her knew he was once more steering her away from her pointed questions. "Your men tattle like little children."

"And with no end of stories to tell in order to pass the time aboard ship this past week," Spencer told her, pushing back the mass of sunset-red hair that had blown across her cheek. "You were very brave."

"I was very frightened," she admitted, looking up into his face. He'd added another layer of golden tan to his face aboard ship and it suited him. "All I could do was to think, what would Papa do if he were in this position? And then I did it. Except he probably would have shot MacTavish without warning him. In a situation like the one we found ourselves in, every man must pull his weight or pay the price. Besides, MacTavish ate entirely too much of our limited rations."

"I would have liked your father. A pity we never met."

"He admired you," Mariah told him, their gazes still locked, mostly, she thought, because she was finding it impossible to look away. "For knocking down Proctor. It was long overdue, according to Papa. I cannot help but blame the general for my father's death. For all those deaths."

"It's a guilt Proctor will carry with him, no matter that he's been officially reinstated. But we must all go on and leave what happened where it is, behind us." He slipped an arm around her shoulders and pulled her close against his side. He liked her like this, close against his side. "Now, unless there is something else you wish to accuse me of or tell me about, I suggest we get out of this wind. I can already smell the rain."

Mariah liked the feel of his arm around her shoulders, the warmth of his body against hers. She actually began walking with him, feeling in charity with him. For the length of about ten steps.

"No, wait. People have been *handling* me since I arrived here and I'm not going to let you do it, too. I want the truth. My son is under that roof over there. Are you smugglers? Were you all pirates years ago, before you came here? I won't tell anyone, I promise, not that there's anyone to tell. But this is not a simple country house, Spencer, and yours is not a simple country family. Only a fool would believe that."

"And you're not a fool, are you?"

"I wonder about that, whenever I think too hard about this place, and then simply go down to dinner and allow myself to be entertained by Rian as he parries verbal thrusts from Fanny, or sit and draw with Eleanor and let her lie to me in that sweet way of hers. I wonder why I am not gathering up my son and stealing away from here in the dead of night. I wonder why—" she lowered her head and mumbled the last words "—why I am not running from you."

Spencer put a finger beneath her chin and raised her face to his. "I'd be flattered, save that you've precious little elsewhere to go, Mariah. I had a dream the other night, or a memory. My poor, battered head, pillowed against the softness of your breasts, your arms fast around me, lending me both your comfort and your strength. Was it a memory, Mariah, or just a fanciful dream?"

"Don't…"

"I've never remembered anything, not since I was wounded. Hair like fire in the sun. A cool, clipped voice and the words *failed lieutenant*. That was all and I didn't know what either thing meant. And now this."

Mariah bit her lips between her teeth at the words he said. "I'm sorry for that, Spencer. I needed to rally the men, not have them looking at you, their fallen leader, believing they were lost without you in command. I needed them to think of you as dispensable."

"But not you," Spencer said, smiling. "You, Miss Rutledge, they needed to believe in, didn't they? Your father did a very good job raising you. I'm only grateful you didn't prove me dispensable by leaving me behind when it was time to move northward."

"I…I considered it, sacrificing you for the sake of the rest once Anguish and a few others were recovered enough to move on and you still just lay there unconscious. But what separates us from savages, Spencer, if not our compassion for a wounded soldier? Especially one who had bloodied General Proctor's nose?" She took a deep breath, then let out her next words in a rush. "I'm trustworthy, Spencer. I'm rational, practical and I can keep a secret, I promise you. And I, by damn, didn't save your life just to have my son's father hang. Please—are the Beckets smugglers?"

Family first, Spencer knew. That truth had been ingrained into his soul. And, fetching as this woman was, alluring as this woman was, as much as he was grateful to her and longed to have her in his bed, she was not family. Not yet. He looked deeply into her eyes, his expression as earnest as he could make it. "No, Mariah, we are not."

Mariah's knees went weak with relief and she clung to the lapels of his greatcoat. "I'm sorry. I've been…fanciful."

At last, he smiled at her. Indulgently, forgivingly, invitingly. He was, he knew, a bastard of the first water, all the way to the marrow of his bones. "Yes, you have, haven't you? I don't know that I will be able to forgive you. No, wait, I have an idea. I'll take a kiss."

"Spencer," Mariah said, backing up a pace. But she hadn't let go of his greatcoat. She noticed that immediately—that her body wasn't totally in tune with what her mind was attempting to tell it to do.

"*Spencer,*" he repeated, singsong. "And now I will say, *Mariah*. Come, what is another kiss between us? We created a child between us, remember?"

"I do but you don't," Mariah said, wishing there were a way to bite off her own tongue before she said anything else, one more single word.

"True. But the first faint stirrings of memory are there now. Perhaps if you were to give me something else to help remind me?"

"You're laughing at me," Mariah said, shaking back her head because the wind had blown her hair every which way and it now whipped around her, even tangled against the wool of his greatcoat.

He stroked her cheek with the back of his hand and then caught a lock of her hair between his fingers. "It's a long life we face, Mariah, without having to live together and be alone," he told her, surprised to hear the conviction in his voice. It would be more than a long life if he had to be this vibrant woman's husband and yet not bed her—it would be an eternity, with death a blessed relief from his torment. "But I'm not asking for everything now. A kiss, Mariah. Our first was interesting but I took you unawares. I want your full concentration now. Just one kiss, given freely. Please, Mariah. Welcome me home."

She must be mad. Or desperately lonely. Or even both. Mariah lifted her chin and pursed her lips together, closing her eyes. Waiting.

Spencer shook his head, marveling at this woman who remained a virgin in all but fact, and more than a little bit worried that, whatever they had done that night in the deep woods, he definitely hadn't been shown to his best advantage. The woman looked positively *resigned* to his kiss, as if it was something to be endured. How unflattering…and how challenging.

Mariah opened her eyes, her lips still pursed. She saw his fairly mocking smile and she reacted to it. She slapped him, hard, across the face.

Something snapped inside Spencer, releasing the rogue civilization had never quite banished. He grabbed at her wrist and twisted her arm against her back, pulling her toward him at the same time, crashing their bodies together, taking her mouth hungrily, greedily, his other hand on her breast even as he coaxed her lips open and slid his tongue into her warmth.

With the wind blowing around them, with her hair tangling about them both, weaving a web that held him in the middle of her living fire, with the rain beginning to sting at them from an angry sky, Spencer heard Mariah moan softly against his mouth even as she struggled to free her wrist from his grasp.

He let her escape him and her arms were around him, pulling him against her even as he molded her body against his. Hot, violent, damn near a union of all their senses, right here, right now on this windswept beach, with all the world and heaven only knew who else watching, with her not quite two weeks out of childbed.

And the devil with all of it!

"Mariah." He breathed against her neck as he at last broke their kiss, his breath labored, her trembling body now his anchor, as he was hers. "By God, we'll make new memories. Together."

Mariah concentrated on regulating her breathing, her breasts heaving as she tried to control herself and the passion that filled her, frightened her. "I must be mad. I...I don't even know you."

She was right. She didn't know him. And he'd just lied to her a second time. No, they weren't smugglers. Not in the strictest sense of the word. But they were the Black Ghost Gang, aiding the local freetraders, guarding them, facilitating them. Hell, because of the Beckets one of the King's own Waterguard lay beneath the shifting sands she'd seen him walk with Rian. They were not innocent. Good intentions be damned, they were now and had always been considerably less than law-abiding subjects of the Crown.

And this is what he had to offer Mariah, to offer his son. A life of secrecy, a life of isolation and a past that could not ever be exposed. A life of danger always lurking, ready to strike.

It wasn't enough.

He put her from him, his face now as dark as any

thundercloud. "The rain is coming harder. We need to get inside."

Mariah looked at him, confused. That was all he had to say to her? Why? Was he ashamed of his reaction to her? *Her reaction to him?*

Suddenly she felt soiled, something she hadn't felt the night he'd reached for her beneath the damp, ragged blanket, the night she'd given herself to him in the hope that she would then feel alive, believe she could go on living.

"I need to check on William," she said tightly, walking away quickly as he stood there watching her.

"Mariah…"

She lifted her skirts and began to run.

For now, for the moment, he knew he had to let her go. He had to stop lying, stop reacting as a Becket always careful to hide their dangerous secrets and begin acting as the man who would be her husband. He had to begin telling her the truth and hope she would share his vision for them both—and for young William.

He had to get Edmund Beales out of their lives, so that they would all be free to live….

CHAPTER SEVEN

THE WEEKS MOVED on into July, then to the middle of July, with Mariah keeping herself occupied with William—hiding behind her own child—and Spencer busy either in the village or on weekly trips to Dover, many of them lasting several days.

They met at the dinner table and sometimes crossed paths in the dressing room that was William's nursery, as they did now, with the child already sound asleep after Sheila Whiting had filled his belly for him.

"I've come to say goodbye. I leave in the morning. Again," Spencer said as Mariah, who had been leaning over the cradle, straightened at the sound of the door to the hallway closing behind her. Strange how attractively maternal she looked bending over the cradle to gaze at their son, and how his mind immediately saw the difference, and the different sort of attraction she presented when she was looking at him, the man who would soon be her husband.

Mariah nodded, drawing her dressing gown more closely over her breasts, and turned to enter her bed-chamber, Spencer following after her. Once inside and still carefully a good twenty feet away from the bed, she turned to confront him.

He was dressed informally in just form-fitting dark brown country breeches, tall black boots and a full-sleeved white shirt open at the neck. But she was barefoot, clad only in her night rail and dressing gown, which made him seem positively overdressed...and her underdressed. In other words, he held an advantage over her, and she didn't much care for the feeling.

"And when do we see this magnificent ship, Spencer? I should think a fleet could have been built in all this time."

"Miss me when I'm gone?" he asked, grinning at her.

"As I'd miss a pebble in my shoe."

Spencer pressed a hand to his chest in mock pain, the two of them now used to this constant thrust and parry, for they had spent many hours together, usually with William as their chaperon, just as she'd teased. But they were getting to know each other and he hoped she liked him as much as he liked her, as a person.

They'd kissed again a time or two. But those kisses had been few and chaste. He hadn't pushed, had held back his desires, and he truly believed that she became more relaxed with him every day. Less fearful that he would simply *pounce* on her, as he was beginning to think he must have done when they'd come together under that blanket in the forest.

But they were still a long way from the sort of relationship Chance and Julia shared, or Elly and Jack had or Morgan and Ethan had. They still had such a long way to go. Until he was certain he could trust her. Until she was certain she could trust him.

"Ah, a mortal wound," he said, still rubbing at his chest. And then he sobered, for he had come here for a specific reason and needed to keep their conversation civil. "Ainsley cornered me after dinner tonight, Mariah. In his opinion, we've put off the wedding long enough. I agree. I should be back by Friday evening and we'll be married on Saturday morning and William baptized, as well, as long as the vicar is handy. Please consider allowing Callie to stand beside you for the marriage ceremony, as she's a very romantical child."

Mariah's heart ridiculously began racing in her chest and she silently admonished it to return to its regular beat, a feat not easily accomplished as long as Spencer looked at her the way he was doing now. "And who stands behind you, with a pistol pressed to your ribs?"

"You think so little of your attractions, Mariah?" he asked her, taking two steps forward. God, how he wanted her. It had been six long weeks now, surely enough time for her to have fully recovered from William's birth. But no, he would wait. He'd waited this long.

With some effort, Mariah stood her ground. "Stop smiling like that, you look the idiot. And step back, you're looming."

"Looming? Surely not. I'm fully five feet away from you."

She pulled the dressing gown sash tighter. "It feels as if you're looming. You *are* looming over me."

"Menacingly so? Or provocatively so? This looming I'm doing, that you think I'm doing. You and I together, alone in your bedchamber. Does it frighten you, Mariah…or excite you? It's something I've wondered, something I've longed to ask."

"Oh, don't be so smug."

Now Spencer grinned, beginning to enjoy himself very much. She stood toe-to-toe with him, never afraid, and he admired her for that. "Looming *and* smug. Shame on me."

"Yes, shame on you. Shame on all of you. You just…you just take it for granted that I should be so very grateful to you and then do anything you say. Perhaps I've been using giving birth as an excuse. Perhaps I don't want to marry you. Perhaps I'm even considering the benefits of being a fallen woman. Perhaps I'm—stop *looming*." She pointed in the general direction of the fireplace and the chairs that flanked it. "Go. Over there. Sit down."

"Yes, ma'am," Spencer said, shaking his head. God, she was remarkable. "If it pleases you, ma'am. God knows I don't want another hole added to *my* head."

"And don't be facetious. I hate when people are facetious. I only did what had to be done," Mariah said, following after him and then sitting down in the facing chair. "Now, about this marriage."

"Yes, something else to be done only because it has

to be done. That is how you see it, isn't it, Mariah? Or is it a question of religion, the choice of celebrant? Or perhaps one of marriage settlements? You wish to discuss an allowance?"

Mariah bit her lip for a moment at that last question. "An allowance? I hadn't considered any of that. Should I?"

Spencer shrugged. "I have no idea. You'll be my wife, Mariah. Anything you want, anything you wish, I'll provide for you. I've no intention of being cheese-paring or even stern. Although being stern does hold some small appeal. You know all of that business about you obeying me, being subservient to your husband in all things? That is in the vows, I believe. I could probably enjoy that."

"Oh, for heaven's sakes. And I thought we two could have a reasonable, mature discussion? I must have been out of my mind. You know, Spence, if it weren't for that child in there—"

"If it weren't for *our* child in there," Spencer interrupted, turning serious. "Nothing else can be more important than William. No one else can come first for either of us."

Mariah felt herself beginning to soften toward Spencer. Again. If William grew up with half the man's charm, they'd be beating young women away from him with stout sticks. "At least we agree on something."

"And William should not grow up alone," Spencer

said, pushing his point while he felt he had the advantage.

"Alone? Becket Hall is not exactly uninhabited. For such a large house, it's nearly impossible to walk more than ten feet in any direction without bumping into somebody."

"But he'll need brothers, sisters. As a child, I enjoyed being a part of a large family."

Mariah nodded. "It was always just my father and I. It would have been nice to have a sister or brother for company at some of the more isolated posts where my father served. But wanting and having are two different things, Spence. You can't ask me to agree to…to be a wife to you in all things." Then she closed her eyes and ceded him some ground on their personal battlefield. Not complete surrender but definitely a yielding, an offer to renegotiate terms. "Not yet."

A wise man does not gloat when victory is in sight and a very wise man is careful to at least feign compromise. "There's a fairly good-size dressing room connected to my bedchamber. I'll sleep there for now and William will be moved to the nursery and someone will be with him there at all times. Do you have anyone in mind for the position of nanny?"

Mariah tried to speak, but found that her mouth was dry. She swallowed, coughed slightly and then nodded once more. "Onatah, of course. And Edyth, if she's agreeable, to spell her from time to time."

Spencer smiled. "There. We're being civilized.

Making decisions. Or does that make me smug again, pointing this out?"

"No. Merely vaguely irritating," Mariah said without stopping to think before she spoke and then she smiled. "What will you do once the trips to Dover are no longer necessary? What is your…your role, here at Becket Hall?"

It was a good question. It would have been better, Spencer believed, if he had an answer for her. "We all just lend a hand where it's needed. I've spent many years firmly under Jacko's not quite tender tutelage, learning about the sea, and others learning about the land." *And still more, learning how to fight,* he added mentally but didn't actually say the words. "I've been gone for nearly two years and returned home wounded, so I haven't really been doing much of anything, frankly. That's why I was happy to help out with the trips to Dover. Are you going to put forth suggestions as to how I might occupy my time?"

"No," Mariah said, sighing. "But to just stay here for the rest of your life? Living under your father's roofs? Your brother Chance left to establish his own residence. Morgan left to live with her husband."

"And Eleanor stayed, along with her husband, who now seems to be Ainsley's second right-hand after Courtland, a change that took place during my absence. So what you're asking, Mariah, is if you and I are to remain here for, as you said so portentously, the rest of our lives. I take it the prospect doesn't appeal?"

"I don't know, Spence. Eleanor is very much in charge of the day-to-day running of the household and Courtland and Jack are in charge of most everything else—with Ainsley overseeing it all. I'm used to running my father's—" She'd nearly said *life*. "That is, being in charge of a household. Granted, a small one. But I was in charge. Here? Here, I'm as useless as…as…"

"A wart on the end of Prinney's nose?" Spencer suggested helpfully. "And if you were going to say that you were used to running your father's *life* before you thought better of it, please be contented in the knowledge that I fully understand that you aren't the sort of woman who is happy merely tending to her knitting and that I'm up for the challenge. So, what do you suggest?"

"I have no idea." She looked at him intently. "You will be the head of our small household. Those decisions rest with you."

"Ouch!" he exclaimed, pretending to cringe. "That must have hurt, saying that. Very well, I'll give what we've discussed some thought and then render my decision, hopefully with all the gravitas incumbent upon me as the head of the household. Does that please you?"

"No, it doesn't," she said honestly. "I am handing my son and myself over to a man I barely know and then trusting him to do what is right for all of us. Would you be pleased, were you to be standing in my shoes?"

Spencer fought the urge to squirm in his chair.

"You're making me look at myself, Mariah, and that isn't pleasant, not when I know that as a man grown I'm now completely superfluous here and useless anywhere else. When Chance left to live in London we had no idea our circumstances would change." *We had no idea Edmund Beales was still above ground to recognize any of us, so now I'm fairly well stuck here at Becket Hall, even as Chance is stuck at his country estate, until Beales is eliminated.* That, he did not say.

Mariah twisted her hands together in her lap as she struggled to understand what he was telling her and what he seemed to be attempting to avoid telling her. "I don't understand. Is it…is it a matter of money?"

Now Spencer laughed. "Money? Oh, no, never money. That has never been a problem, not for any of us. Ainsley has made ample provisions for each of his children. Agreeing to *take* that money is something else. I would prefer to earn it, not have it handed to me on the proverbial silver platter."

At last Mariah felt they were getting somewhere, making some sort of progress between them. Her soon-to-be husband was a proud man, a man with a conscience, a man who wished to succeed on his own merits. She liked that. "That's very commendable, Spence. And how would you wish to earn that money if you are, as you say, superfluous here at Becket Hall? And what would you do with that money?"

He looked at her for a long time, wondering what she might say if he told her what he'd been thinking about for the past few years, for the entire time he was with the Army and most especially since his return to Becket Hall to see Jack Eastwood fitting so comfortably into the place he'd always thought would fall to him. Would she laugh at him? Would she be horrified? *Would she refuse to marry him?*

Was it time for the truth? Yes, it was. It was time he trusted her with his dream just as he trusted her with his son. It was time to learn if the strengths she'd shown after Moraviantown extended to taking his hand and stepping out into the unknown at his side.

"Have you ever heard of a place called Hampton Roads, Mariah?"

She shook her head. "No. Oh, wait. Yes. Yes, I have. Wasn't Jamestown established near Hampton Roads? That first, failed English settlement in the colonies so many years ago?"

"I think so, yes. The entire area is now called Virginia," Spencer said, relaxing somewhat. After all, it was only his dream, not yet an accomplished fact. "A few years ago I very briefly met someone who lives in Hampton Roads. A ship's captain by the name of Abraham. An interesting man, Mariah, a freed slave. We've since corresponded, only a few times I'm afraid, before the war put a stop to our letters. But Abraham's powers of description make it almost possible for me to see what he tells me are the green, rolling hills of Virginia. Canada was green and so were the parts of America I saw, but Virginia draws me more with its warmer climate and with a friend there to greet me. I have no desire to return to the islands, Mariah, and England has never really felt like home to me. But a new land, fresh and clean and still with opportunity for anyone willing to work hard, build his own dynasty, his own future? England will give up this war soon and I'll be able to travel there, see it all for myself."

He smiled at her, attempting to gauge her reaction to his words. "Do you look at me and see a gentleman farmer, Mariah? Crops, cattle, horses—even sheep? Do you see me, see yourself, in America? A new land, Mariah. A fresh start. A home and a life to build. Something of us to give into William's hands one day, to all of our children?"

Mariah didn't know what to say to him. His words had come to her seemingly from out of the blue, totally unexpected. She could hear the intensity in his voice and a hint of uncertainty, as if he wasn't sure of her reaction. *A new land. A fresh start.* God, what did the man need to put behind him?

Then again, what was here for him, a younger son, in Romney Marsh? His large family, for one thing. Perhaps too large? Perhaps even crushing him beneath its collective weight? To leave Becket Hall, this she could understand. But to leave England?

Perhaps he was looking for a home he felt was his.

And he was offering to take her and William with him.

"I…I have nothing and no one holding me here,

Spencer," she said at last, realizing that this was the truth. She had only William. She'd never had a home that was hers, but only a series of posts, traveling with her father, saving for the few years she'd had to stay behind in the Lake District while he served on the Peninsula.

She had no roots other than the ones she longed to put down somewhere for herself, for her son. A home of her own. A husband and family of her own. A place to build on for the future.

"Yes, Spencer," she said at last. "I can see both of us—all three of us—in America. Building something of value for William. But the war continues."

Spencer got to his feet, unable to sit still any longer, excitement coursing through him, not realizing how young he looked, how eager…and how vulnerable. "Ainsley tells me quiet negotiations are already underway to end the war. Don't ask how he knows this. He always knows everything and I'm convinced he's right. With Bonaparte banished, England is tired of war and nearly bankrupt with it. No one will win or lose in America. It will, in the end, be as if nothing had ever happened and no one had died over there."

"My father died over there, Spencer. His body is buried over there among so many others, where I cannot even hope to find his grave again let alone put flowers on it," Mariah said tightly. "I detest war."

"And I agree. The entire exercise has been one of futility and holding on to lands already our own, lands that weren't even threatened when we began the whole horrible mistake. In the end, the only ones to lose will be Tecumseh's Five Nations and the whole Indian population. I know this, Mariah, just as I believe he did, but I don't want to personally watch that inevitability, which is another reason to choose Virginia, far from the conflicts with the Indians that are bound to be small, bloody wars that last for years. But Virginia is already solidly in the hands of the Americans. I would find it difficult to aim down my rifle at an Indian, knowing Tecumseh's arguments about the land were sound, if futile."

Mariah twisted in her chair to watch Spencer as he spoke and paced. "You truly have given this a great deal of thought, haven't you? And you wouldn't miss your family too much?"

Spencer stopped, looked at her. "All of them would be a mere five- or six-week voyage away, and Ainsley is already investing rather heavily in those new steamships that will one day soon make the journey even shorter. It's not as if we'd have traveled to the opposite end of the earth. But only Ainsley—Papa—knows how I feel, what I want. I have his blessing. And I will earn the money he'll give me in order to travel to Virginia, buy land, build my house—our house. He knows I feel I have that obligation and has made…arrangements for me to earn whatever he gives me. I wouldn't feel comfortable about taking his money any other way."

"Earn it," Mariah said, also getting to her feet. "By

overseeing the building of his new ship? That's very commendable, Spencer. Is that why you've been gone so much? Earning your way to…to freedom?"

Now it was Spencer who lowered his gaze to the carpet at his feet, thinking of Edmund Beales, but then he recovered just as quickly and looked at her. "I wouldn't want to leave here until I knew everyone else was…settled. I owe that to Ainsley for all he's done for me. But, as he reminded me when I began stammering and stuttering out my dreams, he did not take us in to be his possessions, but only to guide us as we grew and then let us go our own way if that's what we wished. It's…it's difficult to explain Ainsley. He's an extraordinary man."

And a very secretive one, Mariah reminded herself, although she didn't say that to Spencer. It was enough that they were speaking, actually getting along, getting to know each other better.

And Virginia was a long, long way from whatever was going on here, at Becket Hall. She'd believed Spencer when he said that the Beckets weren't smugglers. She'd believed that for at least four and twenty hours, until she'd overheard Fanny in a whispered argument with Rian about how he'd conveniently forgotten to tell her that *he* was riding out as the Black Ghost to meet the luggers instead of Spencer.

The Black Ghost? The name sounded romantic; what that Black Ghost did sounded so very dangerous. How Mariah longed to confront Spencer with what she knew…except that she knew so little and he lied so smoothly.

Yes, Virginia and a new, fresh start seemed the perfect answer.

Now to worry about whatever it was Spencer seemed to think he still *owed* Ainsley before they could leave…

"Mariah?"

She shook herself back to attention, to realize that William was crying in the next room. "Oh, our voices must have woken him."

"Should I go find Sheila Whiting?"

"No, that's not necessary. He nursed only a short while ago. I'll just walk with him for a while, until he goes back to sleep."

"You shouldn't have to do that," Spencer told her, following her into the dressing room. "He should be in the nursery."

Mariah scooped the crying child up and onto her shoulder, patting his back as she rocked from side to side. William began to settle himself almost immediately. "Nonsense. He's my son. And I'm no grand society lady who only sees her children when she happens to turn down the wrong hallway in her great London mansion."

Spencer laughed. "We're going to rub along together just fine, aren't we, Mariah, you and I." He stepped closer, ran the back of his fingers down her smooth cheek. "Thank you again for saving my life and for giving me William. Thank you for…for listening to me."

Mariah didn't know how to answer him. She fairly basked in his nearness, gloried in his love for his son and had at last begun to believe the three of them could become a real family. If only she hadn't overheard Fanny and Rian. If only she could pretend that she didn't know Spencer had looked firmly into her eyes and then lied to her and would probably continue to lie to her until whatever hold Becket Hall and Ainsley Becket held over him was satisfied.

What good was anything, any one place, if she and Spencer couldn't seem to trust each other enough to be entirely honest with one another?

"Spencer," she began, still not quite sure what she was going to say and then there was a knock on the door to the hallway and Jacko's voice could be heard through the thick wood.

"Do your mooning over the fruit of your loins another time, bucko. Cap'n wants you downstairs in his study. Now. And dress warm, it'll be nippy out in the Channel."

"Damn the man," Spencer said at the interruption, sure something had gone wrong just when one thing in his life seemed to at last be going right.

"Spencer? You're going out now? Tonight? Why?"

His expression had closed, become unreadable after so many wonderful minutes during which she was sure he was at last showing her at least a piece of his heart. "I have no idea. But duty appears to be calling me." He cupped a hand around her neck as he bent to kiss the top of William's head and then kissed her forehead, as well. "Saturday morning, Mariah. And, after the ceremony…Saturday night and beyond. You'll think about the rest of our lives?"

"I…I…"

"The word was *now,* bucko," Jacko called out loudly in his deep, booming voice and William began to cry once more.

Spencer kissed her open mouth. "I ask only that you think about it," he said and then left her, pausing with his hand on the door handle to look back at his soon-to-be wife and their son, his heart aching—a reaction he needed time to think about, time he didn't have now. "A whole new life, Mariah."

Then he pulled open the door, stepped into the wide hallway and glared at Jacko, who was grinning at him, his eyebrows raised, his hands stuck deep into his pockets, the great big bear attempting to look sheepish. "I woke young William? I didn't mean to do that."

Spencer closed the door behind him, unimpressed by Jacko's show of embarrassment. "You didn't mean to do anything, Jacko. You never do. Unless it's watching the rest of us jump through hoops for your amusement. It's well after ten. What's wrong?"

"Word's just come from Calais. Seems you, together with Ainsley's bits of gold, have finally done it. There's someone important come to town, hiding his face inside a fancy black closed coach escorted by eight ugly-looking bastards on horseback, and being sneaked up the back stairs at the best hotel in the whole Frenchie town."

Spencer almost asked Jacko when someone was going to tell him that he hadn't been the only one crossing the Channel on the hunt for Edmund Beales, but held back in time. He should have realized that fact on his own. Ainsley Becket left little to chance and had probably had someone watching his son's back, guarding him, the entire time he'd thought he was on his own. He could be angry about that, but Ainsley was just being Ainsley. Careful. And always thinking.

"I'll assume the crew has already been alerted. Luckily, the sky is full of stars tonight to guide us across the Channel. Give me five minutes to change and collect Clovis and Anguish and I'll be ready to leave."

"Not before you talk to the Cap'n. He's waiting on you in his study."

William held close against her shoulder, Mariah stepped back from the door, having had her ear pressed to it for the past minute or more. She kissed the sleeping infant and placed him back in his cradle with hands she wished weren't trembling, before tiptoeing back into her bedchamber, heading straight for her clothespress. A moment to dress, another to find Onatah to tell her to sit with William and she could be heading down the servant stairs to the back hallway and Ainsley's study.

CHAPTER EIGHT

WHEN SPENCER ENTERED the study it was to see Ainsley Becket sitting behind his desk, dressed in his customary black, his elbow on the arm of his chair, slowly rubbing at his chin. *The spider sitting smack in the middle of his web.*

"Can we be sure it's Beales?" Spencer asked without preamble, taking up one of the chairs that had been placed on the far side of the desk. He wanted it to be Beales. He wanted this to be over. He wanted to be free to go to Mariah, tell her everything, and then set out with her, with William, to build a new life. One without shadows.

Ainsley stared into space for another moment, probably reliving something Spencer didn't want to know, and then sat forward, leaning his elbows on the desktop. "Not at all, Spencer. We may have raised an entirely different monster out of the muck and mire of conspiracy that always surrounds these things. We may even be facing someone who only wants your gold, and Bonaparte and his resurrection be damned."

"But you don't think so."

"No, I don't. At the very least, we've flushed out someone who is interested in freeing Bonaparte from his Elba and setting him loose in Europe yet again. Because this person truly believes France will be better with Bonaparte than without him, or because this person has even higher aspirations."

"As Bonaparte, just because of his successes in France, may inspire the unhappy here in England to mount a revolution of their own, as peace certainly has yet to translate to prosperity for most Englishmen." Spencer went on as Jacko settled himself on the couch behind him. "Which could even end with a new order here in England, one without a king. I've been thinking about that, Papa. Wouldn't our royal family simply then be replaced by the Emperor Napoleon?"

"Ah, but would it?" Ainsley picked up the brass paperweight and began idly palming it as he spoke. "Try, if you will, to think like a man who desires power more than anything else. Power and, of course, money."

Spencer stood up and went to the drinks table, pouring himself a glass of wine. "Bonaparte, not as emperor, not as the new ruler of England and its empire, but merely as a means to an end?"

"Most everything and anyone can be considered a means to an end, if that end is one that benefits only your own ambitions, yes," Ainsley agreed, taking a small sip from his own wineglass. "I don't believe overtly ruling nearly half the world would be

Edmund's passion. He might be happier with someone else in the seeming position of power while he stood in the shadows and pulled all the strings. Tell me, Spencer, from what we know of Napoléon Bonaparte—do you think he would be content to be a figurehead?"

"No," Spencer said. "A ruler rules and that would be how Bonaparte would see himself. So, if we believe this tapestry you're weaving, Papa, Bonaparte becomes a means to an end. And dispensable at some point, to be replaced with someone more…amiable. If this is Beales, if this is truly how he thinks, he plays a dangerous game, with very large chess pieces."

Ainsley nodded. "That's always been his ambition. I very much remember a conversation, a series of conversations, I once had with Edmund. Coming to the islands at all, privateering, was a means to an end. Turning pirate from time to time was a means to an end in a world where our enemies seemed to change almost daily. Attack a French ship one day and you're a privateer, acting within the law. Attack a French ship another day and you're a pirate, acting outside the law. Especially as we were carrying Letters of Marque from more than one country, which put us outside everyone's laws."

"It was a different time, Cap'n."

"True, Jacko, but still regrettable."

"Ah, Cap'n, time blurs things, doesn't it? You don't see me doing penance, do you? We were bad men in a worse world and I'm still proud of that."

At last, Ainsley smiled. "True, Jacko. We were bad men, weren't we, and we enjoyed ourselves mightily for a time. But we're discussing the means to an end. That end for me, as I eventually learned to my considerable surprise, was security for my family, for my men and their families, and an eventual return to England and respectability. But that was never enough for Edmund."

"Nothing was ever enough for that bastard, Cap'n."

"Again, true, Jacko. The man's love of money is only exceeded by his love of power. He asked me once if I'd rather be a king or the man who controlled a king and, through that king, controlled everything and everyone else. Kings, you see, still have to answer to laws, to the people. The man behind the scenes, tugging all the strings? He's a law unto himself. Edmund greatly admired Richelieu, you know, warning only that, unlike the cardinal, he would never trust anyone and would never be reticent to act in his own best interests. I should have believed him, should have realized that he didn't exclude me, supposedly his most trusted friend and partner, from those he found expendable."

"Don't go beating up on yourself for that again, Cap'n. He fooled us all, for more than a dozen years," Jacko said quietly.

"No, Jacko, he didn't," Ainsley said on a sigh. "Knowing what I knew, I *allowed* myself to be fooled. But to get back to Edmund and those he admired, as we should know a man by knowing those he admires. Machiavelli was another. Edmund carried copies of *The Prince* and the *Discourses on Livy* with him everywhere, wherein Machiavelli put forth his belief that a healthy body politic is kept strong by means of social friction and even conflict, not rigid stability."

"Conflict—war. Power for the sake of power," Spencer said, cudgeling his brain for memories of the man. "But didn't you teach us, Papa, that Machiavelli's fault was that all he could do was amass power and more power, but that he never knew what to do with what he'd won—so that was all he was left with, always striving for more and more power? Conflict results in winners, even more wealth and, of course, power. Peace, stability, in that case, would be the worst enemy of his aims."

"Very good, Spencer. How comforting to know that I haven't been speaking into a void with you children all these years. Edmund never planned on making Machiavelli's mistake, either. He would concern himself only with power and the accumulation of riches and let others fall while governing, always with his eyes on the next winner, the next prize. He builds nothing, Spencer, he only destroys. Has destroyed…"

Spencer, for just a moment, felt he could actually see the destruction Beales had brought to the island. To all their lives. "I…I thought he wanted Isabella. I thought that was why he did what he did."

"Easy, Cap'n." Jacko slid in smoothly from his seat on the couch. "The boy means no harm."

Spencer turned in his seat to look at Jacko. It wasn't often the man protected any of them, preferring that they stand or fall on their own. What had he said? And was he protecting Spencer or Ainsley?

Ainsley stood up and walked over to the window to look out into the darkness, but he saw only his own reflection in the glass; his hands clasped tightly together behind his back. "My wife was someone he wanted, yes. We were leaving, Spencer, giving up the life. Taking what we had and leaving. Edmund couldn't allow that. Not us leaving and most certainly not me taking my share of—of our profits."

He turned away from the window to look at Spencer. "In the end, he came away with neither...yet we were the ones who lost everything of importance."

It was quiet for a long time after that, until a log fell in the grate. Spencer got to his feet, understanding so much more now than when he'd first entered the room. "Tell me exactly what it is you want me to do, Papa."

Ainsley seemed to shake himself back from wherever he had gone yet again...a dark hell that hadn't faded even after sixteen long years.

"Show yourself in your usual places. Wait to be contacted. Don't be subservient, but don't overplay your hand, either. Listen rather than talk, and speak only to dangle promises and number your conditions. Observe."

Jacko spoke from behind him. "Billy'll be nosing around the men our stranger brought with him.

Drinking in the same tavern, his sharp eyes watching, his elephant ears flapping in the breeze, picking up anything he can."

"Billy?" Spencer smiled. "That bandy-legged old seadog? I thought he was still with Chance, playing the protector."

"You know Billy," Jacko said, grinning. "He can be anywhere. With the chance of bringing down Beales, we couldn't much have this party without my good friend and shipmate, could we? And nobody notices. Forgettable, that's our Billy boy. And he won't let Beales see him."

"I didn't see him, that's for certain," Spencer said, shaking his head. "All right. So I listen, don't say much—and arrange another meeting, promising to bring along my superior, as well?"

"Unless he looks at the man and sees the boy," Jacko pointed out cheerily. "Then you'll be fish bait, won't you?"

"It is a risk, Spencer. You were only about ten years old and only on the island for a few months, but the possibility he'll recognize you is always there," Ainsley told him.

"We don't even know if this is Beales, if he's involved at all, or if he'd come to Calais himself rather than send one of his hirelings." Spencer thought about Mariah for a moment, his son for two more, and then shook his head. "No, sir. I've come this far. I'll go the rest of the way."

"All right then," Ainsley said, retaking his seat behind the desk. "You'll recognize him?"

Spencer sat down, as well. "Tall. Thin. Black hair, black eyes. Hungry eyes that constantly darted everywhere, missed nothing. He spoke quickly, almost too fast for me to understand him. A certain…greasiness about all of him, no matter that he always seemed to dress well. Oh, and always chewing on some dark green leaves he carried with him. Strange, the things a child remembers."

"Coca leaves," Ainsley said, nodding. "Edmund believed they increased his intelligence and abilities. He may continue the habit and it would be a good way to recognize him after all these years."

"Yes, I'll keep that in mind. But, truly, I remember the Frenchman more. He thought I was looking at him too hard one day and picked me up at the neck with one hand, breathed his foul breath into my face as I choked and turned blue, kicking to get free. He asked me if I wanted to die with his knife in my ribs—*avant que vous ayez baisé une femme, peu de pousse.*"

He gave a single shake of his head. "I asked Odette what that meant and she slapped my mouth, then told me. That's about the only French I can remember, not that that particular phrase came in all that handy while I was in Montreal. Yes, I remember the Frenchman better."

"Before you'd fucked a woman, little sprout?" Jacko said, then laughed. "Did you piss your pants then, *peu de pousse?*"

"Damn near," Spencer admitted, smiling. "He's mine, by the way, if he's still above ground."

"S'il vous satisfait," Ainsley said, *if it pleases you,* and then sighed as he leaned back in his chair. "I'd forgotten the observant Jules. It could be him, you know. Can you hold your temper if it is?"

"Jules, Beales, whoever it is, I know what I need to do. Promise everything and arrange another meeting. And you'll really travel to France?"

If it were possible to crush the brass paperweight, it would have buckled beneath Ainsley's white-knuckled grip. "At once, if that was all that needed doing. But it isn't, Spencer. If this is Edmund, whatever he's up to, we need to know his plans, which may very well involve others and be far enough along to go forward without him. My mind tells me he's planning Bonaparte's escape from Elba, to unleash him on Europe at the least and England, too, at the worst. I broke many laws in the past, Spencer, did things I'm not proud of, and now, at last, I may have the opportunity to make some sort of peace with the world. Personal revenge has to wait on destroying Edmund's plans. We have to be sure. That will take patience."

"Even when it's over, I am still to leave Edmund Beales for you," Spencer said, getting to his feet once more. "I understand that. More now than ever. Is there anything else?"

"Let out your string slowly, Spencer," Ainsley called

after him as he headed for the hallway. "Be receptive but careful, and plan another meeting in a fortnight to turn over the bulk of the funds you say you can deliver. You still need to be convinced and, for that, Edmund or his representative is going to have to tell you what he's doing with this gold you'll be giving him. Remember to contain that temper of yours. The plan may go on without him, and I owe England more than that."

Ainsley had repeated himself, something he never did. His blood was running, his apprehension concerning Spencer showing. He must really believe it was Beales who had come to Calais in that closed coach....

"I'll come back whole, Papa," Spencer said with the hint of a smile. "I promise."

Jacko followed Spencer into the hallway where Clovis and Anguish were waiting. He pulled him aside, glaring at the other two men until they backed a good six feet away.

"He's convinced it's Beales, you know," Jacko whispered in his own gruff way. "Me, I'm not so sure. I'm not so sure I even want it to be Beales. Lot of memories here, bucko, none of them lovely. And a lot to lose."

"Gentlemen, I agree."

Both Spencer and Jacko turned to see Jack Eastwood standing behind them, a thin, unlit cheroot clamped between his teeth. Tall, slim, with lines cut into his cheeks and a way of measuring a man with his narrowed eyes—Spencer had seen those same sharp eyes soften whenever Eleanor came into view. A man's man but also a man in love.

"Courtland's pacing in the drawing room like an old woman. He wants to talk to you before you leave, Spencer," Jack said before turning to head back down the hallway.

Spencer swore under his breath. He liked Jack, not that he knew that much about him. He did not like being summoned.

Jacko started to follow, but Spencer grabbed his arm, held him back. "Jack said he agrees. He knows? He's that far into the family?"

Jacko shrugged. "He's Elly's husband, Spence, and not half-smart. She trusts him so who are we to say no?"

"So the same should be true for Mariah, who is shortly to be my wife. She asks so many questions," Spencer said as they headed down the hallway once more.

"Questions you can't answer, Spence. Jack proved himself, putting himself in danger for us," Jacko reminded him. "The girl has yet to even be tested."

Spencer bit down on his temper. "Tested? And how do you propose we go about that, Jacko?"

"And now you've hit on it, haven't you, boyo? How, indeed? But we'll not risk us all until we can be sure of her, a soldier's daughter and loyal to the Crown. She could hang us all. It's, as the Cap'n says, a conundrum."

"I'm so bloody sick of secrets," Spencer said as he

all but slammed into the drawing room to see his brother standing in front of the large fireplace, legs spread, hands hidden behind his back, that damn short beard making him look like a headmaster about to deliver a homily. "Court? You sent for me?"

Courtland, at twenty-nine, was the second-oldest of the four Becket sons. It had been a younger Court whom a defeated, returning Cap'n—then known as Geoffrey Baskin—and the crews of his two ships had seen standing knee-deep in the clear blue surf protectively clasping the infant Callie to his chest, the carnage Edmund Beales had left behind spread out behind him on the once-white sands. Courtland Becket, who rarely smiled, who worked hard, who was loyal to a fault. Calm, clearheaded, careful, responsible Court.

Spencer loved him as the brother he'd become. Admired him, looked up to him. But what a damn bore.

Court frowned, most probably at Spencer's tone or because Court simply liked to frown, and then pulled his right hand out from behind his back—a flat, silver and mother-of-pearl cylinder about an inch wide and four inches long in his palm. "I know you're hot to leave, but I'd like you to take this with you."

Spencer hefted the thing in his hand. It weighed next to nothing. "What is it?"

"Push that small lever at the one end. See it?"

Spencer did and nearly dropped the thing when an

evil-looking four-inch, two-sided blade instantly swung out, locking into place. "Jesus, Court! You could have warned me."

Courtland smiled one of his rare smiles. "Forgive me. Waylon made it in the smithy, to my specifications. Simply one of my random ideas. There's a mechanism that goes along with it to secure the thing up under your sleeve. I've already discussed this with Clovis, who will fit it on you once you're aboard ship. A careful shrug of your shoulder and the knife will slide down onto your palm, ready to use. I haven't completely perfected the harness yet so it's still rather bulky. Luckily, you're not in love with your tailor and your jacket will be loose enough to conceal that bulk."

Spencer didn't know what to say as he pocketed the strange knife. "Thank you, Court. You don't mind that Ainsley's sending me rather than you?"

"No," Courtland said quietly. "He chose the right man. Beales would remember me, at any rate. I was older and he'd known me years longer."

"Even with that hideous growth on your face?" Spencer asked, grinning.

Courtland rubbed at the light brown fuzz. "Please. Callie hates it. That alone makes it marvelous and worth the occasional itch."

Spencer nodded at the oft-told joke, understanding. Fanny and her insistence on following Rian wherever he went. Callie worshipping Court like some wide-eyed puppy. They had to get this business with Beales settled, get those two silly girls away from Becket Hall and into the world to find more suitable mates. And the same for Rian and Courtland. Becket Hall had been their sanctuary, their prison, much too long.

"You'll watch over Mariah and William for me? If anything should happen?"

Court put his arm around Spencer's shoulder. "If America didn't kill you, nothing else will. But we'll keep your lucky charms safe until you return, at any rate."

Jack Eastwood stepped forward, his right hand extended. "Godspeed, Spencer. I wish I could go with you. It's been a while since I've been out to play." He stepped back, raised his hands. "Not that I'm complaining. Married life holds its own rewards, as you'll soon discover."

"And you're terrified of Elly, just like the rest of us," Spencer said, grinning and feeling in charity with this new brother. "All right, I'm off."

Then a now grim-faced, hard-eyed Spencer Becket was out in the hallway once more, to where Clovis and Anguish waited, and Clovis was tossing a greatcoat up and onto his shoulders before smartly saluting his lieutenant. The three men stepped out of the house into a moonless night and a rising mist, striding silently toward the beach, the *Respite* and the unknown.

CHAPTER NINE

SPENCER SAT at the small table bolted to the deck in the captain's quarters as the sloop cut through the choppy waters of the Channel, testing and retesting the knife Courtland had given him, smiling at the thought that his brother could be a dead bore. Dead bores don't get ideas like this weapon in their heads. Perhaps Court's time spent riding out as the Black Ghost hadn't all been for the unselfish sake of the residents of Romney Marsh. Staid, proper Courtland Becket might just have enjoyed cutting a dash in that cape and mask—the devil. What was that saying about still waters?

"Spencer?"

He was on his feet and turned about in less than a second, the chair toppling backward on the wooden deck, the knife still open in his hand. "Mariah, what in bloody hell—"

She held her hands out in front of her, the door to a cabinet behind her still hanging open on its hinges. "Put that thing away, please. I've been punished enough, cramped up in that cabinet for the past several hours," she said, and then waited until he'd done so. "Thank you."

"You might not want to thank me," he said, righting the chair and motioning for her to sit in it—which she didn't do and he probably should never have expected her to do, damn it all to hell, anyway. *Obey* might be a part of the marriage vows they'd take on Saturday morning, but that's all it ever would be to Mariah. A word. "How did you get aboard ship? Is there a body I may be tripping over soon?"

She shook her head, trying not to smile even if what she'd done wasn't all that amusing. He was so upset. "Jacob Whiting is neatly tied up, I'll grant you, but he's safe enough. He's in a cabinet in the other cabin. A smallish cabinet, so his knees are touching his ears, poor thing. Don't be angry with him. I was holding a pistol on him from beneath my cloak as he rowed me to the ship. It was tricky as I climbed the rope ladder onto the deck, but he believed me when I told him I'd shoot his nose off for him if he betrayed me. I can see why your sister Morgan found it easy to lead him around by that nose, as Sheila does now."

Spencer rolled his eyes heavenward. "Jesus. And this is the mother of my child?"

He wasn't the only angry person in this cabin. Mariah was more than ready to dismiss the subject of Jacob Whiting and get down to the business at hand. "And this is the father of my child, deliberately lying again and again to the mother of his child, haring off to risk his life and that of this crew in order to clean up Ainsley Becket's mistakes for him? He was a *pirate* when you lived on that island with him, Spence. He broke the King's law."

If she wasn't going to sit down, he was. "Where were you?"

"In the hallway outside Ainsley's study, until I had to hide in a corner when I heard Jack walking down the hallway. You'd left the door open behind you when you went in to see your father," Mariah said, not bothering to dissemble. She, at least, told the truth. "Spencer—what is all this about? Is this the way you think you'll *earn* your way out of the family, how you'll *earn* your freedom? By putting yourself in danger, jeopardizing your own future to make up for whatever terrible past is clearly Ainsley's responsibility? I heard him say it, he was a bad man who'd done bad things. This isn't your fight, Spence. It's his."

"No, Mariah," Spencer said, oddly calm now, his blood suddenly so cold it barely moved through his veins. "It's our fight. All of us. You heard what you heard but you can have no conception of what happened, what so many suffered. Old men. Women, children—babies. Not a few casualties of a fight between partners who'd had a falling out. Not even a fight. A massacre, Mariah. Torture, when Beales didn't get the answers he wanted. Venting his rage once Ainsley's Isabella was dead and lost to him, because Beales had wanted her for his own. And the rage went on forever, while those few Odette could rescue hid deep within the trees and listened to the screams. A bloodlust that fed on itself until there was no person, no animal, *nothing* left alive to destroy."

He scrubbed at his face with one hand and then pushed his fingers through his hair, trying to wipe away the mental portrait he had just painted for her. But this had to be said if she was to understand the enemy they faced, and damn his family for making him keep such a secret from her. Maybe he had to say it for himself, too, as he had forced the memory from his mind for too long, tried to deny that terrible day had ever happened at all.

It was time to bring the memories out and deal with them. Not to defend Ainsley or any of them. But to explain. Until Mariah, he hadn't found anyone else he had wanted to tell. Had trusted enough to tell.

"There were more than forty children on the island when Ainsley's supposedly trusted partner and his men dropped anchor in the harbor that day. Fourteen sailed with us to England. *Fourteen,* Mariah. I was one of them. Sometimes we would wish we'd died that day, so we wouldn't have to remember what we saw, what we heard. I've spent the last sixteen years trying to forget it. All those bodies wrapped in sailcloth, silently slipping into the sea once we reached open water, one after another after another, as if we'd mark our route all the way to England with the bodies we left behind us. Sweet Jesus, there wasn't enough sailcloth, so we had to wrap the babies with the mothers."

"Spencer, I—"

"No, you need to hear this, if you're going to accuse Ainsley. Let me finish. Aboard ship, night after night, I'd hear the other children crying for their mothers. Grown men sobbing, cursing God as they shouted at the stars. Hell on earth, Mariah. Two ships, manned by dead men who still breathed and only held together—eventually made whole again—by the man I most admire in this world. You can't know what it was like and I don't want you to know what it was like. But don't tell me ridding the world of Edmund Beales is not my fight."

Mariah thought of William, snug and safe in his cradle, and wrapped her arms about her waist, feeling physically ill. "How could he…how could *anybody*…?"

"I don't know," Spencer said honestly. "There's more to it, I'm sure, and I don't know it all. We never talk about it. Tonight was the first time I'd ever really heard Ainsley say anything to the point about what happened. I'd always thought Beales did it simply because he wanted Isabella and Ainsley was leaving, taking her to England. And when she died trying to escape him, screaming to us to run, to hide, then tumbling down the stairs, he simply went mad and killed everyone. But that's not all of it. I hadn't thought much about their profits or that they could have been hidden on our island. I assumed he'd been after Ainsley's share, but that's all."

"But Ainsley said this Beales person didn't find the—the booty, is it called?"

Spencer nodded, thinking back to what Ainsley had said. He'd seemed to hesitate before he'd said the words. What in bloody hell was included in that *profit?*

"The crew—the husbands and fathers—they wanted to stay, fight, but Ainsley knew they all just wanted to die so he wouldn't allow it. Instead, we repaired the ships—there'd been a battle at sea, something you haven't heard, another piece of this whole long nightmare of Beales's making—and we left for England and the house Ainsley had ordered built years ago, safe at the back end of nowhere. Beales supposedly was dead, anyway; his own crews turned on him when he couldn't find the fortune he'd promised them shares of as their reward for attacking the island."

He sat back in the chair, spreading his arms wide; a weight he hadn't known he'd been carrying seemed to have lifted off his shoulders, just by talking to Mariah, sharing his burden with her, a woman who had lost someone she loved in another senseless, stupid battle.

"The past is over, Mariah. It's done. The why of what happened doesn't really matter now and Ainsley has been doing his penance for too many years. What matters is that Edmund Beales is alive. We've known that, believed we've known that at any rate, for about a year, but he went to ground and we've been waiting for him to surface once more. If Ainsley's right, Beales has and he's gone far beyond attacking one small island. He's plotting to unleash Bonaparte to make a living hell out of half of Europe. More battles, more deaths. You said you hate war, Mariah. We both do. That's all I can think about right now. The rest, with Beales, happens when it happens. Our revenge has already waited for sixteen long years. But right now I have to think about something else, don't I? I have to think about how I'm going to find myself another impossible, flame-haired witch after I bloody well break your neck for being here."

Mariah went down on her knees in front of him. He had to let her help, now more than ever. "No, no, you don't. I heard what you said to Ainsley, Spencer. You don't speak French."

"So?"

"So, Spencer, that's why I'm here. Because I do. We were stationed in Montreal for three years. I can be your ears when you meet with this person. Possibly hear things they don't want you to hear, comments they might make about you and their plans for you. And I can shoot. I wasn't threatening anything with MacTavish that I couldn't do. I could have your back while nobody bothers to consider me important at all. I can help you."

Spencer looked down into her serious, intense face for a moment, then threw back his head and laughed out loud. "How? First you'll have to find a way to get yourself untied, madam, and off this ship."

She gripped his knees tightly. "No, Spencer, please, *listen* to me. I heard what Ainsley said. And, hiding at the back of the hallway, I heard what Jacko said. I haven't been tested. I haven't…I haven't *proven myself*. If I'm to be a Becket, I don't want to be held at arm's length. Not by your family…*not by you*."

"And hiding yourself in this cabin is proving yourself?"

"No! Going into Calais with you would be proving myself. Nobody would think twice about your having a woman with you. It might even serve to allay anyone's fears if they thought you might be out to betray them. I mean, they may believe you're an idiot, taking time to…to diddle a woman when you're planning Bonaparte's rescue from Elba, but they'd be less inclined to believe you had some other motive for seeking them out. You'll just be the idiot Englishman who wants an adventure and not a danger to them."

"Diddle a woman?" Spencer rubbed at his forehead, sure the world had just turned upside-down. "Where in bloody hell was your father when you were growing up in all these army postings?"

Mariah relaxed slightly. "Our quarters were often very small, with my cot tucked up in a loft open to the ground floor where Papa and his friends sat around the hearth in the evenings telling tall tales. And little pitchers have big ears. Please, Spencer, let me go ashore with you. I can be *your* ears. If we're to have that future you talked about, let me help you finish this, gain your freedom. I…I want to *earn* my way, too."

"Ainsley never put conditions on any of us."

"I'm sure he didn't. You put those conditions on yourself because that's the sort of man you are. That's honorable, Spence. I admire you for that, I truly do," Mariah said quickly. "But the dream, Spence. Just tonight you finally spoke to me honestly, openly. You told me your dream and it's a wonderful dream. You offered to make William and me a part of that dream and I thank you for that. But please, don't ask me to know you're in danger, that the dream is in danger, and then stand back, do nothing. You're meeting with Frenchmen. I speak French, you don't. It's that simple. You *need* me."

"William…"

"Will be safe with your family until we return tomorrow or the next day. Please, Spence, let me help. I don't intend to die. And I damn well didn't save your life so you can throw it away."

"I'm never going to live that down, am I?" he asked, pulling her to her feet as he stood. "Maybe I should find a way to save your life so that we're even and you won't have that to hang over my head for the next fifty years. But it damn well won't be by dragging you into the middle of this."

She placed her hands on his forearms, aware of how small this cabin was, how near he was, how much she couldn't ignore the fact that his safety meant more to her than her own and probably had from that first moment she'd touched his brow and he'd looked up at her without really seeing her. "I found my way to safety after my father was killed. I found my way to Becket Hall while heavy with your child. I have found my way onto this ship, Spencer Becket, and I'll damn well find my way to your rooms in Calais. You know I will. I don't give up easily."

Spencer sighed in frustration. "Julia poked her nose in all sorts of places it didn't belong. And while anyone would expect Morgan to do the same, even Elly volunteered to—you're right. Chance never won nor did Ethan or Jack. Why am I fighting this? All right, Mariah. You can come with me. But only if you obey me without question, without argument. Agreed?"

"Agreed," Mariah promised quickly. "As long as you give reasonable orders."

They stood there, gazes locked, each trying to exert their will on the other, as Anguish knocked on the door. "Kinsey is saying as how we'll be dropping anchor within the hour, sir."

Spencer continued to look into Mariah's eyes. "Thank you, Anguish. I have a few things to attend to here but I'll be up on deck in good time."

Mariah tightened her grip on his forearms. "Spencer? Please? I'm going to be a Becket in a few days. My son is a Becket. That makes this my fight, too."

He'd burn in hell for this. "You don't look like some low tavern wench. You look like my son's mother."

Made nearly giddy with relief, she quickly raised her hands to her hair, roughly pulled out pins and let them drop to the floor, then ran her fingers through the deep waves that tumbled into her face, onto her shoulders. She shook her head and one thick lock of fire-kissed sunlight hair came to rest over her left eye. "There, is that better?"

Spencer felt a tightening in his loins. "The gown...the gown isn't right."

"Oh, for heaven's sake, Spence," Mariah said, unbuttoning the top three buttons of the old gown she'd chosen because she could then dress herself without assistance. "Now?"

He could just glimpse a hint of the enticing curves hidden by the plain gray material. "Being a fallen woman entails more than a few opened buttons, Mariah," he said as he eased four more buttons from their moorings and then spread the material, tucking the ends under themselves, to reveal the modest, lace-topped shift she wore beneath it. "Better," he said, "but I think we'll have to untie this as well," he said, reaching for the strings that held the shift closed.

Mariah shut her eyes, her skin burning as Spencer's fingers worked at the bow, and he smiled when those eyes flew open again as he slid his hands beneath the shift, cupping her bare breasts in his hands.

"Don't..." she breathed quietly.

He moved the pads on his thumbs across her nipples, which responded immediately to his touch. He'd been thinking about—dreaming about—touching her like this ever since the day he'd walked in on her so soon after William's birth. The image and the longing hadn't cooled with the passage of time but had driven deeper and deeper into his brain, making that longing even more intense.

And now he had her here, was touching her, and he wasn't idiot enough to believe she wasn't responding to him. He needed her now, needed a release after all he'd thought and said in the past hours. He told himself that she might feel the same.

He bent his head and captured her nipple in his mouth, the rasp of his tongue replacing the drag of his thumb…and Mariah seemed to collapse against him, allowing him this new freedom.

He moved his head, sliding his mouth into the valley between her breasts, licking at her, tasting her, his thumbs busy once more as Mariah clasped his shoulders, threw her head back, whimpered low in her throat.

The lightning bolt of passion evident to them from that day on the beach shot through them both again now in this small cabin, and Mariah didn't protest, couldn't even think to protest as Spencer turned her about, backed her against the wooden table in the center of the room.

So much need, all coming together in the form of a passion neither could deny.…

His mouth was on hers. His hands were bunching up the material of her gown, pushing the hem up, up, out of his way. She worked frantically at the buttons of his breeches, her mind whirling, her senses swimming, her common sense departing without so much as a cautionary note of farewell.

Spencer ripped at her undergarment as he half lifted her onto the table, still ripping at the damn material, pushing himself between her legs as she freed him from his breeches. He came into her, hard and fast, pulling her against him, his teeth nipping at the side of her neck as she gripped him tightly at the shoulders.

This was no weakened Spencer Becket in need of comfort, roughly, clumsily reaching out to that comfort. This was a dark and dangerous man, a fully potent man, taking what he wanted. But it was also what Mariah wanted. She hadn't known that when she'd stowed away in his cabin. That what she felt certain had almost begun in her bedchamber a few hours earlier and was culminating now was what she wanted more than anything on this earth, now or ever.

But it was.

The heat of it. The fierceness of it. The raw hunger of it. Building. Building. Like a spring coiling tighter and tighter deep inside her, filling her with a tension that transformed itself and her into this wildly wanton creature that wanted nothing more than to hold on to Spencer Becket and take all that he could give her.

Take all that she could take....

"Mariah," Spencer breathed against her mouth before sealing his against her, his hands on her buttocks as he pulled her hard against him, moving

deep inside her again and again as she wrapped her legs around his back, until he felt her clenching around him, heard her whimpered cry of surprise and allowed himself his own release.

Madness. Divine madness....

"Lieutenant?"

Spencer swallowed down hard, trying to bring his breathing back under control as Mariah buried her head against his shoulder. "In a minute, Clovis, in a minute."

"You want me to help you with the knife harness, sir?" Clovis called from the other side of the door...and Mariah's arms tightened even more around him.

"No...no thank you, I can manage. And Kinsey won't run us aground. This isn't our first trip to Calais. Now go—I'll be right there."

"Sir," Clovis said, his tone rather injured at this dismissal.

"Is he gone?" Mariah whispered as Spencer stepped slightly away from her, held her steady as she seemed to collapse against the table edge.

"Yes, thank God," Spencer said, grabbing a length of toweling from the bunk in the cabin, using it and then tossing it to Mariah before turning his back, giving her some sense of privacy. "Ainsley designed a fine sloop but he neglected to put a lock on that door. Jesus God, Mariah, we're both out of our minds."

He turned to look at her again and saw her smile as

she stood there, holding up her white lawn pantaloons, now ruined beyond repair.

"I don't have any other clothing with me, you know. You can be a generous protector and buy me more when we land, but nobody but you can be allowed in the longboat before I've climbed down the ladder. Now, do I still look like the mother of your child, Spencer?" she asked him, feeling delicious, even as she wrapped her arms tightly about herself because otherwise she'd be throwing those arms around him, holding on tight.

The corners of his mouth twitched as he looked at her. "Your hair is wild, your mouth is pink and swollen, your gown looks as if you dressed without a candle in the dark and we both probably smell of sex. No, Mariah, you don't look like the mother of my child. But I'm damn glad you are."

She wasn't as sophisticated or as wanton as she'd like him to believe. "Is there…is there time to wash?"

Now he chuckled low in his throat. "No, there's not. I thought you were only recently thinking about the benefits of becoming a fallen woman, as I think you called it. So—does the idea still hold as much appeal?"

"Now you're making fun of me," Mariah said, suddenly more than ready to get back to the business at hand and ignoring the slight soreness between her legs, the almost pleasurable heaviness low in her body. "And we're wasting precious time. Let me see this harness Clovis mentioned. What is it—what does it do?"

"Nothing. A small toy Court thought up some long winter night." He picked up the knife, slipped it up inside his sleeve to engage it and then held out his hand, his arm lowered. "Watch." Pressing his arm against his side three times, the knife appeared; a push on the lever exposed the blade.

Mariah goggled at the blade. "You call that a toy? Then you are expecting trouble."

"To not be prepared for trouble, as Ainsley says, is to invite it in and offer it a chair," Spencer said, repositioning the blade inside his sleeve. "No, don't smooth your hair, leave it as it is. Did you think to bring a cloak, madam, or just a pistol?"

Mariah shot him a look he felt fairly sure a wise man would do his best to avoid inciting again, and then retrieved a dark, hooded cloak from the cabinet she'd hidden herself in earlier. "What will the men…your crew say?"

"Ah, let me think. Women onboard are bad luck? Are you out of your mind, Spence? *You lucky sod?* Yes, looking at you, probably that last one."

Mariah felt her cheeks going hot. She'd go up on deck and every man there would know what had happened in this cabin. Very well. All right. Staring them down would be good practice, wouldn't it, if she was to play her part successfully when Spencer met whomever he was to meet. She would simply have to raise her chin, ignore the flutterings in her stomach and do what had to be done.

That's what her father had taught her. A person does what has to be done. Execute the order given. No thought, no question. Fear, indecision, could prove fatal.

"If you would be so kind as to wipe that inane grin off your face, Mr. Becket, let's be on with it. The sooner we begin, the sooner we finish."

"And the sooner we'll be back aboard ship. There is a bed in here, you know."

"Not that you remembered earlier."

Spencer nodded, acknowledging the hit. "You have no idea what it is to make love, do you, Mariah? Not really. First the fumblings of a man lost in his own fevered head and then the rutting boar of a few minutes ago. You've no notion of what it is to lie in a man's arms as he leisurely kisses you, strokes your naked body, wakes you, makes you yearn for the unknown. Brings you pleasures that spin you both into another realm, where there's nothing but your two bodies and the moment. And that's my fault, my mistake. One I intend to correct the moment we're back at Becket Hall."

He took three steps in her direction—all that was needed in this small cabin to bring him close to her. He put a finger beneath her chin and lifted her face to within a breath of his, devouring her with his hot gaze, wanting her again and again and again. "I promise you, I'm not always so clumsy. I'm going to make love to you one day soon, Mariah, until the world goes away. Long and slow, until we're both mad with it, until you understand what it is to float above the earth, spin off into the stars, even as the world grows wonderfully small, centers on you…centers on me…and then explodes around us, between us…deep, deep inside us."

Mariah closed her eyes, swayed where she stood. "Don't…"

"Yes. *Don't.* You keep saying that, Mariah. And I never listen."

Thank God. But she didn't say the words. It was possible she'd lost the power of speech forever. As long as she didn't lose her eyesight or else she'd never see this glorious, intense man again. That would be heartbreak….

The sound of the anchor chain unwinding, the anchor breaking the surface of the water, shattered the moment that Mariah believed might otherwise never end, she might want to never end.

"Are you ready?" Spencer asked, tying her cloak around her shoulders before reaching for his own. "We'll breakfast in the public room to make our presence noticed, then sleep for a few hours. Wait for our quarry to contact us. With any luck, we'll be back on board tonight or tomorrow morning with all the answers Ainsley seems to think he needs."

"Unless this Beales person or this Jules person recognizes you and you're fish bait," Mariah said, her fears returning even as she retrieved the pistol she'd *borrowed* and tucked it into the pocket of her cloak. "If you let that happen, Spencer, I'll never forgive you."

"A consequence I fear more than anything, madam," Spencer said. Then he opened the door and moved his arm in a flourish as he bowed her out of the cabin ahead of him.

The sun had already risen and Mariah squinted, shielding her eyes with her hand as she mounted the last stair and stepped out onto the deck.

"Miss Rutledge?"

She turned to see Anguish standing nearby looking, well, anguished. The man's name suited him. "Good morning, Anguish. Lovely day, isn't it?"

"I…um…that it is, Miss Rutledge, it is that, indeed. Par…um…pardon me, ma'am," he stammered, backing up all the while until he collided with Clovis.

"Here now, catch yourself up, lad. It's an arm you lost, not a leg," Clovis said, righting him. His grip on the man's upper arms seemed to freeze in place for long moments as he caught sight of Mariah. "Ma'am," he finally said, looking past her to Spencer. "Lieutenant, sir. It's…I…that is…forgive the interruption earlier, sir. Beggin' your pardon."

"Don't mention it, Clovis," Spencer said, slipping an arm around Mariah's waist and pulling her close against his side. "And I mean that, most sincerely. Now, the name is *Mr. Abbott,* remember, not *lieutenant,* and this is not Miss Rutledge but—"

"Lily," Mariah said quickly, grabbing at her mother's name and hoping lightning bolts weren't about to come crashing out of the sky to strike her dead. "You're to address me as Lily, Clovis. I'm…I'm his…that is, I'm—"

"Allow me, please," Spencer cut in, returning interruption for interruption. "Lily here, Clovis, is my doxy, my light-o-love, my recreation. She will be at my side at all times, making a perfect spectacle of herself as she lends credence to the notion that I am a very foolish man with more money than sense—and one who will probably end with a whacking great dose of the clap for his indulgence before this short visit is completed. Anguish, close your mouth and check on the longboat. I want to be onshore in the next fifteen minutes or know the reason why I'm not."

He kept a smile on his face, doing his best to ignore the fact that Mariah had been surreptitiously grinding the heel of her half boot into the top of his foot since he had begun speaking.

"Yes, sir, Mr. Abbott, sir," Anguish said before turning about smartly and making himself scarce.

"Clovis, if you'd be so kind as to go down to the cabin next to mine and retrieve Jacob Whiting from the cabinet and untie him—and then forget you've done either thing?"

Clovis took in a deep breath, let it out slowly. "For-gettin' a lot, sir, it seems. Shoulda listened to my ma, sir, and stayed home in Dorset, working in the cobbler shop like my da before me, if this is what wantin' to go out and see the world gets for a person."

"And what would that be that you get, Clovis?" Mariah asked, unable to hold back a smile.

"Troubles, Miss—Lily. Piles and heaps of troubles."

By this time the rest of the crew had been alerted via whispers and surreptitiously pointed fingers that Miss Rutledge was aboard and looking a bit queer and bawdylike while she was at it, too.

But these were Ainsley's men, Becket men, and they asked no questions. They just went back to the rigging, the lowering of the longboat. After all, they'd seen stranger things and would probably see stranger things still before they were finally carried off to bed on six men's shoulders.

CHAPTER TEN

THEY WALKED across the hard-packed sands toward the city spread out in front of them. An alert Clovis and Anguish followed a good ten paces behind, Spencer holding tight to Mariah's hand as he pointed toward Notre Dame Church, then Fort Risban and the impressive Tour de Guet.

They could have been only two more of the several dozen recent, obviously English, arrivals, stopping only briefly in Calais before heading on to frolic in a Bonaparte-free Paris, a Bonaparte-free Europe. A carnival atmosphere filled the air, save for a few well-dressed ladies who still appeared to be feeling the effects of a choppy crossing of the Channel only to wilt even more beneath the hot Calais sun.

As they left the sands Mariah's ears were assaulted with a dozen different languages; they all blended together, one indistinguishable from the other.

On the streets, the women of the city all seemed to wear silly high caps that covered every bit of their hair and tight, short jackets, looking far different than she did in her hard-worn cloak and bare head. Even the men were more exotic birds; a few of them wore earrings in their ears, and one remarkable fellow had a colorful tattoo decorating his face from his cheeks upward to his hairline. Happily, everyone seemed to smile as they passed by, welcoming them to Calais.

The smell of frying sausages set Mariah's stomach to rumbling and when she saw a cart on the street she stopped to take in a deep breath.

"If you're not opposed to taking your meal standing up in the street, we could have some of those sausages, then adjourn to the shops," Spencer told her. "I'm finding, madam, that I cannot quite banish the knowledge of your state of undress beneath that skirt."

"And your mind should be on the business at hand," Mariah agreed, squeezing his hand tightly as she began pulling him toward the cart.

Ten minutes later, the roof of her mouth only slightly singed from the half-raw, half-burned sausage she'd downed more quickly than she should have, Mariah found herself inside a small bow-window fronted shop filled with shelves crowded with bolts of material that stretched from floor to ceiling. There were large pots on the floor, jammed full with tall, multi-colored feathers and open boxes spilling over with lengths of ribbon and fine lace.

"We don't have time to commission anything, Spencer," she said, looking longingly at a length of emerald green silk she felt certain would flatter her hair and complexion.

"True, but the shops along this street are aware that we English don't linger in Calais, and are also prepared with goods already sewn and ready to sell. I'll leave you to it, shall I, and return in an hour."

He reached into his pocket and extracted a small but heavy purse as a tiny, grey-haired woman bustled out from the back of the shop. "Feel free to allow her to rob us blind. You need at least two gowns, much better shoes, a new cape—and undergarments." He smiled down at her. "And nothing in the least bit practical, Mariah. Nor modest, if you can help it. May I suggest lace and silk for your most intimate apparel? You know the French—they are famous for their fine fashions. Montreal or wherever your wardrobe was sewn, my dear, if you'll forgive me, is not."

"You…you're not going to stay here with me?" Mariah asked, feeling nervous for the first time, nervous enough to ignore his insult to what, as it happened, was her own expertise with the needle. "Where are you going?"

"As I've trusted Kinsey to deal with the harbormaster, it is left to me to secure our rooms, arrange for a private dining room and, hopefully, show my shining face where its appearance will be reported back to the man we wish to meet. *Madame,*" he then said, bowing in the old woman's direction. "My—" he hesitated just long enough to give the woman the intended impression as to Mariah's morals or the lack of them "—*com-*

panion wishes your kind assistance. Make me smile, *Madame,* make me happy."

"I could hate you," Mariah said as the old woman frowned at Mariah as if she didn't want her in her shop, that frown tilting upwards into a smile as Mariah, gritting her teeth, displayed the purse in her hand.

"Coming ashore was your choice, *Lily,*" Spencer reminded her tightly, his dark eyes hooded. He still couldn't quite believe he had allowed her to leave the *Respite.* He could, however, believe what he planned for her when the summons came to the meeting Ainsley had pinned so much of his hope on. "Clovis will be standing just outside that window. Enjoy yourself."

As the door to the shop closed behind him, Mariah turned back to see the woman still smiling, her black-bean eyes dancing in her head as she asked, *"Celui-là, un tigre dans les feuilles, oui?"*

The French she'd learned in Montreal differed somewhat from the woman's speech and accent, but Mariah was fairly certain she knew what had been said. *That one, a tiger in the sheets, yes?*

Begin as you plan to go on, Mariah knew; take the upper hand away from this leering creature. She made her expression stern even as she fluffed at her hair as she had seen some of the women who followed the army do when they wished to insult another female. *"Une femme regardant pour la remplir des poches maintient sa bouche fermement fermée, Madame. Tout que j'ai besoin, de la peau dehors, deux fois. Et cette soie verte. Rapidement, la Madame, la patience n'est pas l'une de mes vertus."*

Yes, it had been the right thing to say, Mariah complimented herself as she immediately was led back behind the curtain to a small dressing room in the rear of the shop. *A woman looking to fill her pockets keeps her mouth firmly shut, madame. Everything I need, from the skin out, twice. And that emerald silk. Quickly, madame, patience is not one of my virtues.*

It was only a pity her knowledge of the language didn't extend to the vulgar insult. A pithy curse or two, perhaps. That would truly have been impressive....

When next she saw Spencer—he was a man of his word and had returned in an hour—it was to see an involuntary widening of his eyes, lasting less than a moment, as he took in the sight of her in one of her new gowns. He'd been correct. After she'd chosen the gowns she liked from an impressive array presented to her, a small army of giggling young women had measured and sewn up the hems and set the last stitches at the side seams.

She turned in a full circle in front of Spencer, refusing to give in to the urge to hold her hands protectively in front of her nearly exposed breasts above the peach-colored silk that fit tightly beneath those breasts, then fell nearly straight to the tops of the neat black satin slippers on her feet. Madame LeClaire had said she looked like a flame in the sun, a reference to her hair that was beginning to pale badly on Mariah, who had heard this much too often. Why was it that people were so taken by the color of her hair? She'd always envied those with brown or black hair— nobody thought to scold them that their tempers matched their hair.

Madame LeClaire settled a long peach and moss-green paisley shawl over Mariah's shoulders, rather ruthlessly tugged it down so that it rested in the crooks of her elbows and then looked to Spencer for his approval.

"And all in the first stare of French fashion, I'm sure. How much of that purse did you give this woman?" he asked Mariah.

"Before you deserted me you said money has never been a problem," Mariah told him, lifting her chin in defiance. "So I gave her all of it."

"And worth every last coin," he told her, enjoying her anger. He extended his right arm to her, elbow bent, only to have her load that arm down with two large bandboxes. Heavy bandboxes. "You are definitely a woman of *my* word, aren't you, *Lily?* How do you propose to pay me back?" he asked as they left the shop and turned to their left to head down the flagway, a gape-jawed Clovis and Anguish falling in behind them.

"Pay you back?" Mariah shot him a searing look.

She thought of the coins still in her pocket, as she had counted out only half to the shopkeeper. She wasn't a complete fool and it was comforting to know she was no longer penniless. She also, she realized, wasn't quite honest. But she was living with former pirates, current smugglers. There were levels of honesty and it would seem she was…adaptable.

"Yes, most assuredly," Spencer said and a happier, luckier man had rarely strolled this flagway, he was fairly certain. And he might as well enjoy the feeling, because he knew her happy congeniality wasn't going to last. "If my question puts you at a loss, I do have a few suggestions…"

"This is a side of you I haven't seen before, *Mr. Abbott,*" Mariah told him sweetly as they turned the corner and approached a large building she assumed was their hotel. "The annoyingly obnoxious side, in case I haven't as yet made myself quite clear on that point."

"Have I told you that you are the most beautiful woman in this entire, clogged metropolis?"

"Oh no, Mr. Abbott, don't think you can deflect me. You're taking all of this entirely too lightly. We are here on an important and dangerous mission if you'll recall. Grinning, and making absurd statements, does not lend the gravity to the exercise I believe your father would expect from you."

She was right. But, damn, she was also glorious, gorgeous, outrageous, and he was a bastard for wanting nothing more than to take her to their rooms and bury himself deep inside her, hold her until the entire world went away.

They stepped inside the cavernous lobby of the fairly elegant hotel and Clovis brushed past them, heading for a sour-faced man standing behind the front desk. "Here now! Messages for Mr. Joseph Abbott, froggie—*toot sweet.*"

"He lacks a certain élan," Spencer whispered to Mariah, who had finally given up her indignation and was beginning to think that Spencer's lighthearted performance was a carefully cultivated act he played out very well indeed. "Ah, but you'll notice that he is also successful. For me, Clovis? Heaven will reward you, my son," he said, holding out his hand for the folded note the other man promptly placed in his palm.

"You play the idiot as if you've done it before," Mariah told him quietly as he escorted her to a wide staircase and they climbed two floors before turning down a long hallway. "And this place is immense. Is…he here, too? In this hotel?"

Spencer raised his eyebrows as he put a finger to his lips, waiting until they were locked inside the suite before answering her. She might be a willing accomplice but he had played this game for several long weeks. "He is, according to information I received from an old friend almost the moment I left you. I had planned for us to be elsewhere, my usual lodgings these past weeks, but a woman would be more comfortable here."

Mariah took a turn about the large, well-appointed rooms, peering into the bedchamber with its single high tester bed, pausing in front of one of the well-appointed windows to look down at the narrow side street below. Gilt and heavy blue velvet were everywhere.

"A veritable hovel after Becket Hall, but I do suppose I'll manage somehow," she said, smiling at him, knowing this room was a far cry from a small cabin half buried in snow, with only a single room and a curtain to seal off an area for her to sleep, or even the three-room cottage she and her father had called their home in the Lake District. "And now?"

Spencer had already shrugged out of his cloak and jacket, exposing the leather harness encasing his right arm and shoulder. He was very careful to look at her as he spoke. Honest. Even guileless. "And now, I'm going to take a nap. I suggest you do the same."

Nightclothes. She hadn't purchased any nightclothes! Dressing her *from the skin out—twice—*hadn't included nightclothes. Damn and blast! Mariah spied a marble-backed book on a nearby table and retrieved it. "Thank you, but I believe I'm too excited to think of sleep. Oh, look, *The Life and Strange Surprising Adventures of Robinson Crusoe.* One of my favorites. I'll just sit here and read for a while, if that's all right with you?"

Good. Just the sort of answer he'd hoped for. Spencer walked over to her and traced a single finger along the enticing skin just above the opening of her bodice. "It's not, Mariah, but as this is neither the time nor the place for what I do want, I'll leave you your privacy now. Clovis will have a meal sent up to us around five. Now, ask what you are longing to ask."

Mariah stepped away from him, relieved and disappointed at the same time. "The note. What was in it?"

"A place and a time," Spencer told her, taking the note from his pocket, crushing it into a ball and tossing it toward the small fire in the hearth. "Eight o'clock, here, in this hotel. I'll be sent for."

"And me? I'm coming with you."

"Just as we've planned. You'll be my small surprise." He looked at her bodice once more. "And a considerable diversion, I believe. You know, Mariah, this might just work."

He was being so…so nice. So adaptable, even complimentary.

Mariah immediately smelled a rat.

Once the door to the bedchamber closed behind him, Mariah raced over to the fireplace, grabbed the poker and managed to save most of the note Spencer had thrown into the hearth.

Sucking on her fingers, for she'd used them to snuff out the still-smoldering edges, she carefully spread the crumpled paper on a tabletop and read the contents of the note.

She ran to the door to the bedchamber and yanked at the latch. Locked.

She looked to the door to the hallway, then ran to

it, already knowing what she'd find. The latch refused to move under her hand.

"I *knew* he was being too amenable."

But she was wasting time. She ran to the table and read the message again.

Hôtel Calais. Room Eighteen. Two of the o'clock.

Spencer was already on his way to the meeting.

She didn't have to see the inside of the bedchamber to know that it had to contain a second door to the hallway. The clock on the mantel noted the time: just lacking fifteen minutes to two o'clock.

He'd planned this from the moment she'd demanded to accompany him. He hadn't trusted her. He'd thought she'd be in the way. He worried for her safety.

No matter what she believed his reason, she was locked in this hotel room and he was out there, somewhere, without her.

Mariah ran to the window she'd looked out of earlier, already knowing that the drop to the narrow street below would either maim her or kill her outright.

And there was no sense trying to overcome the lock to the door leading into the hallway or the one to the bedchamber, because either Clovis or Anguish undoubtedly was standing outside those doors, just waiting for her to do so. Both men were soldiers and wouldn't succumb so easily to the sight of her holding a pistol as had Jacob Whiting. Besides, she couldn't actually shoot either Clovis or Anguish, could she?

She was trapped, locked up tight, banished as the encumbrance Spencer obviously believed her to be. Buy the foolish woman some fancy new clothes; that will be enough. Tell her you want her in your bed, sigh with disappointment, yawn with fatigue…lie straight to her face with all the ease of a pig slipping in its own mud and then lock her up where she couldn't cause any trouble.

"I shouldn't care what happens to him, I simply shouldn't," she gritted out from between clenched teeth, then sighed. "But I do, damn him!" She returned to the first window, then moved to the next, and the next, all of them showing her a drop straight down to the flagway.

But the room was located at the end of the hallway, at one of the corners of the hotel. There were two more large windows cut into the other wall. Could that wall be at the front of the hotel? Hadn't she seen a fancy wrought-iron balcony when she'd looked up at the facade?

"Please…please…" she begged as she pushed back the heavy draperies tightly shut against the early afternoon sun and her prayers—or her curses—were rewarded. Not windows this time but a pair of French doors. There was a balcony outside that ran along the entire width of the building, overlooking the wider, busier street at the front of the hotel.

She held her breath as she reached for the latch holding the door shut and it depressed easily.

"Not quite so smart as you think yourself, Spencer

Becket. And I'm not so easily defeated as you'd like to believe."

But then she dropped her hand to her side, frowning as she realized she had no idea what to do next. Escaping the room proved that she could follow him if she wanted to, if she put her mind to it. But would that even be wise? Could she be putting him in danger, just by her own obstinacy?

She could, most definitely. She could not go chasing herself up the steps to Room Eighteen. Not without putting Spencer and the entire plan in jeopardy.

But the balcony was out there. If nothing else, she could possibly knock on another set of doors along its length and ask to be allowed through to the hallway. From the hallway she could go down the stairs to the large, ornate foyer, perhaps to have someone bring her a dish of tea and an iced cake. Spencer could keep her from attending the meeting with him, but he would not get past her and onto the street without taking her wherever he went.

It was petty, bordering on willful and even stupid. But she'd do it, just to prove that she could, just to see the look on his face when he finally found her.

Somewhere, she thought with a quick smile, her father was sighing and nodding his head, telling the angel on the next cloud, "Yes, that's my Mariah…."

She flung her ridiculous shawl over her shoulders, shrugged so that it fell into the crooks of her arms, opened the French door to the balcony, took a deep, steadying breath and stepped outside.

Nobody on the street below seemed to notice her, not that it would be all that strange to have a guest of the hotel take some afternoon air, in any case.

She turned to her left and walked down the balcony, skirting the white wicker chairs that seemed to have been placed along it willy-nilly. She and Spencer were staying in Room Four. It had two sets of French doors facing the street. She counted down and knocked at the first set of French doors that did not belong to her own suite.

There was no answer, so she moved on, counting down two more doors and knocking again. No one answered her knock. And there were only two more French doors fronting on the balcony.

Her last chance.

She raised a hand to a windowpane and knocked sharply on the glass, then stood back, hoping for the best.

Moments later she saw a hand push back the heavy draperies and a man's face appeared at the window. He had thick, light-brown hair that was cut to reach halfway down over his ears. His eyebrows were low and straight above pale blue eyes; his nose well-formed but rather sharp and prominent; his mouth a wide slash with a full bottom lip above a square jaw that hinted of a cleft. He was dressed in pantaloons, a workman-like brown coat and a high-necked black ribbed sweater. A sailor? Perhaps. And definitely very French.

Mariah tipped her head to one side, fluffed at her hair and smiled.

The man smiled back at her, showing a fine set of straight white teeth, and opened the door before bowing her inside.

"Oh, thank you, thank you," Mariah gushed as she stepped past him and into a room that looked remarkably similar to the one she had seen when she'd poked her head into the bedchamber of her suite.

Good God! She'd expected a sitting room but she'd just invited herself into a stranger's bedchamber!

"Forgive me, please, sir," she said quickly, belatedly attempting to look demure and maidenly, which was all but impossible in this gown, with her hair blown about her head by the breeze on the balcony. "It seems that I stepped outside for a breath of air and the door closed and latched behind me."

She spread her arms in a gesture of feminine helplessness. "I've been frantically knocking on doors all up and down this balcony, hoping someone would save me. I feel so very windblown. And embarrassingly stupid, of course. Would it please be possible for me to pass through your rooms to the hallway and then hopefully someone from the staff will give me access back into my own rooms?"

"Now, now, we can't have you tripping about the hotel hallways unaccompanied, not a lovely young lady like yourself," the man drawled in accented English. And he was positively leering at her. "Much better that I ring for someone and order that someone to fetch a key for you. And what number would that be, Miss—?"

"Jenkins," Mariah said, borrowing her mother's maiden name, as well. "Lily Jenkins. Oh and what else did you ask? Ah, I remember." She smiled at him, looked at him from beneath her lashes and continued to lie as smoothly as Spencer had lied to her. "That would be Room Six, sir. And I don't believe we've been introduced?"

His smile faded slightly and his eyes went cold, hard. But then he smiled again. "No, we haven't, have we. Nicolette!"

Mariah's eyes widened in surprise as the covers on the unmade bed shifted and a woman's head and thin shoulders appeared, her long, almost white-blond hair a tangle around her narrow face, her bare breasts small and pink-tipped. Her voice was low, husky, heavy with sleep. She spoke in French. "Jesus. You're still here? You said you had an appointment to attend to. Not now, Renard. I'm exhausted and I feel as if I've had a nettle rubbed between my legs. Go rut with someone else and bloody well leave me a—" She blinked twice, pushed her hair out of her eyes. "Ah, so that's the way of it? This is your so important appointment? Very well, bring her here. But this time I only watch...."

The blonde head subsided once more into the mass of pillows and rumpled coverlet.

"I...I'm so prodigiously sorry, sir. I don't speak

French, but it's obvious I've disturbed your lady wife. Please give her my apologies. I'll go now," Mariah stammered, backing toward the balcony. Nicolette was a *real* doxy! *Damn!* This wasn't working out at all the way she'd supposed.

"No matter, Miss Jenkins," he said as she stepped outside the room. "And please pardon my...wife. She's never at her best before nightfall. I'd escort you downstairs, but Nicolette has just reminded me that, alas, I have an important meeting to attend to in just a few moments. I will, however, send someone to unlock your doors for you. Good day, miss."

Mariah's cheeks were burning, she was sure of that, as she ran back down the length of the balcony, looking back to make sure he wasn't watching her and then quickly stepping inside her own suite, locking the French doors behind her. Her back to the doors, she took several deep breaths, trying to slow her rapidly beating heart, and then opened her eyes wide.

What was she doing here? Nicolette said the man had an appointment. Had she just come face-to-face with the man Spencer was to meet in a few minutes?

She had to go back, take another look.

"I'm ripe for an asylum," Mariah muttered as she stepped out onto the balcony, tiptoeing her way down its length once more, relieved to see that the man named Renard hadn't bothered to pull the drapes shut again. Even better, the door was slightly ajar. *How could she be so lucky?*

She stayed close to the wall of the building, hoping Renard and Nicolette would speak some more, say anything of importance, but all she heard was the startling, sickening sound of flesh connecting with flesh and Nicolette's squeals of pain.

"Quiet! Never question me again, you ditchwater drab," Renard ordered in harsh, guttural French. *"Never."*

Nicolette's answer was barely a whimper. "But, Renard, I only asked—"

"You only *asked,* Nicolette?" His voice lowered even more but now he seemed amused, making him truly frightening. "No, my cabbage. You only ask do you like this, Renard? Do you want me to turn onto my belly like the bitch I am and wriggle my pasty white buttocks for you, Renard? Do I please you enough *that you'll let me live another day,* Renard?" And with each filthy suggestion accompanied by the sound of yet another open-handed blow landing on bare flesh.

"Renard, no. Stop. Anything—I'll do anything, you know I will. Here, let me show you. Look, look. See? I'm all wet for you. Ready for you. You're excited now? Please, Renard, let me—*no, Christ, don't hurt me. Don't do that. God, no, don't do—*"

Mariah bit her bottom lip between her teeth, part of her wanting to rush inside the bedchamber and rescue the hapless Nicolette and the other part of her knowing that would be madness.

And then all was quiet inside the room.

Mariah chanced another quick look through the glass doors, just in time to see Renard position himself in front of a mirror, adjust the collar of his strange coat and then pull a black silk hood over his thatch of light brown hair before leaning forward to peer more closely into the mirror. Satisfied, she assumed, he removed the hood and stuffed it into his pocket and then exited the room.

He was the man. The man who was on his way to meet Spencer—she was sure of it.

Moments later, she heard Nicolette begin to cry. Thank God; at least the unfortunate creature was still alive to cry.

Mariah whispered a silent *I'm sorry* to the woman and then headed back down the balcony once more.

There hadn't even been holes cut in the hood for the man's eyes, so she imagined he could see through the material, although anyone looking at him, anyone like Spencer Becket, couldn't possibly see his features well enough to identify him if Renard passed him in the hallway an hour later, dressed in other clothes.

Nobody, that was, except her.

Which comforted her not at all as, realizing how foolish she'd been, how lucky she'd been, she hurriedly tossed a bouquet of lovely white roses onto the floor, dropped to her knees and vomited into the vase.

CHAPTER ELEVEN

MARIAH WAS ASLEEP on one of the couches when Spencer unlocked the door from the bedchamber and came into the room, the door swinging back so wildly against the wall that she half jumped from the couch to confront him.

"We're leaving as soon as you can make yourself ready," he told her, looking toward the bandboxes in the center of the room. "Good, you haven't unpacked. Clovis has a closed coach waiting in the alleyway. Mariah? Don't stand there gawking at me. I want to catch the wind before it has a chance to turn."

"I'm not gawking, I'm exhausted." Mariah rubbed at her eyes, then read the time on the mantel clock. Just past four. "What...what happened?"

Spencer picked up the bandboxes even as he tossed the paisley shawl at her so that she automatically reached out and caught it. "It's not what happened, Mariah. It's what's going to happen. Quickly, before they discuss the thing and decide I might take it into my head to disappear."

She would have thought he was being melodramatic had she not seen Renard for herself. As it was, she wanted nothing more than to be shed of this hotel, this place, the memory of Nicolette's pleadings, the sounds of Renard beating her.

Anguish led them down steep servants' stairs and through the boiling-hot kitchens of the hotel, the smell of roasting chickens fairly turning Mariah's stomach, and then she was all but tossed into the dark interior of a nondescript coach with the side windows covered.

Spencer sat in the seat facing hers, dropping one of the shades to keep a watch out of one window for the few minutes it took for the coach to push through the crowds of people and vehicles before the horses were pulled up and the coach stopped, the off-wheel sinking low into a small ditch.

Such a fine beginning. Such an ignoble ending.

Then it was a barely controlled dash across the wide, still-bustling beach to the longboat and the half dozen seamen waiting inside it to row them out into the harbor to where the *Athena*-dubbed *Respite* waited. As they reached the side and the rope ladder, it was to see the anchor already being hauled up, the sails unfurling and flapping loudly, filling with the constant breeze from the Channel.

It was the retreat from Detroit all over again. Only better managed, thank God.

Mariah put up her hand to be hoisted aboard and felt her wrist clasped tightly and given a hearty yank. She scrambled the last few feet and landed with a thump on her knees on the deck, thoroughly winded and more than a little upset.

"You weren't hauling up wood, you know," she muttered, shaking back the hood of her cloak as she stood up to glare at the bandy-legged little man who was grinning at her as if she was the most amusing thing he'd ever seen.

"Ah, now look at that hair, would you, buckos. Like living, breathing flame, ain't it?"

Mariah narrowed her eyes, any vestiges of civilization flown out of her head at the man's comment, which had filled her cup of patience to overflowing. "Oh, stubble it, you old fool," she said flatly. "Spencer? I'll wait for you in our...your cabin."

Spencer stepped back to bow as she brushed past him before shaking his head at Billy. "Lucky for you my bride-to-be doesn't carry a knife, *you old fool*." He headed for the wheel then, barking out commands as he went, and the *Respite* was soon threading its way through the ships clogging the harbor and out into the open sea. Had half of England anchored here on their way to see Paris?

"I can take it from here, Spence, if you want."

"Thanks, Kinsey. Don't spare the sail and get us home before full dark if you can," Spencer said, turning the wheel over to Billy, who was still busy greeting old friends he hadn't seen in a while and telling them how he couldn't wait to get back to Becket Hall and a good joint of beef because "those bloody frogs eat snails, it's no lie I'm telling you, buckos, no lie at all."

Spencer stripped off his cloak, folding it over his arm as he nimbly jumped down the short flight of steps and strode toward the captain's cabin, pushing open the door to see Mariah standing in the middle of the room, still wearing her own cloak and looking faintly dazed. But she hadn't questioned him; she'd swiftly obeyed him. Definitely a soldier's daughter.

"Madam," he said, smiling at her as he picked up the crystal decanter and poured them both glasses of wine. "I apologize for the rude treatment, but we needed to be shed of Calais as quickly and quietly as possible. I'm afraid I may have worn out my welcome."

She'd thought it had been something like that. "How? What did you do? Did you lose your temper? Renard suspects you?"

Spencer was about to answer her when he realized all that she had said. "Renard? If that's French for dangerous bastard, then yes, I'm fairly certain he does suspect me."

Suddenly Mariah felt mulish. Childishly, stupidly mulish. "You lied to me and then locked me in that hotel room. I told you I wanted to help. How could you do that to me?"

Spencer set down his glass, shook his head. "*How, Mariah?* What else was I to do with you? I couldn't let you come traipsing along to my meeting with—

never mind that. You don't stay where I put you, anyway, so what does it matter? Now, who or what is Renard?"

Mariah took a sip of her wine, hoping it would build her courage because she'd need it once she'd told Spencer what she'd done. "Renard is the man I encountered once I'd found my way out of the hotel room. You forgot to lock the doors leading to the balcony."

"Sweet Jesus. Not me. Clovis. But it's still my fault. I should have tied you to the bedpost. You did warn me, after all. Tell me what you did."

"I shouldn't. It was stupid of me, even dangerous." She lifted her chin. "But I didn't know it was going to be dangerous when I did it. I just wanted to prove to you that I could follow you if I'd wished it. I was *so* angry with you."

"My apologies. I'd do it again—better, I should hope—but my apologies at any rate. Now, go on. You went out onto the balcony? Why?"

Mariah concentrated her gaze on the wineglass in her hand. "I thought I could knock on one of the other doors along the balcony and someone would allow me to pass through to the hallway. After that I'd—well, I'm not quite sure what I planned to do once I was free." She looked at him, smiled. "I think I mostly wanted to annoy you."

Spencer didn't return her smile. "In that case, madam, my congratulations. You succeeded."

Obviously Spencer had never been dressed-down by her father. But she had. Her papa could make the rafters shake with just the sound of his voice. "Oh, stop scowling. I'm not in the least impressed. Now, where was I?"

"Out on the balcony, knocking on doors," Spencer said, subsiding into a chair. "Obviously, someone answered your knock. And, just to show you that I'm an inept gaoler, but not completely obtuse—that someone who answered your knock was a man. A man named Renard."

Mariah nodded furiously. "I suppose I was hoping the person who heard my knock would be a woman. And that the door I knocked on would be to a parlor, not a bedchamber."

Spencer leaned his elbow on the table and pinched the bridge of his nose with thumb and forefinger. "You knocked on the door of a strange man's bedchamber? Go on, this gets better and better."

"Actually, Spence, it does," Mariah told him, slipping into the chair across the table from his, her palms flat on the tabletop. "Except for Nicolette. Things certainly didn't get better for her, poor thing."

Spencer looked across the table at her. "You're not going to make this easy for me, are you? *Who* is Nicolette?"

"You know, if you stopped asking questions and just let me speak, we could be done with this," Mariah pointed out.

Spencer held up his hands in defeat. "Amazing, isn't it, how the blame for everything you've done, stowing away aboard ship, knocking on the doors of unknown men—all of it—keeps landing on *my* shoulders. But, please, tell your story."

All right, so perhaps it wasn't exactly jolly, having Spencer be so calm. So even-tempered, instead of blustering, the way her papa would do. But that was only, she believed, because she could *feel* Spencer's temper beneath the calm and knew that his anger was simmering there, ready to burst into flames.

So she told him quickly and as dispassionately as she could. "Then," she ended in a rush, "I went back to peek in the room again and he was...he was beating the woman for something she'd said, for asking about an appointment he had. I still wasn't sure, but when I saw him slip a black hood over his head and then check his reflection to make sure he couldn't be recognized before stuffing the hood in his pocket, I knew he was the man you were going to meet."

"Oh, God. Oh, sweet Jesus," Spencer said, getting to his feet, all but slamming his chair against the wall. "Mariah, we can't tell anyone about this, do you understand? I can't allow you to be involved."

"But, Spencer—I *saw* him. I'll recognize him when I see him again. This is *good* news." She hesitated, seeing the dark storm in his eyes. "Isn't it?"

"No, Mariah, it's not. In fact, it's not any news at all because nobody can know you saw the man's face.

You're done, you've proven yourself or whatever in bloody hell you thought you were doing by following me. But nothing more. Swear it, Mariah."

"How can I swear to that when I can help you now? I'll admit it, I was frightened when I realized who Renard was—and he's a mean, terrible man. But I didn't give myself away."

"No, you didn't. Because, Mariah, if you had, you'd be dead and we wouldn't be having this conversation," Spencer said, his heart pounding as he realized how empty his world would be if this infuriating woman were no longer in it. "Swear to me."

Mariah knew when she was defeated. "I swear," she said quietly. "But tell me what happened, please, because the man I saw in that bedchamber couldn't be Ainsley's old enemy. He was too young, not much older than you, Spence. So this is something entirely different you've discovered, something that doesn't involve that man?"

He took a deep breath, then let it out slowly, trying to find the words that would let her know what he knew. "It's worse than anything I imagined, anything even Ainsley imagined."

"Tell me."

Spencer gave in, pulling the chair back to the table and sitting down once more. "I don't know. My age, you said? With the hood and situated as he was in shadows in the bedchamber of the suite when I was finally ushered in, it was impossible to say for sure.

But I sensed that he wasn't much older than I. There was a Frenchman with him, which means nothing, because I only heard his voice for a few moments and he was also standing in the shadows. It could have been Jules, I suppose. It could have been any of ten thousand Frenchmen. But it doesn't matter if this Renard is one of Edmund Beales's men, Mariah, or if Edmund Beales is involved at all. What these men are planning is so diabolical…"

"Bonaparte's escape from Elba," Mariah said, nodding her head.

"Yes, that's part of this ambitious, two-pronged plan. Hell, there may be even more he didn't tell me."

"Only part of it? What else could there be?"

Spencer looked into her eyes, acknowledging the intelligence there. He could trust her; they all could trust her. Just as she'd wanted to do, she'd proved herself. He might as well tell her everything. "The Prince Regent's damnable spectacle, that's what. They're all coming together for some grand celebration or are already here. Alexander, Czar of all the Russias. Prussia's King Frederick, as well as Blücher. All the allies and most of the generals, Mariah. Wellington, the entire Royal family, all of them gathered in one place in London to gloat, to celebrate peace and victory in very public venues. Imagine Bonaparte loose in Europe again, Mariah, and then imagine he and his *Grande Armeé* loose in Europe…and the leaders of the Russias, Great

Britain and Prussia and their generals assassinated as they stand together to enjoy one of Prinney's absurd parties."

"All those men, dead? Murdered? There would be mourning, confusion—anarchy. Everywhere," Mariah said, her fingers tightening on the stem of her wineglass. "And this Renard, he told you all of this? Why?"

Spencer smiled ruefully. "When you already have given a man five thousand pounds in good faith, and promised that man fifty thousand pounds sterling more if his answers please you, Mariah, you are allowed, even expected, to ask a few questions. And you get a few answers. Unfortunately, not quite enough answers. He kept insisting to paint in only very broad strokes, veiled hints. I don't know *how* they're going to free Bonaparte. I don't know *how* they plan to assassinate Prinney and the rest during the celebrations. Only the date, the first of August—the same day they plan to move Bonaparte from Elba. Two-pronged, Mariah. And, even more unfortunately, I'm afraid I asked too many pointed questions, went too far, pushed too hard. The one you call Renard was about to answer one of those questions when the Frenchman stopped him— that's probably the only reason I heard his voice at all, not that I understood him. After that, I was quickly dismissed and told I would be contacted later tonight. By a knife to the throat, I believe, which is why we're on our way back to Becket Hall. I couldn't risk not getting this information to Ainsley. And I couldn't risk you."

"No, no, you were right to leave. The Prince Regent must be warned. What did he say, this Frenchman?"

Spencer rubbed at the back of his neck, which still tingled as it had when he'd turned and walked out of the meeting, half convinced a knife would find its way between his shoulder blades before he reached the hallway. "I'm not sure. I remember only the simplest words. Something like *un lion pours*—no, damn it all to hell, that's not it. *Un lion pour effray*—then something else, and then—*un loups?*"

Mariah got to her feet and began to pace the small space. Spencer's accent was atrocious, but she thought she knew what he was trying to say. *Un lion pour effray?* No. Effrayer? *To frighten?* Yes, that was it. "Lions and wolves, Spencer. He was saying something about lions and wolves. Lions and wolves frightening someone?"

"I don't know." Spencer stabbed his fingers through his hair. "Whatever he said, it was a warning to the other man to stop talking, no more than that. The entire tone of the meeting shifted from congenial to near-threatening and I pretended to storm out, telling them to contact me again when they could agree to talk plainly to me. I might have stayed at the hotel, seen what happened next, how the evening played out, but I had to get you out of there, out of danger. Little knowing, of course," he added, smiling weakly, "that you'd already seen the man without his hood, had even spoken to him. How in bloody hell am I going to explain any of this to Ainsley?"

But Mariah wasn't listening. "Lions and wolves, Spencer. And Renard? Renard means fox. Did you know that?"

"Isn't that wonderful," he said, far from pleased. "We'll soon have all the animals in the Tower Menagerie. What does it matter? Or did you think Renard was really this bastard's name?"

Mariah's optimism deflated quickly, but then she rallied. "Perhaps not, but Nicolette would still be Nicolette, wouldn't she?"

"And?"

Mariah pulled out the chair across from his, dragging its weight across the wooden floor, and sat down heavily. "And I don't know what that means. In any event, you won't be traveling to Calais again. They won't be getting their fifty thousand pounds sterling. Perhaps that's the end of it. Without the funds you'd promised them, they might not be able to pay anyone to facilitate Bonaparte's escape or hire anyone to attack the Prince Regent and the others. When you first went to Calais it was to attract the attention of those who wished Bonaparte back in power, believing that someone might be Edmund Beales. Perhaps all you did was raise some dreamers and now their dream has died."

"Dreamers? Don't exclude yourself, Mariah, when you speak of dreamers. Because, if I'm right, they were about to eliminate me *before* I could give them their fifty thousand pounds, which tells me the plan is a serious one and will go forward no matter whether they have my money or not. And think about this, Mariah. What if they are only partially successful? What if they only mange to either wound or kill the Prince Regent, or only the czar? Does it matter? There'd still be chaos, especially with Bonaparte on the loose."

"I hadn't thought of that, but you're right. Someone is planning to turn the entire world on its head. What are we going to do?"

He helped her to her feet, bent to kiss her cheek. "You look tired. Why not try to sleep and I'll wake you when we arrive back at Becket Hall?"

"But…where will you be?"

He wanted nothing more than to stay down here with her, to hold her, to forget what he knew, to talk about his own dream—that of Virginia, of a new life, a very different life for his son than the one his father lived. But he was a Becket and that would never change. "Up on deck," he told her, turning for the door, "…where I bloody well belong."

CHAPTER TWELVE

"THEY'RE BACK, already making their way across the beach," Courtland said, walking into Ainsley's study, Rian and Jack behind him. Courtland shrugged completely into the jacket he'd carried into the room with him and then tried to smooth his hair. "Billy, too. They're back so soon, not even a full night and day gone. I wonder if that means good news or bad."

Ainsley motioned them all to chairs. "Perhaps I should ring for refreshments, a plate of cakes? Rian, tuck in your shirt, if you please. Are you hungry?"

Rian grinned as he perched himself on the wide wood of a window embrasure. "Only for adventure, Papa."

Ainsley gave an elaborate sigh. "This must be the price a man pays for having sons. Daughters wouldn't be so eager to expose themselves to danger."

"Fanny would. Morgan, too, if she wasn't a mother now," Rian said, then lost his grin as Courtland glared meaningfully at him. "Um…do you think Bonaparte will actually be able to escape Elba? That's why Spence went to Calais, right, to find out? There'd be war again with England, if that were to happen."

"Don't make me sorry I woke you, Rian. If all you can do is to point out the obvious," Courtland told him tightly, "perhaps you'd be wise to just sit there quietly, before you're sent back to the nursery."

"That will be enough, thank you, Courtland," Ainsley said placidly as he heard voices in the hallway and then got to his feet as Spencer stood back to allow Mariah to enter the study ahead of him. They might not have tarried long in Calais, but somehow she seemed to have acquired a new gown. "Miss Rutledge," he said, inclining his head slightly as they walked across the room to stand directly in front of his desk, "your son is upstairs."

"True enough, sir, and I'm anxious to see him, even as I know he's been in capable hands," Mariah said, her gaze sweeping the large room as she mentally toted up the number of occupants. "I've come here first, to apologize for what I've done. It was stupid of me, sir, and even selfish."

"Not to mention reckless. But you'd do it again, wouldn't you, Mariah?" Ainsley asked her kindly and Mariah's shoulders sagged with relief.

"Yes, sir, I would. If I'm to be a part of this family, I feel I should first prove myself worthy."

"By first, I'll assume, listening at keyholes, and then stowing away on the *Respite*—and giving Spencer here fits, I'm sure," Ainsley said drily, wondering if he'd ever been that young and impulsive. "So tell me, Mariah, did you prove yourself worthy?"

She opened her mouth just as Spencer put his hand on her arm and stepped half in front of her. "I locked her in my hotel room the moment we got to Calais. She didn't do any harm, I promise."

"Except to your pocketbook," Jack remarked from the couch across the room. "That gown's a French design, isn't it? I seem to remember Eleanor showing me a pattern much like it in one of her magazines. Did you even get a sniff of the man we're after or did you spend all your time in the shops?"

Mariah looked up at Spencer, watching the tic that had begun to work in his cheek. She'd made a fool of him, embarrassed him. "I'm so sorry," she whispered as Rian laughed at Jack's comment. "Please, let me tell them about—"

"No," Spencer told her quietly. "I don't want you involved in this. Go tend to your son."

"Don't order me about like one of your crew. *You* go tend to him if you think he's been mistreated in the single day we've been gone."

"That's not the point."

"Well, then, what *is* the point?"

Ainsley had leaned forward in his chair, resting his chin in one hand as he watched the quick, terse exchange between his son and Mariah. He couldn't hear what they were saying but he was fairly certain they weren't whispering sweet words of love to each other, not if he could measure their feelings by the stubborn expressions on both their faces.

"Ahem," Ainsley said at last, when it appeared that the pair in front of him had lapsed into a staring match. "Why don't you two sit down. Spencer, you tell me what happened in Calais. As Mariah said, William is in good hands."

"Yes, Spence, you look ready to explode," Rian commented from his perch. "Will there be an attempt to free Bonaparte? Will there be war again? What have you learned?"

"More than any of us hoped to know, Rian, and if believable, none of it good," Spencer told his brother as he watched Mariah take the chair directly in front of Ainsley's desk.

The next half hour passed quickly in a round of explanations, questions, answers and yet more questions. Glasses of wine were passed around, a grumbling Rian was sent to the kitchens for meat and cheese and Mariah watched Ainsley Becket's face as often as possible, trying to gauge his reaction to the information they'd brought to him.

But his expression told her nothing, not until she told him about the few words of French Spencer had heard and her thoughts on them.

"Lions and wolves?" Ainsley repeated. "Being afraid of lions and wolves?" He sat back in his chair, rubbing at his chin. "Spencer. Your full attention if you please? *On doit donc être un renard pour identifier des pièges et un lion pour effrayer des loups.* Does that sound familiar?"

"Again, sir, please," Spencer said, aware that Ainsley's eyes had grown cold. When Ainsley repeated what he'd said, Spencer nodded. "Yes…yes, I think that's it. That's what I heard the man say. What is it? What does it mean?"

Mariah answered for Ainsley, who was now looking toward the dark beyond the window where Rian sat chewing on a thick slice of cheese. "I hope I have this correctly. What your father said is that one must be a fox to recognize traps and a lion to frighten wolves. Is…is that correct, sir?"

"It is. Very good, Mariah."

"Ainsley?" Jack Eastwood asked, getting to his feet. "I don't like the way you're looking, sir. What does this mean?"

Ainsley looked at Mariah, wondering how much she'd overheard the previous evening, how much else Spencer had told her. But what did it matter, *what did anything else matter, now?* "The quote is one I've heard before, Jack, many times, taken from Machiavelli's *The Prince.* 'A prince being thus obliged to know well how to act as a beast must imitate the fox and the lion, for the lion cannot protect himself from traps, and the fox cannot defend himself from wolves. One must therefore be a fox to recognize traps, and a lion to frighten wolves.'"

Mariah was fascinated. "So the one man was reminding the other to protect himself when Spencer's questions delved too deeply, worried that Spencer was setting some sort of trap for them?"

"Shh, Mariah, not now," Spencer said, laying his hand on her arm. He felt certain he knew what Ainsley was thinking the moment he'd said the name Machiavelli. "Papa?"

"It could have been Jules. He often sat with Edmund and myself on long nights, with Edmund reading to us, arguing that Machiavelli had the right of it—that all that was needed to succeed were your own brains and the stupidity of others. And, of course, there's the plan itself as you've outlined it, Spencer. That, too, would appeal to Edmund. The sheer audacity of it. Cut off the head and the body has no power, leaving all that power for the man clever enough to gather it up. It's a shame you couldn't see their faces, Spencer."

Mariah leaned forward and laid her hands on the desktop. "Sir, I—"

Spencer's temper, held in check so long, finally broke free. "Damn it, Mariah, I said no!"

Once again Ainsley cupped his chin in his hand and watched as the two of them glared at each other and spoke to each other in hushed, hissing whispers, Spencer gesturing, Mariah stone-faced. Theirs was not going to be a placid marriage....

"Oh, all right," Spencer said at last, literally throwing up his arms. "You'll just tell him the moment my back is turned, anyway. Papa—Mariah saw him. She saw Renard without his mask."

Mariah sighed in relief, even as she knew there'd be

the devil to pay later, when she and Spencer were alone. "Rian? Please be kind enough to fetch me a pad of Eleanor's drawing paper and some colored chalks. I want to make a drawing while my memory is still fresh."

"Do that, Rian," Ainsley said, "and then go wake Jacko, if you please. Renard, you said? I'd like Jacko's opinion once the drawing is complete. Courtland, your opinion, as well."

Spencer looked at Ainsley in curiosity, his anger momentarily forgotten. "Why? What are you thinking? Jacko and Court might know this Renard?"

"That remains to be seen, Spencer. Why don't you have another cake? Bumble's outdone himself, don't you think?"

Spencer shook his head, grinned. "I think you're more wily than any *renard,* that's what I think. And I'll be damned if I know what you *think* Mariah's drawing is going to show any of you."

A full half hour later, time spent informing Jacko of everything Spencer had learned in Calais, Mariah put down the last colored chalk and nodded to Ainsley.

"I've no need to see the drawing, thank you, Mariah. You may pass it to Jacko. Jacko? By now you know what I suspect, I'm sure."

Jacko took the drawing pad and then pulled out a pair of spectacles and propped them on his nose. Everyone watched him as he squinted at the page, looked overtop his spectacles at Ainsley, looked at the page again. "It could be him, sir, if he were a good twenty years younger."

"Could be whom?" Spencer asked as Courtland stood close to Jacko to look down at the drawing. "Let me see that."

Courtland handed Spencer the drawing pad. "It's a very good likeness, most especially the nose. You're very talented, Mariah, nearly on a par with Elly. Papa? Didn't he leave us a good six months before the—that is, didn't he use his share to open a tavern in Saint Kitts, giving up the life?"

Spencer felt his temper rising once more and got to his feet. "What are you all talking about—who are you talking about? You had me traveling back and forth to Calais for weeks, not knowing what I should even have been looking for—*whom* I should have been looking for. Damn it, what haven't I been told?"

"Oh, sit down, Spencer," Mariah said, understanding his anger but also anxious to hear about this man she had drawn. This terrible, cruel monster.

"Ha! Hear that, Cap'n? Not even bracketed yet, and she's got a stout ring in his nose to pull him around by," Jacko said, then sobered. "Could be the whelp. He had one, remember? The age would be about right."

Ainsley nodded, and then smiled thinly at Spencer. "I'm sorry, son. I hid nothing from you. We're learning this just as you are. It was Mariah who first made me suspect, giving us a name. *Renard.* The Fox. Not his real name—many of us took other names when we came to the islands, hoping to one day return to England and go back to a more normal existence. There was something about the man that made him fit the name."

"The nose," Mariah said, nodding. "The sharp features."

"He'd been with us for years," Courtland said. "Ever since I arrived on the island, at least. So you think he turned traitor, went over to Edmund?"

Jacko snorted. "If there was enough money in it, Georgie Fox would have wiped the devil's own ass for him—um, your pardon, Miss Rutledge."

"There's no point in dissembling, as I think we all know what we're discussing. George Fox, Mariah," Ainsley explained, "was the man I trusted to keep our accounts for us. Each ship we took as licensed privateers, each cargo we captured…in other ways. The men in the crews shared their portion of our profits equally and Fox wrote everything down, figured out those portions. What went to the Crown, what went to the men, what came to me as Captain. A bookkeeper, you'd say."

"Got sick as a dog aboard ship," Jacko said from behind her. "Worthless for anything save numbers. But he knew everything, Cap'n."

"Not quite everything, Jacko," Ainsley reminded him. "Only you, Billy, Pike and I knew the location of our—" he looked at Mariah "—bank. If he had known, possibly Isabella and everyone else would still be alive."

"No, sir," Courtland said, refilling Ainsley's wineglass. "Beales was there to kill, no matter what. If he couldn't torture for answers, he would have tortured for sport. And now he's back, most definitely back, or at least Georgie Fox's son is. Mariah's drawing proves that. There can be no question."

"Just as there can be no question that it was Edmund Beales who risked Eleanor's life by tricking the Black Ghost into attacking her ship as it was bound for England," Jack added, not looking at Jacko as he spoke. "If you're handing out chances to have a piece of the man, Ainsley, I'm in for whatever it takes."

Mariah kept her expression blank, even as she longed to ask a thousand questions about Edmund Beales, the Black Ghost, what had happened to Eleanor.

Spencer shifted uncomfortably in his chair. Jack had just as good as said that Ainsley had been guilty of attacking an English ship—the worst crime possible. They all seemed to have completely accepted Mariah into this conversation, into the most private secrets any family could ever have—secrets that, if revealed, could end with them all hanged in chains.

They'd accepted her because she'd been brave, fearless actually, and because she had brought them important if damning information. But her involvement had to end now.

"We've got less a week in which to prepare," Spencer said, breaking the silence that had taken over the room once more. "Let's consider a plan that came to me on the trip back from Calais." He turned in his chair. "Court, you and Rian and Jacko take the *Respite* and the *Spectre* at first light and make for the waters around Elba. Kinsey is preparing the ships and two crews. The crews are probably already loading provisions. By my reckoning, if you catch a good wind and stay close to the shore, you can make it in four days, five at the most."

"To do what, Spence? Watch helplessly as Napoléon sails past us? Wave to the ships, perhaps? The Emperor's got close to one thousand well-trained soldiers on that island with him and, from reports we've read, there are enough ships in the harbor to transport them all."

Ainsley got to his feet and walked over to the table where dozens of maps were always spread out for him to study. He placed a fingertip on one of the maps. "No, Court, Spencer's right. Two obviously well-armed sloops lying close to the island and making themselves extremely visible would attract considerable attention. Even a fool such as the man supposedly acting as Bonaparte's gaoler would put his ships and the men on the island itself on the alert, increase their patrols. Bonaparte will leave Elba at some point in time, of this I'm certain—but his escape could be delayed. And a plan delayed is more often than not a plan destroyed."

"What do we do if they ask to board us?"

Ainsley, still leaning over the map table, turned his

head toward Courtland and smiled, his eyes alert, alive, a part of the young and daring Geoffrey Baskin in those eyes. "Why, Courtland, you'll invite them to tea, of course. You're merely curious citizens like so many others, come to gawk at the Little Corporal in his cage. You might allude to the fact that you'd heard rumors that Bonaparte was planning an escape quite soon and you thought it would be great good fun to watch."

"Be idiots, you mean, Cap'n," Jacko grumbled from his seat. "Rich, brainless fools with more hair than wit, out for a lark. We can do that easy enough. We'll just let Rian do all the talking."

Rian tossed the remainder of his bit of cheese at the grinning man; Jacko snagged it out of the air and took a healthy bite out of it.

Spencer and Mariah exchanged glances and she put her hand on his arm. This man had shown her a future and she'd be damned if she'd let him die before they and their son could see it. "You plan to go to London, don't you?" she asked him in a whisper. "I'm going with you."

Spencer looked Ainsley, then leaned in close to whisper back at her. "No, you're not. I'll take Rian, who obviously doesn't want to sail to Elba. Thanks to your drawing, we'll all recognize this Renard bastard now when we see him."

"But I've seen Nicolette. She'll be there, too. Renard brought her to Calais. It stands to reason he'll bring her to London, too."

"Then you'll draw us another picture. You're so good with the chalks, remember? But you're not going to London."

"I'll follow you at any rate, Spencer. You know I'll find a way."

He looked at her for a long moment and she didn't blink. Damn.

"Spencer?"

"Yes, sir?" he said, turning his attention back to Ainsley.

"I'll assume you plan to travel to London for the celebrations?"

Spencer nodded. "We could leave tomorrow. Meet with Chance at his house in Upper Brook Street, make it our headquarters while we're there. Chance wouldn't want to miss this and he and Julia would be expected to attend the festivities if they're in town. Billy has already agreed to go to his country house and fetch him to London to at least meet with us."

"I agree that Chance has to be involved," Ainsley said, returning to his chair, "but I hesitate to bring Julia into this, so that decision will be left to Chance."

"To Julia, you mean," Jacko said, chuckling.

"True enough. Ethan and Morgan are somewhere in Shropshire, presenting the twins to a pair of his maiden aunts, so they're lost to us. And neither Jack nor Eleanor can show their faces, I'm afraid, not after what happened last year. It might be better to have Chance speak with his former superiors at the War Office, alert them as to what he believes to be a plot against His Royal Highness and the others. But, before you argue with me, Spencer, I agree that we're too personally involved to simply inform the War Office and then do nothing but hope for the best. Rian, you may forgo the sea voyage and travel to London with Spencer, as you've already been there and know Chance's location."

"Yes, sir!" Rian said, getting to his feet, looking ready to leave within the minute.

"If I might say something, sir?" Mariah folded her hands in her lap and looked levelly at Ainsley Becket. "I know nothing about what happened with Eleanor and her husband, and won't pry, but having another woman present would make us an unremarkable party as we, um, reconnoiter the areas where the celebrations are to take place. We'd simply be another interested party of gawkers and celebrators, even as we watch for Renard." She turned to glare at Spencer before looking to Ainsley once more. "Or his woman, Nicolette. I saw her, as well."

"No," Spencer said. "I forbid it. You have a son, madam."

"How very tiresome you are. *We* have a son, *sir,*" Mariah shot back at him. "I want him to grow and thrive in a world of peace."

"Then I fear you are destined for disappointment, my dear," Ainsley said, his tone somber. "There will always be ambitious monsters like Edmund Beales and the world will never be truly at peace. It is up to the rest of us to acknowledge that fact and always be alert, waiting and watching for the next Edmund Beales, and the next. Spencer—she travels with you, she's earned the right twice over. But first, we'll have the wedding ceremony, tomorrow, rather than Saturday, and you'll leave for London the next day, giving Chance time to be there to meet you." He got to his feet. "I think we're done now, and your fiancée looks asleep on her feet. You're all excused."

"Thank you, sir," Mariah said as she stood, more than eager to escape to her bedchamber without any further argument from Spencer. Besides, she felt this crushing need to see William, to hold him in her arms. She and her soon-to-be husband could take up their argument again tomorrow.

"And the rest of you, as well. You heard the Cap'n," Jacko said, already heading for the door to open it, watch as they all passed by him, into the hallway. He closed the door behind the last of them, Rian, who looked as pleased as a boy heading for a party.

"Ah, youth," Jacko said, returning to the drinks table to pour he and Ainsley more wine. "All Rian sees is adventure, but he'll learn soon enough. We all do, don't we, Cap'n, for some of us the lesson's harder than for others?"

Ainsley had his elbows on the desktop as he rubbed at the back of his neck with both hands. "George Fox, Jacko. I don't know what I'd thought to hear from

Spencer, but I hadn't expected to hear that. I trusted him. How blind I was, not to see, not to know. Edmund must have been planning for months, years, to betray me. To do what he did."

"You were crazy in love, Cap'n," Jacko said, putting the wineglass next to Ainsley's elbow. "And planning to leave for England, take your share and leave the life behind in exchange for a new one. I'm the one who should have known, should have realized the little clerk was turning his coat. But we can't neither of us think too long on any of that, Cap'n, what happened all those years ago. We're sending boys to do a man's work. Boys and little girls, God help us all."

"You think I should go to London."

Jacko sighed, rolling his heavy shoulders. "Will Beales be there?"

Ainsley sat back in his chair, looking up at the ceiling. He hadn't left Becket Hall in sixteen long years. When he did leave, as he'd begun to consider, he'd never imaged London as his destination; that dream had died the day he'd been tricked into sending an English ship to the bottom. "No, I don't think so, Jacko, at least not yet. I listened to Edmund weave fantasies with his grand ideas and schemes for more than a dozen years. I know, unfortunately, how he thinks, the sort of webs he weaves, even as I still learn of the depths of his treachery and vile ambitions. But I most definitely know his capacity for evil, his genius for evil. And, God forgive me, I helped make him rich enough to live out his plans."

Jacko grinned now. "But not as rich as he'd planned, Cap'n, not even by half. That must still stick in his craw, that we have our fair share of our takings—and the other—and not him."

"That *other* you speak of, Jacko, cost me my wife, cost too many innocent lives. And, sadly, men like Edmund always find another way to gather wealth to them."

They both turned toward the door at the sound of a knock to see Spencer already walking into the study. "Excuse me, but I found several mentions of the Grand Jubilee in the newspaper someone left in the main drawing room. The celebration will include Hyde Park, Saint James's and Green Park. Half the world will be there. And we'll be looking for one man in the middle of all of this. How many men will you allow me to take with us?"

Ainsley considered the question. "Nobody who sailed with us, of course, or they could be recognized. After all, we have no idea how many of the men who sailed with Beales are still with him. We already know George Fox's son is with him. Twenty, thirty at the most? Chance will find out where the dignitaries will be situated to view the celebrations and you can then concentrate everyone close by, alert for anything."

"But alert for what? An armed attack? That doesn't seem feasible."

"Think like your enemy, Spencer. Decisions must be made as to how you will proceed, Spencer, and as

I considered the thing, how I would manage the affair, I have already decided on an explosive discharge when most of the dignitaries are together in one place, remembering Guy Fawkes and his legendary attempt to blow up Parliament."

"I'm not taking Mariah with me," Spencer said, thinking of the destruction and death that would be caused by a large explosion of black powder. "I doubt Chance will allow Julia to accompany him, either. It's too dangerous."

"Miss Rutledge says she can recognize the woman traveling with Fox," Ainsley reminded him with a smile. "She also, as I'm sure I don't have to remind you, found her way aboard the *Respite*. It may be safer to keep her where you can see her, as we can't chain her to a wall, you know."

Jacko's stomach rose and fell as he chuckled. "Well, Cap'n, we *could*."

"I'll ignore that, Jacko. And I'll enjoy speaking with her at length once this is over. I'm convinced our Miss Mariah Rutledge has lived a rather unorthodox life."

"Our Lady of the Swamp," Spencer said, gathering up the newspapers. "I should be grateful, I know, but it's rather unnerving to see a woman so...so..."

"Independent? Resourceful? Adventurous? Fairly fearless? So much like yourself?" Ainsley suggested, not all that helpfully in Spencer's opinion.

"I was thinking hotheaded and impulsive,

actually—which, I suppose, is also a lot like me, thank you," Spencer grumbled, subsiding into a chair, his long legs flung out in front of him. "I, um, I told her about Virginia."

"And?" Ainsley asked him, his expression carefully guarded.

"And she said yes, she'd accompany me." Spencer raised his head to look at Ainsley. If there was one man he could always speak the truth to, bare his soul to, it was this man. "The idea of beginning a new life seems to appeal to her. But whether it's me or Virginia and a home of her own that made her say yes—that I don't know. She may just want what she believes will be a safe place for William and herself, away from Romney Marsh, and I'm merely a means to an end."

Jacko slapped his hands on his thighs and got to his feet. "I don't know what that means, bucko, but I think my bed's calling me—and that you may think too much."

Spencer watched the older man leave the room, then turned back to Ainsley. "She's a strange woman. Willful, I guess. But I can't deny her bravery or her good heart."

"You're not discussing a loyal hound, Spencer," Ainsley said, smiling at his son. "Isabella was what you call willful. She called it knowing what—and whom—she wanted. Thankfully, she wanted me. I never understood why. Could that be your problem?"

Spencer rubbed at his forehead, smiling behind his hand. "No, I think Mariah's my problem, and I understand why. I can't seem to keep my hands off her, even when I know I should. We'd better both live a long, long time, because I think it's going to take a lot of years before either of us knows why we act the way we do when we're together. Running hot…running hotter." He lowered his hand, looked earnestly at Ainsley. "But we won't leave here, Papa, not until this is settled, not until Edmund Beales is dead and none of you are locked up here, worrying about the bastard."

Ainsley's voice was a soft purr. "This may surprise you, Spencer, but not all of us consider Becket Hall a prison."

"I know, Papa, I know," Spencer said, getting to his feet once more. "I sound ungrateful and I apologize."

"Don't. We each have to find our own place, our own happiness. But I think, son, your happiness might not be a place. Your happiness might actually be that hotheaded and fairly fearless young woman who is currently so unnerving you. Now go to bed. You'll be marrying that young woman in the morning, remember?"

CHAPTER THIRTEEN

THIS WAS ALL PERFECTLY silly. Here she was, already a mother, yet dressing for her wedding to her son's father. She wasn't facing a joyous ceremony. She and Spencer were only making *proper* what they'd obviously already done without the blessings of church or state.

What did any church or state have to do with a man and a woman and what happened between them, anyway, what they did in private? Honestly, it was all just too silly.

And she was so damnably nervous.

And fussing.

Fussing with her gown, the second of the pair she had brought back from Calais; a simple thing the color of newly churned butter; cunningly simple, but fashioned of the finest silk and in what she had been told was the first stare of fashion.

Fussing with her unruly hair, tying it up on top of her head, then pulling out the pins to let it hang loose, then tying it up again, but only half of it this time, so that some of it waved down over her shoulders. Then tearing out the ribbon and tossing it to the floor in disgust while trying to convince herself that she was *not* going to dissolve into tears like some petulant child over something so silly as how she wore her hair.

Callie retrieved the ribbon now and tied Mariah's hair back one more time, then put her hands on Mariah's shoulders, holding her in the dressing table chair with considerable force. "Touch it again and I'll use the ribbon to tie your hands behind your back, I swear I will, Mariah. And wouldn't that look just fine as I push you into the drawing room to meet your bridegroom?"

"I don't know if it would look just fine, Callie," Mariah told her, grimacing. "But it most certainly would convey my feelings quite well. This marriage is being forced on Spencer. And on me."

"Oh, pooh," Callie said, half pushing Mariah out of the chair so that she could sit down and check her own reflection in the mirror. "You have William. Of course you have to be married. It only makes sense. Even Fanny says so. You're only nervous about everyone watching you as you say your vows, but you'll soon forget all of that. I so envy you, traveling to London for your wedding trip. I never go anywhere. Do you want me to put a flower in your hair? I think brides wear flowers in their hair."

"No, no flowers, Callie. The ribbon is fine. And I'm fine, truly I am. Let's take William downstairs with us now, all right? It isn't every child who can say he was a witness to his parents' nuptials."

She opened the door to the dressing room to see Eleanor Eastwood bending over the cradle, her hand resting lightly on William's stomach. She straightened quickly, blinking back what Mariah was sure were tears.

"I…I thought I'd come take William down to the drawing room, if that's all right?" she said, smiling at Mariah.

Mariah nodded, returning the smile. Eleanor Eastwood was a beautiful woman, a beautiful *lady*. Petite, her bone structure that of a princess, Mariah had thought more than once. Made a bit fragile by some unnamed old injury that caused her to limp when she walked, yet strong in her own quiet way. A woman wed only a year, very much in love with her husband…and yet there had been more than a trace of sadness in her lovely eyes when she'd been looking at William.

"Callie?" Mariah said, turning to the younger woman. "If you'd please, go downstairs and tell everyone that Eleanor and I will be joining them directly."

Callie looked past Mariah to her sister, and suddenly the girl who was part silly child, part young woman, had a soft, sad look in her own eyes that had banished the silly child completely. "Yes, of course. But don't tarry, or Odette will come up here after you and I know neither of you wants that."

Mariah waited until Callie had gone and then approached Eleanor. "Is something wrong?"

"No, not at all," Eleanor said, quickly brushing at her cheeks as she smiled at Mariah. "It's just…it's just that William is so wonderful, isn't he? So small, so marvelously perfect."

Just like any other proud mother, Mariah was quick to agree and thanked Eleanor for her kind words, only to hear the woman's involuntary sob as she pressed a hand over her mouth. "Elly? Something's obviously wrong. Please, let me help."

"No, there's nothing you can do, thank you, Mariah. I'm just being maudlin. Selfish. Entirely unreasonable. I…I began my monthly flux this morning, that's all. It sometimes makes me weepy."

Mariah felt she understood. "You and Jack…you want a baby?"

Eleanor fought to bring her emotions back under her control, where she'd always worked hard to keep them, except with Jack. "It's more than a year…and nothing. You…you don't even love Spencer and you have a baby. Without even trying, you have this beautiful baby. I love Jack with all my heart and soul, and yet we…we…oh, I didn't mean that. I truly didn't mean that. I'm so sorry, Mariah. So sorry."

"No, don't be," Mariah said, wondering if she should put her arms around the smaller woman and then holding back, fairly certain that a physical expression of sympathy might dissolve Eleanor in tears.

"What happened with Spencer, with William, was an accident, or so I believed at the time. But now it's as if William was destined to be born. Your time will come, Eleanor, I'm sure of it. What…what does Odette say?"

Eleanor wiped at her eyes one last time and then took a deep breath, squared her slim shoulders. "Odette? She's very vague, actually. She says she sees children for us, but when I ask her when, when does she see them, she only smiles and says I'll know. It's silly. I'm silly, wanting assurances from Odette, who is the first to say that she's not always right, she doesn't always…see. But I vow, Mariah, if she told me to walk around Becket Hall backward five times at sunrise and then spit in the Channel, I'd do it—anything to have a child."

Mariah smiled, because she knew she was supposed to, and then she lifted the sleeping William from his cradle and handed him to Eleanor. "Here, why don't you carry him downstairs for me? I forgot something in my chamber and need to fetch it."

Eleanor tucked William close against her breast. "Thank you, Mariah. And I'll watch over him while you and Spencer are in London. Please, stay safe. No matter what may or may not happen, coming back here to William is more important than anything or anyone else. One way or another, as Papa has said, the world will go on."

"We'll be fine, I promise. The, um, the plan? It's already going forward?"

Eleanor nodded, suddenly very businesslike. "Court and Jack and Jacko lifted anchor hours before dawn and Billy is already well on his way to Chance's estate. The men who will accompany you and Spencer and Rian to London have been chosen and are being prepared. And your bridegroom is cooling his heels in the drawing room, waiting for his bride. I know you must feel rushed, but Papa was adamant about this marriage, that it not be delayed any longer. He can be quite…sentimental."

Mariah wasn't surprised that Eleanor knew their plans, even as Callie had only been told that they were taking a wedding trip to the metropolis. Callie was still a child, and her father's own child at that. As Mariah returned to her chamber to gather what she'd forgotten, she wondered if Ainsley Becket would ever be able to let Callie go…the child of his beloved and tragically lost Isabella.

"And that's enough thinking for the moment," Mariah told herself sternly. "It's time to face going downstairs to marry the man who has threatened to make love to you until the entire world fades away."

When she entered the drawing room it was to see all of the Beckets still in residence already there, chatting with each other and then turning as one to look at her as she made her entrance. It was a small but fine-looking gathering of people, all strong and confident people, all united in a way that most families bound by blood would envy.

She looked to Fanny, whom she'd barely gotten to know, and the girl smiled back at her, then winked. Mariah took that to mean that she'd been accepted, and that was nice.

But then Spencer stepped forward and she forgot anyone else was in the room.

He was dressed in a fine dark-blue jacket and fawn pantaloons, the lace at his throat as white as Canadian snow, his eyes and his barely tamed hair as dark as a moonless night, his skin as golden as the sun and his heritage made it.

She'd seen this man wounded and vulnerable. She'd seen him both careless and carefree. She'd experienced his anger, watched him play the fool, marveled at the sight of him up on the deck of the *Respite,* looking longingly out to sea. And now she saw him in the trappings of a gentleman, his fire scarcely tamed, only marginally contained. This was the man who'd made William with her, the man whose blood flowed in her son's veins. He was so many men, this Spencer Becket, and she wanted to know all of them…all of him. *Until the world fades away.…*

"Here," he said, handing her a large bouquet of flowers. "Jacko cut them for you personally before he set sail. I'd say this means he's officially approved of you. It's up to you whether you want to feel flattered or turn on your heels and run from here as fast as possible."

Mariah sniffed at a pale pink rose nestled in with

several others. "What a strange man he is, isn't he? I have to remember to thank him when he returns."

Spencer held out his hand to her, as she held out hers to him and allowed him to lead her toward the grey-haired stranger standing in front of the fireplace, an open prayer book in his hands.

But before the vicar could say a word, Odette, dressed all in white from the enormous scarf wound about her head to the slippers on her feet, approached them to lay colorful silk scarves around their shoulders. She then recited a prayer in a mix of French and some language Mariah could not understand, moved her right hand in the air to sketch the sign of a cross and bowed to them before returning to the side of the room where Onatah stood, her wizened, small, walnut-shell face solemn yet shining.

After that, the ceremony was blessedly brief, with Spencer squeezing her hand as the vicar intoned the word *obey,* and her returning that squeeze while trying not to giggle. Giggles then became the furthest thing from her mind as Spencer slipped a gold and emerald ring onto her finger, the weight of the thing telling her of its worth and the seriousness of the bond that was now between them.

And when the ceremony was over she barely had time to think about Spencer's quick, hard kiss as she was passed from one Becket to another, all of them kissing her cheeks, hugging her, welcoming her to the family.

Anyone would think she hadn't shown up on their

doorstep heavy with child, all but forcing this day on them.

And then William was christened, still held tight in Eleanor's arms, but with every Becket sibling also standing for the child who would never be lacking in family love and protection. That thought alone was enough to bring tears to Mariah's eyes and she took hold of Spencer's hand and urged him out into the hallway.

"Is something wrong? I know we can be a bit overpowering at times…"

"No, no, I like your family very much. Even Odette, who I most sincerely hope was blessing us," Mariah assured him, stepping away from the open doorway as she reached into the pocket of her gown. "It's just that I wanted to give you this," she said, holding out her father's pocket watch and fob, the man's most treasured possession, which she'd taken from his still-warm body that day outside of Moraviantown. "I miss him so very much."

"I know, Mariah. I…we'll all do our best to protect you for him. We're your family now, which should frighten you not a little bit," he said, smiling at her, trying to ease her pain.

Mariah nodded, took a steadying breath. "One day, when he's grown, you can give it to William."

Spencer looked down at the watch, then closed his fingers around it. Why couldn't he relax? He felt so stiff, so formal. He hadn't even told Mariah how beautiful she looked. "I'm honored, Mariah. And humbled. And, until that day, I'll wear it in remembrance of a good man."

Mariah smiled, releasing her breath in relief. "I know it's not much, not worth a pittance compared to this ring..." She stopped speaking as a thought struck at her, looked at him seriously. "Was this ring...was it part of...?"

Spencer didn't pretend not to know what she was asking. "The gold was fashioned here, in our smithy, Mariah," he told her. "But that emerald definitely sailed an ocean at one time and landed at a destination not intended by its original owner. Do you mind?"

Mariah looked down at the ring, the huge stone. "Well, at least you're honest about your thievery," she told him, and then grinned. "Papa won his watch in a card game with a wealthy, well-born and very stupid captain of the Guards."

"Now I'm doubly honored to have it," Spencer told her, slipping the watch into the pocket of his waistcoat, attaching the fob. He sensed her nervousness, wished it away, just as he wished his own away, and turned serious. "Just as I'm honored to be your husband, Mariah. I know we're still strangers with so much to learn about each other, but now we've got the rest of our lives, don't we? The rest of our honest and upstanding lives."

Mariah bit her bottom lip between her teeth as she nodded. "Eleanor...Eleanor told me to remember that the world goes on no matter what and that we need to protect ourselves so that we come back here to William. But we owe it to William to give him the best world possible, don't we? Not a world of complete peace, because Ainsley was right, that's impossible. But the very best world we can give our son."

"One without Edmund Beales in it, yes." Spencer cupped her chin in his hand, his dark eyes smoldering as he looked at her intensely. "You don't have to go to London with me tomorrow, Mariah. You know I don't want you to go, in any case. William needs at least one of us."

She pulled her head away from him. "One of us? He'll have both of us, Spencer. And he'll have Virginia and a whole new world of promise. You said so and you damn well had better have meant it."

Spencer smiled while once again silently questioning whether she wanted him or merely a safe home in Virginia. "Married less than an hour and already arguing. Does this bode well for our next fifty years, wife?"

She almost softened, but then quickly glared up at him. "Oh, no. Don't think you can change the subject, Spencer Becket. You all think you're such masters of diverting me, but it won't work. When I wake tomorrow morning, it will be to see you lying beside me."

He was more than happy to tease her. "Ah, this gets better and better. An invitation."

She refused to rise to his bait or be embarrassed by

his words. She had to know that he wasn't going to trick her, escape to London without her. "No, a command. If I don't wake up to see you, if you've left without me, watch your back in London, Spencer, because it won't be just Renard who will be aiming at that back."

Onatah, who felt most comfortable in Odette's rooms, swept past them down the hall, muttering something in her own tongue as she went. Something that had Mariah flushing to the roots of her hair.

"Don't tell me. Making an honest woman of you or not, I'm still the fornicating son of a three-legged cur, correct?"

Mariah lowered her head, shook it. "No. She reminded me that I am your woman now, and should not speak to my master with the sharp tongue of the serpent if I wish for many cooking pots and bear-skins."

Spencer's smile was wide and delighted. "I knew that woman was a treasure the first time I saw her. You'd be wise to listen to her, although I don't think you should pin your hopes on a bearskin, as bears are in rather short supply on Romney Marsh. I do know where to find some fairly good cooking pots, however."

"Oh, go to the devil," Mariah told her bridegroom of less than an hour and flounced back into the drawing room, where she surrounded herself with Becket women for the next several hours.

CHAPTER FOURTEEN

SPENCER ENTERED his dressing room to see Clovis and Anguish waiting for him, standing at attention…although Anguish rather listed to port, more than slightly the worse for drink.

"We're here to drink to you and your bride before turning in for the night, Lieutenant," Clovis said, turning smartly to retrieve a silver tray from one of the tables, a tray bearing a decanter and three crude glasses meant more for ale than French brandy. Apparently Clovis's larceny didn't extend to fine crystal.

"That's some of Ainsley's best, gentlemen, smuggled here from France by the good men of Romney Marsh at great peril to their lives and limbs. Do you expect us all to just throw it back like water?"

"And isn't that still the best way, sir," Anguish said with a broad wink, accepting a glass from Clovis and running it beneath his reddened, bulbous nose as he took an appreciative sniff of its contents. "Ah, and I can already feel it warming my thin Irish blood."

Clovis pulled a face. "He's been feeling one strong spirit or another warm his thin Irish blood for hours now, sir, drinking to your health. Surprised he can feel anything at all."

"Now, now, Clovis, not just to the lieutenant's health, but his lady's, as well." He lifted his glass. "To Our Lady of the Swamp—a long and happy life to her!"

"Hear, hear!" Clovis said, tossing back his own glass.

"Agreed," Spencer said, then joined them in their salute to his bride. "Now, if you gentlemen will excuse me?"

"Oh, yes, sir, that we will," Anguish said, holding out his glass to Clovis. "Only one more drink, sir, and that's to me."

"Really? You're getting married, then?" Spencer asked as Clovis poured them each another two inches of costly brandy.

"Me, sir? Oh, no, sir. I'm not that balmy—er, not yet found the lady, sir, so it's a bachelor boy I am for now. Not but a few years past forty, sir, there's still time enough," Anguish told him, rocking slightly on the balls of his feet. "It's a new name I've got tonight, sir, thanks to Mr. Becket."

Spencer looked to Clovis for an explanation, as Anguish now seemed to be having some slight difficulty focusing.

"It's like this, Lieutenant," Clovis explained. "Our Anguish here—"

"Aloysius," Anguish corrected, then loudly burped. "Ah…needed that, I did."

"Yes, Anguish…that is, sir, our Aloysius here figured that if Mr. Becket had given you a name, or so Bumble told us, and most of the others, too, then maybe he could gift Ang—Aloysius with a new name, as well, seeing as how the one he had might have some bad luck attached to it."

"And most of my good right arm *not* attached anymore, if you're taking my drift. Sir," Anguish said, nodding. "So now I'm Aloysius Nulty. A fine name, that. Solid. And all my bad luck behind me." He lifted his glass. "A great day, sir, all around!"

"And I'll be happy to drink to that, Aloysius," Spencer said solemnly, not smiling until he'd downed the brandy and turned to his tall dressing bureau to begin stripping off his neck cloth. "Long life and good luck to you. Um…Clovis?"

"Taking him off to his bed, sir," Clovis said, turning the newly christened Aloysius at the shoulders and frog-marching him to the door. "You're all packed and ready, Lieutenant, and the coaches will be ready at nine of the morning. A good night to you, sir."

Spencer shook his head at his two loyal companions as he stripped off his jacket and waistcoat, then unclipped Mariah's father's watch and fob and held them in his hand for a long moment, looking at his bride's gift to him. "I promise, sir," he said quietly, "I'll keep her safe for you." Then smiled as he added, "Even if I have to kill her to do it."

He set the watch on top of the bureau and opened

his shirt buttons at his throat, removed the studs from his cuffs, pulled his shirttails free of his pantaloons and rid himself of hose and shoes. He slept in the buff and had done so since childhood, but for tonight he believed he'd be best served by greeting his bride while still fairly decent.

She was in the dressing room on the other side of his bedchamber even now, with Onatah in attendance, probably filling her with dire warnings about obedience and cooking pots, none of which Mariah, he felt sure, would take to heart.

He poured some still fairly warm water into a wash basin and splashed his face, ran his damp hands over his hair, washed his hands, cleaned his teeth—the sweetness of the tooth powder jarred badly with the lingering taste of brandy—and then examined his reflection in the small mirror that topped his dressing bureau, hoping to see the man and not the wharf rat.

She'd seen him worse, God knew. But he hadn't promised her a long, slow lovemaking then, had he? Loneliness, grief and fear had led to their first encounter. Passion and excitement had led to their second. But this was a beginning, the beginning of a lifetime together.

And he'd damn well better get it right.

Taking a deep breath, cursing himself for a fool, he opened the door to his bedchamber just in time to see Mariah entering the chamber from the opposite side.

She saw him and paused, her hand still on the door

handle, her long, perfect form outlined inside the thin, white gown by the candles behind her, still lit in the dressing room, her unbound hair a halo of living fire tumbling to her bare shoulders.

"Spencer," Mariah said, letting go of the handle as she took three steps into the large chamber.

"Mariah," he answered, inclining his head in a rather self-mocking bow.

Screaming, running, hiding. Options Mariah quickly considered, then discarded, as she wasn't afraid of the man. She already *knew* the man, in a most intimate way. This night was no different from the nights after Moraviantown, from that almost embarrassing coming together aboard the *Respite.* What was a bed, after all? How did a bed make anything different? How did vows spoken under duress make anything different?

But they did. And it was. And she was all but trembling from nerves. *Damn the man!*

Spencer walked slowly toward her in the soft yellow glow cast by candles and firelight, his gaze locked with hers, his heart pounding in a way that told him he was taking his first steps toward his future, her future. Their future, theirs and their son's, the children she would give him, the life they would make together in a new land. A new beginning, away from the dark and dangerous shadows of the past; a place where they would *belong.*

Tomorrow he would think of that past and how

what had happened in the islands still haunted them all, and the dangers they faced in trying to banish that past and its demons forever.

Tonight? Tonight he would do his best not to think at all....

Mariah walked toward him, saying without words that she would meet him halfway, that they would try for William's sake, perhaps even for their own, to make this marriage between them work as more than a mere convenience, a nod to propriety.

"You're beautiful," Spencer breathed softly as he stood in front of her and raised one hand to cup the curve of her cheek. "Frightened?"

Mariah closed her eyes, her body turning boneless as she pressed her cheek against his hand. "Terrified."

"Me, too." Spencer dipped his head to touch his lips to hers; gently, lightly, even hesitantly. Their bodies still separate, their only connection the kiss they shared. That kiss. And the next. And the next....

He stepped closer, clasped her waist lightly with one hand as he trailed his fingers slowly down the side of her throat, along the sweep of her shoulder, down the length of her arm, where he entwined his fingers with hers.

Mariah sighed audibly, raised her other hand to press her palm against his chest to feel his beating heart. Her own heart felt like a trapped bird in her breast, beating its wings furiously fast, frantic to be free. To fly. To soar.

Her terror melted away to be replaced by a yearning, a hunger, a curiosity heightened by a swiftly rising passion.

Her lips parted seemingly of their own volition and Spencer eased his tongue inside, meshing their mouths more firmly together as he let go of her hand and raised his arms to push his spread fingers up into the warm, fiery hair at her nape, to hold her head as he deepened the kiss; take and give, take and give.

Her senses swimming with sensations familiar and yet new, Mariah slipped her arms around him, curling her fingertips into his back, clinging to him as he lifted her in his arms and carried her over to the high, wide bed that had been turned down for them, welcoming them.

"Still terrified?" he asked, breathing the question softly into her ear.

She bit her bottom lip for a moment, then said, "Could we…could we possibly discuss this later?"

Spencer dipped his tongue into her ear, tracing the perfect curve of it. "Later?"

Mariah moved beneath the heat of him, raising a hand to cup his neck. "Yes. Much later…"

He kissed her hair, her eyelids, suckled lightly on her velvet-soft earlobes, licked at the sensitive skin at the base of her throat. His mouth followed his hands, his fingers busy unbuttoning the modest night rail, lifting her slightly so that he could slip it up and over her head. He covered her nakedness with his body, rousing her with long, drugging kisses that she returned tentatively at first, then with building passion.

Mariah caught her breath in shock and pleasure as he cupped her breasts in his palms, his gaze steady on her as he licked at her nipples, nipped lightly, drew her into his mouth as he flicked at her with his tongue, rubbed her sensitive nipple between finger and thumb.

His eyes were so dark, filled with passion that seemed to enhance her own. She was sure he would take her now, give release to the passion building inside them both. But he didn't.

Instead, he moved slightly away from her, stripped off his clothes without concern for buttons and fastenings and then returned to her, to kiss her shoulders, the crooks of her elbows, the palms of her hands.

She moved beneath him, wordlessly telling him she was ready, but he ignored her, his fingers now busy stroking her rib cage that rose and fell with her quick, shallow breaths. He dipped his tongue into her navel, curling something tight, deep in her belly. His hands skimmed her hips even as he moved lower, lifted her leg to nibble the soft flesh on the inside of her thigh.

"Spence, please…"

Her skin was so fair, the sunlit fire of her hair spilling across the snow-white pillow, nestled so cunningly between her legs, drawing him into her fire. He could touch her all night, kiss her all the night long, watch the emotions on her candlelit face, see the wonder, the need, the realization.

He drew his tongue across the skin behind her knee, kneaded the creaminess of her thighs, drew himself back up to the center of her, the heart and heat of her.

"I...Spencer..."

"Shh, sweetings," he told her, his fingers already spreading her. "I promised...until the world goes away..."

Mariah watched as he slipped his hands beneath her buttocks, raised her slightly, then lowered his head to her. This was impossible, unbelievable, *surely forbidden.* But he was touching her, exploring her. She felt his warm breath against her skin. Shivered as his tongue glided over her, again and again and again.

Her head fell back against the pillows when he covered her with his open mouth, drawing her into his mouth, into his world, even as he moved his long fingers deep inside her.

She lifted herself to him as her world got smaller, centering only on what he was doing to her, how her body was reacting to what he was doing to her. There was nowhere else, there was nothing else. There was no one else but Spencer and herself...and the sweet tension building, building. Spreading. Flowering.

Her limbs went limp, all but numb. Now there was only Spencer's mouth, Spencer's fingers. Spencer, moving the world far away, building a new world with room only for the two of them.

She had let her legs fall open, giving her strong mind, indomitable spirit and sensitized body entirely over to him. Trusting him. Allowing him. Giving to him. Spencer knew it was time. He found her center, sucking at her as he flicked his tongue faster and faster, buried his fingers deep inside her, felt her explode around him, clench him, take from him.

"Now take me with you," he whispered to her as he raised himself between her legs, slid into her, felt her arms grasp him tightly even as she lifted her legs up and around his hips. "Into the fire, Mariah...take me into your fire..."

They built their own world and stayed it in until dawn before they finally slept in each other's arms, waking only slowly, reluctantly, as sounds of the household coming to life invaded the bedchamber.

"Good morning, wife," Spencer said, stroking her tangled mass of sun-kissed hair as she lay against him, her head on his chest. "Is it much later?"

Mariah blinked to clear her brain of a dream that had featured Spencer quite prominently, to find that she had her arms and legs wrapped around the reality of him. "Is it what?"

"Later. Much later. You said we'd discuss...well, I don't think we need to have that discussion now, do we? As a matter of fact," he said, twining one long, sleep-warm curl round his finger, "I think we've found at least one part of our married lives that will be completely free of problems."

Mariah pushed herself up on her elbows—one of them, hopefully, taking a bit of the hot air out of the man as she dug it into his side—to look at him through the veil of her hair. "Oh, you do, do you? And I suppose, delighted as you are about…about that *one part,* you now expect every other part to simply fall into line, making me a compliant wife and yours an easy life, yes?"

Spencer pushed himself up against the pillows, fairly certain he had just stepped at least one foot into quicksand. "I said all that? I don't think I did."

"Well, maybe you didn't," Mariah said, suddenly unsure of herself. "But you are looking smug, you know."

"Ah, but I'm not looming," he pointed out, grinning at her.

"And I'm not going to stay here at Becket Hall while you go haring off to London."

"Did I ask that?"

"No, but you were going to, weren't you?"

Spencer decided that the least he could be was honest. "Yes, I was. We have a son, Mariah—"

"Yes, we do. And I would very much appreciate it if you would not *hang* him over my head every time I want to do something you don't want me to do. I can *help,* Spencer. I won't do anything foolish. But I can play the silly woman and hang on your arm as we go about London looking for Renard and Nicolette. I can do this, I really can. We can help keep this new peace between the world and France. We can possibly avert a disaster in London. We can find this Edmund Beales and none of you will have to hide anymore. And then we can—"

"And then we can leave here, go to Virginia," Spencer finished for her. "Which of those things holds the most appeal, Mariah?"

She sat back, feeling threatened, as if her answer would either free her or damn her. "Can't...can't it be all of them?"

Spencer threw back the covers and left the bed, pulling on his dressing gown. "I suppose so. And I'm an idiot for asking so much of you when we've just married, when we, hell, when we barely know each other...what we really think, what we really feel."

What was the matter with the man? Mariah reached for her own dressing gown, lying at the bottom of the bed, and pushed her arms into it before sliding her feet to the floor, hastily tying the sash at her waist. "What's wrong, Spence? Oh. Wait. I see it now. You think...you think I'm only thinking of myself, of William, and not of you. Don't you?"

She marched around the bed to confront him, but he wouldn't meet her eyes.

"Don't you, Spence? Perhaps you even think I deliberately set out to bear your child, knowing you lived in a place so grand it was known by your family name? You think I came here already knowing the size of this house, the fortune that built it—and now all I want is to be taken care of, William and I? Oh, and *Virginia!* What a coup that is, isn't it? My own home in a new land? I've certainly landed on my feet, haven't I? Is *that* what you think?"

He took hold of her at the shoulders, gave her a quick, short shake. "No! No, damn it, I don't. I—"

"You *did*," Mariah said accusingly, cutting him off. "Admit it, Spence. You might not think it now, now that I've dragged it all out for an airing, but you *did*." She smiled, painfully. "Well, isn't this above all things wonderful? Your family accepts me, your family trusts me. But my *husband?* My husband still wonders, doesn't he? I never should have married you."

"Mariah, I'm sorry. I'm an idiot, I'll admit it. I can't explain myself to you. That's impossible. I'm a part of this family, yes. But a part of me has always been alone, separate. I don't know why. Hell, I don't even remember my life before I was a Becket." He shook his head slowly, trying to banish the fog that crowded his brain. "I've spent my entire life being…angry…feeling apart from everyone else… longing to go my own way. I just never…I just never thought anyone would want to go there with me."

Mariah raised her hand to his face, stroked his cheek. Such a complicated man, living such a secretive, complicated life. "You have a son now," she told him quietly. "And, for good or ill, you have a wife. Is that really so terrible? To not be alone anymore?"

He shook off his melancholy mood, not without effort, and smiled at her, covered her hand with his own. "I've been reading one of the books in Ainsley's study, and I think I can probably find a bearskin for you in Virginia."

Mariah's heart did a small flip in her chest. She

wouldn't push at him anymore, but just follow his lead. They had their lifetimes to talk about the past. "And cooking pots? Fine cooking pots? I'm afraid I'll have to insist on the very best cooking pots."

They were standing so close together, in more than a physical way, perhaps even standing on the brink of something wonderful. Spencer sensed it…and then he ruined it. "Don't go to London with me, Mariah. Don't make me worry about you when I should be concentrating on finding Renard."

"Oh, Spencer," Mariah said, closing her eyes. "If we're ever to have a future together, you're going to have to understand that I'm going to walk beside you, not behind you."

Then she turned away from him and walked to her dressing room. She'd be gowned and ready before he was, and sitting in the coach, ready to leave for London, even if that meant missing her breakfast.

"You'll drive a man to drink," Spencer called after her.

She stopped, then turned to face him, her smile wide and genuine. "My father said that all the time. You really should have known him. Then, maybe, you'd understand me."

Spencer stood alone in his bedchamber for a full minute, attempting to figure out what in hell was happening to his life, his solitary life. But then the mantel clock struck the hour and he realized he had to get ready to leave for London or, hell's bells, Mariah would go without *him.*

So they'd start off on their wedding trip to the metropolis, one that would be filled with deceit, treachery, danger and the very real possibility of disaster. That was life. That was being a Becket. And, damn him, now that there was a possibility that life could be different, he resented the hell out it.

CHAPTER FIFTEEN

"CHURCH STEEPLE ahead! Another change of horses coming up fast, Lieutenant!" Clovis yelled down through the opened portal cut into the roof of the traveling coach.

Or, as Mariah considered it, the man had *bellowed* the warning just when she'd found a comfortable position on the velvet squabs and had dozed off for a few minutes. Her wedding night had been wonderful, but she hadn't spent very much of it asleep.

"He still calls you Lieutenant," Mariah grumbled, pushing herself into a more upright position. "Does that mean you can order him shot?"

Spencer, sitting on the facing seat, reading the newspaper he'd found in the posting inn in the last village they'd passed, learning as much as he could about the coming Grand Jubilee, put down the paper and grinned at his wife. "This is only our third stop, Mariah. Between now and tomorrow evening you'll sleep in this coach and take your meals here, as well. We've got horses posted all along the way and will stop only to change teams and mounts. I warned you that this wouldn't be an easy journey. I can put you down here with a man to guard you or hire a coach to return you to Becket Hall."

"You wouldn't dare and I'd never agree," she told him, adjusting her bonnet, fearing she'd sadly crushed one side of it by leaning her head against the side of the coach. "I've been on forced marches before, Spencer Becket, more than once. Your threats don't bother me. Just make sure you can keep up."

"I think I'll ride Fernando between this stop and the next, bear Rian company," Spencer said prudently, folding the newspaper and placing it beside him on the cushion. "It may be safer."

"It most certainly may be," Mariah told him, wondering what maggot she'd gotten into her head that made her think she even *liked* the man. "And we'll stop at this inn long enough for me to step inside it for at least five minutes."

"Mariah, I told you—"

"Oh, for pity's sake, Spence, I need to relieve myself. Something, by the way, you never considered when you locked me in that parlor in Calais. You men may be able to step behind a convenient tree or building, but I am female enough to insist on at least some semblance of civilization."

Spencer felt hot color running up the back of his neck as the coach halted in the yard of the inn. His hand was on the door latch before the wheels had stopped turning. "Clovis will assist you from the coach. I'll go ahead and secure a private dining room for us. We'll stay here for an hour. No longer, Mariah."

She folded her hands in her lap, smiling sweetly at him. "I wouldn't dream of it, Spencer."

He shot her a dark look and slammed out of the coach. This journey couldn't end soon enough for him.

It was nearing dusk and raining a day later as their party of a pair of traveling coaches and slightly less than two score men on horseback made its way into London. Mariah rode in the first coach; the second was loaded with baggage and an assortment of weapons and munitions. The coaches were accompanied by six outriders; the remainder maneuvered separately through twisted streets on their way to the mews and the back entrance to Chance Becket's townhouse in Upper Brook Street, three doors down from Hyde Park.

The knocker wasn't on the door to discourage visitors, but there were candles burning in one of the upper windows. A liveried footman opened the door at Spencer's knock, ushering everyone inside and to the back of the house, where a fire burned in the fireplace of Chance's study.

Chance rose from his seat behind a large desk and came around to clasp Spencer and Rian to him, one after the other, welcoming them to his home, telling them that he and Julia had only beaten them to town by a few hours.

There was good humor and backslapping all around

and Mariah watched, yawning behind her hand. She'd had only one victory during their journey, had seen the inside of only one inn for more than the five minutes Spencer had allotted her to, as he said, "Do what you have to do," just as if a more reasonable woman could override nature.

No, the bride and groom were not currently on the best of terms. And Mariah was too tired to care.

Now she attempted to take the measure of the man who, Spencer had told her during one of the rare times he'd chosen to ride inside the coach with her, had been the first orphan Ainsley had brought to his island home. Island headquarters. Whatever that accursed, unnamed island had been called.

Mariah was now Spencer's wife, shared his bed, but it was clear that this didn't mean that he and his family would now be an open book to her, not if he wouldn't even tell her the name of the island. She wanted his trust, if not his love, and that was why she had tearfully kissed her small son goodbye and insisted upon accompanying her new husband to London. To earn her way into this family and perhaps into Spencer's carefully guarded heart. Couldn't the stupid, thickheaded man understand that?

Besides, she wasn't the sort of fainthearted woman who could sit home and slice up sheets for bandages, waiting for the outcome of a battle. It wasn't in her nature. That part of her, Spencer also would simply have to get used to, because if she could accept him, his family, his foibles, then he would have to accept hers, as well.

She continued to visually examine Spencer's oldest brother. He'd already told her that Chance had sailed with Ainsley, pirated with Ainsley and later been estranged from Ainsley as he attempted to make himself into a gentleman and to forget who and what he had been.

"But don't let his outside fool you, because it didn't quite work," Spencer had told her with a grin. "He's still Chance, still ripe for adventure."

Mariah looked at the man and saw that he was still fairly young, probably not much more than a few years on the shady side of thirty. He must have been little more than a boy when he'd sailed with Ainsley Becket. There couldn't have been much opportunity for a childhood, living a life like that. And, she realized, for all his youth, he commanded this small room with his presence. He wore his dark blond hair long, tied back at his nape, not the fashion, she felt sure, but it suited him. In all, Chance Becket had the look of a man who noticed everything.

And now, once he'd congratulated Spencer on his marriage and rubbed at Rian's dark curls, suggesting he grow a beard like Courtland's to lose that look of a pretty baby, Chance turned those intense, all-noticing green eyes on her.

"Mrs. Becket," he said, bowing. "An honor. And may I offer you my heartfelt sympathies?"

"Accepted with thanks, Mr. Becket," Mariah said cheekily, dropping into a curtsy as Spencer gave a mock growl.

"Please, that would be Chance. And my wife will be down shortly to collect you, take you to the chamber we've ordered prepared and then quiz you on your marriage and on all of the inhabitants of Becket Hall. And, even if you don't believe me now, within an hour you will have told her things you didn't even know you knew."

"I heard that, darling."

Mariah turned at the sound of another female voice, to see a tall, handsome blond woman with a thin, intelligent face glide into the room. "Spencer! Rian! How good to see you both. Now go upstairs and wash away your travel dirt and I promise you food in the dining room in a half hour. Nothing hot, I'm afraid, as we're still settling in ourselves. You are hungry, aren't you?"

Spencer looked to Chance, eager to speak with him about their plans. But he knew better than to ignore Julia Becket's velvet-wrapped order. After all, the woman who could tame Chance Becket, call him to heel with no more than a smile, was not a woman to be lightly disobeyed. "Julia, if you'd please grant me time to allow me to introduce you to my bride, Mariah."

"Yes, yes, I know who she is. Don't growl at me, Spencer, we'll be fine. I don't bite, after all, no matter what my husband tells you. Now shoo—this poor girl looks ready to drop. I don't suppose you spared the horses on your way here and I know how she feels, as Chance shares this same inexcusable rush for speed over horrendously bad roads. Mariah, do you agree? Would you like to leave all these rough-and-tumble gentlemen to their dirt and come upstairs to have your meal in bed?"

Mariah and Spencer exchanged quick glances and then Spencer shrugged in a way that had Mariah laughing as she obediently turned and followed Julia out of the study, more than ready for a good wash, her night rail and a meal taken once she was tucked up in bed.

"I'd have served under Julia without a qualm," Spencer told Chance as he sank into one of the soft leather chairs in front of the fire. "A passable general, your wife."

"Yet you're still here, not marching upstairs to clean up your dirt. You're hoping I have news, aren't you?" Chance retook his chair behind the desk, picking up a round silver paperweight, to begin turning it in his hand. He did not in the least resemble Ainsley physically, yet he had many of the same mannerisms. Spencer wondered if Chance even realized that and decided he didn't. "Billy told me everything and Ainsley's letter filled in the areas Billy missed. So Ainsley believes it's really Beales and not just some intrigue you've stumbled on by spreading gold around Calais?"

Spencer shook his head, both at Chance's question and Rian's offer of wine. "We can't know. I heard a man speak French, quote something Beales used to say. That's not much evidence."

"Jules. It could have been Jules," Chance said, nodding. "I've been making some inquiries over the past year about the man Jack saw, the man we're assuming is Beales. In the end, I located a few servants from the house our supposed enemy resided in while in London, and learned a few things. One most important thing that I've kept from Ainsley these past months. He's worried enough as it is. I suppose the time has come to share that information."

Spencer sat forward in his chair. For a year they'd known about the man Jack had seen, the real leader of the Red Men Gang, and they'd taken precautions, kept their faces out of sight, believing that man to be their old nemesis, Edmund Beales. But proof? No. They'd never had absolute proof. "Tell me."

"Remember, Spence, I'm telling you, not Ainsley. Billy and I managed to run down one of the maids who served in the man's household. She had little to say, had never even seen the man—our mysterious man in black that Jack saw—but she did clean up after him."

"And?" Spencer watched Chance's face, but saw no emotion, none at all. How Spencer envied Chance his control. Cold-blooded, that was Chance, his hard edge probably a result of what he'd done in the past, what he'd seen in the islands…what he'd seen that last day.

But even as his eyes stayed hard, alert, Spencer had seen how they softened whenever his wife or children were present. If Spencer could someday find that same measure of peace with Mariah and William, he'd take it and be grateful.

"And, brothers mine, she complained about the mess on the carpets, on the tabletops, the couches, even in the man's bed. Bits and pieces of chewed-up leaves he'd spit everywhere."

Spencer released a breath he didn't realize he'd been holding. "Coca leaves. Jesus, God—it is him." Then he frowned. "When in bloody hell were you going to tell Ainsley and the rest of us?"

"Never, if I didn't have to, if I could find and dispose of Beales on my own," Chance said, smiling without mirth. "Ainsley's finally crawled out of that black hole he's been living in all these years, Spence. I didn't want to take the chance of sending him back into it, eating himself up inside, knowing for certain that Beales is still aboveground, and yet unable to find him. In truth, I've more than once imagined bringing him Beales's head in a box."

"Us, protecting Ainsley?" Spencer shook his head. "I don't know about that, Chance. He won't thank us for it."

"No, he won't. He wants to be in on the kill, you know," Rian said, settling into a chair with the bunch of grapes he'd lifted from a silver platter. "So, Chance, do you think he's past it?"

Spencer and Chance exchanged smiles before Chance said, "Rian, you pup, you probably think *I'm* past it, don't you? Ah, to be so young again."

Rian tossed a grape at him. "Well, at least Jacko's past it. His belly enters the room a good five seconds before the rest of him, for all his fine bluster and bragging over the man he once was. I pinked him, you know, the last time he thought he could teach me a lesson with the foils. That never happened before, not for any of us. Of course, I'm probably better with a sword, a pistol and a rifle than any of you. There is that to consider."

Spencer got up, went to the drinks table. "Our pup wants to go out and fight, Chance. I think he half wants Bonaparte free of Elba, just so he can take up arms and go chasing him. Not to mention how pretty he'd look in uniform."

Another grape was launched, this time in Spencer's direction.

"Have you ever noticed, Spencer," Chance said, "how much those who have never fought embrace the idea of war to solve any problem and how much those of us who have fought, who have seen the reality of violence, of war, want nothing more than to find a way to a fair peace? It's why I'd rather take my orders from a Captain, like Ainsley, than trust my fate and that of my family to an ambitious politician or a vainglorious king."

"Oh, the devil with you both. Maudlin, prosing old women, the pair of you. I'm going upstairs to change," Rian said, throwing down the grapes and leaving the room.

"Our little boy is growing up, Mother," Chance said, sighing theatrically.

"Wrong, brother mine. He is grown up. He insisted on coming here to help us. I think he believes the real fighting, if we have to fight, will be here in London, as Ainsley ordered Court to retreat if Bonaparte's ships left port, and hie themselves back to Becket Hall without attempting to engage them, go down to certain defeat. No sport in that, correct? I felt the way Rian feels, two years ago. All I wanted was a good fight, a chance to prove myself. And the adventure of the thing. I won't lie and deny that. Is it fair to deprive Rian of the same opportunity to learn the hard way that war doesn't turn a boy to a man, but only steals his youth?"

Chance looked levelly at his brother. "I heard about Moraviantown, and the rest of it. And now we've extended our naval blockade all the way up the American coast, thanks to ships freed from fighting Bonaparte. We may not be winning this war, but it seems we're as yet not prepared to lose it, not if we've sent many of Wellington's best soldiers over there."

Mention of the blockade reminded Spencer of something he'd learned. "Ainsley has been keeping up a correspondence with that American woman Ethan brought to Becket Hall. What do you make of that?"

"Mrs. Warren? I don't know, Spence. It has been

sixteen years. And, unless we can be rid of Beales, Romney Marsh might not be the haven Ainsley thought it would be, not for much longer. He'd built the pile for his return to respectability, you know, but that was before Beales turned us all into enemies of the Crown. The sheer isolation has served us well, but now that one by one we're all growing and leaving? None of us will be his responsibility for much longer. It may be time for him to move on, as well. You do know he turned down what I thought was his best chance for a pardon?"

Spencer sat forward in his chair. "No, I *don't* know that."

Chance picked up a silver letter opener, began turning it in his hand—another unconscious gesture that was much like Ainsley's. "England is always mad for new maps, new charts of waters where we sailed. You know Ainsley—he's made dozens of charts, detailed maps of the coastlines we traveled, where the channels are deep enough for larger ships. Others have exchanged valuable knowledge like that for pardons, to have the slate wiped clean. But he wouldn't hear of it. He had me forward copies of everything he had to the War Office anonymously. I don't know if he didn't want to take the risk of being tried and hanged anyway or if he felt that gaining a pardon for himself, without pardons for the rest of the crews, would be a form of betrayal. In any event, that opportunity is now lost to him."

"He could return to the islands." As soon as Spencer

said the words he knew that was impossible. "No, he wouldn't do that. That time is past, not just for us, but probably for the world, as well. It was another time, wasn't it? A time now nearly gone. There are no more true privateers, only pirates. Let's talk about Beales, shall we, and what I learned in Calais. We're rapidly running out of days."

Chance opened the middle drawer of his desk and pulled out several clippings from London newspapers. "Since you've been living at the back end of beyond and busy wooing the mother of your child, you may not know where things stand now. The Czar is here, as are several other heads of state, all to play a part in Prinney's grand party. Nearly all the generals have crowded into the city, including Blücher, and our own Iron Duke, who has been called back from Paris for the celebrations. They want him to go to America, you know, to take command of our forces there, but he's resisting the order and will probably be sent to the Congress in Vienna instead. At least for the moment. Paris, I hear, is becoming dangerous."

Spencer was surprised. "Wellington would really go to America?"

"He will, eventually. He may be a Duke now, but he's still a soldier, subject to orders. A good friend from the War Office has written to tell me that Wellington has at last agreed to travel there this coming March. It should prove interesting, the Iron Duke marching his beloved boys toward the American capitol. Then they'll know we're serious, won't they?"

Spencer couldn't restrain his smile. "Clearly, Chance, you don't know the Americans. They believe in themselves and no one else. And they know how to fight."

Chance shrugged. "In any event, Carleton House has been lit up every night as they drink and carouse, and a reviewing stand has been constructed in Hyde Park, with a view to both Green Park and St. James's Park in the distance. I understand this inventor, Congreve, has prepared a fireworks display of rather epic proportions for the first night of the Grand Jubilee. Rockets used for war being set off in the middle of London, for the supposed beauty of them. I think we're all mad."

Spencer nodded his agreement. "We haven't much time, if we hope to put a spoke in this particular wheel of Beales's plans. Less than four days now, Chance. To find them, to stop them."

"I know. We'll reconnoiter the area, but as you've never been to London, I'll tell you now that Hyde Park begins across from Kensington Palace and extends in this direction, funneling down past the Serpentine— where we're going to be treated to miniature ships re-enacting Nelson's victory at Trafalgar, if you can believe that ridiculousness—and ends at the Stanhope Gate, about six or seven blocks south of here, with the other, smaller parks to the west. It's a large area to cover effectively. Too large, I'm afraid, especially when we really don't know what we're looking for, do we?"

"Ainsley seems to think the most efficient way to eliminate everyone is with explosives."

Chance considered this. "Black powder? That's certainly one option. Enough of it, hidden beneath the reviewing stands, could cause considerable damage. Go wash up, get rid of your travel dirt, round up Rian, and we'll discuss this more over some bread and cheese."

Spencer made his way back to the front of the narrow house, where a footman directed him up the stairs to the third floor and to the last door at the end of the hallway. He knocked twice, then pushed open the door to see Mariah curled up on her right side in the bed, still dressed in her travel clothes, fast asleep, an untouched plate of meat, bread and cheese on the nightstand beside her. She had her fisted left hand lightly pressed to her mouth, just the way William did in his sleep, and Spencer felt his heart lurch at the sight.

What a maddening, stubborn woman. What a remarkable, courageous woman.

He spied a soft cashmere throw hanging over the back of a chair next to the fireplace and retrieved it, then laid it over Mariah before bending to smooth her hair back from her cheek and press a kiss against her temple.

Tomorrow, and the days after that, could be dangerous. Deadly dangerous.

What would he do with her, to keep her safe? What would he ever do without her, if he failed? *How, damn it all, had she become so important to him, to his hap-*

piness? He was actually angry with her, angry with her that she'd become so necessary to him. Angry with himself for wanting to forget the world and just lie down beside her, hold her in his arms, listen to her breathe.

He closed the door behind him and made his way to Rian's chamber at the other end of the hall, to use his washbasin so as not to disturb Mariah, all the time thinking of Ainsley and his lost Isabella. How had the man survived her death? Why had he survived?

For his children. Yes, Spencer understood that now. You survive, for your children. But, perhaps, with your heart buried, lost to you.

"Spence? You're at the other end of the hall," Rian said as his brother walked into the bedchamber where Rian was standing at the window, inspecting the scenery outside his window; London, sliding into a misty, smoky dusk. "Uh-oh," he said, pulling a face. "I've seen that particular dark look before. Just remember, I'm your brother, and you're not really angry with me, don't really want to hit me, or at least I don't think you do. Go punch a pillow, or even that wall over there. There's a good fellow."

"Rian, I want you to promise me something," Spencer said, slipping out of his jacket, exposing the harness Courtland had made for the knife. "If we get into the thick of anything and it begins to look bad for us, I want you to grab Mariah and get her the hell away, get her to safety, straight back to Becket Hall. Are we agreed? Just leave us and go."

Rian hopped up onto the high tester bed, reclining against the tall headboard, his long legs stretched out, his arms crossed over his chest. "Oh, I don't think so. I'm not here to be your wife's nursemaid, Spence. Tie her to the bedpost, if you can't control her. She shouldn't be here, or Julia, either. I'll say this at least for Fanny. Much as she thinks she's responsible for me, she knows where she belongs."

Spencer rubbed at his aching head. "I don't remember asking your opinion, Rian."

The younger Becket grinned. "No, I suppose you don't. Just don't ask me to play nanny, Spence. And I still don't know what help Julia or Mariah could possibly be in any of this. War is a man's work."

"True, Rian, my grand and intelligent brother. But peace is everyone's work."

"Was that supposed to be profound? And if you and Chance want personal peace, you'll do whatever your wives say, correct? And you all ask me why I want a good war to run to? It's a great disappointment my brothers are, a grievous disappointment, and I wish to point out that you're not exactly shining examples for a impressionable young man such as myself."

"You know, Rian, you wouldn't look half so pretty with your front teeth gone missing," Spencer warned, but his heart wasn't really in the threat. God, had marriage turned him mellow? That would be a hell of a thing, wouldn't it? "Let's go downstairs and feed our bellies. Then we can start planning just how we'll attack our problem in the morning. We'll begin by strolling out with the ladies, I think, to see what foolishness his royal highness is planning in the parks…"

CHAPTER SIXTEEN

MARIAH WOKE SLOWLY, reluctant to leave the dream that had brought a smile to her lips. Spencer was touching her, sliding his hand over her, not in a demanding way but the way a blind man might, trying to learn her.

She opened her eyes to a dark room and a dying fire and turned over onto her back, to see the outline of Spencer's head as he lay beside her, his head propped up on his hand.

"It's time you change out of your clothes and go under the covers, wife," he told her and then she saw the white of his teeth as he smiled. "I thought I could volunteer my assistance."

Mariah felt something begin to curl deliciously in her lower belly. "Oh, you did, did you? What time is it? And, by the way, you're *looming* again."

"It's my new mission in life. To loom over you. Do you hate it?"

She stifled a yawn. "I'm still deciding. Now tell me the time."

"It was past three when Rian and I left Chance.

And, as you seem to have this obsession with the time, we'll all be leaving the house at ten to begin our reconnoiter of the parks."

Mariah's chest rose and fell in a sigh. "And this is what you woke me from a sound sleep to tell me?" She turned her back to him. "Go away."

Instead of obeying her, he began loosening the buttons on the back of her gown. Pressing his lips to the skin he revealed each time another button was eased free of its mooring.

"Spencer...no," Mariah half pleaded, and then sat up, knowing she couldn't go to sleep again. "I'm hungry."

He freed three more buttons. "Not shy, are you, wife?"

Mariah swung a fist behind her, hoping to connect with solid flesh, which she did. "For *food,* Spencer. For pity's sake."

"Ah," he said, jackknifing to a sitting position himself, "but you knew what I meant. Not being a gentleman, may I tell you how happy I am that you may be a lady but also a bit of a hellion?"

"Hellion?" Mariah slid to her feet on the carpet and grabbed the plate of food, taking it with her to one of the chairs in front of the low fire. "I traveled with my father, Spence, to some places where the only other female companionship were the women politely known as camp followers. I'm probably considerably more than a hellion, thank you. And *not* a lady at all."

Spencer followed her, taking the plate from her and breaking off a piece of cheese, which he promptly fed to her as he propped himself on the arm of the chair. "As I've admitted I'm no gentleman, I suppose that's only fair. Eleanor's our lady, you know—she can't seem to help herself. And now Morgan is *supposed* to be a lady, seeing as how she's Ethan's countess and they move in Society. But I don't think she'll ever be Society's idea of a lady."

"Julia told me Morgan and Ethan are traveling and won't know anything about what we're doing until it's all over. Until we've either succeeded or failed. And if we fail, the entire world will know."

Spencer put the dish in her lap and sat down in the facing chair. "But only we will know that we've personally failed. That's…that's…"

"Quite a burden," Mariah finished for him. "We have to tell someone, someone else, someone in a position of power."

Spencer opened the top two buttons of his shirt, his neck cloth long since discarded. He decided not to tell her what he and Chance and Rian had planned for early in the morning. "Chance told me that he'd hinted to several of his former colleagues at the War Office that the true head of the Red Men Gang was still at large. He told them that last year, when he helped Jack and Eleanor capture the nominal leader and turn him over to the authorities. According to Chance, a few people laughed at his warning, a few more dismissed the idea as nonsense and a few more were curiously silent. Two days later, while Chance was still in town, someone took a shot at him on his way home from his club. That was enough to get him back to his estate and to tell him that not everyone wanted him talking about Nathaniel Beatty."

Mariah ripped off a small piece of bread and held it in front of her mouth. "Who is Nathaniel Beatty?"

"If we're right, Edmund Beales. That was the name he used last year. He had begun to move in Society, only discreetly. We can only wonder who his friends are and who is in his pocket—how high in the government these new friends may be. So, you see, we're a little reluctant to share our suspicions with anyone."

"Leaving us with the responsibility to save the Prince Regent and the others." Mariah shook her head. "No, we can't do that, Spencer. It's too dangerous. Surely there's someone we can trust."

She was like a dog with a bone, his wife, and quite correct. "All right, I give up. We have thought of one person we're confident we can trust. Wellington."

Mariah put the plate on the table next to her and eagerly leaned forward in her chair. "Oh, yes. Wellington. He'd be perfect. The man is a true hero and a true patriot. How do you plan to contact him?"

"*You?* Not *we?* You're a constant surprise, Mariah. I'd thought you'd demand to be a part of that plan, too." Spencer leaned over and took the small loaf from the plate, breaking off a piece for himself. "He supposedly rides in Hyde Park every morning just after daybreak. Hell, people line the streets every morning just to cheer him as he passes. At any rate, his charger, the famous Copenhagen, enjoys a good gallop from what we hear. Chance and I will be waiting for him this morning. If we can't approach him directly, Chance's own mount, Jacmel, will do the trick for him. Wellington admires fine horseflesh and when Chance gives Jacmel his head the Duke will notice, or so my brother hopes. After that it's up to Chance to convince the man of the truth of what we believe."

"So you're saying that the future of the world as we know it could possibly depend on a horse?"

Spencer smiled. "A horse and the way Chance rides him, which is fairly magnificent in itself. I agree, it sounds insane. But there's no other way to approach the man in relative privacy, not in these few days, and we've convinced Rian that kidnapping the fellow is out of the question. It would be easier if Ethan were here to throw around his title and consequence, but he isn't."

"I wish my father could be here. He served with Wellington on the Peninsula, before he was made a quarter-master. They spoke several times. Perhaps if I were to approach the duke, to tell him about my father…"

Spencer shook his head. "Ah, there it is. I knew you'd find some way to have yourself included. But truthfully? If Chance's idea doesn't work, we could think about that. But you'll need a few more gowns, Mariah. You'll need them in any event, but especially if you want to try to get us an audience with the Iron Duke."

Mariah felt her temper rising. "So you're going to shunt me off, send me shopping with Julia?"

"Actually, I thought we'd go to Bond Street together tomorrow, you and I."

"Oh." Mariah was nonplussed and rather amazed at the way her heart did a small flip in her chest. "Really? Just the two of us?"

Spencer smiled. "Just the two of us and please realize the enormity of my sacrifice. I'd rather face a dozen howling Americans than set foot in any shop filled with lace and satins. However, at my count, you own two presentable gowns, Mariah, as I won't consider anything you brought with you when you arrived at Becket Hall. And I'm most certainly not including what you're wearing now."

She took his hand and stood up, pretending not to notice how handsome he looked in the orange glow of the fire. "What's wrong with—oh, never mind. It's obvious what's wrong with it," she said, looking down at her much let-out and then nipped in again grey gown that was now travel stained and wrinkled from having slept in it. "All right, I suppose I will have to go shopping for a few more things such as we found in Calais. But not until the afternoon, please. I want to go to the park with you to reconnoiter. I have a fairly good military mind, you know."

"I believe I will spend the next fifty years learning the scope of your talents, yes. I'll be interested in just where you think we should set our perimeter. According to Clovis, you personally positioned the guards each night after Moraviantown."

Mariah nodded, remembering those weeks; in the swamp, on the way north to safety. "Papa and I spent many a long winter's night discussing battles both recent and ancient. I know where Alexander made his mistakes, where Caesar overextended his troops, how the Americans turned defeat into victory during their revolt. Papa had wanted a son, I believe," she ended, smiling, "but when he got me, he eventually decided to make the best of the situation. I only wish I'd learned how to ride. I was always stuck in a wagon with the supplies, you understand. And I hated being inside that coach on our way here, instead of riding with you."

Spencer stepped closer to her, stroked her cheek with the back of his hand. "Once we're done with Beales, and Morgan and Ethan are home again, I'll take you to Tanner's Roost. They raise horses, you know. You'll have your pick, as my wedding gift to you, and I'll teach you to ride."

"I...I'd like that," Mariah said, aware of the dark fire that had come into Spencer's eyes as he continued to look at her, as he cupped her chin in his hands. "Mostly, I think I like talking about a time beyond this monster, Edmund Beales, a time for us to...to get to know one another."

Spencer slid an arm around her waist, drawing her closer. He hadn't come to her tonight with the intent of being serious but some things had to be said. "I already know one thing, Mariah. I know I want you in my life. A few months ago, I didn't even know you or William existed. But I felt your absence. I felt the need for you both. I just didn't recognize that need—that emptiness—for what it was. The part of me that was missing, has been missing all my life."

"Spencer, I…" Mariah said, raising her hands to his cheeks. "Thank you."

He gave a small chuckle. "Thank you? Am I frightening you at last, Mariah? I'll admit that I'm frightened."

"Then I suppose…I suppose it's better that we be frightened together?"

"I'm sorry about the other night. For thinking you were only looking for…for a safe haven."

Mariah bit her bottom lip, nodded. "But I was, Spencer. Think of it. Alone, nearly penniless, carrying a child—even responsible for Onatah. I didn't know what I'd find when I found you, found Becket Hall. I didn't, couldn't, expect to fall into one of the deepest gravy boats in all of England, be welcomed so openly—even given the promise of a new life in Virginia. How could I have known that? But I'll be honest. I didn't travel halfway around the world because I longed for nothing more than to see your smiling face again."

Spencer grinned down at her. "Oh, now I'm crushed."

"No, you're not," she told him seriously. "We did what we had to do. For William. But I'll try to be a good wife to you, Spencer, I promise. I'm going to try very hard to be a good wife."

Spencer laughed, then scooped her up into his arms and carried her over to the bed, dropping her so that she actually bounced on the soft mattress. "Very well, good wife. For starters, let's see how obedient you can be when you put your mind to it, shall we? I suggest we begin with getting rid of that horrible gown."

Mariah sat up, looking at him through her spill of flaming hair. "Horrible? No, not horrible. *Horrendous*. And there are *so* many tiresome buttons."

"Now *that's* an invitation," Spencer said, stripping off his shirt as he joined her on the bed, turned her onto her stomach. "And just to make sure you're never tempted to wear this *horrendous* gown again, I believe it's time you were shed of the thing, once and for all."

She felt his hands at the middle of her back, as he'd already opened several of the buttons, and then felt a sharp tug as he pulled at either side of the gown, ripping it straight down past her waist, buttons flying everywhere, the aged material giving easily under his strength.

There was need on both sides. There was apprehension on both sides. There was the moment without knowing what the next days would bring. There was their future, tantalizingly close, dangerously far away, possibly out of reach.

With so little in their control, they took the moment they had. Coming together with a heat born of that moment, knowing that danger and possible disaster loomed in their futures, ready to rip away all that they had, all that they might hope to have.

It was a mutual devouring, an explosion of the senses. Touch. Taste.

Mariah allowed Spencer to be the aggressor that first mind-shattering night of their marriage. She'd experienced, savored, marveled, enjoyed.

But they were equals now, each knowing the limits to the pleasure they could give each other and knowing that the pleasure was limitless.

What he had done, she did now, sliding down his body, learning it, touching…tasting.

There was no shame, no hesitancy, no fear. After all, morning might never come. Why not take all that the night could hold for them?

Spencer's kisses were long, drugging, and returned with a new daring that surprised them both.

Her hands learned him, shaped him, cupped him, brought forth a response that made Mariah feel powerful, if not in complete control.

He would teach her to ride, he'd said, and he began his lessons when she thought she was sated, ready to curl against him and find sleep once more. But sleep was the last thing on her mind when he rolled onto his back, taking her with him. Encouraged her to straddle him, move with him, move against him even as he held tight to her waist, guiding her onto him, into her.

He was so deep inside her, filling her so completely, but she wanted more. More, harder, faster.

As he skimmed her rib cage with the lightest touch, then teased at her nipples, she lost all thought and could only react. Moving against him, grinding against him, throwing back her head as she rode him, drove him, straining to take him deeper.

"Hold me…hold me…please," she begged him and he lifted himself up, pulling her tight against him as she swung her long legs out and then wrapped them around him even as she dug her fingers into his strong back, nipped at and kissed the side of his neck, suckled hard at the sweat-slick skin; not knowing why, just that he tasted so good.

They moved together, rose together, hung suspended together, exploded and crashed through the universe together and then fell back against the mattress, reluctant to let each other go, even as they slowly recaptured their breath and slipped into sleep….

Spencer heard the knock on the door and willed it away, willed the world away.

"Lieutenant, sir? All pardon, sir, but you said to wake you all prompt at five. Mr. Chance is already downstairs and halfway through a fine mess of coddled eggs. You'd best hurry, sir."

"Yes, thank you, Clovis," Spencer called out, already easing from beneath Mariah, who still lay half on top of him, some of her long hair caught under his shoulder. "Sorry, sweetings," he said as she moaned softly and then turned onto her side.

Gathering up his clothes, he slipped off to the dressing room, splashed cold water on his face, then quickly washed, ran his wet fingers through his hair and pulled on the clean linen Clovis had laid out for him the previous evening. He all but dove into his hacking jacket and breeches and then carried his boots into the hallway, to put on once he was downstairs, and saw Chance waiting for him at the front door.

"Well, don't you have the look of a happily married man," Chance said, watching as Spencer sat down on the third step from the bottom and pulled on his boots. "And injured in battle, I see, as well."

Spencer looked at him owlishly.

Chance raised his hand, pointed to the side of his own neck. "You've a lovely advertisement of your wife's ardor, just there. I'd pull my neck cloth higher, were I you, to spare your bride's blushes—and Rian's, if he should see it. He's such an impressionable lad."

Spencer clapped a hand to the side of his neck. "Jesus. Do you have to notice everything?"

"Not really, no. But what I miss, Julia catches, so now you're twice warned. Are you sure you don't want to go back upstairs? I could manage this without you, you know."

"Perhaps," Spencer said, getting to his feet, taking the gloves, hat and riding crop that a red-faced, clearly in-awe Clovis held out for him. "But how many men can say they've spoken directly to the Duke of Wellington?"

"Thousands, probably," Chance told him as a footman opened the door and they stepped out to the flagway where their mounts waited, Jacmel giving the groom fits as he danced in place and fought to be free. Spencer's bay stood docilely, but that didn't mean the horse wasn't ready to run. Fernando just played his cards closer to the vest, as it were, and wouldn't try to bolt until Spence was on his back. "The trick, I'm afraid, will be in having the man speak to us in return. Shall we?"

Jacmel settled once Chance had his feet in the stirrups, which was when the bay, with Spencer just sliding his left foot into the stirrup, tossed his head and reared up on his back legs.

"As wild as his master," Chance said as Spencer fought the horse back under control. "Or is it that he's still taking revenge for getting him shot?"

Spencer drew up alongside Chance, grinning. "No, he bit me for that, so we've called it even. God's teeth, Chance, this city stinks. It smells old and filthy and everything is yellow with dust. How do you stand it?"

"All cities smell," his brother said as they made their way to the park gate. "It's why we have parks. Sometimes, if we're lucky, we can even look up in a park and see the sky without a chimney pot in the way."

They reined in their mounts just inside the gate and

Chance swore under his breath. "But not today. God, look at this mess."

Spencer half-stood in the stirrups as they walked the horses forward, to see wooden booths and stalls and endless rows of tiered plank seating being nosily hammered into existence on every side. Banners were being hung; cooking pots were strapped on the backs of strong men in leather aprons; lanterns were being carried up tall ladders and tied to tree branches. There were already at least three dozen small replicas of ships floating at the edge of the waters of the Serpentine. As far as he could see, the perimeter of the large park was being cluttered with clever distractions and lined with convenient places for assassins to hide. Add several thousand people to the mix in a few days, and their task was beginning to seem impossible.

"What are those buildings in the distance?" he asked as a group of laborers in white smocks cut across their path, leading a string of donkeys with bales and sacks strapped to their sides.

"Just a small conglomeration, although there is one building that might concern us. The last one on the right—the powder magazine."

Spencer didn't like that. "Munitions are stored here in the park? Isn't that convenient."

"I know. When we get closer, you'll see that I've already stationed ten of our men in the area. But it's a fine mess, isn't it? It's no wonder we're the only ones here to exercise our horses. We can only hope Wellington hasn't decided his Copenhagen would be happier in Richmond Park. At any rate, let's give them their heads. From here to that first group of plane trees over there," he said, pointing with his riding crop. "Do you see where I mean? Just past the banner proclaiming that stall as the home of the Veteran Prince Blücher Ices and Stout, no less."

Spencer didn't answer, as he'd already put his heels to Fernando's flanks and was off in an immediate gallop. He wasn't being unfair; he simply knew that Jacmel would have Chance at the trees in time for his master to dismount, light a cheroot and probably smoke half of it before Spencer arrived, because the stallion was built for speed, the bay for endurance.

And exactly as he'd supposed, Chance and his mount went flying by a few moments later, just as a group of five uniformed men on horseback cantered toward them from the opposite direction. The man in front was taller than the rest, his uniform the most elaborate. When he held up his gloved hand the men with him immediately reined in their horses and they all watched Jacmel race across the ground, scattering startled workers and kicking up large clumps of dew-wet turf, Chance sitting him low, moving as one with the horse, as if slicing a battlefield in half.

"Ah, brother, I'll say this for you, you do know how to bait your hook," Spencer murmured as the tall man whose distinctive features had been captured in a thousand broadsheets urged his large, full-chested charger to follow where Chance had led. By the time Spencer joined them, it was to be introduced to the Iron Duke, who scarcely seemed to notice him.

"An honor, sir," Spencer said, tipping his hat as he inclined his head in a small bow.

"Yes, yes," Wellington said off-handedly, his eyes still on Jacmel. "Not for sale, you say? Not at any price?"

"No, sir," Chance told him, winking at Spencer before adding, "This horse has no price, even if many men have theirs. If I might have a moment, sir? Forgive me, but I have deliberately set out this morning to speak to you on a matter of grave importance. I have news I feel safe only for your ears, your grace. News that makes me fear for the life of our Prince Regent."

Wellington finally drew his attention away from the horse and up to the face of the man on that horse's back. "You do, do you? So do I, who has to watch him stuff his face with victuals and drink all the night long, until his face is beet red and his eyes all but bulge out of his head. A man can't live long, not if he lives by his stomach. Not that he's a patch on France's new king, who is so rotund he has to be carried everywhere. I don't think the man's seen his own feet in twenty years."

He raised a hand as he added, "Forgive me. My head is splitting, as it does each morning, thanks to the long nights of food and drink and overheated rooms, and then I rise to see this…this *debacle* being executed here in my beloved Hyde Park. I'm being indiscreet.

But, damn, I'd rather a battle than another state dinner or overblown celebration, gentlemen, I swear it."

Spencer bit his lips together to keep from laughing and calling attention to himself, but it was difficult to look at this straight-backed, slightly hatchet-faced yet handsome man and reconcile the fierce look to the fairly whining complaints coming from his mouth.

Wellington shook his head, clearly a man disgusted. "Louis-Stanislas-Xavier. *Louis le Desiré,* his few fierce friends call him. I call him a perfect walking sore, not a part of his body sound. Even his head lets out a sort of humour. He's a blight on Paris, a blight on France, and Bonaparte—*Napoléon le Grand* to his *Louis le Gros*—must look better to the French with each passing day. Don't travel to Paris, Mr. Becket. It is not a pretty sight."

"Many of our fellow countrymen and women are flocking there," Chance said, allowing the fellow his head, insinuating himself with the great and, apparently, unhappy man.

Wellington smiled, the smile looking more of a gash in his stern face. "Many of our fellow countrymen and women are bloody fools, Mr. Becket. Paris forces its gaiety where it can, but cannot hide that it has the sad appearance now of an old, ravaged woman. Houses in ruins, gutters running with mud and offal. Bonaparte's once-fine army in tatters of both mind and body. Poor bastards, skulking in the streets, muttering that their

Emperor will return with the violets in the spring to rid them of the fat, gouty brother of the man they'd sent to the guillotine and to restore France's power across Europe. They were once fine fighting men, worthy enemies—now reduced to the starving dregs of a ruined society."

It was just the sort of opening Chance and Spencer had been hoping for, and Spencer was the first to push his way in. "Yes, sir, poor bastards. Many would be happier to have the Little Corporal back. Many more see their own advantage in having him back and other leaders gone, other revolutions begun elsewhere."

Chance, who had learned how to approach those in power during his time at the War Office, rolled his eyes at Spencer's directness. "Well, brother, that was subtle. Your grace, if I might suggest we three go somewhere quiet to have a private conversation? My brother here would say it is a matter of life and death, your own included, but he's young and still fairly hot-blooded. Unfortunately, I agree with his sentiments."

"Will you sell me the horse?" the duke asked.

"No, sir, I will not," Chance told him, smiling. "But my brother and I might save your life."

"Or take it," Wellington said, looking at Spencer, who knew he was scowling but didn't really care. "No, I think not, gentlemen, although I'll admit the horse was a clever ruse."

"Oh, bloody hell," Spencer said, Fernando sensing his mood and dancing beneath him. "It's not my neck at risk, and nobody much likes the Prince Regent, anyway. Maybe watching them all blow to bits will be just the entertainment the citizens want. Come on, Chance. We can't help someone too stupid to listen."

"Hold where you are, son," Wellington ordered sharply, raising a hand to Spencer, looking at him intensely. "Stupid, is it? Not at all in awe of me, are you, or used to taking commands?"

"I served under Henry Proctor, your grace, at the River Raisin at Moraviantown. Would you be in awe of those in command, sir, were you I?"

Wellington's shoulders stiffened and then he relaxed slightly, shook his head. "Point taken, Mr. Becket. But I'll ask you not to insult me by ranking me with General Proctor or his ilk. I believe I have honorably earned my own reputation."

"Yes, sir, you have," Spencer said, his temper still running high, considerably higher than his awe at being in the great Iron Duke's presence. Chance might think him a hotheaded fool, but he preferred to see himself as someone who did not gladly suffer fools. And time was running short. "They'll build a fine statue or three to you here in London once you're dead and gone. The question is, sir, how soon do you wish them to begin?"

"Jesus, Spence…"

"No," Spencer said, the agitated bay barely under his control. "We don't have time to dance around this, Chance, play the gentlemen. The world could very well go to hell in a handbasket a bloody few days from now, and we've got work of our own to do. He's either with us or he's not."

CHAPTER SEVENTEEN

MARIAH LOWERED her head as she sat at table in the Becket morning room beside her new sister-in-law, Julia, covering her mouth with her hand to hide her smile as Chance told them about Spencer's audacious outburst in front of the important Duke of Wellington. She could have told Chance that her new husband was not the sort to tiptoe about anything nor to pay attention to convention, the niceties of dealing with authority—not when he was in a rush for results.

"I still can't believe you went without me," Rian said, nursing his bruised sensibilities with the help of a heavily buttered scone. "I told you to wake me up in time. The Iron Duke—and I missed him."

"If you wouldn't sleep like the dead, you could have met him," Spencer told him. "Some fine soldier you'd make, snoring through cannon fire."

"I would not. And I can't take it into my head that you actually spoke to Wellington that way. Look at Chance. He's still shaking his own head. You don't talk to a duke that way, Spence, not a hero. As good as calling him stupid, demanding he listen to you."

"At least he didn't knock him down, bloody the man's eagle beak of a nose for him and get you both clapped in irons. You can be grateful for that, Chance," Mariah said after a moment and then laughed when Spencer's cheeks flushed beneath his tanned skin. "And you did say he let you tell him about Edmund Beales."

"Yes," Chance agreed, "and although we had to necessarily be vague, I think he believed us. At least enough to assign more of his most trusted troops to the celebrations, concentrating them near the viewing stands from now until after the Grand Jubilee, as he agrees that would make the best target for an anarchist, as he terms Beales. Of course, there are problems associated with that solution."

Spencer popped a miniature strawberry tart into his mouth and spoke around it. "Our own men will now look damned suspicious if they loiter in the area. But if you're suggesting we all just turn around and go home now, Chance, you already know my answer to that."

"As you know mine, Spence," Chance said, grabbing the last strawberry tart for himself. "But now we're free to spend the next days combing London, watching for Renard or any other familiar face, knowing we've done all we could do to alert Wellington to Beales's possible plan, even if it's too late for him to send a message to Bonaparte's gaoler about the other half of that plan. We can only hope Court and Jacko will soon be making considerable pests of themselves just off the shores of Elba. And that all said, ladies, and with at least a measure of the load shifted off our shoulders, may I suggest that you visit the shops?"

Julia Becket nudged Mariah in the ribs just as she was lifting her teacup to her mouth so that she had to grab the cup with both hands to save her gown. "They're pitiful, aren't they? Trying to make us believe that everything is all just fine now and we should go enjoy ourselves, spend their money—something I'm not entirely opposed to—and not worry our heads about Edmund Beales because, surely, they're not thinking of him at all. Men are so transparent."

"They may be, Julia, but I believe I would very much like to visit Bond Street, as even I've heard how wonderful it is. And my wardrobe is virtually in *shreds.*" She turned to grin at Spencer. "Isn't it?"

Spencer choked on the last bit of strawberry tart. "Chance, I've decided that these two shouldn't be together without one of us present. Not ever. And now that I'm considering it, Morgan will not be allowed in the house at all. However, Julia, I believe that last night, in a weak moment I volunteered to take my wife round the shops. If you don't mind?"

"Oh ye of faint heart." Julia was already getting to her feet. "And, no, I don't mind at all, as I have much to occupy myself with here. This house has been closed up for months. Oh, and you'd best not go to Bond Street, as Mariah cannot wait weeks for her new gowns. You can leave Bond Street for after we've saved the world, and take Mariah to visit Oxford Street for her most immediate needs. You'll be unfashionably early but the shops will be less crowded."

Mariah ran upstairs to fetch her bonnet and shawl before Spencer could change his mind and, after a short discussion on the merits of calling for the coach to go a distance of only a few blocks, they walked to Oxford Street.

"Do you think we should drop breadcrumbs, in order to find our way back?" Spencer asked her as she slipped her arm through his. "I think Julia does, given the lengthy directions she forced on us since I've never before been to London."

"I've never been to London, either, you know," she said as they turned the corner onto Oxford Street and she looked, wide-eyed, at all the shops lining both sides of the street. "Oh, my goodness, so many shops. Perhaps Bonaparte was right and England *is* a nation of shopkeepers."

"And yet he is on Elba and we're still here. All right, Mariah, from here on out, you're in command. Where to first?"

She looked at him in sheer panic. She'd managed her father for years, had borne up under many hardships—but the sight of all these shops frightened her to her toes. "I have no idea. You pick. Please?"

"There's a gown displayed in that window over there, across the street," Spencer told her, pointing.

"It's as good a starting point as any, don't you think, to find a gown for you?"

Mariah regained some of her confidence. "Only one? I had considered a half dozen, at the least. And shoes. And gloves. Oh, and most definitely a few bonnets. We are, after all, in London. We can't always be thinking dire thoughts."

Spencer could only manfully suppress a groan and lead her across the street.

In the next two hours more than one gown was quickly found, along with a pair of black kid slippers that fit Mariah beautifully, a soft wool cloak in scarlet—not quite town wear, but perfect for walking the shore at Becket Hall—and even a beaded reticule she was not afraid to admit to have fallen in love with at first sight.

It was wonderful not to have to worry about every penny and rather than feel guilty about her purchases, Mariah refused to even ask the cost of anything. Although she did, as Spencer escaped a shop to stand outside and smoke a cheroot, spend what was probably an unconscionable amount of time poring over an assortment of grosgrain ribbons until she found what she considered the perfect ribbon to attach to her father's watch, as Spencer had been true to his word and wore the watch every day.

Carrying several bandboxes, they were on their way back down Oxford Street when Spencer spied a window filled with a glorious assortment of fresh fruit and they went inside to make a few additional purchases, hoping the drizzle that had begun would stop again shortly.

Spencer was inspecting a pyramid of pineapples, struck by the arrangement that reminded him unhappily of pyramids of cannon balls when Mariah cried out, "Oh, my God—Spence. It's her! It's Nicolette!"

"Mariah, wait," Spencer told her, but Mariah was already out the door and running madly down the crowded flagway.

Spencer tossed a coin at the hovering clerk, ordered him to watch the bandboxes and followed after her at a dead run.

Uncaring of shocked looks and a few nasty comments, Mariah hiked up her skirts as she dodged a few gentlemen and their oversize umbrellas, stepped neatly around a young man carrying a plate of meat pies, skidded to a halt at the corner, then turned to her left and took off once more, her heart pounding in her chest.

She stopped halfway down the flagway, attempting to get her bearings, as she no longer saw Nicolette anywhere. Perhaps she'd stepped into one of the shops? No, there were no shops on this narrow side street, save a tobacco shop. But she had come this way, Mariah was sure of it.

"Mariah? God's teeth, I lost you for a moment in the crowds."

She turned gratefully to Spencer, who had caught

up with her. "It was her, Spence. I know it was her. But now I can't see her."

"And you're sure she turned this way?"

A handsome black coach pulled away from the curbing just then, its windows covered, so that Mariah could not look inside.

The coach was indistinguishable from any other on the street, so she concentrated instead on the horses pulling it and the driver up on the box. The man's livery was as black as his complexion, as were his hat and gloves, the only bit of color a cockade stuck in the lapel of his sodden greatcoat. This, too, Mariah committed to memory, and then quickly averted her face as the coachman noticed that she'd been staring at him.

"Spence—that coach! No, don't look! If the coachman sees us, we could put Nicolette in danger."

Spencer pulled Mariah across the flagway and beneath a canopy hanging outside the tobacco shop. "It's raining harder. You're getting drenched. Mariah? Are you sure it was her? There's more than one blond woman in London, you know."

Mariah wrapped her arms around herself, suddenly chilled. "It was her, I know it. Oh, Spence, they're here. They're really here and it's really happening." Then she turned around, peered into the window of the tobacco shop. "But that doesn't mean she was in that coach. She could be in here, couldn't she?"

Spencer looked up and down the narrow side street.

"It's the only shop. But, Mariah, there are at least a dozen houses on either side of this street and she could be in any one of them. Come on, we'll retrieve your bandboxes, find a hackney, get you out of this rain and go back to Upper Brook Street to tell the others. We can assign at least a half dozen men to this street, watching everyone who comes and goes."

"Unless Nicolette was taken up in that coach," Mariah pointed out as Spencer took her hand, leading her back to Oxford Street where there would be a better chance to hail a hack. "Oh, wait! She was carrying a bandbox, too. It was covered in blue and white stripes, just like one we've got. Maybe the shopkeeper remembers her."

"That is also possible, Mariah," Spencer said. "Do you remember the shop?"

"Loathe as I am to admit this, yes, I do. There's a lovely bonnet I saw in it earlier, but as I'd already purchased two, I didn't tell you. You think the shopkeeper will remember her?" Mariah asked as they rapidly walked along the increasingly deserted flagway, as rain seemed to chase Londoners inside before they melted or some such thing.

"That is also possible. And we can hope that your Nicolette placed an order for a bonnet she plans to return to collect at some time before the Grand Jubilee."

He stepped in front of her to open the door to the shop and Mariah stepped inside ahead of him, sparing a moment to take another peek at the natural straw bonnet on the second shelf to her left, the one with the large pink cabbage roses attached to the brim. Ah, well, she would have looked silly in it, anyway.

She left it to Spencer to approach the clerk, a small, sallow man with a rather dyspeptic expression on his narrow face.

"Excuse me," Spencer said, once again showing a talent for lying that Mariah longed to applaud, "but just a few moments ago my wife espied a young woman she met a few years ago in school and although we couldn't quite catch up to her, my wife did recognize the bandbox she was carrying as one of yours. So it occurred to me that my wife's friend may have ordered something from you and left her address with you. Or perhaps she's planning to return?"

The clerk looked at Mariah, at her damp skirt, her damp, bedraggled bonnet. "I don't think I can possibly divulge such information about one of my patrons, no. So sorry, madam."

Spencer mentally hit himself. He reached into his pocket and withdrew his purse, tossing a coin onto the glass-topped counter. "Surely you can make an exception, my good fellow," he said, smiling at the clerk— or baring his teeth at the sallow-faced little ferret. It was one of those, he was sure.

"Uh...um...if madam would perhaps care to describe her friend?"

Mariah grinned at Spencer. Truly, the man was a genius. And he hadn't grabbed the shopkeeper by the throat, threatening to shake answers out of him. That could be considered an improvement, couldn't it? "I would be delighted. My friend is French, blond, slight although tall. Her Christian name is Nicolette, but I'm afraid that I've heard that she married since I last had the pleasure of seeing her and I cannot tell you her husband's name. You have an address for her? She'll be returning, possibly? I really do need to contact her."

The clerk's sallow face turned fairly pale. "No, I'm sorry. I cannot…cannot remember, that is. I wish I could help you, I truly do, but—"

Suddenly the shopkeeper was off his feet, thanks to the strong, one-handed grip Spencer had on his neck cloth as he half dragged the man across the top of the counter, going nose-to-nose with him. "Apply yourself."

Mariah just rocked back and forth on her heels and grinned.

CHAPTER EIGHTEEN

ONCE BACK in Upper Brook Street, Mariah made several drawings of both Nicolette and Renard, so that whoever was assigned to watch the area around Oxford Street had copies of those drawings tucked up in their jackets, ready to be drawn out and compared to patrons frequenting the shop.

They also watched the houses along the side street, hoping for a bit of good luck. In the chance the shop-keeper, who had told them of Nicolette bringing a companion with her on her first visit—a male companion who the clearly frightened man seemed to believe held all the power of the devil—had lied to Mariah and Spencer about the expected date of her return to the shop to claim a bonnet she'd ordered, the same day as the Grand Jubilee. In the chance that she wouldn't return alone or that someone else might arrive to retrieve the bonnet in her stead.

Even Julia had the drawings tucked up in her reticule as the others went about town, acting the part of rejoicing Londoners out to enjoy themselves, but always alert for the sight of a blond head, a glimpse of a closed black coach and its fairly singular coachman.

There was an air of carefully concealed optimism now. Nobody said that this could be the end of Edmund Beales, of their long nightmare—but everyone thought it, hoped for it, prayed for it.

Mariah had been confined to Upper Brook Street, much to her chagrin. But if she could recognize Nicolette, it stood to reason that Nicolette could likewise recognize her. As Renard could recognize her.

The last thing anyone wanted was to alert Renard and possibly send him scurrying away before they could corner him, *convince* him to give up Beales's whereabouts.

So, while Spencer and Rian and Julia spent the succeeding days and evenings on the hunt, Chance, who could also be recognized because he'd been nearly grown when last he'd seen Beales and Jules, bore Mariah company in the small drawing room in Upper Brook Street.

Chance sat at his ease on one of the couches, watching as Mariah paced the carpet, reminding him very much of his brother, but in female form. "How did you and Spence meet in North America, Mariah? I ask this only because Julia wants to know, just as she longs to know everything."

Mariah turned to him and smiled. "I have noticed that about her. She's rather like a more kindly Spanish Inquisition. Oh," she added quickly, "but I quite like her. I quite like all the Beckets. Even the ones I haven't yet met, as Elly makes them all sound fascinating."

Chance took a sip from his wineglass. "Have you considered volunteering to work for the Crown, Mariah? You'd make an admirable diplomat."

"Not really," she admitted, sitting down on the facing couch, frowning at him. "If I would, I wouldn't be sitting here smiling at you and plotting ways to be outside on the streets searching for Nicolette."

"Ah, but that's what diplomats do," Chance told her. "Smile quite happily, while busily plotting all sorts of devious things. I'd be out there, too, Mariah, if I didn't know that I could end up doing more harm than good. Now, tell me how you and Spencer met in America."

Mariah kept her mouth firmly shut for a moment, looking at the man. How could she dress this up in fine linen? In truth, she couldn't. "Spencer was injured and feverish, delusional, and I crawled under his blanket with him to calm him and…and now there's William. Spencer can't even remember the event, but I can. Not with much fondness."

Chance took another sip from his wineglass, fighting the impulse to drain its contents in one long gulp. "Well, that will teach me to leave Inquisitions to my wife, won't it? Spence really doesn't remember…any of this?"

Mariah shook her head, getting to her feet once more to pace the carpet. "I'm glad he doesn't. It's better that…that we make a fresh start of things, don't you think?"

Chance shifted forward on the couch to look at Mariah, who had her back to him. "No, I don't think so, my dear. Do you blame him for what happened?"

Mariah whirled around to face him, shocked by the question. "Me? Do I blame *him?* No, of course not. *I* was the one who—"

"So you blame yourself," Chance said, looking down at his wineglass to see that he had in fact gulped down its contents. Not only that, but another drink was probably in order. "Spencer's an odd duck, not one to share his feelings easily—excuse the candor—but he doesn't seem particularly unhappy in his marriage. Frankly, if he hadn't wanted to marry you, he would have said no to Ainsley and meant it."

"We have a son," Mariah said, blinking rapidly, surprised by the sting of tears in her eyes.

"Ah, I see. So, he married you to give a name to his son. Now, *that* does sound like Spencer. Of course, it doesn't explain your presence here, now does it?" *Or the love bite on my brother's neck the other morning,* Chance thought, but wasn't stupid enough to say.

Mariah smiled a watery smile. "He couldn't help it, Chance. I kept chasing after him. I chased him to Romney Marsh, I chased him to Calais and he knew I'd chase him here."

"My poor beleaguered brother. Mariah," he said,

settling himself back on the couch once more, "do you really think Spencer couldn't…outrun you?"

She pressed her hands to her cheeks. "No, I suppose not. He's…he's got quite a temper, doesn't he? Then again, I'm not particularly…placid. I fear for our son's temperament."

Chance knew it was time to draw back from such a personal discussion. "You'll have your hands full if your William is anything like Spencer. Let me tell you something about your new husband. Years ago, I think he was no more than twelve, Spence decided to build a boat and sail off to China."

Mariah grinned, subsiding onto the couch once more. She knew so little about Spencer. "Twelve? Really? Why would he want to do that?"

Chance shrugged. "He hated us and wanted to be gone. I don't remember why he hated us that time. There were so many times. Court and I were older, Rian was always with Fanny. Morgan and Elly and Callie were, well, they were *females*. And Ainsley? He was there but kept to himself, really not paying attention—something he regrets now. So Spencer was pretty much on his own, I guess. Poor little bastard."

Mariah felt a pang of sympathy for the young Spencer Becket. "So, like many children, he decided to run away from home? But to China? That was rather ambitious, don't you think?"

"But that's Spencer. He thought—thinks— anywhere that isn't Becket Hall has got to be better.

He loves us as we love him, but you can't make a family out of so many disparate parts and expect all those parts to fit. At least not completely. He still wants to leave, make his own way in the world," Chance said, looking at her carefully. "Doesn't he?"

Mariah kept her gaze steady. "You'd have to ask him that, Chance. For now, please tell me what happened when Spencer built his boat. He did build it, didn't he? I doubt he gave up and forgot the idea."

"Yes, he built it, and he didn't want anyone's help, either. So, over the course of a few weeks, he built himself his boat, commandeered food from the kitchens and set out into the Channel one morning without so much as a farewell to anyone. It's the only time Ainsley ever went out on the water since we'd arrived in Romney Marsh. He took one of the long-boats, he and Billy, and they rowed after Spencer, who was bailing his little boat frantically as it began to sink about fifty yards offshore."

Tears stung at Mariah's eyes once more. "He must have hated being rescued."

"Oh, Ainsley didn't rescue him. He just rowed alongside Spencer as he swam back to shore, and then he stared down everyone on the shore so that none of us dared to say a word as Spence laid there, vomiting up half the Channel. The very next day Ainsley and Spencer and Pike—he was the ship's carpenter then, before he…died—were back out on the shingle, building another boat."

Mariah was incredulous. "So Spencer could attempt to sail to China again?"

"No, he never tried that particular escape again. I think he'd learned his lesson—the hard way, as Spencer seems to always learn the hard way—and then, of his own accord, he gave the boat as a gift to one of the local freetraders who'd lost his in a storm. The man's probably still using it. That damn thing was a good, solid boat."

"I think that story was supposed to be about Spencer, but it was also about Ainsley and all of the Beckets, wasn't it? Still, if one day William attempts to sail to China, I'll know that Spencer will handle the problem brilliantly."

"Yes, I think he will. Spence is a good man, Mariah, even if he can occasionally run a bit…hot. I do want you to know that. And, bless his passionate Spanish heart, he *can* learn."

"Maybe…maybe one day he'll learn that he doesn't have to be alone," Mariah said quietly. "Maybe, one day, we'll have more than William and our two stubborn natures between us."

Chance smiled. "Oh, I think there's already more than that between you."

Mariah could feel a flush of heat running up her cheeks and was happy to hear the sound of the door opening on the ground floor and footsteps on the stairs. "They're back. I hope they have good news for us."

But when Spencer entered the room to say that Julia

was continuing upstairs to wash her face and hands, and Rian had stayed in Green Park—presumably to look for Renard or Nicolette but, as Spencer suspected, more to watch the balloon being set up for its grand ascension—he looked tired and worn and more than a little discouraged.

"No luck," he said rather unnecessarily, collapsing onto the couch beside Mariah. "There was one coach I hoped might be the one we're looking for, but the coachman was English and wore no cockade. Still, I followed it on foot for three blocks before it stopped, letting down some grande dame who could no more plot against the Crown than see sixty again. Oh, and one thing more—I think every second person in this city wears one cockade or another. Damn stupid things. There should be a law against them."

Chance and Mariah exchanged small smiles as Spencer levered himself to his feet and stomped over to the drinks table to pour himself a glass of wine. Yes, Spencer Becket sometimes *ran hot.*

It had been Julia who had given them all a short history of cockades, the ribbons worn to advertise their wearer's allegiance to a political faction or cause. The recently reinstated Bourbon dynasty's cockade was white, as was the English cockade for those favoring the restoration of a Jacobite monarchy. Not to be outdone, those men and women who wished to see the Hanoverian monarchy of the Georges maintained wore black cockades.

"During the revolution in France, men and women added to the white cockades, pinning on circles of red and blue, making them tricolor," Julia had explained, drawing two increasingly smaller circles inside a larger circle, showing the division of the three colors. "But Mariah saw a white cockade with a red circle on top and a *black* circle at the center. I have *no* idea what that combination means."

But Chance had a theory. "Edmund's personal flag, a tri-corner thing, was always flown from the masthead of his ships. It was black, with a red skull and two white bones crossed beneath. I don't think we need seek further evidence, do you? The cockade Mariah saw displayed an allegiance to Edmund Beales," he'd said and they'd all gone back to work, searching the streets of London. Watching. Always watching.

And nothing. If Renard and Nicolette were staying in London, they were doing a commendable job of playing least-in-sight.

The carnival atmosphere in London had doubled and redoubled, as had the crowds in the streets. William Congreve's scores of various fireworks, rockets and pinwheels on stakes, and Catherine wheels tied in the trees, were tantalizing reminders of the spectacle planned once the sun had set tonight. More booths and stalls, kiosks and arcades, follies of every sort, were still being hastily constructed everywhere; a half dozen elephants were now eating their heads off in Hyde Park.

Rowboats decorated to resemble grand ships had been floated in the canal as it ran through St. James's Park, ready to reenact the Battle of the Nile. A supposed Temple of Discord had been constructed in Green Park, as well, but it didn't hold a candle to the yellow bridge ornamented with slashing black lines that had been erected across the canal, dotted with four matching pavilions and centered with a seven-story, blue-roofed Chinese pagoda, the significance of either the pagoda or its blue roof not quite clear to anyone except, one could suppose, the spendthrift Prince Regent himself.

And Mariah was missing all of it, stuck in the house on Upper Brook Street, only reading about the celebration in the newspapers.

Spencer returned to the couch, carrying his glass of wine. "So, what have you two been doing in our absence?"

"I've been telling tales of your checkered youth," Chance told him amicably. "But I believe Mariah has been plotting how to be a part of our party tonight."

Spencer turned to look at Mariah, who was already looking at him, her chin stuck out mulishly. "Oh she has, has she?"

"Spence, I'm going," Chance pointed out, hoping to avoid an argument. "Julia is going. We were right to be prudent these past few days but now is the time for action. We wouldn't even know who we're looking for if it hadn't been for your wife. She's earned the right to go with us this evening."

Mariah tilted her head to one side, waiting to hear what Spencer would say.

"Madam, we'll do this privately," he said and stood, heading for the foyer, and the stairs to their bedchamber.

Chance shook his head. "Thick as a plank, that boy. And you think he doesn't care for you, Mariah? Think again."

By the time Mariah climbed the two flights of stairs it was to find that Spencer was seated in one of the chairs flanking the fireplace, the newspaper unfolded and lifted high enough to cover his face. Honestly, she could just box his ears for him.

"Spencer, don't be obnoxious," she told him, plunking herself down in the facing chair.

He lowered the newspaper and peered at her overtop it. "At least I'm not *looming.*"

Why did she think he was adorable? She should be grabbing that newspaper from him, rolling it into a makeshift club and beating him to flinders with it. "Then what *are* you doing?"

"I'm controlling my temper, Mariah. Please, let me do this." He raised the newspaper once more. "Ah," he said. "Here's an item about one James Stadler—he'd be the one managing the ascension, and a quite famous balloonist, to read this. And, once the balloon is on the ascent, he and others in the balloon will be dropping programs listing the order of events as well as favors and fairings to the crowd assembled below." He set down the newspaper. "There will be rioting, people will be trampled, all to catch a prize. Don't those idiots realize anything?"

Mariah kept her hands carefully folded in her lap. If he was going to try to leash his temper, she could only do the same. "I already read today's newspapers from one end to the other, thank you. And may I remind you that you're asking this question of a royal prince who orders forty-seven courses for a state dinner for six hundred people?"

"No more than five hundred, and I think it was a mere thirty courses. Our great Iron Duke must be in agony this morning," Spencer said, then carefully folded the newspaper, calmly, precisely, before smashing it into a ball and throwing it, with some violence, into the fireplace. "Damn it—and them—all to hell!"

Mariah was fairly certain a reasonable person would retire from the field for a space, but she found herself more amused than upset. She certainly wasn't afraid of the man or his temper. "My goodness," she said, crossing one leg over the other as she sat back at her ease, "I think I'm trembling in my shoes. I couldn't possibly be insane enough to bring up the subject of tonight and my intention to go with you to the park. Except that I am—bringing up the subject, that is. *And* going with you."

He glared at her with those dark black eyes.

She smiled at him. "Should I fetch you something else to throw? I'm sure Julia wouldn't mind the loss of one of these vases on the mantel, for instance. In a good cause."

Spencer looked at his wife. Shook his head. Felt the fool. And then moved even more swiftly than he could think, grabbing her up and carrying her over to the bed, following her down until they were belly-to-belly, nose-to-nose, her glorious hair slipping free of its pins to fan out round her head. "There isn't another person in the world who would talk to me like that," he told her, the corners of his mouth twitching in his growing good humor. "I feel as dangerous as a cannon with its fuse pulled free. How do you manage it? How do you manage me?"

Mariah slipped her arms around his back. "I'd never dream to *manage* you, Spence. Who on earth would wish a docile lap pet for a husband?"

He rolled onto his back, taking her with him, so that her hair formed a living curtain of fire around them. "And who would wish a docile lap pet for a wife? Not me, it would seem," he said before sealing his mouth against hers.

Mariah felt a flood of feeling threatening to drown her as she gave her mouth to him, gave herself over to him, allowed him to be the aggressor, the *man,* the *husband.* His passion, his frustration; he'd brought them both to her. She soothed him as he sought release from both; she aided him and guided him, her own passion rising with each kiss, each fevered caress.

The feelings were the same. The heat, the hunger.

But there was also something new, something different, and when the passion burst around them they held on tightly long after that passion was spent, Mariah nestled into the curve of his shoulder, Spencer lightly stroking her hair.

"Spence?" she hazarded, the thought coming into her mind without her seeking it out. "Do you trust me?"

"I don't sleep with a knife under my pillow, if that's what you mean," he told her, yawning. Between searching London from one end to the other all day and making love to his bride whenever he could, he was beginning to believe he'd never feel completely awake again.

"You're so amusing," Mariah said drily. "But I'm serious. Do you trust me?"

Spencer reached down to tip up her chin. "I trust you, Mariah Becket. With my son, with my life, with the lives of my family. You've done as you said you wanted to do—you've proven yourself. There, is that sincere enough for you?"

Mariah blinked back tears. But then she pushed, because that was her nature. "It's a beginning. I suppose I'd like you to trust me with more than what happened when Beales betrayed you all. You…you could begin with telling me the name of the island. Is that such a terrible secret?"

"Ah, women. Always feeling it necessary to know every small detail," Spencer said, then held up his hands to ward off a blow that didn't come. "I'm not hiding anything from you, Mariah. The island never had a name. It was just what I said—the island."

Mariah didn't understand. "But…but Ainsley lived there for a number of years. And he never named the island? His home?"

"Think about it for a moment, Mariah. If he'd named the island, then it would be possible for one of the crew to be overheard saying that he was going to return to Victory Island, or Saint Christopher's Island or whatever name you could think of to give an island. Soon there would be maps and the island picked out on those maps, named on those maps. Ainsley's enemies could find him, or follow one of the crew from Port-au-Prince or wherever he might happen to be at the time. Believe me, the island wasn't named because of any lack of imagination but out of a large portion of self-protection. Not everything is a puzzle. Now, is there anything else?"

Mariah grinned up at him. "Well, of course there is. I'm a woman, aren't I?"

So they talked about Virginia, Spencer telling her of books he'd read, letters from his friend Abraham. About the crops grown there, the climate, the animals, even the government. He promised to let her see those books when they got back to Becket Hall. They even discussed the merits of brick as opposed to wood houses.

They talked about William, how they both missed him—and wasn't that strange, considering that not three months ago he hadn't really existed. Not to

Spencer, who hadn't known about Mariah's pregnancy, and not even to Mariah, who had been more concerned with how she would feed the child, clothe the child, leaving little time to think about herself as a mother.

Spencer pressed a kiss against her temple. "I wish I could remember what happened in America. I wish I could remember you, how magnificent you were. Clovis remains quite in awe, you know."

Mariah ran her hand over Spencer's chest, the soft hairs that tickled at her palm. "I'm glad you don't remember," she told him quietly.

He could feel her body tensing, held her against him as she tried to move away, sit up. "Don't," he said. "I think we need to talk about this, just the once. Did…did I hurt you?"

Mariah closed her eyes, took in a breath and let it out slowly. "I would suppose that was inevitable. I was a virgin. Which is no excuse. You were feverish, out of your mind with that fever. I could have overpowered you, pushed you away. I didn't."

"And I hurt you."

Now she did struggle out of his arms, to raise herself up, look at him through the wild curtain of her hair. "You held me. You made me feel alive. You frightened me and you saved me. Your touch told me I was a woman, that my life wasn't over, that there were still things for me live for, to experience. What…what if there had been no William? What would I have done?

Because I don't know, Spencer, I really don't. Once we were safe in Canada, there was nothing for me. Nowhere to go, no one for me to take care of—no one to care for me."

She pressed a fist into her abdomen. "You didn't hurt me, Spencer. Not in any way that counts. You very possibly may have saved me."

He pulled her down against him once more, relief flooding him as he realized how much he'd needed to hear her say those words. "As you saved me."

Mariah smiled, her heart lightened. "Yes, I did, didn't I? My, aren't we both marvelous creatures?"

Spencer threw back his head and laughed, then pushed Mariah over onto her back and kissed her. And kissed her. And then kissed her again....

They were lying together once more, still breathing rather heavily from a mutually pleasurable exertion, when Chance knocked on the door and called through the thick wood. "There'll be no dinner gong tonight, as Julia insists on sampling every booth in the park. Be ready to leave in an hour, all right?"

Spencer called back his agreement even as Mariah climbed out of the bed, dragging the sheet with her and wrapping it around her body, throwing one end up and over her shoulder. "You look like a Greek statue come to life, wife."

Mariah was momentarily diverted, flattered. But just because she was still feeling warm and rosy from his lovemaking didn't mean she was about to allow him to sneak away to the park without her. "Thank you. Now get dressed, please, so you can help me back on with my gown. We don't want to keep everyone else waiting, do we?"

Spencer opened his mouth to protest and then just waved his hands in front of him as if to erase what he'd almost said. "They don't have to wait for us. I chose the long straw, and we'll be cooling our heels in St. James's Park while Chance and Julia position themselves within sight of the Prince Regent and Rian and Billy make their rounds in Green Park."

Mariah paused, half bent over, reaching to retrieve her undergarments from the floor, then gave up any notion of modesty, letting the sheet drop as she picked up her shift. "St. James's Park? But why? I can understand you and Chance shuffling poor Rian off to where he'll be safe. I know we have to divide our forces, keep watching for Renard and Nicolette, even though she hasn't yet returned to the shop as she said she would to retrieve her new bonnet. But why would we expect anything to happen in St. James's Park?"

"And why would I think you'd be happy just to be included in the plans? I should have known better. And, General Becket, we're doing it this way because Chance received a note from Wellington late last night. It seems that the Czar has voiced a wish to personally inspect the Chinese pagoda at some point tonight, and now they'll all be riding over there in state coaches. If we know this, we can't be sure Renard doesn't also know, so somebody is already guarding the pagoda and keeping an eye on the area."

She pulled her gown over her head, let it drop around her shoulders. "Oh. Well, I suppose that's a credible reason."

"I'll tell Chance you've agreed. I'm sure it will greatly relieve his mind to know that Our Lady of the Swamp has approved his plan."

"Yes, he should be," Mariah said, ignoring Spencer's sarcasm. "Wait here. Don't say another word." Holding her unbuttoned gown at the shoulders, she raced into her dressing room to retrieve a fresh pair of white silk stockings. Perching on the end of one of the chairs in front of the fireplace, she began smoothing them up over her foot and leg.

Spencer pushed his arms into the sleeves of his coat and then simply watched her as she finished with her right leg and began slipping the silk onto the left. "Would you consider wearing those to bed?" he asked, then laughed when she shot him a shocked look. "And no, I'm not looming this time, Mariah. I'm *leering*. Let me help you with the fastenings on your gown."

"I don't think so, Spencer Becket, or the Prince Regent will be starting his Grand Jubilee without us. I'll meet you downstairs. Oh, wait."

"Good thing you aren't leading this particular army. Chance is waiting for me."

"Yes, yes," she told him, hurrying back over to the bedside table. "But you can't go without this." She held up the *gad* he'd taken off because he hadn't wanted the alligator tooth amulet to scratch Mariah's fair skin. He lowered his head as she slipped the thin leather strip over it, patted the tooth as it laid against his shirt. "There. Now you can go."

Spencer tucked the *gad* beneath his hastily tied neck cloth. "You really believe in Odette's nonsense?"

"I believe in anything that might help us. I've been wearing my own *gad* pinned to my undergarments since the day Odette gave it to me."

Spencer nodded, his mind suddenly and completely concentrated on the night ahead of them. "You're right. We'll believe in anything that might help us."

CHAPTER NINETEEN

ALL OF LONDON pushed into the parks for the first night of the Grand Jubilee, members of the *ton* rubbing shoulders with chimney sweeps, the smells of food, costly perfumes, horse dung and sweat mingling together to have Mariah reaching for her handkerchief, pressing its scented linen against her nose and mouth as she held on to Spencer's arm and did her best to not step in anything more vile than the mud churned up by ten thousand pairs of feet that had already destroyed every blade of grass in St. James's Park.

Nicolette hadn't returned to the millinery shop to take delivery of her bonnet that afternoon, which proved that either the shopkeeper had lied about the day she was to return or that she hadn't been able to return. That last worried Mariah more than a little bit.

It all would have been so easy—see Nicolette, follow her as she left the shop, capture Renard and convince him to lead them to Edmund Beales. Mariah didn't know precisely how the Beckets would convince the man, and didn't want to know. She just wanted this over and her life with Spencer and William to begin in earnest, with no shadows of the past able to reach out and hurt them.

"Would it be terrible of me to beg you to buy me a pint of stout?" she asked. Spencer avoided a mug that a burly man in a leather apron was swinging about as he spoke to a companion. "It's so warm in this crush and Papa let me drink a bit of stout from his glass on very hot summer days."

"A sip is not a pint, Mariah," Spencer pointed out, already elbowing his way toward a stall selling stout and ale, both of which would probably cause less damage than a glass of water. "You can drink a little from mine, all right?"

"Are you afraid I'll go all tipsy and begin singing bawdy songs?" she asked him, feeling petulant. She was just *hot* after spending several hours in this mad crush of people, so very hot, and wishing everyone else would simply go home. Mostly, she was angry that she and Spencer were trapped here in Green Park, when anyone with any sense knew that whatever was going to happen would happen in Hyde Park.

Spencer dropped a few coins on the wooden counter and grabbed a pint, easing them back into a less crowded area. "Are you telling me you know bawdy songs?"

Mariah took two quick sips of stout and then sang out in a clear, strong voice, *"As I walked out one May morning, one May morning so early, I overtook a handsome maid just as the sun was rising."*

"Oh, God," Spencer said, rolling his eyes, but then joined her in the chorus. *"With my rue dum day, Fol the diddle dol, Fol the dol the diddle dum the day!"*

Behind them, Clovis took up the second verse. *"Her shoes were bright, her stockings white, her buckles shone like silver. She had a black and roving eye, and her hair hung down her shoulder."*

By the time they'd reached the chorus once more, Aloysius, née Anguish, had begun to dance a jig and several others nearby had lifted their mugs—undoubtedly not their first of the evening—to sing along.

*"With my rue dum day, Fol the diddle dol, Fol the dol the diddle—*where are we going?" Mariah asked as Spencer took her arm and began dragging her through the crowd. "I love the next verse. *How old are you? My fair pretty maid. How old are you, my honey? She answered me right cheerfully, I'm seventeen come Sunday. With my rue dum day, Fol the diddle—*would you *stop* dragging at me! You're spilling the stout."

"Damn the stout," Spencer gritted out from between clenched teeth, not stopping until they were at the fringes of the crowd, a worried Clovis and Aloysius joining them a few moments later. "Is this how we watch for Renard?"

Mariah dipped her head, mumbled her apologies. "We both know Renard won't be showing up here, Spence. Besides, you did ask if I knew any drinking songs."

"I didn't expect you to break into verse, madam,

with the rest of the world and his drunken wife joining in," he told her, stabbing his fingers through his hair. "Oh, hell, and yes, you're right. We should leave here, go to Hyde Park and the viewing stand, no matter what Chance said, and just follow everyone back here when they come to see the pagoda. At least, there, we can watch the royal viewing stand. The only way to see anyone here would be to be up in that damn balloon."

"About that, Lieutenant, sir," Clovis said, holding his hat in his hands, fairly wringing the cloth. "I saw over there where someone is selling rides on one of those pachyderm beasts. High above the crowd that would put you, sir, you and your lady wife. You could see a good fair lot, atop a pachyderm."

Spencer looked across the canal, where the Battle of the Nile was now raging, complete with flaming boats and small fireworks meant to resemble cannon fire. He could see an elephant that had been decked out with some sort of large open-topped box tied to its back, the box filled with no fewer than a dozen people, most of whom appeared to be hanging on for dear life while rethinking their bravery. Put Mariah up in a basket like that? "I don't think so, Clovis…"

"Oh, come on, Spencer, we'll be like Hannibal, crossing the Alps," Mariah begged, more than happy to have her feet somewhere other than where they were, surrounded by puddles, with only half of them, she worried, being mud puddles and the rest created in ways she could have only guessed at before she'd seen a red-faced, clearly drunken young man clad in the first stare of fashion bent over, his hands on his knees as he cast up his accounts in a fit of violent retching. "And Clovis is correct. We would be higher than anyone else, according us a much better view."

After indulging in a short mental vision of commandeering an elephant and riding it through the throng, hard on the heels of a fleeing Renard and Nicolette, Spencer sighed and nodded his agreement. And a few minutes after that, he was handing a dark-skinned old man in a turban and baggy pants a shilling each for he and Mariah, then watching in amazement as Mariah nimbly ascended the wooden ladder propped against the side of the now-kneeling elephant. Was there anything the woman wouldn't dare?

He joined her in the box that was covered in an assortment of rather moldy carpets and he looked out over the park, toward the Chinese pagoda, now lit on all seven stories with what had to be more than a thousand flickering lights. "I hesitate to point this out, Mariah, but this elephant's hind leg is shackled to a fairly stout stake hammered into the ground. We're going nowhere."

Mariah, heady with the height, the thrill of the thing, turned to grin at him. "And where did you want to go, Spencer? We'd be trampling the villagers, as I've heard happens in India, if the elephant broke loose. I hope the stake is very heavy and hammered into the ground at least three feet or more. Oh, look—there's Aloysius, waving up at us. *Yoohoo, Aloysius! Here we are!*"

"Oh, for the love of—Mariah, I know I said I doubted anything was going to happen here in St. James's tonight, but if Chance knew I'd spent precious time perched on a damn elephant, I wouldn't blame him for knocking me down."

"You're just upset because we've been banished here, that's all," Mariah told him. "So am I, truthfully, and the pistol is banging painfully against my leg when I walk, so I'm not all that delighted to be here, either. Just let's make the best of it, all right?"

Spencer turned her to face him, ran his hands down over her hips and found the outline of the pistol. The large pistol. "How in bloody hell—?"

"I took a page from Courtland's book of brilliance and fashioned a sort of *harness* for it from strips of my petticoat. As you're already *pawing* me in public, perhaps you'll find the seam I opened enough to reach my hand inside my gown and extract it, if necessary."

"I'm definitely never letting you anywhere near my sister Morgan," Spencer grumbled, turning his attention to the fireworks that had begun in a small way, with Catherine wheels spinning colored flame in the trees to the sounds of *oohs* and *ahhs* from the increasingly drunken crowd.

"You didn't bring a pistol, Spencer?"

"Clovis has it, tied around his neck together with his own, beneath his coat. I can have it at a moment's notice."

Mariah stepped closer to him as the elephant seemed to decide he needed to shift his weight about somewhat, and slipped her hands beneath Spencer's jacket, her fingers closing around the leather harness holding the mechanism for his knife. "Well, I suppose that's all right, then. We neither of us expect to be a part of whatever happens tonight, but at least we're prepared."

The dark sky above them suddenly lit with the explosion of larger fireworks—Congreve rockets especially made to be all flash and dash, rather than the destructive rockets he'd invented for warfare. Mariah rested her head against Spencer's shoulder as she looked into the sky above their heads. "Oh, look, aren't they beautiful!"

The crowd no longer milled below them, but had all stopped where they were, to cheer each new explosion, those emanating from the area behind the bridge holding the Chinese pagoda as well as more bright explosions in the distance—in Green Park, even as far away as Hyde Park itself.

Spencer felt a tug of disappointment that he wouldn't see the large Temple of Discord be enveloped in fireworks as the entire top of the Temple was craftily revolved to reveal, as the smoke from the explosions cleared, a new name for the structure, the *Temple of Concord*. He'd have to hear Rian tell him about the thing, probably at least a dozen times.

As much as Spencer believed this entire celebration was nonsense, an expense England could not afford after a long war had depleted the Treasury, an affront, almost a *goad* to Bonaparte to prove the celebration premature, he could not deny that the evening itself was fairly close to spectacular. A fete so grand, nothing close to its scope and grandeur would probably be seen again for several generations. They were celebrating victory, after twenty long years of war across the continent. This was history in the making, a thrilling and glorious time to be alive.

The dawn of a new peace, please God, a lasting peace.

"Maybe Prinney isn't as silly as I believed him. Maybe we all do need something like this grand spectacle right now," Spencer said, drawing Mariah close against his side, smiling as the bright colors of the fireworks seemed to be reflecting in his wife's shining eyes.

And then he tensed, his arm going more tightly around her.

"What's wrong, Spence?" Mariah asked him, immediately sensing his sudden alertness.

"Did you hear it? God knows I've heard that sound enough."

"It's the *bang* of the fireworks exploding, that's all," Mariah told him, but she was already following him as he pushed aside people sharing the basket with them, heading for the ladder. "Isn't it?"

"Not that last one, no, and it sounded close by,"

Spencer said, whistling the attendant over to make the elephant kneel, then holding the ladder still as he helped Mariah over the railing of the basket. She quickly climbed down and he joined her almost immediately, ignoring the short ladder as he jumped to the ground. "Clovis, Anguish—to me!"

"Er…that's Aloysius, sir."

"Bloody hell, Anguish, now's not the time. Did you two hear the difference in one of the explosions? Just a minute ago. *There!* There's another one, coming from somewhere behind us," he said, looking up at the sky in time to see one of Congreve's rockets shooting overhead, heading for Green Park…or perhaps even Hyde Park itself.

"Those…those are *real* rockets?" Mariah asked. "My God, Spence!"

He grabbed her hand and began pushing his way through the crowd toward the Chinese Pagoda, Clovis, Aloysius and five strapping sons of former members of the Black Ghost crew running ahead to help clear the way.

Mariah used her free hand to hold the pistol still at her side as she ran, not that her leg wouldn't be bruised badly by the time she awoke tomorrow…if she awoke tomorrow. "Oh, excuse me!" she said, as Spencer was pulling her along willy-nilly and she'd crashed into a blowsy-looking woman in red satin and green-dyed feathers, knocking her to the ground.

"Here, now, look what you did, knocking my

Maisie on her rump! How about I knock you down, you flame-haired bitch!"

Spencer didn't actually stop so much as he paused, pushing Mariah behind him even as he stepped forward and pushed out his right arm in a short, economical movement that had his fist connecting with the protesting man's jaw and the man's rump connecting with a large puddle on the ground, just beside his Maisie.

"Be more careful, Mariah," Spencer said, dragging her along again.

"Me? You're the one who *rammed* me into the poor woman. Oh, I don't have the breath for this," she complained as she hiked her skirts nearly to her knees and tried to keep up.

She longed to ask Spencer where they were going, other than in the general direction of the Chinese pagoda, and what he expected to do when they got there.

But there was no time for questions.

They ran along the canal, the decorated rowboats flying French flags still burning down to their waterlines, Catherine wheels spinning colored fire, smoke hugging the ground around them, thin shafts of hot color shooting up into the sky—riots of color, like cabbage roses, blooming over their heads.

And the occasional rocket that sang over their heads, not exploding in a shower of pretty colors but heading somewhere else…somewhere deadly.

The battering ram that was the men from Becket

Hall cut a swatch through the revelers who still laughed and cheered each rocket, and at last they were clear of the worst of the congestion and within sight of the yellow bridge.

Spencer skidded to a halt and looked at Mariah even as a nearly breathless Clovis handed over his pistol. "You stay here with Clovis, you hear me?"

"No! I don't know where you think you're going, Spencer Becket, but I'm going with you and you can't stop me. I mean it, Spence, you—"

He took hold of her upper arms, breathing heavily as was she, and crushed her mouth in a short, hard kiss before looking at her, his dark eyes intense. "I love you, Mariah Becket."

Mariah looked up at him, unable to move, unable to say a word, her head positively spinning. He loved her? He *loved* her!

"Yes," he said, grinning at her. "I thought that would do it. Clovis, take her. And if she tries to follow me— tackle her if you have to!"

"Um…sure thing, Lieutenant," Clovis said, his hands now clamped on Mariah's upper arms as he stood in front of her, his smile apologetic and a bit sickly. "Please don't make me tackle you, Missus," he begged as Spencer took Aloysius and two others with him, directing the remaining three men to his left so that they would come up on the area behind the bridge on both flanks.

"Clovis?" Mariah asked, regaining her bearings.

"Yes, Missus," he said, his hands still tight on her arms.

"I've got a pistol, Clovis. Feel it? I will use it on you, or I will use it to help my husband. My husband who loves me. Which would you like me to do?"

"Ah, now, Missus, you wouldn't do that to—"

Her hand inserted through the slit in her gown, Mariah pushed the barrel of the pistol more firmly against the body part Clovis probably cherished more than all others in this world. "I would, Clovis. You were with me in the swamp. You know I don't threaten. Not more than once. Now, Corporal Meechum, I've given you an order. Take your hands off me, Clovis...*now*."

"No, Missus, I can't do that. He loves you. I heard him, too. So I'm guessin' you'll just have to kill me, because the lieutenant will, if you don't."

"Oh, for pity's sake! Clovis, you love him, don't you?"

"Yes, Missus. He's my lieutenant."

"And I love him. He's my husband. So? Are we both just going to keep standing here?" She looked up as that peculiar sound, so different from the rockets meant to carry only fireworks, boomed and whistled yet again. And still nobody else seemed to notice. "Are we, Clovis?"

Clovis dropped his hands away from her. "He went that way, Missus."

Mariah didn't run, as she knew enough to be aware that the worst thing that could happen would be to inadvertently put Clovis and herself between Spencer and whoever was sending those deadly rockets into the air. So, instead of a full, frontal assault on the area, she cut far to the right side of the bridge, then circled around through the cover of a small stand of plane trees, hoping to come up behind Spencer as she called his name as quietly as possible.

Stopping behind one of the trees, she raised a hand to signal Clovis to halt and peered out into the cleared area where many of the fireworks had been assembled, lined up in clay pots all across the rear of the bridge and the Chinese Pagoda at its center. Several men holding brightly burning torches stood behind the rows of pots and, as she watched, one of them lowered his torch to the thick wick trailing away from one of the pots and, moments later, a white-hot fireball shot nearly straight into the air.

"Fireworks. They're simply setting off the fireworks. The real rockets must be somewhere else," she told Clovis, signaling that he should follow her as she threaded her way through the trees once more, still circling behind the bridge. "Damn! There goes another one. Did you see where it came from, Clovis?"

"I did that, Missus," Clovis said, pointing to a smaller clearing just now visible as they crept out of the trees, keeping behind some tall bushes that smelled slightly singed from all the gunpowder.

Even as Mariah watched, Spencer, Aloysius and two of the Becket Hall men crashed into the clearing, pistols drawn. There were no loud reports of gunshots, not that the noise would be remarkable with all the cheering and shouting coming from the main area of the park. Mariah shot a triumphant fist into the air as she could see the three men dressed all in black quickly lay down their torches and raise their hands in surrender—what her father would have called a bloodless coup of sorts, she supposed.

"Don't shoot, Spencer," she called out as she and Clovis emerged from the bushes, even as the rest of the Becket men joined the small group and began kicking over the metal stands holding three-foot-tall rockets aimed up and over the Chinese pagoda.

Spencer had just turned to look at Mariah, his mouth opening to tell her he knew full well that she'd never stay where he'd put her, when two men, also dressed in black, their lower faces covered by black silk, stepped out of the trees behind her. One of them knocked Clovis to the ground with the barrel of his pistol; the other grabbed Mariah and twisted her pistol out of her hand.

"We meet again, Mr. Joseph Abbott," the slighter man drawled, tightening his grip on Mariah, who knew she was being employed as a human shield and wasn't exactly willing to be that cooperative. "Later, *mon chérie doux,*" he whispered into her ear, "you may wriggle all you wish beneath me as I delight you past all bearing and then strangle you with your own fiery hair. I've thought about that a time or two, since last we met. But for now you will remain still *or your Mr. Abbott dies.*"

CHAPTER TWENTY

MARIAH CEASED her struggles and looked to Spencer.

"Let her go," Spencer ordered, leveling his pistol at the man. "Cowards, the pair of you, hiding your faces, hiding behind a woman. But it's Renard, isn't it? I think I can hear the same slime in your voice as I did in Calais."

"You would have known more than my voice had you stayed in Calais as you were supposed to, Mr. Abbott, or whatever your true name might be. I had so anticipated slicing your throat once we'd had a small chat as to the name of your employer. The War Office? You work for them, I suppose?"

The second man spoke. *"Tenez un moment, Renard, ne le tuez pas. Je connais ces yeux foncés, ce regard féroce. La mémoire vient clairement à moi maintenant. Spencer? Les dents du Christ, c'est la petite pousse, un des bâtards orphelins de notre vieux Geoffrey d'ami. Lui et moi ont beaucoup à parler. Je vous promets, Edmund embrasserai vos deux joues pour ceci."*

Mariah's heart, already beating quickly, threatened to burst out of her chest as she translated the man's words in her head. *Hold a moment, Renard, don't kill him. I know those dark eyes, that fierce look. The memory comes clear to me now. Spencer? Christ's teeth, it's the little sprout, one of our old friend Geoffrey's orphan bastards. He and I have much to talk about. I promise you, Edmund will kiss both your cheeks for this.*

"He knows!" Mariah shouted in warning. "Spencer, he knows who you are. Oh, God—"

Renard's forearm, tight against her throat, silenced Mariah, but didn't stop her from kicking back frantically with her heel, banging hard against the man's shin. Once, twice.

He reciprocated by slamming the butt of his pistol against the side of her head and she dropped to the ground beside Clovis.

"Bastard!" Spencer yelled, his opponent's shield gone now, and he leveled his pistol, fired from no more than six feet away, the ball making a small black hole in the center of Renard's forehead.

One of the Becket men with him tossed Spencer his pistol, which Spencer immediately pointed at the second Frenchman. But it was too late. The large man had pulled Mariah up by her hair and was now shielding himself with her limp, unconscious body even as he held a pistol pressed into her ribs.

"Well met, little sprout," the Frenchman said, already backing toward the bridge. "And Geoffrey? He lives? The coward lives?"

"He's no coward, Jules," Spencer said, daring a step forward, his pistol still trained on the man, not trusting himself to look at Mariah. "Beales is the coward. The cowardly murderer."

"Oh, yes, yes, the murderer. How terrible. Missed you, though, sprout, didn't we? Pity, that. Now," he said, hefting Mariah's body slightly as he ground the pistol barrel into her side, "we have us a dilemma of sorts here, don't we, sprout? I most certainly can't hold this woman much longer, especially if she begins to rouse, and I think you may care for her. Lacking a third arm, I can't easily snap her neck, now can I, keeping my pistol for you, and if I kill her, I die." He sighed theatrically. "What to do, what to do? Perhaps I'll merely choke her. Just a little bit."

"Just let her go, Jules, and I'll let you go," Spencer said, his intense gaze locked on Mariah, his prayer that she wouldn't begin to rouse, to struggle. "After all, we can't know if your plan has succeeded, can we? Do you really want to die not knowing if one of your rockets has killed the Prince Regent and the others?"

"The rockets?" Jules laughed out loud. "A diversion only, little sprout. No one can know for certain where one of Congreve's inventive toys might land, although we were assured that at least half of them would reach Hyde Park. No. It is as all those fat, panicked old men and their painted women race to protect themselves that my men will strike. Quickly, out of the darkness, a full two score of trained assassins. Martyrs all to the cause, willing to die, but not before their assigned targets are dead. I would have been with them, Renard and I both, save for the part about the martyrdom. Only fools die for what they are taught to believe is a grand, even holy purpose. Your fat prince may already be gutted, God willing. Sweet Jesus, this bitch becomes heavy."

"Then let her go. I promise, Jules, I won't shoot you," Spencer said, tossing his own pistol to the ground, aware that, behind Jules, Clovis had begun to wake up. Please God, don't let Clovis decide after years of avoiding such a thing that he wanted to play the hero. "See? You and I, we'll meet another day."

"Ah, but my good friend Edmund would not be happy if I told him I'd seen you, seen the little sprout, and then let him go. I fear we are at an impasse. So you will come with me. Have your loyal men put down their weapons as my loyal men regain theirs. That is, if you want this pretty little baggage to live."

"Agreed," Spencer said, motioning for his men to throw down their remaining weapons.

"Sir?" Aloysius all but bleated. "It's thinking, I am, that you've had better ideas, sir."

"Do as I said, Anguish," Spencer spat quickly and then added for Clovis's benefit, as the man had now gotten to his hands and knees behind Jules, "We will not do anything that might endanger Mariah any further. Not a single movement without a surety of success. *Do you understand?*"

Clovis slowly sank back down on the ground.

"But Mr. Chance, sir," Aloysius persisted. "What do we tell him?"

"Mr. Chance?" Jules stepped back several more paces, past Clovis, closer to the end of the bridge, dragging Mariah along with him, his forearm hard across her windpipe. "Oh, if that isn't wonderful. Geoffrey's favorite bastard whelp. You're all here in London? And Billy? The inestimable Jacko? All of your miserable, cowardly crew? Geoffrey lives, doesn't he? How delicious. Come along, sprout—we have so much to talk about."

"Anguish—relieve our friend Jules of his burden, if you please," Spencer said, ignoring the Frenchman's delight. "Jules? You should have no problem with allowing a one-armed man close to you. Even a cowardly cur like yourself could overpower a one-armed man."

"Oh, here now, sir, it's not as if I'm entirely helpless," Aloysius complained. "And it's Aloysius, if you'll please remember."

"You'll leave your man behind, Jules?" Spencer asked, gesturing toward the deceased Renard. "His father might not be happy with you."

Jules glanced down at Renard's body. "You're right, damn it all. Raoul, Pierre—take hold of his legs and drag the stupid bastard, if you will." He then staggered slightly under Mariah's weight, for he'd been holding her up against him for some time now. "Here, take her," he commanded now that his men, four in all, had joined him. He aimed his pistol at Spencer's head. "Now, if you've no other requests, little sprout, I think we'll be leaving."

Mariah moaned softly as Aloysius caught her clumsily, the two of them falling to the ground, and Spencer had the satisfaction of knowing she was not dead, thank God. Now to make Clovis understand what he needed everyone to do.

"Everyone, remain where you are, stay with Mariah. Obey me, Clovis, Anguish, just as you know I always obeyed General Proctor," he told his men and then allowed two of Jules's men to each take hold of one of his arms as they retreated from the scene.

Aloysius scratched at the side of his head. "Now, when did the lieutenant ever obey the—Clovis?"

But Clovis had understood Spencer's words, just as he had realized what his lieutenant had been about, worrying over one dead froggie. And Clovis could add: two men dragging the dead frog by his heels, two men holding on to the lieutenant, which left only the pig who'd been using Miss Mariah as a shield free to use the pistol in his hand.

Not a single movement without a surety of success. That's what the lieutenant had said. Well, it wasn't a surety, but the odds weren't too terrible.

"Forward!" Clovis yelled as he sprang to his feet with all the agility of a man who'd never see fifty again, and Aloysius and the men from Becket Hall picked up his shout, repeating it as they charged, weaponless, at the small knot of Frenchmen.

The two men dragging Renard's body let go of his legs and fired their weapons directly at the men running full tilt at them.

Spencer rammed his elbows out at either side, catching one of the men holding him in the ribs hard enough to have him let go his grip on Spencer's arm long enough for him to plow the fist at the end of that freed arm into the face of his other captor, neatly breaking the man's nose. He was getting very good at breaking noses....

Jules was already running, leaving his men to their fate, and Spencer took off after him. He couldn't let the bastard get away, return to Edmund Beales, tell him that Geoffrey Baskin and his men still lived. But Spencer didn't want the man dead, either, for he had to know where Beales was, know all of the man's plans.

Jules, for all his age and bulk, braced his hands on the railing at the end of the bridge and vaulted over it onto the bridge itself, then ran toward the Chinese pagoda.

Good.

Trapped animals always climb. That's their fatal flaw. Spencer heard Ainsley's voice, one of the many lessons he had taught his children, and he followed Jules slowly, giving the man time to well and truly tree himself high in the pagoda. He spared a moment, a very quick moment, to look down from the bridge to see how his men were faring.

Clovis was in a fistfight with one of the men while Anguish, bless him, sat astride another. Young Johnny Keeler was down, holding on to his left shoulder. The other men from Becket Hall were having some difficulty subduing the other two, but they seemed to be getting the upper hand, and the rest of the Becket Hall men would be on the scene soon, leaving Spencer free to take on Jules by himself...which was just the way he wanted it.

What he didn't want was to have the last thing he saw in this world be Mariah, lying motionless as she was now on the night-wet grass....

The pagoda was a fairly flimsy construction, as hastily erected as the rest of the structures ordered by the Prince Regent, all flash and bright paint on the outside, its interior all but hollow, a set of twisting, turning stairs taking up the center and rising the full seven stories, planking around the inside of the walls serving as a way for servants to light the gas lights shining in each of the multitude of windows.

"Nowhere to go, Jules!" Spencer called out, holding on to the first section of banister as he peered upward, blinking against the fairly intense light reflected off the whitewashed walls inside the pagoda. "You say Beales will have questions for me? Think of the answers Geoffrey will want from you—and the way Jacko will make sure you answer them, one way or another. Poor bastard, you might be happier dead."

"You think so?" Jules called down to him, and Spencer strained to catch sight of the man's feet, something, high above him. "I stand at this window, sprout, my pistol aimed at the ground. No, not the ground, sprout. At the woman lying on the ground. Would I miss from this distance? Anything is possible, sprout. But do you want to take that chance?"

Spencer cursed under his breath, then yelled, "You always hide behind women, Jules?" He sat down on the bottom step and pulled off his boots, not without considerable effort, and carefully laid them aside. "You should wear skirts, Jules, if you long to hide with women. But that ugly face would give you away, wouldn't it? And that smell you carry with you."

"You smell your own death, sprout," Jules called down to him as Spencer carefully made his way up to the next level of the pagoda, still straining to locate the Frenchman by the sound of his voice.

The staircase twisted again, winding its way upward, Spencer reaching each new level and then pressing his back against the wood, trying to peer first left, then right, toward the planking that ringed the inside of each floor. He wouldn't speak anymore, not willing to give away his own location, and only wished that he couldn't hear himself breathe; he wondered if Jules could hear him breathing, as well.

"Coming, sir! You get him yet?"

"Anguish, no!" Spencer called out, willing Aloysius back down the steps he was climbing in his enthusiasm to be in on the final capture.

"It's all right, sir. Missus Mariah, she's sittin' up now, askin' for you, and I figured I'd fetch you. Still good for somethin', with my one good arm. Got a brace of pistols with me, too, iffen you were to need them. Step out, sir, where are—"

The soldier's question was cut off by the sound of a pistol shot and Spencer was on the move again, climbing, praying Jules didn't have another pistol, but not much caring if he did.

He'd reached yet another landing when Jules' empty pistol sailed past his head, followed quickly by the man himself, and together, Spencer and Jules tumbled down to the lower landing.

Spencer regained his feet first, his hands balled into fists as he waited for Jules to rise just far enough so that he could knock him down again. But Jules didn't try to stand. He flew forward from a low crouch, tackling Spencer below the knees, so that once more the two of them were locked together, rolling along the planking that was all that separated them from a four story fall to the base of the staircase.

Jules did not fight like a gentleman, but Spencer had been taught at the gentle hand of Jacko, who had shown him tricks that could make a grown man blush—if he wasn't fighting for his life.

When Jules got his hands around Spencer's neck,

grinning at him as he head-butted him, then squeezed his fingers tight, Spencer answered by reaching between the Frenchman's legs and grabbing the man's testicles, giving them a violent twist.

Jules called out in agony and let go his grip on Spencer's neck, staggering back toward one of the windows, knocking into a precariously balanced gas lamp, smashing the glass around it, catching the sleeve of his coat on fire.

He stripped off the loose coat and flung it away from him, then gave a guttural growl and ran at Spencer once more, even as Spencer still struggled to regain the breath Jules had nearly choked out of him.

The fight continued; Jules bit deep into the back of Spencer's hand even as Spencer, knowing he was in the fight of his life against a man who obeyed no rules, ground one of his fingers into the Frenchman's ear.

They rolled together, nearly falling from the planking, Spencer having the upper hand one moment, Jules the next.

Spencer was well aware of the knife tucked up his sleeve, but he needed Jules alive. A dead man couldn't tell him where Edmund Beales was hiding. At the same time, he knew he couldn't allow Jules to best him, kill him. He had too much to live for—*his wife, his son, their future.*

There was an explosion behind them, the force of it rolled them over yet again, followed by the fierce heat of the flames now licking at the wooden structure.

Within seconds the staircase was on fire, the only escape from the pagoda.

"You can't kill me, not if you want me to tell you where Edmund is, remember? You want to cook, little sprout?" Jules asked, grinning down in Spencer's face as he freed one arm enough to clamp a hand around Spencer's neck yet again. "Let me kill you first, so the burning will not hurt. And you think I have no kindness in me?"

Spencer, fighting the panic that had robbed him of some of his strength, brought up his knee, but Jules had been a street fighter too long to have the same trick work twice. He had more than twenty years on Spencer, but those were twenty years of experience, and he had a lack of fear born of a life led without scruples, without conscience.

Spencer had made a nearly fatal mistake. He'd been thinking of Mariah, of William. Ainsley seemed to speak to him again. *I expect you home here in one piece. To be too careful is to invite disaster.*

"Not today, Jules," Spencer said, his voice hoarse and whispery as Jules pressed down on his windpipe. "I'm not the one who dies today. You can take your damn secrets with you to hell." Spencer squeezed the muscles of his arm against his side once, twice, a quick third time; the knife slid into his palm. A push on the button and the blade shot free, even as Spencer felt himself losing consciousness between the pressure cutting off his air and the smoke and heat of the fire.

With one last surge of strength, he sank the blade into the side of the Frenchman's neck, to the hilt.

Jules's eyes widened in shock even as his tight grip on Spencer's neck relaxed and a moment later Spencer's face was covered with the blood gurgling hot and fast from the Frenchman's mouth.

Spencer pushed himself free of the body, rolling over the planking to the stairwell that was now almost entirely wrapped in flames. He grabbed on to the bottom of the railing, swinging himself free of the planking, hanging suspended four stories above the ground. He kicked out, trying to find purchase on one of the lower stairs.

Once.

Twice.

The third time he felt the wood of one of the treads beneath his stockinged feet and he began moving his hands, first one, then the other, lower on the twisting banister.

The fire chased him down, intensifying as more of the gas lamps exploded, the hiss of gas warning him to hurry, *hurry.*

When he reached the landing on the second level, he was able to swing up and onto the stairs and was only one floor from safety when a loud pop was followed by a rush of hot air that hit him squarely in the back, throwing him off the stairs and down onto the hard floor ten feet below.

Or it would have, if Clovis hadn't been standing

there. As it was, Spencer landed half on his loyal friend and their worst injury was that the wind was knocked out of them both, so that they were helpless to do more than allow themselves to be dragged out of the pagoda as Mariah called out orders.

Spencer half staggered to his feet, supported by one of the men from Becket Hall, and they all fought their way off the bridge, dodging flaming bits of the Chinese pagoda that was rapidly breaking apart. By the time they were clear, standing in the trees, the pagoda was collapsing on itself, slowly, almost gracefully, to the cheers and whistles of the throng in St. James's Park, all of whom seemed to think the fire was simply another part of the Grand Jubilee.

"Ang—Anguish," Spencer managed before bending nearly in half to cough up the smoke he had swallowed.

"Gone, sir," Clovis said sadly. "He was gone when I found him." He looked toward the hungry flames. "He's still in there. We can't help him now, sir."

"Sweet Jesus," Spencer said as Mariah stood close beside him, rubbing at his back.

"Spencer, we have to get away from here," she said, hating that she had to be sensible. "Someone will come investigating soon, when they figure out this fire was not part of the celebrations. We have to go back to Upper Brook Street, and hope Chance is there soon, with good news."

"I know, I know," he told her, taking her hand in his. "How's your head? That bastard hit you fairly hard."

"Not really," she told him, trying to push thoughts of Aloysius away, at least for the moment. "I was stunned, I agree, but I think the entire time that Jules person was holding me I was awake, and trying to make myself as heavy as possible. I think he hurt me more when he threw me at…at Aloysius. *Oh, Spence…*"

"I know." He squeezed her hand, then winced as he finally felt the pain from the burns on his hands. "Clovis, I'm putting you in charge. Get us out of here, including our prisoners. I don't know how you're going to do it, but find a way."

"Yes, sir, Lieutenant!" Clovis said, saluting smartly, tears for his friend still coursing down his smoke-blackened face.

"Wait!" Spencer said, collecting his thoughts. "Renard. He's got a bullet hole in the middle of his face. We can't leave him here. Too many questions."

"That's a bit trickier, sir, if I may be so bold," Clovis said, but when he snapped his fingers, the men from Becket Hall retrieved Renard's body, Clovis already planning to drop it a few feet inside the first alleyway they passed on their way back to Upper Brook Street. This was London, after all. There must be people tripping over dead bodies in London alleyways every day.…

EPILOGUE

THE BECKETS SAT in the drawing room in Upper Brook Street two mornings later, with nothing much to add to the newspaper recounting that Mariah had just read to them concerning the destruction of the Chinese pagoda in St. James's.

There had been no explanation for the fire other than that one of the fireworks may have ignited the wooden facade or the gaslights had malfunctioned in some way. Yes, those gathered in the park had been unaware for several minutes that the fire had not been planned as a part of the festivities, but when workmen belatedly attempted to put out the blaze it was too late to save the structure. Several workmen had been injured in the attempt and, sadly, when the fire was at last out, the bodies of two workmen were discovered in the ashes. It was doubtful their identities would ever be known.

The article had ended with a tribute, not to the injured and deceased workmen, but in a sad farewell to a number of Royal swans in the canal that had succumbed to the smoke and fire.

"It's over then," Rian said at last, sitting on the arm of one of the couches, his right leg swinging in agitation. "What a sad fiasco all around. The rockets scattered the Prince Regent and the others, made some holes in the ground and caught one of the Hyde Park stalls on fire, but Wellington's men quickly surrounded everyone and got them all to safety without so much as a single blow struck. I suppose that's all right. Good thing we did, you know, alerting the Iron Duke. We're heroes, that's what. But nobody will ever know. Just a couple of rockets gone wrong, that's all."

"That still smarts, does it, Rian?" Julia asked, smiling slightly. "His Grace did tell us that several men in black were captured as they attempted a run at the Czar as he was being spirited away to his carriage. And, remember, it wasn't as if we were wrong. It's just that we were only nearly right. Still, I think we can be proud that, without us warning the Duke, things could have been a lot worse."

"The men we turned over to the Duke were nothing but minions," Chance said. "Hired assassins who know nothing of Edmund Beales, more's the pity. Young Johnny Keeler will be fine in time. But the loss of even one man is one too many."

Spencer looked down at his hands, both wrapped in layers of white linen. "I want Aloysius's body. I want him back at Becket Hall. Some spot where he can face the sea."

Mariah leaned her head against his shoulder. "He'd

like that. With nothing but nothing to do today and nothing more to do again tomorrow."

"I've already spoken to the Duke in confidence, Spence, and everything is arranged for Billy to transport the body back to Becket Hall tomorrow," Chance said, looking at the buttered scone in his hand, then replacing it on the tray, his appetite gone. "Jules's body can rot wherever someone puts it. You know, Ainsley must be wearing out his carpet, waiting for news."

"And we'll have none on Courtland's success or failure for several more days," Spencer said, dragging his thoughts away from Aloysius. Poor, brave Anguish. A change of name hadn't altered his bad luck, had it?

"I wonder if it matters whether they were successful or not," Mariah said, feeling very much the doomsayer, even if she felt she had reason, that the world turned upside-down much too often for her liking. "Unless this Congress of Vienna that supposedly convenes soon has the sense to listen to those demanding that Bonaparte be moved to that other island, he can probably leave Elba anytime he feels the need to have the sheets changed in his palace in Paris."

"Saint Helena," Julia said, nodding her agreement. "But I think that plea is falling on deaf ears. I wonder why."

Chance smiled at his wife. "That's what's left to us, darling. To watch and to wonder why those in power do what they do. So many things we could have learned from Jules if we could have taken him prisoner."

"Forgive me," Spencer said wryly. "I wanted both he and Renard alive, but they refused to cooperate."

Once more, they all lapsed into silence, broken now only by the sound of the dice hitting the tabletop as Rian, always easily bored, began rolling a pair of dice, his left hand against his right. His right, he announced a few minutes later, was pounding the flinders out of his left.

"What about Nicolette?" Mariah said at last, shifting in her seat. "If we could find *her?* She might know more about Edmund Beales, where he is—Spencer, why haven't we thought of that before?"

Spencer and Chance exchanged looks, and Mariah, who didn't miss much, saw the exchange.

"What aren't you telling us? Julia? Do you know what they're not telling us?"

Spencer bent down to retrieve the newspaper from the floor, swearing softly when he couldn't quite grasp it, so that Rian hastened to pick it up, then folded it over before handing it to his sister-in-law. "It's a very small story, Mariah, at the bottom of the page."

Mariah looked at him curiously, and then dropped her gaze to the newspaper, already sensing what she would read did not bode well for Nicolette.

The body of a young woman was Most Unfortunately Discovered in a cupboard at Grillon's Hotel at NO. 7 Ablemarle Street two nights previous by a parlourmaid in search of a broom. The woman, found with a thin cord Knotted

Tightly about her neck, had been a Guest of The Hotel along with her Husband, one Monsieur Lyon, who has Mysteriously Disappeared Without Notice, or settling his accounts with the hotel. Misadventure is suspected.

"He killed her," Mariah said dully, handing the newspaper back to Spencer. "I should have spoken to her that day in Calais, convinced her to escape him. It was clear to me that he didn't care for her."

"We all choose our own paths, Mariah," Julia said, getting to her feet, her hand in Chance's so that he stood up with her. "We've decided to go collect the children tomorrow and visit Becket Hall in the next week. There's a lot to talk about now that we know Edmund Beales has such grandiose plans."

Spencer and Mariah stood, as well, leaving Rian to scoop up his dice and fall back over the arm of the couch, tucking a pillow beneath his head as he settled against the cushions. "Yes, that's it. You all go off somewhere to think heavy thoughts," he told them. "Me? I'm going to rest my weary bones for a while, and then Clovis and I are going to take ourselves out to Hyde Park for the day and the night, to eat a bite of everything being sold there, and drink a bit of everything that is being poured there. Tomorrow is soon enough for heavy thoughts. For today, Clovis needs to find his way into a half dozen bottles."

"Thank you, Rian," Spencer said, and then smiled. "I know what a sacrifice this is for you."

"Well, seeing as how you can't hold a pint with those bandages and Mariah wouldn't let you go at any rate, I thought I'd do my part."

Mariah rolled her eyes and led the way into the foyer, Spencer following her up the stairs to their bedchamber.

"I should change those bandages again," she told him as she helped him unbutton his shirt, as he'd insisted on trying to hold his coffee cup with his bandaged hands and his shirtfront was the worse for the effort.

"I'd rather you didn't, thank you. The damn things stick to my skin and pulling them loose hurts like the very devil."

"Baby," Mariah said, stepping up on tiptoe to kiss him. "Spencer?"

He leaned forward for another kiss, but she placed her hands on his chest, holding him off. "Uh-oh," he said, wincing. "We're married such a short time, and already I believe I recognize that look and that tone. You want me to say yes to something, don't you? Do you want me to tell you again that I love you, how much I love you? I will, if only to hear you tell me you love me."

"I love you, Spence. I love you, love you, love you." She blinked back unexpected tears. "But I want to go to Becket Hall, Spence. Now, this morning. I know we were going to leave tomorrow, but tomorrow is so far away. William is so far away. I love you, I really do, but...but I need to hold William. I need the world to make sense again. Do you mind?"

Spencer pulled her close, careful of his hands, although his burns would heal. Someday, even the world might heal, and although both his hands and the world would forever bear the scars of war, he wanted to believe that seeing those cruel reminders, understanding them, would help his son and others learn not to repeat the same mistakes that had led to those scars.

Some day, they'd be free to sail to Virginia, start a new life. Some day, when Edmund Beales was finally out of their lives. But until that day, he and his small family would remain at Becket Hall.

And he'd no longer chafe to be gone from there. Because no matter where he lived, as long as Mariah was in his life, he would be content.

He kissed wife's head, took in the sweet smell of her, the soft, warm promise of her, his heart aching, but full. "You're right, Mariah. Let's go home...."

* * * * *

1815: The Year of Waterloo.
At last Rian Becket finds the battle he longs for,
even as Fanny Becket runs off to find him,
fight by his side...or so she believes.
THE BECKETS OF ROMNEY MARSH *saga*
continues in September 2007 from HQN with
A RECKLESS BEAUTY.
Turn the page for a sneak peek.

BECKET HALL, ROMNEY MARSH

Dinner over, Ainsley Becket relaxed in his favorite chair in the drawing room, listening to his children as they discussed Bonaparte's adventures since he escaped Elba several weeks earlier.

Breakfast, lunch, dinner, the conversation never seemed to vary. What will Bonaparte do? Where will he strike first? Will the Allies cede all command to the Iron Duke? Will Wellington be able to defeat the man he had, remarkably, never before met in battle?

Ainsley let their individual voices fade into the background as he concentrated on his children.

Such a disparate group, all eight of his children; seven of them the children of his heart, and now all of them grown, some of them already gone their own way, with his blessing.

Morgan, a wife and mother now, lived on her husband's estate near London, and her Ethan, Earl of Aylesford, undoubtedly working very long hours at the War Office.

Chance, Ainsley knew from the letter he'd received from his oldest son a week ago, was also back at work in the War Office, as all of England braced itself for the inevitable clash with Bonaparte.

Ainsley sipped at his snifter of brandy, selfishly content that these two men had found a way to serve the Crown without exposing themselves to battle, and stole a look at his son Spencer, who was bouncing his young son, William, on his leg as Mariah Becket smiled at them both.

Would Spencer willingly leave his small family and go to war again? Ainsley planned a quiet talk with the boy, who had sacrificed enough in America and needed to think first of his wife and son—and the second child Mariah now carried.

Eleanor and her husband, Jack, sat close together near the fireplace, a stack of Paris newspapers Ainsley had acquired in his usual secretive, inventive ways piled in Eleanor's lap. There still was no baby to be held in her arms, a sorrow she hid most times, but one that Ainsley knew ate at his oldest daughter.

Callie, the youngest, and the only child born to Ainsley and his lost Isabella, continued her argument with her brother Courtland about the latter's assertion that he should buy a commission in the army Wellington was hastily forming to confront the French emperor, now that the majority of the Field Marshal's troops had been sent to fight the Americans. As it was, foreign troops would outnumber English troops two-to-one.

Courtland, always the solid one, the rock of the Beckets, firmly believed in duty.

Callie, with all the surety of a seventeen-year-old, firmly believed Courtland belonged to her.

"You and Jack have enough on your plates," Ainsley said quietly now, making his point without overtly referring to the roles the two men played aiding the local smugglers, and Courtland nodded his reluctant agreement.

"I know, sir, but I believe you and Jacko are still reasonably capable and can run Becket Hall in our absence. Besides, we'll have Boney corralled and in a cage in a few months, if not weeks."

Callie, always sharp, sharper than most young girls were raised to be, spoke up. "In a cage, you say, Court? I believe—you'll correct me if I'm wrong, Papa—that it was Marshal Ney who promised the now-displaced King Louis that he would bring Bonaparte to him in an iron cage, and place him before Louis's throne."

She grinned at Court. "Would that be the same iron cage, Courtland, hmm? Especially now that Ney is back to perching on a cushion at Bonaparte's feet, apologetically licking his boots?"

Mariah Becket laughed as she took young William from her husband and lifted him into her arms. "She's got you there, Court. You men. So much bluster, so many promises. Spencer? I'll see you upstairs and meet you with a book tossed at your head if you dare to even hint that you'll attempt to follow the drum again."

Everyone waited until Mariah had left the drawing room before bursting into laughter at Spencer's expense.

"Well and truly tied to the apron strings, aren't you, old fellow?" Jack Eastwood asked, earning himself a speaking look from the love of his life. Morgan or Mariah would have delivered a sharp jab to his ribs, but the petite, ladylike Eleanor needed only to send a level look from her speaking eyes and Jack subsided, murmuring a quiet, "Sorry, Spence."

"It's all right," Spencer said, going to over to the drinks table to pour himself a glass of wine. "I know I can't go. And neither can you two, not when the Black Ghost has to ride out with regularity and definitely not when we still don't know where our old friend Edmund Beales might next show his face—and recognize yours. What if he's acting as Talleyrand has, and has thrown in his lot with the Alliance, abandoning Bonaparte after the fiasco that was his attempt to free him from Elba last August? Bonaparte might not be quite in love with the man now, you know."

Mention of Edmund Beales cast the room into silence for some moments, and Ainsley was, as always, thrown back into time, remembering the days when he'd considered Edmund his best friend and partner. Before Edmund's betrayal. Before Isabella's death at Edmund's hands. Before the massacre on the island that had brought the Beckets to England and the protective isolation of Romney Marsh seventeen years ago. Before they'd learned that Edmund still lived, and had taken his study of Machiavelli's mad genius to heart, believing himself destined to rule half the world. Before…before… before….

"It's true," Callie said, breaking the silence, as she saw the shadows in her papa's eyes, and wanted them gone. "None of you can be seen by Beales, as he's seen all of your faces at one time or another. So you can relax, Papa, nobody is running off to war. Except Rian, of course," she added, her pretty face marred by a frown as she thought about the day, a few weeks earlier, Rian had made his farewells and ridden away with an eagerness he couldn't quite disguise, his commission in his pocket.

"Our brother is so damn hot to play the hero, the fool," Spencer said, shaking his head. "We can only hope he'll stay cooling his heels in Belgium and never even set foot on French soil."

"Amen to that, Spencer. I still find it difficult to believe the way the French have embraced Bonaparte, after damning him just over a year ago," Eleanor said, paging through the newspapers she'd been holding on her lap. "Just look at these, for pity's sake. Let me read the titles of the stories written over the course of the past weeks by the *Moniteur,* once so loyal to the Emperor. Here, darling, help me before they all slide to the floor."

She passed some of the newspapers to Jack, whom she asked to read the oldest one first.

"It would be my pleasure. Ah, here we go. 'The Corsican werewolf has landed at Cannes.'"

"Yes," Eleanor said. "Now this one is next, only a few short days later. 'The tiger appeared at Gap, troops were sent against him, the wretched adventurer ended his career in the mountains.' They said he'd been killed, for pity's sake."

Jack reached for another newspaper. "'The fiend has actually, thanks to treachery, been able to get as far as Grenoble.'"

Eleanor continued with the title of a later story, "'The tyrant has reached Lyon, where horror paralyzed all attempts at resistance.' But, Papa, haven't your agents in France already told you Bonaparte was greeted with cheers?"

Ainsley nodded. "Elly, you really expect truth from a newspaper controlled by the state? I thought I'd taught you to be more discerning than that. Read the rest, if you please. They are amusing, in a rather macabre way."

Jack lifted another newspaper, scanned it, and smiled ruefully. "Ah, no longer the werewolf, I see, but actually at last referred to by name. And in just a few days' time. 'Bonaparte moves northward with rapid strides, but he will never reach Paris.'"

"And these last two," Eleanor said, shaking her head. "'Tomorrow Napoléon will be at our gates.' And, lastly, this. 'His Majesty is at Fontainebleau.' His Majesty? From werewolf to their most beloved Emperor in a few days' time? Hypocrites, all of them! But if that's how rapidly the French can turn their coats, can Bonaparte sleep easy at night?"

Ainsley drained the last of his brandy and stood, ready to return to his study and the maps he'd been poring over since first he heard of Bonaparte's escape, comparing those maps to the steady stream of information his money so cleverly bought. He'd correctly picked Cannes as the man's initial destination. Now he looked to the area around Brussels, feeling that to be the logical ground for Wellington and the Emperor to at last meet across a battlefield. He'd already forwarded his thoughts to Chance and Ethan, with little hope such a necessarily anonymous warning would be heeded by their superiors.

And Rian, God help them, was already on his way to Belgium.

"Remy," he said, referring to his informant in Paris, "has written me that Bonaparte paused on the steps of his palace the day of his arrival, to look out on the quiet city, and said, 'They have let me come, just as they let the others go.' So, if that answers your question, Elly, I would say that the man knows his rule is tenuous, at best. Which I believe, sadly, means he will march out of Paris soon to confront the Allies, rather than wait for them to come to him."

Courtland, who had spent many hours poring over the same communiqués and maps as Ainsley, disagreed. "It will be near the end of July before the Russians and Austrians can meet up with our own army, and neither we English nor the Prussians will be fool enough to engage Bonaparte until all of the Allies are together."

Ainsley smiled indulgently. "Don't think of rosy scenarios, where the world works to your hopes, Court. Better to think like your enemy. Can you conceive of a better reason for Bonaparte to move now? His people will want to see a victory, a bit of the old soldier in his battle-worn green greatcoat, the hero they have followed for so long. It's not enough, Court, to parade in a Coronation coach, wear fine white plumes, even to declare democratic constitutions. He needs to give them a victory, even if that means coming out with a smaller army than he'd like. And I do not believe he wants that initial fight to be a defensive action, one that takes place on French soil. No, Bonaparte is first and foremost a soldier. War may have been declared on him, but he will take the initiative, attack. If only the fools in the War Office could understand this."

"Pray God they will, Papa. So...so Rian could be closer to this first battle, when it comes, than we believe?" Eleanor asked, slipping her hand into Jack's.

"That blasted girl!"

All heads turned to look at Mariah, who was standing in the doorway, her cheeks flushed, and clutching a thick lock of light blond hair. She held it aloft, shook it with some fury.

Ainsley looked at the hank of hair and felt a frightening chill, as if a goose had just walked over his grave. "Fanny?"

Mariah nodded, scarcely able to speak. Fanny

Becket had pushed back from the dinner table the previous evening, complaining of the headache, and gone to her rooms. "I knocked on her door a few times today, but there was no answer. You know how she can be, sulking ever since Rian left, and I decided—Eleanor and I decided—to simply let her stay locked up in there until her stomach finally forced her out again. But tonight, well, enough is enough, so I commandeered a key and...and she's not there."

Callie turned in her chair to ask, "She's run away? Did she leave a note?"

"She didn't have to," Ainsley said, sitting down heavily, feeling all of his years. "We all know where your sister has gone."

Fanny Becket hid herself just at the entrance to a foul-smelling alley fronting on the bustling wharf where soldiers and horses milled about as dusk fell, waiting for the order to take ship. She nervously fingered the *gad* hanging around her neck from a gold chain, the especially prepared alligator tooth her old nurse and voodoo priestess, Odette, insisted all the Beckets wear.

It was a silly thing, but Odette renewed the protective magic in each *gad* every spring. How could Fanny leave such a potent weapon against the bad *loa,* bad spirits, behind as she went off to war?

She'd ridden through the night and day to make Dover before anyone could catch her, drag her home, but she'd been standing in this alley for the past two hours, not knowing what to do next. Because Dover wasn't Ostend, and she knew she had to get herself across the Channel to Ostend before she could travel inland, to Brussels.

To Rian.

Her mare, Molly, stood obediently behind her, nuzzling at Fanny's neck, hoping for a treat. Fanny dug into the pocket of Rian's cloak for the last broken bit of carrot she had brought with her, handing it up to the horse.

It was a mad scheme she was considering now, but desperate times call for desperate actions. After all, Rian had told her she was pretty, even as he laughed at her, pretended not to love her as anything more than his sister, even though they were not related by blood.

But they'd always been together, for as long as Fanny could remember. From that day when, at no more than three years old, she had knelt beside her mother in the pretty, whitewashed island church, and the priest was holding up the chalice, and her mother bowed her head, striking her breast three times, once for each time the bell was rung on the altar.

Just as the bell rang that third time, the cannon had exploded all around them and Fanny had looked up, seen the blue sky, seen bits of the roof raining down on them before being pushed to the floor, her mother lying on top of her, protecting her.

That's where the man later to christen himself

Ainsley Becket had found her, still half-crushed beneath her mother's body. There were others, other survivors of the Spanish pirate's attack that had come from the sea without warning, Rian among them. Three of the women still lived in Becket Village, but other mothers and their children, and the four other orphans of that day, had survived only to die several months later, when Edmund Beales attacked their island.

Pirates. Brigands. Warm white sands and clear blue waters. Death. Death everywhere; once and then again. Fanny barely remembered any of it. Just watching her mother beat at her breast as the bell rang, calling down the roof onto their heads...and Rian, only a few years her senior, but always there, always holding her hand, protecting her, swooping her up into his own thin arms that last day and carrying her deep into the trees, away from Edmund Beales's treachery.

She'd do anything to protect him, as well.

Even see if he was right, that she was pretty. A pretty girl.

Fanny tested the knot holding the colored scarf around her head, hiding her badly butchered blond hair, and flipped the edges of her cloak back over her shoulders, the better to display the rumpled gown she'd donned over her breeches once reaching Dover.

"Don't follow, Molly," she admonished the mare, who hung her head as if she understood and she probably did, for Molly was very intelligent and Fanny had trained her well.

Then Fanny stepped out of the shadows, heading directly toward the slim young boy in the scarlet uniform of the 13th Regiment cavalry. She'd chosen him for his youth, for his size.

"You're to be sailin' off tonight is it, you pretty thing?" she asked him, circling around both him and his horse, effectively cutting the youth from the herd of his fellow soldiers, all of them exhausted after sailing from Cove, their ship damaged enough that they'd had to put in at Dover for both repairs and provisions before following their two other ships to Ostend.

It had been unbelievable good luck, an omen, Odette would have said, that she'd found some of the 13th here, on this overcrowded dock. Rian's own regiment; fine, brave Irishmen from County Cork and beyond. It had seemed fitting to Rian that he fight with the Irish, even if the only thing still Irish about him was his blood and his name. For the past seventeen years, since the age of nine, since that bell had rung a third time, he had been a Becket.

The young boy Fanny had singled out—he seemed such a child—dipped his head at Fanny's question, swallowing down so hard that his Adam's apple seemed ready to collide with his chin. "And that we are, Miss. Off to chase Boney back where he belongs, give him what-for."

Fanny measured him with her eyes. Yes, this was

good. He topped her own not inconsiderable height by only a few inches. "Well, God bless you then, boyo," she said, pushing a lilt into her voice. "Would you be wanting somethin' to take with you, like? A last kiss from a lass late of County Clare? Mayhap a bit more than a kiss?"

The young soldier looked about him, wetting his lips. "I'm not supposin' you'd be offerin' such a thing for free."

Fanny smiled. "And what are you takin' me for, boyo? One of them loose wimmen?" She reached up, stroked his smooth cheek that had only a hint of peach fuzz. What was he? Sixteen? "No brave man should go to fight without first bein' with a willin' lass, now should he?"

"I been," the soldier protested, his cheeks going red. "I been plenty." He clasped his rifle with one hand and took her elbow with the other even as she deftly grabbed on to his mount's bridle, steering her toward the alleyway, which was right where she wanted to go. "But it's quick we'll be, a'fore my sergeant misses me, you hear?"

Fanny felt herself pushed rather roughly against the wet brick as the boy fumbled, one hand holding her still even as he propped his rifle against the wall and began unbuttoning his breeches.

That was helpful. He was giving her a head start, in a way, or so Fanny thought as she closed her eyes, whispered a quick *I'm so sorry,* and brought the heel of the pistol she'd extracted from the pocket of her cloak down hard on the soldier's temple.

Fanny might be young and slim, but she was also tall, and fairly strong. Bending only slightly beneath the dead weight of the soldier, she dragged him deeper into the alleyway and lowered him gently to the ground.

She worked quickly, stripping the boy to his last little bit of clothing, for she was wearing Rian's underclothes, and didn't much care to exchange them for drawers that looked, even in this dim light, capable of standing up by themselves.

Five minutes later, leaving behind a small purse of coins as well as a rough pair of trousers and a shirt for the boy to cover himself with when he awoke, and with her white braces in place across her now red-coated chest, the rifle slung over her shoulder as well as the heavy pack containing the best of the soldier's gear and her own, Fanny emerged from the alleyway once more, leading Molly and the black gelding by the reins of their halters.

She stayed between the two horses and kept her head down as she joined the men just now being formed up to go aboard, wondering if she'd just saved one young Irish life, but never doubting her own fate.

Ostend awaited. Brussels awaited.

Rian, although he didn't know it yet, awaited.

REQUEST YOUR FREE BOOKS!

2 FREE NOVELS
FROM THE ROMANCE/SUSPENSE
COLLECTION PLUS 2 FREE GIFTS!

YES! Please send me 2 FREE novels from the Romance/Suspense Collection and my 2 FREE gifts. After receiving them, if I don't wish to receive any more books, I can return the shipping statement marked "cancel." If I don't cancel, I will receive 4 brand-new novels every month and be billed just $5.49 per book in the U.S., or $5.99 per book in Canada, plus 25¢ shipping and handling per book plus applicable taxes, if any*. That's a savings of at least 20% off the cover price! I understand that accepting the 2 free books and gifts places me under no obligation to buy anything. I can always return a shipment and cancel at any time. Even if I never buy another book from the Reader Service, the two free books and gifts are mine to keep forever.

185 MDN EF5Y   385 MDN EF6C

Name _____ (PLEASE PRINT) _____

Address _____ Apt. # _____

City _____ State/Prov. _____ Zip/Postal Code _____

Signature (if under 18, a parent or guardian must sign) _____

Mail to **The Reader Service:**
IN U.S.A.: P.O. Box 1867, Buffalo, NY 14240-1867
IN CANADA: P.O. Box 609, Fort Erie, Ontario L2A 5X3

Not valid to current subscribers to the Romance Collection,
the Suspense Collection or the Romance/Suspense Collection.

Want to try two free books from another line?
Call 1-800-873-8635 or visit www.morefreebooks.com.

* Terms and prices subject to change without notice. NY residents add applicable sales tax. Canadian residents will be charged applicable provincial taxes and GST. This offer is limited to one order per household. All orders subject to approval. Credit or debit balances in a customer's account(s) may be offset by any other outstanding balance owed by or to the customer. Please allow 4 to 6 weeks for delivery.

Your Privacy: Harlequin is committed to protecting your privacy. Our Privacy Policy is available online at www.eHarlequin.com or upon request from the Reader Service. From time to time we make our lists of customers available to reputable firms who may have a product or service of interest to you. If you would prefer we not share your name and address, please check here. ☐

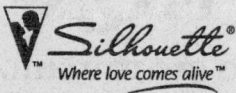

KASEY MICHAELS

77107	BEWARE OF VIRTUOUS WOMEN	___ $6.99 U.S. ___ $8.50 CAN.
77100	A GENTLEMAN BY ANY OTHER NAME	___ $6.99 U.S. ___ $8.50 CAN.
77151	THE DANGEROUS DEBUTANTE	___ $6.99 U.S. ___ $8.50 CAN.
77038	SHALL WE DANCE	___ $6.99 U.S. ___ $8.50 CAN.

(limited quantities available)

TOTAL AMOUNT	$ _____
POSTAGE & HANDLING	$ _____
($1.00 FOR 1 BOOK, 50¢ for each additional)	
APPLICABLE TAXES*	$ _____
TOTAL PAYABLE	$ _____

(check or money order—please do not send cash)

To order, complete this form and send it, along with a check or money order for the total above, payable to HQN Books, to: **In the U.S.:** 3010 Walden Avenue, P.O. Box 9077, Buffalo, NY 14269-9077; **In Canada:** P.O. Box 636, Fort Erie, Ontario, L2A 5X3.

Name: _____
Address: _____ City: _____
State/Prov.: _____ Zip/Postal Code: _____
Account Number (if applicable): _____

075 CSAS

*New York residents remit applicable sales taxes.
*Canadian residents remit applicable GST and provincial taxes.

◆HQN™

We *are* romance™

www.HQNBooks.com

PHKM0407BL